FREE FALL

Relax . . . let yourself go . . . you're in the best of hands . . .

Let **J. F. Bone** tune you into the thought-waves of two reptilian super-creatures as they decide the fate of the human race . . .

Let **Fritz Leiber** show you a future where life is one unending love-in—for those hardy enough to take it . . .

Let **Isaac Asimov** work his famous magic with an unworldly scientist, a rapacious businessman, and an **almost** perfect time machine . . .

Let **Judith Merril** clue you in on what happens when the psychiatrists take over—and people really blow their minds . . .

Here are 13 stories that won't let you stop until you touch down on the very last page.

13 ABOVE THE NIGHT

EDITED BY
GROFF CONKLIN

A DELL BOOK
An Original Volume

Published by
DELL PUBLISHING CO., INC.
750 Third Avenue
New York, N.Y. 10017

Dell ® TM 681510, Dell Publishing Co., Inc.
Printed in the U.S.A.
Previous Dell Edition #8741
New Dell Edition
First printing—November 1969

ACKNOWLEDGMENTS

CONTENTS

INTRODUCTION

PEOPLE ARE ALWAYS ASKING ME HOW SCIENCE FICtion writers can keep on writing science fiction. "Haven't they used up all the ideas?" is the constant question. The constant answer—at least when I am sure I will not be misunderstood—is, *"Sure!"* There never were many basic ideas in the first place, and they were already being explored long before the term "science fiction" was even invented.

It is true, of course, that science fiction has mapped many unfamiliar areas of the world of imagination; but these areas have considerably more to do with backgrounds and paraphernalia than they do with ideas. Ideas? They are as rare as hen's hind molars in any fiction, and science fiction is no exception.

You can name the basic gambits in one breath, so to speak; and I have done it time and again. Indeed, several of my early anthologies were based exactly on these categories of ideas: invasions from space, space travel and possible worlds, parapsychological concepts, time travel and parallel worlds, worlds of tomorrow, and the superscience of man, the latter exemplified by such imaginings as antigravity machines, mutation-causing drugs, and the like. Almost obsolete today is a seventh category that was popular in the childhood of science fiction: earth wonders, so-called—stories of volcanic eruptions destroying the Eastern Seaboard of the United States, "mad molecules" (the actual title of a story!) taking over civilization, etc., etc. Today we consider ourselves too sophisticated for legends of this type, but I must say I miss them. Alas that I was unable to find a suitable up-to-date exemplar of the genre for use in this collection.

However, there still is an enormous wealth of first-rate unreprinted science fiction in the first six categories mentioned, and I am convinced that there always will be. Anthologists will never run out of material for new collections.

In the present anthology there are two alien invasions, two possible worlds, three parapsychological adventures, two tales of tomorrow, and four dimensional stories—the latter unusual for my books, since good examples of time travel are ordinarily difficult to locate. Obviously, then, what you have here are more of the same old basic plot ideas. If you are looking for something glitteringly novel, a breakthrough in science fiction ideas, you are barking up the wrong book. I suspect you will never be able to find absolute novelty, no matter how long and how hard you hunt.

What we do have here is exactly what one finds in any *good* s.f. book—pretested, imaginative storytelling at its best. A really good writer can take any idea from any source and, by his skill in highlighting already established concepts and images, bring new insight and understanding to the reader. And that is exactly what the thirteen talented people I have brought together between the covers of this book have done. They have used the same old basic plots, the same old reliable master molds, to create thirteen genuinely fresh, original variations of the archetypical themes. They have written thirteen good representative s.f. stories, including three strong novelettes.

So stay with it. You will have your mind stretched and your worries stashed away for the time being. You will enjoy escape, which is really what we all want now and then, rather than novelty, which can become dreadfully boring if novelty is all a story has to offer.

And, of course, the bonus for today's reader of good science fiction: many of the stories carry the hot spark of a special meaning for our times. Indeed, one of the best definitions of first-quality science fiction stories is only one word long: they are *parables*. There are several extremely pointed parables in this book. I take pleasure in letting you explore their meaning without any guidance from me.

GROFF CONKLIN

FOUNDING FATHER

J. F. Bone

As a cheerfully pessimistic view of the state of modern civilization and the possibilities of its enduring, this story takes top awards. And the "message" in the vivid picture of extraterrestrial intelligences and their horrified reaction to our vertebrate violence, uncontrollability, and instinct for racial suicide, will give you something to think about long after you've finished reading this magnificent novelette.

"WE NEED DATA," I SAID AS I MANIPULATED THE scanner and surveyed our little domain of rocks and vegetation. "The animate life we have collected so far is of a low order."

"There is nothing here with intelligence," Ven agreed, gesturing at the specimens in front of us. "Although they're obviously related to our race, they're quite incapable of constructing those artifacts we saw on our way down."

"Or of building electone communications or even airboats," I added.

"I expect that there is only one way to get what we want—and that's to go looking for it," Ven said as she smoothed her antennae with a primary digit. "I also expect," she added acidly, "that there might have been other places from which it wouldn't be so hard to start looking. Or did you *have* to set us down in this isolated spot?"

I glared at her and she flushed a delicate lavender. "Do you think I landed here because I *wanted* to?" I asked with some bitterness, inflating my cheek pouches to better express my disgust. "There were less than two vards of useful fuel left on the reels when I cut the drives. There isn't enough to take us across this valley. We came close to not making planetfall here at all."

"Oh," Ven said in a small voice, vocalizing as she always does when she is embarrassed. Like most females, she finds it difficult to project normally when she is under emotional stress. Afraid or angry she can blow a hole in subspace; but embarrassed, her projections are so faint that I have to strain my antennae to receive them.

Her aura turned a shamefaced, nacreous lavender. I couldn't stay angry with her. She was lovely, and I was proud to be her mate. The Eugenics Council had made an unusually good match when they brought us together. The months we had spent aboard ship on our sabbatical had produced no serious personality conflicts. We fitted well, and I was more happy than any Thalassan had a right to be.

"We shall have to try other measures," I said. "Although there aren't very many natives hereabouts, we had better start looking for them rather than wait for them to look for us." I felt disappointed. I was certain that we made enough disturbance coming down for them to be here in droves, which was why I had the robots camouflage the ship to look like the surrounding rocks. There could be such a thing as too much attention.

"They could have mistaken us for a meteor," Ven said.

"Probably," I agreed. "But it would have saved a great deal of trouble if one of them had come to us." I sighed. "Oh well," I added, "it was only a hope, at best."

"I could explore," Ven offered.

"I was about to suggest that," I said. "After all, the atmosphere is breathable although somewhat rich in oxygen, and the gravity is not too severe. It would be best to wait until dark before starting out. There may be danger. After all, this is an alien world, and Authority knows what's out there."

Her antennae dropped, her aura dimmed to gray and her integument turned a greenish black. "It doesn't sound pleasant." she said.

The sun dipped below the horizon with an indecently gaudy display of color. After the last shades of violet had faded, I opened the airlock and watched Ven, a darker blot in the darkness of the night, slip away into the shadows.

She went unarmed. I wanted her to take a blaster, but she refused, saying that she had never fired one, wouldn't know what to do with one—and that its weight would hold her back. I didn't like it. But I was unable to go with her, and it was better that she did as she wished at this time.

I sat for a while in the entrance port watching the slow wheel of the stars across the heavens, and for a moment I wished that I were a female with the rugged physique to withstand this gravity. As it was, the beauty of the night was lost on me. I breathed uncomfortably as the pressure crushed my body and made every joint and muscle ache. Males, I reflected gloomily, weren't what they were in the old days. Too much emphasis on mind, and not enough on body, had made us a sex of physical weaklings.

I wondered bitterly if a brain was as worthwhile as the Council insisted.

The next few hours were miserable. I worried about Ven, imagining a number of unpleasant things which might have happened to her. I dragged myself into the control room and fiddled with the scanners, trying the infra and ultra bands as well as the normal visible spectrum in the hopes of seeing something. And just as I was beginning to feel the twinges of genuine fear, I heard Ven.

Her projection was faint. "Help me, Eu! Help me!"

I stumbled to the entrance port, dragging a blaster with me. "Where are you?" I projected. I couldn't see her, but I could sense her presence.

"Here, Eu. Just below you. Help me. I can't make it any farther!"

Somehow I managed it. I don't know from where the strength came, but I was on the ground lifting her, pushing her onto the flat surface of the airlock—clambering up—dragging her in and closing the lock behind us. I looked down at her with pride. Who would have thought that I, a male, could lift a mature female into a ship's airlock even against normal gravity? I chuckled shakily. Strange things happen to a body when its owner is stressed and its suprarenals are stimulated.

She looked up at me. "Thank you," she said simply. But there was more behind the words than the bare bones of customary gratitude.

I helped her into the refresher and as she restored her tired body I pelted her with numerous questions.

"Did you succeed?" I asked.

"Better than I expected."

"Did you find a native?"

"Two of them." The cubicle glowed a pale green as her strength came back.

"Where?"

"Two vursts from here—down the hill. They're camped near a road. They have a big ground car with them."

"Did you see them?"

"Yes."

"What did they look like."

The radiance in the cubicle flicked out. "They're horrible!" Ven said. "Monstrous! Four or five times our size! I never saw anything so hideous!"

"Did they see you?"

"No, I don't think so. They weren't looking in my direction at first. And I don't think they can sense, because I was frightened and they didn't respond to my projection." She was beginning to recover.

"You couldn't have been too frightened," I said. "I didn't hear you—and you can reach farther than two vursts."

"Mostly I was repelled," Ven admitted.

"Why?"

"I don't know. They smelled bad, but it was more than that. There was something about them that made my antennae lie flat against my ears. Anyway—I did a foolish thing." The cubicle turned a pale embarrassed lavender.

"What did you do?" I demanded.

"I ran away," Ven said. "And I made a lot of noise."

"All right—all right," I said impatiently. "Go ahead and tell the rest of it."

"By the time I stopped running I was down at the bottom of the hill," Ven said. "I was dead tired—and with all that rock to climb to get back to the ship. I didn't really think I'd make it."

"But you did," I said proudly. "You're a real Thalassan—pure green."

The cubicle slowly brightened again.

"Can you find them again?" I asked.

"Of course. I wasn't lost at any time. If I hadn't panicked, I'd have been back a whole lot sooner."

"Can you go now?"

She shivered with distaste. "I can," she said, "but I don't want to."

"That's nonsense. We can't let a little physical revulsion stop us. After all, there are some pretty grim things to be seen in this universe."

"But nothing like this! I tell you, Eu, they're horrible! That's the only word that can describe them."

"Take a stat projector—" I began.

"Aren't you coming?" she asked.

"Two vursts on this planet? What do you think I am?"

Her face hardened. "I don't know," she said coldly, "but I do know this—if you don't come, I won't go."

I groaned. From her aura I could tell she meant every word. It angered me, too, because Thalassan females usually don't defy a male. "Remember," I said icily, "that you're not the only female on Thalassa."

"We're not on Thalassa," she said. Her aura was a curious leaden color, shot through with sullen red flares and blotches.

"I have no right to force you," she went on stubbornly, "but I *can't* handle them alone. You simply *have* to come."

"But, Ven—I'm a physical cipher. This gravity flattens me. I won't make it."

"You will," she said. "I'll help you. But this job needs a male mind."

It was deliberate flattery, I suppose. But there was an

element of truth in it. Ven obviously couldn't do it, and obviously she thought I could. I couldn't help feeling pride in her need for me. I liked the feeling. For, after all, we hadn't been mated so long that there was too great an amount of familiarity in our relationship. The Eugenics Council had taken care of that very effectively when we announced our plans for our sabbatical.

"All right—I'll go." I repeated.

With a quick light movement she touched my antennae with her primary digits. The shock ran through me clear to my pads. "You're good," she said—and the way she said it was an accolade.

II

"THIS WAY," VEN SAID, EMITTING A FAINT YELLOW aura that lighted the area around her. "Follow me." She staggered a little under the weight of the equipment she was carrying. I wished that we had enough power to energize an air sled—but we had none to spare. The robots had used up most of our scanty power metal reserves in camouflaging the ship and the adaptor had taken the rest. This was going to be a miserable trip. It was going to be painful, uncomfortable and perhaps even dangerous.

It was.

We went across rocks, through sharp-twigged brush—across the saw-edged grass of the meadow below us, over more rocks, and downhill along a faint double trail that never seemed to end. I was nearly dead with weariness when Ven's aura flicked off and the dark closed in. My proprioceptors were screaming as I sank to the ground and panted the rich air of this world in and out of my aching chest.

"They're just ahead," Ven whispered. "Around that next group of rocks. Be careful."

We moved forward cautiously. "There was a fire," Ven whispered.

"There isn't now," I said. "I can't sense any heat." The night air blew a rank odor to my nostrils. My spines stiffened! I knew what Ven meant when she said that these natives repelled her. I had smelled that scent before—the scent of our ancestral enemies! So *these* were the natives, the dominant life on this planet! I gagged, my tongue thick in my throat.

"You see?" Ven asked.

I nodded. "It's pretty bad," I said.

"It reminds me of a zoo," Ven answered softly.

I nodded. It did and it was thoroughly unpleasant.

I strained my perception to its limits, pushing it through the gelid darkness, searching until I found the natives. "They're asleep," I said.

"What's that?"

"Suspension of consciousness. Something like estivation."

"Oh. Then we can approach safely?"

"If we are quiet," I replied. "Sleep is broken easily and consciousness returns quickly."

The trail deepened beyond the rocks—two rutted tracks about three vards apart. We moved forward cautiously, our senses keyed to their highest pitch. The night was oppressively still and every movement rasped loudly. My breath came fast and shallow. My heart pounded and my musk glands were actively secreting as I parted the opening to their cloth shelter, and sensed the dim forms within.

"Stat," I projected and Ven handed me the weapon. It was almost more than I could manage in my weakened condition, but I aimed it and fired a full intensity blast at the nearest lumpy figure. It jerked and flopped inside its coverings, and the second form sat up with horrid speed!

A roar of sound came from it as the air was filled with its fetid odor. In panic I triggered a blast at the menacing figure, and it, too, flopped and laid still.

I ran my tongue over the roof of my dry mouth and called to Ven. "They're quiet now. Come in and see what we've got."

"Ugh!" Ven snorted as she entered the tent at my heels. "It stinks!"

"They're not the sweetest life form in the universe," I said as I prodded the huge mound beside me, looking for reflexes that would indicate returning consciousness.

"What are they?" Ven asked.

"Mammals," I said.

"No wonder I thought of a zoo," Ven said. "But they're so big!"

"Not on all planets," I said.

"Obviously," Ven commented. "Well—what's next? Let's get this done. I'm suffocating!"

"Hand me the probe kit," I said.

I selected two of the longest probes and made my way up to the head of the nearest monster. I scanned its braincase until I found the area I wanted and inserted the probes, driving them through the heavy bone and into the brain beneath. I clipped on the short antennae and stepped back. "Turn the control to low," I said. "Place the clips on your antennae. Now think of rising." The bulk beside me stirred and Ven gave a squeak of terror. "It's all right," I assured her. "Turn the control back to zero. This one's secure."

I went to the second and treated it like the first, and felt a justifiable pride as it reacted. Not many men could implant neuroprobes correctly on the first attempt. "All right, Ven. You can go out now. Take the controls with you. I'll see what I can do to get these brutes out of their coverings."

The tent opening swayed as Ven passed through and I bent over the nearest form. The covering was a heavy sack closed with a slide fastener much like the ones we used. I pulled and it opened, sending a flood of rank scent into the fetid air. I coughed, my eyes smarting, and found the fastener of the other sack. Retching with nausea, I staggered out of the tent.

Ven sprang forward, caught me as I was about to fall, and lowered me gently to the ground.

"What are we going to do?" Ven asked as I lay panting at her feet.

"We're going to get them out of there," I said, "and take them back to the ship. I didn't come all this way for nothing." I drew one of the controls toward me, fastened the clips to my antennae, advanced the gain and thought into it. There was a stir of movement inside and a huge form came stumbling out. It stood there clad in loose cloth coverings, reeking with halogen. I looked up at the dark bulk and shivered.

"That smell!" Ven said.

"We can help it a bit," I replied and turned to the control. With its massive forelimbs the brute ripped the cloth from its body as it moved downwind. I made it stand and took the other control.

"Let me do it," Ven said. "You can't handle both of them in your condition."

"All right," I said, "but be careful."

"I will. Now what do I do?"

"Advance the intensity knob and think what you want it to do."

There was a flurry of movement inside the tent, the thrashing of a huge body, and the second mammal burst through the opening and staggered clumsily to a stop.

"Reduce the intensity," I said. "You're projecting too strong a stimulus. Now uncover it and send it over with the other one to cool off. They're more bearable when they're cold. They exude the scent from their skin glands to compensate for temperature."

"I know," Ven said. "I studied biology." She did as I instructed and then dropped beside me. We relaxed, gathering our strength for the climb ahead. But I didn't recover rapidly. I could move, but the exertion made me dizzy. The excitement was over and reaction had set in. "I'll never make it," I said dully.

"I can help," Ven said, "—a little."

"It won't be enough. You don't have the strength to carry me." I looked at the huge bodies of the mammals gleaming pallidly in the darkness, and suddenly I had an idea. The Slaads on Valga domesticated mammals. They were quadrupedal, true enough, but they were still mammals. Why couldn't I ride one of these as they did? Those great masses of muscle should carry me easily. "I think I have a solution," I said.

"What?"

"I'll have one of them carry me."

"You can't!"

"Why not? They're controlled. And they're the only way I'll be able to get back to the ship." I picked up the nearest controller. "Let's see what happens."

Ven squeaked as the monster lifted me in the air and set me across its neck. I crossed my pads and hung on. The ground seemed terribly far away.

"How is it up there?" Ven asked.

"A little unstable," I said, "but I'll manage. Shall we go?"

We moved up the trail to the rocky abutment and turned up the hill. The brute beneath me climbed strongly and easily.

"Wait a minute," Ven said as she turned the corner behind me, "you're going too fast."

"Why don't you ride?" I called down to her. "This one moves easily enough. It's much better than walking."

"I think I will," Ven replied.

"This is all right," Ven said as we moved side by side up the hill. "The fibrils on top of its head—"

"Hair," I corrected.

"The hair of this one is longer than yours. I can hold on nicely."

The big bodies of the natives moved smoothly and powerfully, their giant strides eating up the distance we had so painfully covered some time before. Presently we came out onto the lower edge of the meadow below our ship.

Ven looked at me, her aura glowing pink with excitement. "I'll race you to the ship," she cried, and dashed off with a burst of speed.

Somehow I couldn't resist the challenge in her voice. I advanced the control knob and thought strongly. The brute jumped as though it had been whipped and leaped into a plunging run. I clung desperately for a moment and then relaxed as I caught the rhythm of the driving strides. My heart pounded, but not with fear. I had never known such exhilaration! Machines were pale compared to it. The mammal could run like a frightened skent—and it was faster than Ven's!

I caught her halfway up the meadow, and pulled away, exulting in the powerful muscles moving underneath me. I charged up to the grove of trees that concealed our camouflaged ship, and brought the mammal to a halt. It was panting, trembling, drenched with stinking sweat, but I didn't mind. I was part of it. There was a certain amount of feedback in a bipolar control circuit and I could feel the heat of its body, the beat of the great heart, the rise and fall of the broad chest, the pulse of the blood vessels in the thick neck. It was magnificent! I laughed. I had never before felt the ecstasy of physical strength!

I turned and looked back, still tasting the pleasure of the great body connected to my mind.

Ven drew up beside me. "Hai Yee!" she exclaimed. "What a sensation!"

"You liked it?" I asked.

"Liked it? *Liked* it? I loved it! Didn't you?"

"I think so," I said truthfully.

"I'm going across the meadow again," Ven said as she turned her mammal around.

"No," I said. "We have use for these two and we have no knowledge of how much they can stand. There's no sense damaging them." I frowned as I noticed the bloody scratches on the legs and body of her mammal.

Ven noted the direction of my gaze. "They're not as tough as I thought," she said with sudden contrition. "But they're not too badly damaged, are they?"

"No." I said.

I ordered the mammal to set me down. Dawn was breaking and I could see better what we had captured. They were a male and a female. On the whole, except for their mammalian ancestry, they conformed to dominant-race criteria, being erect, bipedal, predatory types with binocular vision. Their upper extremities were evolved into manipulative organs similar to our primary digits.

The most outstanding difference was the extreme sex dimorphism, which was obviously apparent in the brightening light. The physical differences were carried to such lengths that it was hard to believe that they were members of the same species.

They weren't exactly ugly, yet there was something disturbing about them. Perhaps it was the rank halogen odor of their skin glands that were still secreting despite the coolness of the air. Or perhaps it was merely that they were intelligent mammals. It was as though Authority had, in a moment of cosmic humor, drawn oversized caricatures of Thalassans and endowed them with life. I felt a subtle insult in their presence. I suppose it showed in my aura because Ven came quickly to my side.

"I told you they were disturbing," she said as we looked up at their monstrous forms towering over us.

"I'm glad they're not uncontrolled," I answered, shivering a little as I looked at them. "I suppose it's just species antipathy, but they make me uncomfortable."

"Mammals were exterminated on Thalassa long ago, weren't they?"

"Yes," I said. "They ate our eggs."

Ven walked forward and ran her primary digits over the female's legs. "They're quite well evolved," she said. "The skin hasn't a vestige of scales."

"Neither does yours except at the tip of your tail," I said tartly. "Don't get the idea that they're a primitive life form. Actually they are a *later* evolutionary type than we! If our ancestors had not developed intelligence enough to realize their peril, we would be extinct—and something like them would rule Thalassa today."

Ven shivered, "How horrible! I don't like thinking about it."

"Don't," I advised.

"What are we going to do with them?" Ven asked.

"I was going to analyze them and construct a proxy, but they're far too big to duplicate with our limited resources. I suppose the only thing we can do is to insert control circuits and use them as they are."

"Won't that be painful?"

"Only psychically. Physically they shouldn't suffer a bit. The brain, you know, feels no pain. It merely interprets stimuli from elsewhere."

"In mammals too?"

I shrugged. "I suppose so. Besides, what difference does it make? Once we're through with them we can destroy them if they're too badly damaged."

"That seems unfair."

"It's not a question of fairness. It's survival. If they don't perform properly, we shall have to dispose of them or they'll be back here with a whole herd. Of course, if they operate under control, we'll turn them loose when we're through with them. I doubt that their technology is advanced enough to recognize a bio-circuit if they saw one. And if it is, they will have learned nothing new."

"But why can't we keep them—take them back to Thalassa? They'd make an unusual contribution to the Central Zoo."

"I'm afraid not," I said. "I doubt if they'd survive space. The only part of the ship large enough to hold them would be the cargo storage compartment, and that's not shielded. A hyperjump would kill them. You wouldn't want even them to die *that* way, would you?"

Her aura turned gray. "No, I suppose not."

"There isn't a chance," I said, seizing her thought before it was uttered. "It would take ten of our lifetimes to reach our nearest outpost on normal spacedrive. Forget it."

"But—"

"Come along," I said, "I'll need your help to modify these brutes."

Actually it wasn't a hard job. Their brains were well developed and nicely compartmentalized. With our probes and instruments it was a simple enough matter to implant the necessary organic extensions of our instruments.

"That should do it," I murmured as I disconnected the leads I had jury-rigged into the analyzer. "They're clean as a Fardel's tooth." I was tired, but I had the pleasant feeling of accomplishment that comes from working with organic matter. Possibly if I were not so interested in History, I'd have become a medic. I do have a certain talent along that line.

At any rate, we now had a pair of proxies. With only normal fortune they would be completely undetectable.

"Is it all done?" Ven asked as she looked over my shoulder.

"Yes," I said. "But leave the probes in place until we test

them." I dragged my weary body once again into the control room and tried the headgear and circuits. They functioned absolutely perfectly.

"What do we do now?" Ven's projection came to me.

"Remove the probes and send them back to their camp. There's no sense in leaving them here."

"But, Eu—"

"No," I said. "They are not toys. They're tools. They're to do a job for us. Now stop acting like a child. When they bring us metal, you can play games with them—but not now. They're stressed, tired, and need rest. And they're going to get it."

"Yes, Eu." Her projection was submissive.

"But don't worry," I added kindly. "You can monitor them. I installed two extra circuits, one to the hypothalamus and the other to the tactile centers. You will be able to feel every sensation they experience. It will be just like having an extra body."

"Can I try it now?" she asked eagerly as she came into the control room.

"Go ahead," I said. "Put on a helmet and use the double control. Take them back to their camp and then neutralize the controller. As for me, I'm going to the refresher. I need it."

III

I AWOKE FROM PARTIAL ESTIVATION WITH VEN'S PROjection vibrating my antennae. "Eu! Come quickly! They're awake!"

I groaned. What did she expect? But it might be interesting to see how they behaved. And if they panicked, someone should be there to assume control.

I checked the chronometer. I had rested for eight satts, which should be enough. I felt as well as could be expected, so, with only a few choice Low-Thalassic expletives to help me, I managed to clamber out of the tank and stagger into the control room. Ven already had one of the helmets on. I picked up the other and flicked the switch to "on."

It was the male's—and he was talking. The words were gibberish, but the thoughts behind them were easy to read.

I was part of an entity called Donald G. Carlton, a male mammal of the human species. He was a "writer" and was mated to the female, who was called Edith and who worked in "motion pictures." They lived in a place called Hollywood, in a family-unit structure faintly similar to a children's creche. Custom on this world dictated that the female take one name of her mate, which indicated that the sex was even more subservient than female Thalassans. The male's body ached, but not as badly as I would have expected. And, as I expected, there was no sensitivity in the brain.

"Hey! Edith!" Donald said. "Get up!"

"Leave me alone, Don. I'm miserable," a lighter voice answered from the lumpy sack beside him. "I had the most awful dream."

"It must be the mountain air," he replied. "I did too."

"Whatever made me think this would be fun!" Edith said. "You and your meteor-hunting!" The sack heaved and twisted and her head appeared at one end. "I feel like I've been worked over with a baseball bat. Oh! My legs!"

"You're not alone," he said. "I guess it's the hard ground and these straitjackets they laughingly call sleeping bags."

"About that dream," Edith said. "It was horrible. There was this little green and yellow thing that looked like a cross between a lizard and a human being. It was sitting on my shoulders and I was naked—carrying it around, doing what it wanted me to do! I wanted to throw it off and stamp on it, but I couldn't. I just ran and ran, and all the time that little monster sat with its legs around my neck, hooting like an owl. Now, wasn't that something?"

Donald was very quiet. "You know," he said slowly, "essentially that was the same dream I had."

"But that can't be! People don't have the same nightmares."

"We did."

"Then maybe—maybe it wasn't a nightmare!"

"Nonsense. We're here. We're all right. But I think perhaps we'd better get out of here—oh, Keerist! I'm one solid bruise." He twisted around until he found the fastenings and opened the bag. With a groan he stood up.

Edith looked at him, her eyes wide with sudden terror. "Don," she said in a brittle voice, "didn't you wear pajamas when you went to bed last night?"

"Yes."

"Well, you're not wearing them now." An expression of horror crossed her face. "And neither am I," she added in a small voice.

I could feel the shock in Donald's brain as he looked down at himself. "That's not all I'm not wearing," he said dully. "I'm shaved!"

There was a brief flurry inside the other sleeping bag. "So am I!" Edith's voice was a whisper of fright. "That was no dream! I remember this. The lizard gave me something that I rubbed all over myself—and my hair came off. I didn't want to, but I couldn't help myself." Her hands went to her head and she sighed, "Well, *that's* all there. For a moment I thought—"

"My skin is different," Donald interrupted thoughtfully as he inspected himself. "It feels thicker. And I don't feel cold, although I'll bet it's nearly freezing outside."

"Don! Don't you understand? That dream was real!" Edith said.

"Of course it was—unless *this* is a dream. We could be having a nightmare about a nightmare . . ."

I looked at Ven.

"Just what did you do to them?" I asked.

She glowed guiltily. "I didn't know it would take their hair off," she said. "I was worried about their scratches, and the insects were biting them. So I made them rub on some of our skin conditioner."

I raised my digits toward the sky. "There is an Authority that looks over fools and Thalassan females," I said. "What made you so sure our conditioner would work on them? It might have been poisonous."

"I tried it on the male first," Ven said.

"Genius," I breathed with icy sarcasm, "sheer genius!"

"Well," she said, "it worked!" The eternal pragmatist

had applied her sole criterion. "And what's more they looked and smelled lots better after they used it."

I shrugged, gave it up and turned my attention back to the mammals.

Edith had emerged from her sack and was standing before the male.

"Do I look like a nightmare?" she demanded.

"No. More like a skinned rabbit—ouch! What did you do that for?" He rubbed his face where she struck him with her digits.

"There!" Edith said. *"Now* do you think it's a dream?"

"I never did," he replied mildly. "I've never dreamed in my life. I was just breaking it to you easy. It was real enough—even the blank spaces. I wonder—"

"You wonder what?"

"What their reason was for capturing us and then letting us go. It doesn't make sense. They wouldn't grab us just for fun. They're obviously intelligent, and probably thought we would be useful to them. But they turned us loose. So we couldn't be useful except maybe for amusement—but that doesn't jell. No. They've done something to us. They've let us go for a reason."

"Stop analyzing!" Edith said. "Why don't you just get scared, like I am!"

"I *am,*" he said, "but I like to figure things out. If I know what frightens me, it doesn't bother me so much."

"Do that while we're on the way home. Get your clothes on and let's get out of here! Right away!"

"We have to pack."

"Oh, leave it! Let's get out while we can!"

"I don't think we're in any danger," he said.

"Well—I don't want to stay here a minute longer!"

"All right. We'll go. But we'll pack first. Look at it logically. They had us cold. We didn't escape. We were *let* go. So why, if they didn't want us then, should they want us now?"

"Unless they can get us any time they want us."

"You have a point there, but if that's the case, they can get us anyway. So let's pack."

"You can pack if you want to. I'm leaving!" Edith pulled the opening to the tent and slipped out.

"Edith!" Donald cried. "Wait!"

I touched Ven. "Stop her," I said.

Edith's voice came from outside. "Don!" she called in a tight voice. "Don! Help me! *I can't move!*"

"Try coming back here and see what happens," Donald said slowly.

Edith's head appeared in the entrance. "I'm back," she said in a small voice.

"I thought you would be. Now let's pack and perhaps they'll let us go. It's obvious that we can't run away."

"But why? *What's happened to us?*"

"If I told you, you'd think I'm crazy."

"Tell me anyway. It can't be any worse than this."

"I think," Donald said slowly as he began to roll up his sleeping bag, "That we were kidnapped by extraterrestrials."

"Martians?"

"Not necessarily," he said. "But if I remember my nightmare correctly, they aren't human—and they are obviously smart. So they aren't of this earth. We don't have intelligent reptiles here. And with their ability to control our actions, I'd say that they were from a considerably higher culture than ours. They've done things to us—but I don't think they did them just for fun. They want us to do something."

"What?"

"I don't know. Right now I'd guess they want us to pack our things. Let's do it and get out of here. This place smells like the reptile house in the zoo!"

I was amazed. The native's analysis was as logical as my own would have been under similar circumstances. There was nothing wrong with his mind or with his courage. That big braincase held a smoothly functioning mind and a cold courage I could almost envy. In a similar fix I wasn't sure that I could be so calm.

My respect for him mounted. If there were others like him on this world, his race could be a potential danger spot for the whole Galaxy. And, with the natural antipathy between our races, these creatures could be *trouble* if they ever reached space. I wondered for a moment if Authority had known this when It brought me here. There must be some design that I should land here when this race was still capable of being frustrated.

For the sake of civilization I would have to learn more about these mammals. Much more. But since the male had deduced so much, there was only one logical course of action. I adjusted the filters on my helmet to allow the passage of surface thoughts, twisted the dials on the controller until the meters balanced and projected gently.

"Donald—listen to me," I said.

He stiffened. "I thought you would be somewhere around," he said. "Who are you?"

"My name is Eu Kor, and I am a native of Thalassa."

"Where's that?"

"A good many spatial units from here—a good many of your light years," I amended. "I mean you no harm, but I need your cooperation. My spaceship is crippled. Our fuel has deteriorated. We need more and I want you to get it for us. We captured you because we need your help. Being a native you would not make a ripple in this society. And we would create whirlpools."

"What is this material you want?"

"A metal. Atomic number 50, a white metal used as an alloy component of primitive metallic cultures," I said. "It shouldn't be too hard to get." I didn't realize how hard it was to describe what I wanted. I wasn't getting through, and it bothered me. The culture barrier was almost as bad as though we couldn't contact mind to mind.

"I think you mean tin," he said. I grasped the concept and it seemed right.

"Bring me some and I will run tests," I said.

"And what do I get in return?"

I thought quickly. If he wanted to bargain, perhaps we could reach an agreement. It's always better to have a cooperative proxy. They don't cause nearly the trouble in management. And I had other things to do than monitor natives. There was a great deal of repair work to be done on the ship before she would fly again. The subspace radio power bank had to be rebuilt and the circuits should be checked.

"I can give you knowledge that you wouldn't have for decades—maybe centuries," I said. "And I can adjust your bodies for a longer and happier life." I shot a glance at Ven still immersed in her helmet. "In fact, I have made a few adjustments already."

"So I noticed," Donald thought dryly. "Although whether they're an improvement or not I couldn't say. But did you have to go to all this trouble?"

"Think of us—and discount the fact that you carried us because our bodies are too weak for your heavy world." I said. "Did you like us?"

"No," he said. "You repelled me. I disliked you on sight more than I can say."

"The emotion is mutual," I said. "Yet I can endure you. But with your glandular outlook, you could only think of destroying us."

"That is true. But you treated us like animals."

"You are animals," I said logically.

"We are masters of this world. We recognize no higher authority. We are free people—not slaves. And unless we are treated as free agents, you will get no cooperation from us."

"I can force you to do as I wish," I said.

"Prove it!"

I took over. And while Donald watched with helpless horror his hand picked up a knife and drew it across his arm. The keen edge split the tissues neatly and the blood flowed.

"Don! What are you doing!" Edith screamed and then stiffened as Ven took control.

"Observe," I said as I released control.

"Why, you—" Donald began—and then continued in a tone of wonder. "Why—the cut's closing! There's no more blood—It's gone!"

"It's just one of the improvements I mentioned," I said smugly. "You also had a patch of scar tissue on your left lung and infected kidneys. You do not have them now.

Had you not met us you would have been dead within five of your years."

He was shaken. I could feel it.

"I do have Bright's disease," he said thoughtfully.

"You had it," I corrected.

"All right," he said suddenly, "I'll bargain with you. You've done me a good turn and it deserves a payment. I'll help you get your metal." He grinned ruefully. "I guess I couldn't do anything else."

"It makes it easier this way," I said. I smiled to myself. I was telling him the truth, but not all of it. Nor did I trust him. There was fear and hatred in his lower centers, and a formless feeling in his upper levels that he could outsmart any damn lizard that ever lived. He didn't realize that I could read his surface thoughts.

"Just remember," I said, "I can control you completely, if necessary, and pick your brain for data whether you wish it or not. And forget those ideas of informing your authorities about us. Except with your mate, you cannot communicate to anyone about us. There's a basic block in your brain that will result in irreversible mental damage if you try."

This last was not quite the truth. But I hoped that, by establishing fear, I would prevent talk. "Now find us samples of the metal I want." I withdrew and went back to scanning.

"What was going on there?" Edith said. "You were talking to empty air. And why did you cut yourself?"

"It was one of our reptilian friends," Don said. "Like I thought, they're right with us—every way. He's a weird sort. Wants to trade health and knowledge for tin."

"Tin?"

"Yeah. At least I think it's tin. His description of the metal fits. They use it instead of rocket juice."

"But that knife—your arm?"

"Look. No cut—no blood. That's one of the things they did to us. We've got puncture-proof skin."

"Is that good?"

"It isn't bad. And I don't think I'll ever have to shave again. As I remember I put that stuff on my face. Anyway, we now have a couple of fairy godmothers who ride around in spaceships instead of pumpkin coaches."

"You're mixing your stories," Edith said. "Cinderella traveled in the pumpkin coach, not her fairy godmother. And besides, it's not funny. We're more like those poor souls in the Middle Ages who were possessed by devils—incubuses, I think they called them."

"It makes no difference what you call them," Donald said indifferently. "Whatever they are, we've got them and they're not going to leave until they're damn good and ready. Incidentally, yours is a female, so she's probably a succubus. Now don't start screaming. You'll probably be paralyzed if you do."

"I won't scream," Edith said dully. "I'm too numb to scream."

IV

WE HAD SURPRISINGLY LITTLE TROUBLE WITH THE two natives once they realized we could control them if we wished. Of the two, Edith was the worst. She refused to cooperate and had to be forced into the simplest actions.

"We're going to have trouble with that one," I observed as Ven looked at me with faint exasperation in her yellow eyes.

"Oh, I don't think so," she said. "Not really. This is a normal female reaction. It's a phase. Like the way I felt when the Eugenics Council selected me to be your mate."

"Did you feel like that?" I asked with surprise.

"Of course. I wanted to make my own choice."

"But you never told me."

"There was no need. I came around to the Council's view before I met you. And Edith will come around to mine. Don't worry. I know how to handle this."

And she did.

I helped a little by alerting a few reflex arcs and basic attitudes, but Ven wouldn't allow me to modify the higher centers.

"There's no need to make her a mindless idiot," Ven said. "You didn't do that to Donald."

"Yes, but Donald controls his emotions. He doesn't like me any better than Edith likes you, but he doesn't work himself into an emotional homogenate every time I make a suggestion. We argue it out like rational intelligences. Often I can use his experience and viewpoint. And when I can't agree, he will cooperate rather than operate under control. He's not like that bundle of glands and emotions you are trying to make into a useful proxy."

"She *is* a problem," Ven admitted, "but if I had her here—"

"That can be arranged," I said. "I'll give you two weeks. And if that doesn't work you let me perform a prefrontal block."

"That isn't very long."

"That's all we can afford," I told her.

"All right, I can try. In a month I know I could do it."

Donald protested violently when I told him what we planned for Edith, but when I gave him the alternative, he reluctantly agreed.

He passed a story that Edith would be visiting friends, and brought her to the ship.

At once Ven went systematically to work to reduce the mammal to an acquiescent state that would permit control. Since sleep is unknown to our race but necessary for mammals, the task of breaking down the female's resistance was simplified by physical exhaustion. Ven also found that the mammal's sleeping time could be used to strengthen the new reflex channels built during her waking periods. The results were amazing, even to me, and I'm fairly well trained in neuromanipulation. Halfway through the second week the mammal's surrender was complete.

"Another day and she can go back," Ven said. "I can finish her training at long range. Now that I have the channels established, I don't think she'll be any further trouble."

I took the helmet and scanned Edith. "Hmm," I said.

"Do you know what you've done? You've built yourself into an Authority image."

"I know," Ven said smugly. "She is essentially a dependent type. Her mate was her decision maker. That's why I had to get her alone. It wasn't too hard once I knew where to look. As a girl, her mother made the decisions for her. As a woman, Donald has done it. And when I faced her with situations where she had to decide and where the decisions were invariably wrong, she transferred the decision-making power to me."

I looked at her sharply. "I had no idea that you intended to make a pet out of her," I said. "Otherwise I wouldn't have permitted this."

"Well, it's too late now. And besides, it was the only way I could do it in the time you allotted. But don't worry. She'll be as good a tool as your precious Donald—maybe even a better one—because she'll do things to please me and not merely because they're expedient."

Ven had a point there. But it isn't a good policy to get emotionally involved with alien races. However, the deed was done, and as long as Ven was happy I didn't care. I only hoped that she wouldn't become too attached to the creature.

Donald was much more cooperative and much tougher. He had realized from the start that there was no profit in objecting to my demands. But, unlike Edith, he gave me no handle for leverage. He arranged his life to include the unpleasant fact of my existence, and that was that. Where Ven achieved a form of mastery, I never received anything more than acquiescence. There were levels in Donald I could not touch. At first it irked me, but then I realized that I was the greater gainer. For Donald was a constant challenge, a delight to the mind, an outward collaborator and an inward enemy. Our relationship had all the elements of an armed truce. And I often thought that if I did not have the crushing advantage of control, our contest might have been more even.

Although in time Donald's hatred became modified to a grim sort of tolerance, and his repulsion into something that closely resembled admiration, he never lost the basic species antipathy which separated us. And in that regard our feelings were mutual. The ancient Thalassan proverb that familiarity breeds friendship simply didn't apply. We held a mutual respect for each other, and in a fashion we cooperated, but I never could pierce the armor of resentment that shielded him. I tried, but finally I gave up. There would never be friendship between us. We were too different—

And too alike.

In the days that followed the first contact, I proceeded according to approved methods of investigating alien civilizations. At my request, Donald went to the local book repository and we went through a number of works on law, government, social structure, and finance. I felt that I should have some knowledge of this mammalian culture before attempting to refuel the ship. There was no sense in calling attention to myself any more than necessary. If I could obtain what I wanted and leave quietly, I would be perfectly happy. This world was of interest—but it was too disturbing to contemplate for an extended period of time.

"You were right, Eu Kor," Ven said to me as we scanned the pattern of the mammals' culture. "If you had picked any place less isolated than this, we might have been engulfed in that maelstrom."

I nodded. "It was more luck than design," I said, "but I am happy that we are no closer. This world is not for us. It is too strange, too alien with its uncontrolled emotionalism and frightening energy."

"It reminds me of a malignant neoplasm," Ven said, "growing uncontrolled, destroying the body from which it draws sustenance. Have you ever seen such a seething flux of people—such growth—such appalling waste and carelessness?"

I shook my head. "The only parallel that comes to mind is Sennor."

"But that's a dead world—killed by a suicidal race that achieved technology before it had attained culture."

"Which is precisely the situation we have here. Or have you observed their social inequities and history? Periodically these mammals erupt in merciless riots and slaughters over things that could be settled by reason. And oddly enough, these 'wars,' as humans call them, have the effect of stimulating technology. This is a race that apparently loves death and battle. A barbaric horde of cultural morons, with a civilized technology geared to mutual destruction."

"Frankly, I've been scanning through Edith. I've seen only the technical excellence of their entertainment industry, and the enormous waste which goes into the making of one of their productions."

"We must have a synthesis," I said, "and pool our observations."

Ven nodded.

"I'm not at all happy about this place," I continued. "It makes me uncomfortable."

"Could we modify it?" Ven asked.

I shook my head. "It would take an entire task force to do that. Reeducation of this culture would have to begin at birth after appropriate culling. We would have to start from the beginning. I fear that the council would never authorize such an action on behalf of mammals. We are altruistic . . . but not that altruistic."

"Then they will destroy themselves?"

"I fear so. This culture has a poor prognosis. But it is perhaps better so. Or would you like to see them roaming through the Galaxy?"

Ven shuddered. "Not as they are now. Not these fierce, combative, stupid brutes. Individuals perhaps, but not the race. They would have to learn the rules of civilization first."

"Yet they show no sign of learning. If they can't even cooperate with their own species, how in Authority's name could they ever get along with the dissimilar races of this island universe?"

"They couldn't. We would have to quarantine them."

"So isn't it better to save the expense and let them quarantine themselves?"

"I suppose so." Ven's aura was a dull gray and mine

matched the gloom of hers. It is hard to stand aloof and watch a race condemn itself to death.

We fed our observations into the analyzer, together with all extraneous data we could lay our digits on via our proxies—not to prove our conclusions but to determine the means by which we could obtain the power metal with the least possible repercussions in this society. We both realized it would be fatal to expose ourselves. The mammalian technology was sufficiently advanced for them to duplicate the essential portions of our ship, and chaos could result if they secured a road to the stars. Generations of effort would be required to confine them again to their homeworld.

Thinking in this manner caused me to take certain precautions with the drive mechanism that would ensure no trace of our craft remaining if I projected a certain impulse at a given strength. Ven, of course, was appalled at my action, although she realized its grim necessity.

And in the meantime we worked with our proxies, I attempting to establish some means of quietly obtaining the metal we needed, and Ven doing nothing so far as I could determine that would further our mission. At that, Edith was in no position to obtain metal, and Ven was too young and inexperienced in contact work to attempt a mission of such delicacy. Since Edith amused her, I was content to leave them both to their own devices while I worked with Donald to speed our departure.

"In this society," I said to Donald, "it seems that one can accomplish anything with this medium of exchange you call money."

"That's close to a fundamental truth," Donald replied.

"And you are not too well supplied with it?" I asked.

"Those four ingots I brought you last week put a vicious dent in our savings account."

"Isn't your trade as an author profitable?"

"Only in spurts. It's a feast-famine existence. But it's the only one I care to lead."

"But popular fiction makes money—and you can write."

"I wish you'd tell that to my agent. He seems to have other ideas."

"I have recently read some of your fiction," I said, "and have noticed that it has certain basics that could easily be applied to an analyzer. There is no reason why we could not cooperate and produce a work that would yield a great deal of money."

Donald laughed. "Now I've heard everything!" he said. "You mean to tell me *you* could write a book *humans* would buy?"

"No, you would write the book. I would merely furnish the idea, the research data, the plot, and the general story outline. In your popular fiction," I continued, "there are four basic elements and a plot that can be varied about twenty-five ways. There is small need for philosophy and little need for abstract thought. In fact, there is no need at all for anything but glandular excitation. All that is really necessary is plenty of action, enough understanding of the locale and events to avoid anachronism—and the basics."

"What are these basics?" Donald said. "As a writer I'd like to know them."

"There are four," I ticked them off on my digits. "First, violation of the ethical or moral code of your race; second, adequate amounts of cohabitation between the characters; third, brutality; and fourth—murderous assault."

"Hmm. Sin, sex, sadism and slaughter," Donald commented.

"You know, you might have something there."

"I have prepared an outline and a synopsis of such a book," I said. "It is a historical novel. It should sell. Most historical novels do."

"You've done what?" Donald gasped. Then he laughed. "Of all the insufferable egoists I've ever seen!"

"Listen," I said, ordering him to silence while I outlined the opening chapter.

"I can't stop you," Donald said. "But why should this happen to me? Isn't it bad enough to be bossed around by you lizards without having to be forced to ghost-write your amateur literary efforts?"

"It is laid in the period of your history called the Renaissance," I continued, "and deals with a young man of a noble but impoverished house who rose to power by cleverness, amorality and skill with the sword."

"I suppose the girl is the daughter of the local duke."

"No," I said, "she is the favorite wife of a Saracen corsair."

"Well, that's a switch," Donald said. "Tell me more."

So I did. I outlined the opening and told him the major points of the whole story . . . as the computer had synthesized it out of seven excellent novels of the period and a four-volume set of Renaissance history.

Donald was enthralled. "You're right," he said. "It will sell. It's lousy literature, but it's got appeal. With this story and my writing we can out-Spillane Mickey." He was more enthusiastic than I had ever seen him appear before.

"Who is Spillane?" I asked.

Donald looked at me as though he thought I was crazy and shook his head. "I can get to work on it as soon as I get home," Donald said. "And if I keep at it, it'll be ready for mailing in a couple of weeks. I'll get it off to my agent and we'll see. I hate to admit it, but I think you're right about the yarn. It should sell like hotcakes."

"That is fine. It should provide us with the medium of exchange, which is necessary in this society."

"It's not necessary," Donald grinned. "It's essential."

V

DONALD'S PREDICTION WAS A GOOD ONE. THE BOOK sold—and sold well. Despite the outright plagiarism of ideas and source material, it was hailed as a new novel—one that stimulated thought with its realistic approach to the life of the times. And we prospered amazingly.

With the advance money, I had Donald buy the land on which the ship was resting, together with the valley and rimrock. Having thus secured our landing site I felt a bit more comfortable. The comfort was even greater when, at Donald's suggestion, a fence was placed around the property and electronic telltales were installed. The remainder of the royalties were used to purchase tin and supplies.

But despite our prosperity and the regular supply of tin that came to me as a result of my adventure in fiction, and the certainty that Ven and I would be leaving, Donald was not happy.

As a successful new author he had to travel to meetings in various cities. He had to speak at public gatherings. He had to meet with publishers eager to receive rights to his next book. And Edith did not go with him.

Ven said adamant on this point. "It's bad enough that she is working on this motion picture," she said, "but I'm not going to have her traveling all over the face of this planet. She's the only amusement I have since we must stay cooped up in this place. I'm not going to let her go."

Donald was upset about it. He was so angry that he came to visit me voluntarily, and the sight of Edith's little car parked under the trees below the ship infuriated him even more. It took the controller to make him keep his distance as he stood in front of the airlock and hated me.

"Damn you!" he swore. "You can't do this to me! Edith's my wife and I don't like this relationship between her and that—that *dinosaur!* It isn't healthy."

"It's out of my hands," I said. "Edith is Ven's responsibility."

"It's not only that," he raged. "Ever since you lizards butted into our lives Edith looks at me like I was a stranger." His face twisted. "I'll admit she has her reasons. But that gives her no call to ask Ven's advice rather than mine. When I told her I wanted her to come with me, the first thing she said was that she'd ask Ven. She doesn't do one damn thing without that cold-blooded little monster's consent! She even asks advice on what clothes she should wear!" He laughed harshly. "The blind asking advice from the blind!"

I couldn't help chuckling. Ven, like all Thalassans, had never worn anything in her life except a utility belt. Clothing has never been a feature of our culture. Since it isn't necessary on Thalassa, it was never developed, and since our sex impluses are periodic it has never been useful to attract either males or females. "I can see your point," I said. "Ven's ideas along that line would be zero."

"Not quite," Donald said angrily. "She likes moccasins. Apparently they make feet look more like your pads."

"Well?"

"But that's it! Edith's idea of what a well-dressed housewife should wear is—*moccasins!* She damn near caused a riot the other day when our TV repairman called to fix the set. We'll be lucky if we're not forced to move because of that little incident!"

"I'll speak to Ven," I said. "And if that doesn't work, I'll insert a block against such a thing happening again. I don't want special attention called to you. That sort of thing will stop right now."

"Thanks," Donald said. "But I should be the one to stop it."

"Face it," I replied, "you aren't. Not now. But you will be once we're gone."

"Which can't be too soon to suit me," he said. "I spend every spare moment collecting tin for you. Edie doesn't. She *wants* Ven to stay."

"They seem to be happy with each other. Edith comes up here regularly."

"I know," he said bitterly. "She's here more often that she's home. I can't see what fun she gets out of running around these hills stripped to the skin carrying your mate on her shoulders."

"I wouldn't know," I said. "Certainly you never seem to enjoy performing that service for me."

"I don't even like the thought of it. I'm not an animal, after all."

"But you are," I said. "So am I. The only difference is that I am a superior animal and you, being inferior, conform to my wishes. It is a law of nature that the superior type will inevitably rule. The inferior either conforms or dies. And you have no desire to die."

He shook his head. "But I can still object," he said.

"At that?" I asked pointing across the meadow with a primary digit.

Edith was running, her long yellow hair floating free behind her. Ven, high on her shoulders in a seat the two of them had contrived, waved gaily at us as they came up. Edith was flushed and laughing. Her eyes sparkled and her smooth bronze body gleamed in the sunlight. She lowered Ven to the ground, slipped the harness off her smooth shoulders and stood behind my mate, breathing deeply but not at all distressed.

"Oh, Donald!" she said. "We had a wonderful climb—clear up to the top of the ridge! And coming down was almost like flying! I'll tell you all about it in a minute, right after I take a dip in the pool. Ven doesn't like it when I sweat." She turned and ran down to the little pool in the meadow.

"See what I mean!" Donald gritted.

"She seems happy. She's not hurt. And Ven's little weight doesn't seem to bother her. What are you complaining about?"

Donald growled something unintelligible, turned on his heel and walked away.

I let him go. There was no sense in making him angrier than he was. After a moment the snarl of his car's engine rose to a crescendo then faded away into the distance.

A few minutes later Edith came back to the ship. "Why did Don leave?" she asked.

"Perhaps he had something to do," Ven said.

She pouted. "He's always so busy nowadays," she said sulkily. "He isn't nice like he used to be. Do you think he's tired of me?"

"No, I don't think so. He just doesn't like you spending so much time up here," I said.

"But it's fun—and Ven likes it," she said. "I like it too. And since he isn't home much any more, it's the only place where I can relax and be myself." She brushed the drops of water from her body and shook out her damp hair. "It's wonderful up here—so quiet and peaceful—and Ven's so nice."

My mate's aura glowed a pleased pink as I turned an embarrassed lavender. It was almost criminal, I thought, what Ven had done to the girl. Donald might be my servant, but I had never attempted to condition him into liking it. As much as possible we operated as equals, rather than in this sickening relationship which Ven had imposed upon Edith. To avoid showing my displeasure I went up to the control room, donned my helmet and went into rapport with Donald.

"I'm sorry," I said. "I hadn't realized the true situation. The best thing for both of us is for Ven and me to leave as quickly as possible."

"How quick is that?" he shot back angrily.

"Four thousand pounds more," I said.

"Whew! That can must drink tin."

"It takes a great deal to leave a planet," I said. "And hyperspace demands a great deal more. Once we develop an inertialess drive it will be easier. But we've only been working on it a thousand years. These things take time."

"I imagine. Well, are you going to do anything about Edith?"

"No," I said. "It would only make things worse. The relationship has gone too far. Ven has become an Authority-image."

"You could break it."

"But I won't. I'm fond of Ven."

"You're a damned little tyrant," Donald said. "You like to see a human squirm."

"Be thankful that I'm the worst tyrant you'll see," I answered sharply. "You could really learn about them if the Slaads knew you existed. They're more advanced than you. And, unlike us, they're warlike and predatory. They breed mammals for food. However, I'll put up a marker on your moon before I leave. They respect Thalassa and won't preempt our claims."

"You mean you're going to lay claim to Earth?"

"Only technically. We'll exercise it only if the Governing Council decides it will be to our advantage."

"What would you do if you took over?" Don asked curiously.

"Clean things up," I said. "Stop wars, stabilize the population, increase production and distribution, give you an effective central government and an understandable legal code, and eliminate the unfit. In three generations you'd be Class VI all over your planet."

"It sounds good. What's the catch."

"The catch," I said, "is that you wouldn't like it. You mammals are erratic, emotional and uncontrolled. You do not reason well, and you have no race discipline."

"What's that?"

"The capability of sacrificing units for the benefit of the whole. Eugenics control, culling the unfit."

"You're talking about human beings!" Donald exploded.

"And what makes a human being different from any other animal?" I asked. "Would you hesitate to dispose of an animal that was unfit to breed?"

He sighed. "No," he said. "But that's not the same."

"What's the difference? And realize, it's done for your betterment."

"Just a bunch of murderous little altruists," Donald sneered. "Out of the kindness of your cold-blooded hearts—"

"That's the trouble with you lower orders," I interrupted. "You get emotional. Your observations have no basis in logic. Actually, the Galaxy wouldn't even quiver if the lot of you disappeared tomorrow. Yet you think the universe rotates about your heads."

"I didn't—"

"Don't interrupt," I snapped. "You—your race—your whole pitiful little civilization is ready mentally and almost ready technologically to commit suicide. If we came and saved you, you would owe us eternal gratitude, but I doubt if we'd get it."

"You wouldn't," Donald assured me. "There wouldn't be a human alive who wouldn't hate you."

"I realize that—and that is one of the reasons I should report your world unfavorably to the council. We could hardly take on an altruism mission like this unless we felt that our work would be appreciated. It would be better to let you kill yourselves."

"Altruism!"

"In a sense. At least your race would be the greater gainers. All we'd get would be your excess population."

"And what would you want them for—slaves?"

"Authority, no!" I said, shocked in spite of myself. "We'd merely process them for food."

He was silent after that.

Donald was away again, at a publisher's meeting. Our new book laid in Restoration England was going to be an even greater success than the first if the advance notices were any criterion. Edith was at a studio party celebrating the completion of the picture in which she was working. And Ven was bored.

For a while she sat in on Donald's conference in a city called New York, but that proved to be uninteresting. I was busy with a faulty fuel feed in the drive chamber. The sun was hot, and the day was promising to be extremely warm even though it was not yet noon. It was one of those days when nothing happens, and I was grateful for it. I had had enough of emotional tangles to last me for some time. It was almost soothing to work with the robots on insensate machinery rather than supervise a pair of highly charged mammals and a hardly less unstable mate.

The association with these entities hadn't done Ven a great deal of good. In fact, I could notice a deterioration of her character that bothered me. She no longer looked at me with respect. Indeed, her yellow eyes at times held a pitying amusement that I should be so weak as to argue with Donald. I didn't bother to point out that the three tons of power metal had virtually all been brought aboard through Donald's efforts, and that our conveniences, our defenses, our robots and our very lives were due to the working arrangements I had established.

The only useful thing Edith had done in the past month was to help me change the tube liners in the steering jets. Her size and strength had made the job easy—and it was normally a hard one, since the robots didn't have the flexibility or balance that Edith, with her dancer's body, possessed. The job had taken two days. It would have taken better than a week if I had to use robots.

The mammals, I thought, would be of distinct value as members of spaceport maintenance crews. Their combination of immense strength and high intelligence would be useful to our society. I made a note of it and added it to the data I was assembling for the Council. It was foolish, perhaps, but I couldn't help feeling an interest in these creatures.

I looked across the little valley that was our domain. It was an idyllic life we were leading. Unhurried—peaceful—the sort of life I thoroughly enjoyed. It would have been perfect if it wasn't for the insane and dangerous world on which it was being lived.

Of course it was too good to last. Idylls invariably are. The peace of ours was shattered abruptly when Ven came into the drive room and disturbed my work. Her aura blazed a rich violet.

"Eu," she said. "Come up to the control room. Something's wrong!"

"What," I asked.

"It's Edith. I can't do a thing with her."

"You're not supposed to. She's working now."

"She is not! Her studio has finished the picture and they're having a party."

"That's nice. I hope you're letting her have a good time."

"I told her to. But I never imagined what they'd be doing!" Ven's voice was anguished.

"Well, what *are* they doing?"

"Ingesting ethanol to excess!"

"Ethanol!" I gasped. "Oh no!"

I hadn't realized that normal mammals consumed excess amounts of the stuff, although there were references to it in the literature. I thought that was merely literary exaggeration. After all, we had been here scarcely half a year, and we hadn't really learned too much about the details of mammalian society. Donald's kidneys had forced him to lead a quiet life, and the passing of Edith from his control to Ven's had caused no remarkable alterations in her doings.

I should have paid more attention to their customs. But I had been too busy. I swore as I reached for my control helmet. I'd have to stop this before it became serious. Donald would be of no help to me. He was several thousand vursts away, and even under the best circumstances couldn't be expected back for a day.

I didn't bother to call him, but instead adjusted the controls to Edith's setting.

VI

A HORDE OF GAILY DRESSED MAMMALS SURROUNDED me, their faces and bodies oddly fuzzy and distorted. Edith's voice was equally fuzzy. There was something wrong with her centers. I tapped the helmet and checked the controller just in case it was on our end, but they were functioning perfectly. There was nothing wrong—merely the fact that ethanol was disturbing the biocircuits I had implanted in her brain. I swore a few choice expletives of Low Thalassan and tried to get through by increasing the power. It did no good.

"I c'n still feel that li'l lizard in m' head," Edith announced, "Gimme another drink. I wanna wash her out. Darn li'l lizard makes me do things I dowanna do. It wants me to quit, but I wanna get drunk."

"Take it easy," a fuzzy male face said. "You're loaded. Why does a nice chick like you hafta be loaded? Whyncha get outa here? I gotta nice place over in Santa Monica where—"

The face disappeared.

"Hey! Alice! Golly, I almos' din't reckanize you. Howya doin?"

"Better than you, Edith. You're drunk. And from the looks of you, you're going to be sick if you don't get some fresh air."

"Gotta go spit in the eye of my li'l lizard," Edith said "Y'wanna come with me? I got Don's car. We c'n get outa here an' get some fresh air—an' I c'n tell that li'l lizard what I think of her."

"What are you talking about?"

"You wanna see my li'l lizard. She's got yella eyes, and a li'l tail, and she turns all kindsa colors, and she lives in a rock with a door in it, and she makes me do things I dowanna do. It ain't so bad though. Mosta the time I like it. Not alla time though. That's why I wanna spit in her eye. She c'n tell me all she wants—but she's gotta leave me'n Don alone. I love that guy." Edith started sobbing—why, I couldn't understand.

"She's maudlin," I said to Ven. "No one's going to believe a thing she is saying. But this should be a warning to us. We'll have to put in a block against drinking ethanol. I didn't realize how badly it can affect the biocircuits." I handed the helmet back to Ven. "You can watch this mess if you want to. I'm going to our quarters."

I slipped out of the control chair and walked across the room.

I was stronger now, more accustomed to the gravity, and it didn't bother me unless I had to stand for long periods of time. I turned in the doorway to look at Ven. She had the helmet on again and her aura was a crackling red. I shook my head. Edith was due for a bad time when the effects of that hydrocarbon wore off.

I had hardly fallen into light estivation when Ven's projection crashed through my antennae.

"Eu! Get up! Come here quickly!"

With a groan I came slowly back to full facility and ran to the control room. Ven's face was filled with panic.

"They're coming up here," she said. "A whole carful of them!"

"Who?"

"Edith's drunken friends! Somehow she's collected six of them and they're driving up here to spit in my eye!"

Despite myself, I laughed. Ven looked so outraged I couldn't help it.

"We can close the airlock," I said, "and they can't tell us from a rock."

"I won't! I'm going to teach that girl a lesson she won't forget in a hurry! I've listened to myself being insulted for two hours—and she's still going strong. When she gets up here I'll show her whose eyes she'll spit in!"

Ven was raging. I'd never seen her so emotional before. Her aura swelled and ebbed in ruddy shades as her breath came and went in short gasps.

"And how do you propose to do that?" I asked.

"I'll stat her!" Ven raged. "I'll stat every one of them!"

I blinked. "I wouldn't do that," I said mildly. "What can we do with them? The two we have are bad enough. And if you stat them, we'll have to kill or condition them. We couldn't let them go home with a story like the one they'd tell."

"I don't care," Ven said. "You can do what you like about the rest of them, but that Edith is going to learn a lesson." She was being emotional and quite unwilling to listen to reason—and she was larger and stronger than I. Despite my protests, she jerked a stat projector from the rack and strode toward the open airlock.

"Thalassa!" she exclaimed. "They're coming through the gate! They'll be here in a minute."

I could hear the roar of a protesting engine groaning up the trail to the lower meadow as I hurried after Ven. As I reached the airlock, the gray body of Donald's station wagon poked its nose around the trees below our ship.

Ven stood rigidly in the airlock, waiting, her lips tight and her eyes narrow. She took a firmer grip on the stat as the car stopped and the giggling, half-sober humans tumbled out. I was in a quandary. I didn't want Ven to shoot, but I couldn't close the airlock with her inside it. So I stood, hesitating while the group of gaily dressed mammals came toward us through the trees, their high voices loud in the stillness.

"Gotta find that li'l lizard an tell her to stop meddling with my life," Edith's voice came to my ears.

Ven stiffened beside me as the group broke out of the trees in front of the ship.

"Why, Edie, it's beautiful!" a voice said. "It's a fairy glen! No wonder you'd never tell us where you got that suntan! And that big rock—it's just like you said—And—uh!" The voice never finished as Ven pressed the trigger.

I looked down at the six crumpled mammalian bodies and the lone standing figure that looked stupidly up at us.

"Well," I said. "You've done it this time. Now are you satisfied?

"No," Ven said. "Not half." Her voice was tight with

anger. She looked down at Edith. "Come here!" she said.

"Dowanna," Edith replied uncertainly. "You've made Don leave me. I don't like you." But habit was stronger than alcohol and under the furious lash of Ven's voice she came unsteadily forward.

"Do you understand me, you little sarf!" Ven snapped icily. "I said *come here!*" She took the control box from her waist and viciously twisted the intensity dial to maximum. At this range its force was irresistible, even with alcohol-deadened synapses. Edith shuddered and moved toward us, her hands clumsily tearing at the fabric that covered her.

"I'm comin'! You don' hafta shout. I ain't deaf. I ain't done nothin'!" She sat down beside the airlock and struggled out of her clothing, ripping the thin fabric under the last of Ven's anger until she was completely naked. Then she stood up and reached her hands toward Ven.

"You're not going to try to ride her while she's in that condition?" I said.

"This is my affair," Ven replied grimly. "I'm going to get this settled."

I shrugged.

There was no sense reasoning with her while she was in that mood. And if she wanted to kill herself that was her concern. I watched her drop onto Edith's shoulders, wind one hand viciously into the mammal's long blonde hair and guide the gross body into a shambling walk toward the meadow. Edith swayed dangerously, but somehow she managed to stay on her feet as they disappeared into the trees.

I walked over to the six bodies, gave each of them a light stat to make sure they would remain quiet and sat down beside the nearest one to think.

Ven's anger had left me a sizable problem. What on earth could I do with six human females? I needed them like I needed a broken digit. Time passed and the sun rose toward the zenith, and finally I came to a decision. Since we had them on our hands, we might as well make use of them. Killing would be too dangerous.

And presently Edith came through the trees, a sick,

tired, sober Edith whose face was dirty and tear streaked, carrying a grim Ven whose aura smoldered a reddish brown.

"What did you do to her?" I asked.

"None of your business," Ven snapped. "She's all right now. Aren't you, Edith?"

"Yes, Ven—and I won't do it again. Honest I won't."

"You'd better not," Ven said grimly. "Now I suppose we have some work to do."

"You certainly have," I said. "If it wasn't for your temper we wouldn't have this mess on our hands. Now get moving! Have Edith carry these girls to the ship." I gestured at the prone bodies. "And you, get inside and bring out the control equipment and connect the leads to the computer." I was angry, too. Under the force of my superior will, the two females scurried to obey. "I'm disgusted with you, Ven," I said angrily. "Just because your pet went to a party, you don't have to act childish. Did you expect she'd behave like a Thalassan?"

"I trusted her," Ven said.

"It just goes to show that you can't trust an animal too far," I said. "Now get moving. Bring the probes first. We have a lot of work to do before evening."

It was finished sooner than I expected. The sun was still in the sky, but close to the edge of the hills. The row of mammalian bodies slumbered peacefully beside the airlock. Ven looked down at them speculatively.

"No," I said. "You have one, and that's enough."

"But," Ven said.

"I've humored you," I said. "I've let you act like a lower order. Now I want to see you behave like a civilized being. For unless you do, I shall have to take steps. I'm tired of this childishness."

"I'll be all right now," Ven replied. "We've come to an understanding." She gestured at Edith with her primary digit and the big mammal shivered. I wondered what Ven had done to her. Edith was thoroughly cowed—actually afraid of little Ven, who was less than one fifth her size. In a way, I felt an odd sort of pride in my mate that she should achieve mastery over such an intelligent and potentially dangerous brute. I knew perfectly well that I'd never dare attempt such dominance over Donald unless I was prepared to rob him of the mentality that made him useful. But I consoled myself with the thought that this female was peculiarly susceptible to domination.

"We'd better get that car out of sight," Ven said. She nodded to Edith. The human obediently trotted off in the direction of the car. A few moments later the sound of the motor rose and fell as she concealed it in the trees.

As soon as I could, I contacted Donald and told him what had happened. Fortunately he was alone, so his exclamation of surprise and consternation didn't arouse any suspicion.

"Ethanol, eh?" he said speculatively.

It was easy to follow the trend of his thoughts. "Don't get any ideas," I warned in my best TV-villain manner. "I have Edith up here with me. If you want to see her again, you'd better stay sober."

"I wouldn't think of crossing you," he assured me insincerely. "I'm too close to being rid of you."

"Well—what do we do?" I asked. "You're the expert on this insane society of yours."

"You've done it," he said. "I don't think it was smart of you, but under the circumstances, I can't see how you could have done anything else. I warned you about Ven and Edith," he added—rather gloatingly, I thought. "Now you're in for it." His voice was almost gay.

"How?"

"Six women vanishing all at once is going to cause a stir even in Los Angeles," he said.

"After an ethanol party?" I asked curiously. "Six dancers out of a production that used a hundred? Your city will never miss them."

"But their families will."

Families! I hadn't thought of that. Mammals had strong family ties—probably due to their method of reproduction. We Thalassans, coming as we did from eggs, had none of this. The state incubators and the creches were our only contact with parenthood. We had no families. "Hmm," I said. "I hadn't thought of that."

"Well, you'd better start. I hope it gives you a headache."

"You get nastier every time I talk with you," I complained.

"I have my reasons," he said bitterly. "Now, if you're through with me, little master, I think I'd like to get some sleep. In the meantime you'd better get them back to their homes before they're missed."

"I can't," I confessed. "The controller isn't big enough to handle eight of you—not as individuals."

Donald chuckled grimly. "That's your worry. Remember, unless you find out which of them will be missed and act accordingly, you're going to be very much in the public eye."

I didn't feel too happy as I cut off, but Donald had given me an idea.

One by one I checked the new proxies. Of the six, two were living together. They had the casual emotional involvement with males so characteristic of this species, but they could remain here for several days without causing comment. Of the remaining four, one had a roommate and would be difficult to extract; another was living alone; still another was mated and had an offspring, but she was not living with her mate—a legal action having separated her much as it separates incompatible Thalassans. The offspring, however, was living with her when she wasn't working, a not unusual situation on this world, but one which could have some complications unless she was returned to it very shortly.

The last was living with her parents and was seriously involved emotionally with a male. She was planning to be officially mated in the near future, although it would be legal fiction rather than fact since she was already nurturing a living embryo of some three weeks development. I debated whether to remove it, a simple enough manipulation, but decided against it. It would be interesting to observe a mammalian reproduction. But to remove her from her family and her unofficial mate was a task that might be difficult. I needed help.

I projected a call for Ven, phrasing it imperatively so she could have no doubt about its urgency. Her answer was quick and clear.

"I'm coming," she said.

"Good. I need you. And bring Edith. We have a problem that will require her talents."

"She'll be happy to cooperate." Ven's projection was cheerfully confident.

"You did her no permanent damage, I hope."

"Not a bit. In fact, you'd never know she's been disciplined."

"Well, get in here, both of you, we have work to do."

Edith had trouble squeezing into the control room and, despite her skin conditioning, the place quickly filled with her scent. But Ven and I were old hands now and took it in stride. She grasped the problem instantly. "The only one who might be any trouble is Alice. Her family and her boy friend can be difficult. The others won't need much effort, except for Grace. She'd better be returned to her baby as soon as possible."

"How soon?" I asked.

"The baby isn't living with her," Edith added, "not while she's working, but she sees it regularly. Every day or two, I believe."

I sighed. That solved the biggest problem.

"We had better start at once," Ven said.

I ignored her and looked inquiringly at Edith. "What would you do?" I asked, flashing a cold projection at Ven to stay out of this.

"Well—if I had to do it, I'd send Alice and Grace home. I wouldn't do anything to Alice except block her from talking about this place and what happened. Grace I'd put under full control, have her pick up her baby, go home and pack to leave. As soon as she's ready to go, bring her out here."

"The infant, too?"

"Of course. A baby's no bother."

This, I thought, was something of an understatement.

"And what of the others?" I asked.

"Velma has a nosey roommate. Have her start a fight and leave angry. She hasn't much baggage, and it won't be any trouble for her to collect it. As for the other three, I think Joan's being kept. She can't afford a single apartment on her salary. Loleta and Marian are always out, sometimes for days. Their landlady won't think a thing of it. If they never return, she'll just pack their things and rent the room to someone else. I know that old witch. I'd just keep those three here and not worry about them. Nobody's going to make any fuss about three chorines disappearing. Later on you can make them write letters enclosing money to send their clothes to another city. Then they can be picked up and stored. That should give us a year before anyone gets suspicious enough to look for them."

"Edith," I said, "you're a genius."

"I got you into this mess," Edith said. "So, perhaps I'd better get you out."

"But your fellow mammals—"

"You haven't hurt me—not much, anyway," Edith said. "So I don't suppose you'll hurt them. And, besides, I don't want Ven mad at me like she was this afternoon. Anyway—you'll be gone soon."

"I think I shall regret leaving," I said honestly. "There is a great deal about you mammals I am beginning to suspect I do not know."

"You aren't kidding," she said with faint bitterness so similar to Donald's that my antennae quivered. "But it's been quite an experience. I'll tell my kids when I have them—but they're not going to believe me."

"I hope you have those children—and raise them to maturity," I said.

The tone of my voice caused her to look at me with sudden fear on her face. But at the sight of my impassive features it died away. "You scared me for a moment," she said.

"Did I? I didn't mean to."

VII

THE NEXT WEEK KEPT US BUSY FOLLOWING EDITH'S instructions. I didn't see how they would apply to Alice, but Edith knew her species better than I. Alice's silence and the prying inquisitiveness of her parents and her boy friend worked like magic. Alice finally became angry and after a stormy scene left the house, swearing never to return. Edith picked her up as she walked away; Ven turned on the control and turned the threat to fact. Later I took a leaf from Edith's book and sent Alice to San Francisco, where I had her write a pair of bitter letters to her parents and her extralegal mate. After that I felt more secure.

The others worked out exactly as Edith predicted. No trouble at all. By the time Donald returned from the East with a ton of tin ingots in a small truck, our training schedule was well set up. The robots and I had managed to build a multiplex controller similar to those we used on Thalassa on the state farms, but much smaller. It could handle the proxies en masse or as individuals. While far less sensitive than the one in the ship, it was effective enough for our rather elementary purposes.

Edith, who was running the group under Ven's supervision, had them lined up in a row to greet Donald as he came up the hill toward the ship.

"The place looks like a nudist colony," Donald grumbled. "You haven't improved it any." He eyed the file of mammals trooping down to the truck to unload the tin ingots. "I have another ton lined up for delivery as soon as you get this processed," he said.

"Good," I replied. "We'll leave as soon as it's aboard. I don't like the looks of your recent actions."

"Mine?" I shook my head. "Oh, you mean the world situation." I nodded. "You shouldn't worry about it. You should have seen it this time last year."

I shrugged. I would never really understand these creatures. Their brains functioned differently. "You frighten me with your wild displays of emotion. Someday one of you is going to start something and your world is going to go up in fire."

"I don't think so," he said. "I have some ideas about that. With the money from your stories and with what you have taught me, I think there will be some changes." There was a peculiar expression in his eyes that I couldn't identify. It made me vaguely uneasy. "I've been doing a lot of thinking since you met up with Edie and me. What this world needs is someone who can run it."

"That's obvious," I said. "Until your society catches up with your technology you will be in constant danger. You mammals will have to learn to discipline your emotions."

His face twisted. "I've had a good practical course in that," he said. "Now I'm getting postgraduate training." He gestured at the women coming up the hill carrying the silver tin ingots. "Just how long do you think I can endure something like this?"

"Like what?" I asked.

"Do I have to draw you a diagram?" he asked. "Ever since you lizards came into my life I haven't been able to touch a woman. Not even Edith—and she's my wife. Just how much of this do you think I can take?"

"Oh!" I exclaimed with dawning comprehension. "I think I see."

The situation would have been amusing if it wasn't so stupid. I was surprised that I hadn't realized it before. There was, I knew, a certain amount of feedback in a bipolar control circuit. Obviously enough of Ven's conditioning, and mine, had seeped through to affect Donald and Edith's normal relationships. Mammals were far more preoccupied with sex than we were. Their books, magazines, television and motion pictures reeked of it. It was present in almost every piece of advertising, and four of our six new proxies were living histories of it. Yet Donald and Edith, because of our feedback, had been kept as continent as novitiates for the priesthood of Authority!

"I'm a perfectly normal male," Donald said. "Just what do you think you've been doing to me? I can't drink. I can't make love. I can't do anything except collect tin for you lizards. Just why do you think I hate you? Now you surround me with a whole damned untouchable harem! Are you trying to drive me insane?"

I laughed, and Donald recognized the sound for what it was.

"Oh, *damn* you!" he said bitterly. "How would you like to be married for eight months and for six of them be unable to touch your wife? Just why do you think Edith tried to get drunk? I could kill you cheerfully for what you've done to us!"

"Oh!" I said. There was a world of understanding opening in front of me. Of course, it would do no good to tell him that Ven and I had remained in enforced continence for five years. It was just the Eugenics council working through us—entirely involuntarily. What was bothering Donald and Edith was so absurdly simple that neither Ven nor I would have thought to ask. And the mammals with their peculiar customs and habits would never have told us unless—as had happened—the pressure became too great.

What our mammals needed was a good dose of Va Krul's basic therapy. If Edith were fertilized as a result of it, so much the better. It would keep her attention where it more properly belonged. The thought would never have occurred to me in my present state. Since I was content, I had erroneously assumed that everything was in harmony.

"You might as well go home," I said. "Take Edith with you. We won't need you for several days."

"Why?"

"You'll find things a little different. I'll make a few adjustments on the controller."

To my surprise Don didn't appear happy at all. "Does that mean what I think it does?" he demanded. "Do you think I'll get any satisfaction out of being controlled *even there?*"

"I don't know about the pleasure," I said coldly, "but I do know that it will improve your attitude."

Donald raged at me, his brain white with anger. "So help me God, Eu Kor, someday I'm going to kill you for this! It's the ultimate insult."

"You're not going to do anything," I said calmly. His voice dissolved into obscenity. For a moment I felt sorry for him until I remembered the basic truth that none of us are free—and the most intelligent, naturally, are the least free of all. They are bound by their commitments, their duties, their responsibilities, and by their intelligence itself. If a superior intelligence occasionally exhibits petty lapses —which amuse him or relieve his boredom—it is not the place of the less endowed to construe it as a sign of equality.

Some—like Ven and me—have known their place from birth. Others, like Edith and Alice, learn easily with a minimum amount of pain. Some like Grace learn hard; and some—like Donald—do not learn at all.

Donald was the eternal rebel, complying because he must, yet seething with resentment because he did. He was the personification of drive without innate control, ambition without humility, intelligence without wisdom. As he had been, he was not quite enough. At best he would have been a minor author and a petty domestic tyrant. He would never have been a threat simply because he didn't have the ability or training. But I had given him what he lacked. The knowledge I had impressed upon his mind would give him a tremendous advantage over his fellow mammals, and his tendencies toward domestic tyranny would expand to include others. His glandular attitude would pervert his knowledge to the detriment of humankind. He could become a thing so dangerous that it could destroy this precariously balanced world.

I went into the ship and set up a world matrix on the computer, using all the data I had accumulated, secured the answer, and then inserted Donald's potential into the matrix I then ordered a probability extrapolation for both matrices, equating the solutions with survival.

The answers confirmed my thoughts. With the matrix as it stood, the twenty-year survival prediction was 65 percent, which wasn't too bad since few advanced-technology worlds have better than an 85 percent survival probability. But with Donald in the matrix, the survival prediction was zero!

I knew what I must do. I could not leave him behind as I had planned. Nor could I inflict the senseless cruelty of brainblotting. He would have to be mercifully destroyed.

Although I was fond of Donald, and his death would leave me sick for weeks, it would not be right to let my creation live and condemn the mammal race to death. I could not exterminate a race Authority had created. The guilt syndrome would be shattering. Of course, if they killed each other that was not my concern.

But until we left I would give him all the freedom he could use. Outside of the minimum of control, he would be free to do and act as he pleased. I didn't owe it to him, yet it was not his fault that he had come into my hands. And when I returned to Thalassa I would tell the Council what I had done and ask for justice. Perhaps we could save this world from itself even as we had saved others. The question of gratitude would be immaterial.

With a firm hand to set them on the track, the mammals might learn the values of intelligence and cooperation before it was too late. They might understand the realities of existence rather than fall victim to their glandular fancies. They might. But if they did, one thing would be certain—they would learn it the hard way. Donald was proof of that.

I went to our living quarters, and presently Ven joined me. "They're all in for the night, Eu," she said.

"That's good. How are they coming along?"

"Splendidly. Another week should see the end of the training. Edith was a good experience for me in handling these. I'm not making the mistakes I did. I'm finding the blocks and removing them. One of them, the one called Grace, should be even better than Edith."

"As a mount?" I asked with faint humor. "Or as a working proxy?"

"Both," Ven said promptly. "She's stronger and more intelligent. Yet even so I think I shall always like Edith best."

"One's first dependent is always one's fondest memory," I replied sententiously, "But you'll forget them all when we're back on Thalassa."

"I won't," Ven said. "I'll never forget Edith."

"Never is a long time," I said gently. "I shall even forget the pain of killing Donald some day."

"Then you've decided to eliminate him?" Ven said.

I nodded. "It's necessary," I said. "This world wouldn't be safe with him alive."

"Poor Edith. She's fond of the brute," Ven said. She moved toward the doorway.

"Where are you going?" I asked.

"I want to talk to Edith. Perhaps I can prepare her."

"No. Don't," I said. "Contact her if you wish, but tell her nothing."

"Very well," she said. I smiled as she disappeared. Ven was going to miss her pet once we had left. It was obvious.

"Eu! Quick!" Ven's projection crackled in my brain. "They're fighting! Edith's being hurt, and I can't touch them! They've set up a block!"

I ran for the control room, slapped the helmet on my head, reached for the controls—and stopped, laughing.

"Stop them!" Ven screamed. Her aura blazed a brilliant white and her projection nearly knocked me down. She reached for the control switch, but I slapped her hand away.

"Quiet!" I snapped. "They're not fighting, you little fool! Turn on your audio and listen and stop acting silly!"

Ven did as I told her and her aura changed to a fiery pink. "Oh!" she said in a small voice, "but they never—"

I must have made some mistake in revising the controllers—or feedback was stronger than I suspected—for the Va Krul syndrome came back along our lines of contact with explosive force! Desperately I reached for the switch—but my hand froze in midair as an intolerable wave of emotion drove Ven and me together like two pieces of iron with opposite magnetic charge! The last thing I remember was being enveloped in the flaring golden glow of Ven's aura.

I came to my senses in our living quarters. I was stunned—exhausted—limp and gasping.

"Thalassa!" I said weakly, "we've *really* done it now!"

Ven smiled a pale blue radiance at me. "You have become strong, living on this heavy world," she said. "I like it."

"But—but!" I sputtered. "It was so—it can't—it couldn't—"

"But it did," Ven said softly. "And I'm glad it did."

"I don't mean that. What I mean to say was that it was so—"

"Unexpected?"

"No! So utterly—"

"Satisfying?" she asked.

"Stop interrupting! It was all of that and more. But what I want to say is that we've violated the prime restriction for space travelers. How could we do it?"

"You're forgetting that for some time we have been living upon this emotion-charged world," Ven said. "The steady erosion was more than our conditioning could take. The feedback was merely the last in a whole series of disruptive stimuli. It was the trigger, but our defenses had been weakened long before. Not that I'm sorry," she added quickly. "For weeks I've been wondering what sort of a mate you'd be when this trip was over. I'm not unhappy with the preview." She smiled at me and the whole of our living quarters was filled with a bright tender blue.

"The natives," I said worriedly. "We were in contact with them."

Ven's aura darkened. "I had forgotten them," she said. "I hope that the feedback wasn't intensified and returned to them. I'd better look." She started for the control room and I followed more slowly.

"There's no damage," she said from beneath the helmet. "Edith feels just as I do."

I took my helmet and coded Don's pattern on the selector. Peculiar, I thought with vague wonder. Most peculiar. For the first time Donald and I were in true rapport. His mind was slow, lazy, sluggish—even his ambition was sated for the moment. Could it be, I wondered, that we could find agreement through our *emotions?* Was it frustration that drove him? Whatever the block had been it was gone now. This was a true empathic meeting—something far more satisfying than our previous conflict.

I relaxed in it, feeling the slow langorous questings of his mind even as he felt mine. There was a sense of brotherhood that transcended differences in race and culture. We were down to basics, on the oldest meeting ground of life.

He was wondering idly what the outcome of this might be—conscious of me, but careless. It jolted me. He might be uncertain, but I *knew* Ven was from good family stock, and "good" to a Thalassan meant something entirely different than it commonly did to the natives of this planet!

I disengaged hurriedly and shook Ven out of her rapport with Edith. "We've no time to lose," I said. "We must leave at once! You know what's going to happen!"

"I know," Ven said. "I feel the changes already."

"That's just in your mind," I snapped.

"We're not going home," she said. There was a note of prophecy in her voice. "We'll never make it."

"We can't stay here!"

"I know."

"Then what are we going to do?"

We couldn't stay here. But we couldn't go home either. The trip would take weeks, and hyperspace is fatal to a gravid Thalassan female. That was something we learned long ago, and the principal reason for continence-conditioning for couples in space. What was more, I knew that where Ven stayed, I would stay.

"Remember the fourth planet of this system?" Ven asked.

"Yes. Ideal gravity, adequate oxygen, but too cold."

"And with no intelligent life," Ven added. "That's an advantage—and we can beat the cold. It wouldn't be too hard to build domes. We have plenty of power metal, and a matricizer. We could hatch our clutch there. With the mammals to help us, we should be able to make a comfortable enough life for the forty years it'll take to bring our offspring to maturity. We should be able to do this easily, and still get home before we're strangers."

"Hmm," I said. "It's possible. And we can use this world for a supply base. But would you care to live on that cold, barren planet?"

"There are worse places," she said matter-of-factly. "And we'd be close to everything we'd need."

It did have possibilities. And the mammals could be adapted. They were a more advanced evolutionary from than we, but lower on the adaptive scale—nonspecialized —more so than any other intelligent race I had encountered.

Ven said, "We would actually be doing their race a favor, if the computation of this world's future is correct. Some of them would still survive if this planet commits suicide. And if the prediction is wrong, we would have done no harm. If they reach space, they'll merely find that they've already arrived when they reach the fourth planet."

"Which might be something of a surprise to their explorers," I said with a chuckle. "All right. We'll play it your way."

I was pretty sure how Donald would take this. He was going to be furious, but after all one doesn't make a pet of a wolf and then turn it loose. It's too hard on the livestock. But I didn't think he'd be too unhappy. He'd be the principal human on Mars; and after we left he'd be ruler of a world. And in the meantime he could be a domestic tyrant.

It was fortunate, I thought with a smile, that mammals were essentially polygamous. Donald would make some nasty comments about being a herd sire—but I didn't think his comments would be too sincere. After all, it's not every man that has a chance to become a founding father.

I was still smiling as I turned the dials on the controller and flipped the switch. Founding father—the title was as much mine as his!

MATING CALL

Frank Herbert

It obviously is not advisable that *every* story in a science fiction anthology should be Pregnant with Meaning, like the previous story; such a collection might turn out to be a bore. Why not lets have a feathery-light item for contrast—a tale that is just Pregnant, like this one?

"IF YOU GET CAUGHT WE'LL HAVE TO THROW YOU to the wolves," said Dr. Fladdis. "You understand, of course." Laoconia Wilkinson, senior field agent of the Social Anthropological Service, nodded her narrow head. "Of course," she barked. She rustled the travel and order papers in her lap.

"It was very difficult to get High Council approval for this expedition after the . . . ah . . . unfortunate incident on Monligol," said Dr. Fladdis. "That's why your operating restrictions are so severe."

"I'm permitted to take only this—" she glanced at her papers—"Marie Medill?"

"Well, the basic plan of action was her idea," said Dr. Fladdis. "And we have no one else in the department with her qualifications in music."

"I'm not sure I approve of her plan," muttered Laoconia.

"Ah," said Dr. Fladdis, "but it goes right to the heart of the situation on Rukuchp, and the beauty of it is that it breaks no law. That's a legal quibble, I agree. But what I mean is you'll be within the letter of the law."

"And outside its intent," muttered Laoconia. "Not that I agree with the law. Still—" she shrugged—"music!"

Dr. Fladdis chose to misunderstand. "Miss Medill has her doctorate in music, yes," he said. "A highly educated young woman."

"If it weren't for the fact that this may be our last opportunity to discover how those creatures reproduce—" said Laoconia. She shook her head. "What we really should be doing is going in there with a full staff, capturing representive specimens, putting them through—"

"You will note the prohibition in Section D of the High Council's mandate," said Dr. Fladdis. "*'The Field Agent may not enclose, restrain or otherwise restrict the freedom of any Rukuchp native.'*"

"How bad is their birthrate situation?" asked Laoconia.

"We have only the word of the Rukuchp special spokesman. This Gafka. He said it was critical. That, of course, was the determining factor with the High Council. Rukuchp appealed to *us* for help."

Laoconia got to her feet. "You know what I think of this music idea. But if that's the way we're going to attack it, why don't we just break the law all the way—take in musical recordings, players . . ."

"Please!" snapped Dr. Fladdis.

Laoconia stared at him. She had never before seen the Area Director so agitated.

"The Rukuchp natives say that introduction of *foreign* music has disrupted some valence of their reproductive cycle," said Dr. Fladdis. "At least, that's how we've translated their explanation. This is the reason for the law prohibiting any traffic in music devices."

"I'm not a child!" snapped Laoconia. "You don't have to explain all—"

"We cannot be too careful," said Dr. Fladdis. "With the memory of Monligol still fresh in all minds." He shuddered. "We must return to the spirit of the SocAnth motto: *'For the Greater Good of the Universe.'* We've been warned."

"I don't see how music can be anything but a secondary stimulant," said Laoconia. "However, I shall keep an open mind."

Laoconia Wilkinson looked up from her notes, said: "Marie, was that a noise outside?" She pushed a strand of gray hair from her forehead.

Marie Medill stood at the opposite side of the field hut, staring out one of the two windows. "I only hear the leaves," she said. "They're awfully loud in that wind."

"You're sure it wasn't Gafka?"

Marie sighed and said, "No, it wasn't his namesong."

"Stop calling that monster a him!" snapped Laoconia.

Marie's shoulders stiffened.

Laoconia observed the reflex and thought how wise the Service had been to put a mature veteran anthropologist in command here. A hex-dome hut was too small to confine brittle tempers. And the two women had been confined here for 25 weeks already. Laoconia stared at her companion—such a young romantic, that one.

Marie's pose reflected boredom . . . worry. . . .

Laoconia glanced around the hut's crowded interior. Servo-recorders, night cameras, field computers, meal-mech, collapsible floaters, a desk, two chairs, folding bunks, three wall sections taken up by the transceiver linking them with the mother ship circling in satellite orbit overhead. Everything in its place and a place for everything.

"Somehow, I just can't help calling Gafka a him," said Marie. She shrugged. "I know it's nonsense. Still . . . when Gafka sings . . ."

Laoconia studied the younger woman: a blonde girl in a one-piece green uniform; heavy peasant figure, good strong legs, an oval face with high forehead and dreaming blue eyes.

"Speaking of singing," said Laoconia, "I don't know what I shall do if Gafka doesn't bring permission for us to attend their Big Sing. We can't solve this mess without the facts."

"No doubt," said Marie. She spoke snappishly, trying to keep her attention away from Laoconia. The older woman just sat there. She was always just sitting there—so efficient, so driving, a tall gawk with windburned face, nose too big, mouth too big, chin too big, eyes too small.

Marie turned away.

"With every day that passes I'm more convinced that this music thing is a blind alley," said Laoconia. "The Rukuchp birthrate keeps going down no matter how much of our music you teach them."

"But Gafka agrees," protested Marie. "Everything points to it. Our discovery of this planet brought the Rukuchps into contact with the first alien music they've ever known. Somehow, that's disrupted their breeding cycle. I'm sure of it."

"Breeding cycle," sniffed Laoconia. "For all we know, these creatures could be ambulatory vegetables without even the most rudimentary—"

"I'm so worried," said Marie. "It's music at the root of the problem, I'm sure, but if it ever got out that we smuggled in those education tapes and taught Gafka all our musical forms—"

"We did *not* smuggle anything!" barked Laoconia. "The law is quite clear. It only prohibits any form of *mechanical* reproducer of actual musical sounds. Our tapes are all completely visual."

"I keep thinking of Monligol," said Marie. "I couldn't live with the knowledge that I'd contributed to the extinction of a sentient species. Even indirectly. If our *foreign* music really has disrupted—"

"We don't even know if they breed!"

"But Gafka says—"

"Gafka says! A dumb vegetable. Gafka says!"

"Not so dumb," countered Marie. "He learned to speak our language in less than three weeks, but *we* have only the barest rudiments of songspeech."

"Gafka's an idiot-savant," said Laoconia. "And I'm not certain I'd call what that creature does *speaking*."

"It is too bad that you're tone deaf," said Marie sweetly.

Laoconia frowned. She leveled a finger at Marie. "The thing I note is that we only have their word that their birthrate is declining. They called on us for help, and now they obstruct every attempt at field observation."

"They're so shy," said Marie.

"They're going to be shy one SocAnth field expedition if they don't invite us to that Big Sing," said Laoconia. "Oh! If the Council had only authorized a *full* field expedition with armed support!"

"They couldn't!" protested Marie. "After Monligol, practically every sentient race in the universe is looking on Rukuchp as a final test case. If we mess up another race with our meddling—"

"Meddling!" barked Laoconia. "Young woman, the Social Anthropoligical Service is a holy calling! Erasing ignorance, helping the backward races!"

"And we're the only judges of what's backward," said Marie. "How convenient. Now, you take Monligol, Everyone knows that insects carry disease. So we move in with our insecticides and kill off the symbiotic partner essential to Monligolian reproduction. How uplifting."

"They should have told us," said Laoconia.

"They couldn't," said Marie. "It was a social taboo."

"Well . . ." Laoconia shrugged, "that doesn't apply here."

"How do you know?"

"I've had enough of this silly argument," barked Laoconia. "See if Gafka's coming. He's overdue."

Marie inhaled a trembling breath, stamped across to the field hut's lone door and banged it open. Immediately the tinkle of glazeforest leaves grew louder. The wind brought an odor of peppermint from the stubble plain to her left.

She looked across the plain at the orange ball of Almac sinking toward a flat horizon, swung her glance to the right where the wall of the glazeforest loomed overhead. Rainbow-streaked batwing leaves clashed in the wind, shifting in subtle competition for the last of the day's orange light.

"Do you see *it?*" demanded Laoconia.

Marie dropped her attention to the foot of the forest wall, where stubble spikes crowded against great glasswood trunks. "No."

"What *is* keeping that creature?"

Marie shook her head, setting blonde curls dancing across her uniform collar. "It'll be dark soon," she said. "He said he'd return before it got fully dark."

Laoconia scowled, pushed aside her notes. *Always calling it a him! They're nothing but animated Easter eggs!* If only—She broke the train of thought, attention caught by a distant sound.

"There!" Marie peered down the length of glazeforest wall.

A fluting passage of melody hung on the air. It was the meister-song of a delicate wind instrument. As they listened, the tones deepened to an organ throb while a section of cello strings held the melody. Glazeforest leaves began to tinkle in sympathetic harmony. Slowly, the music faded.

"It's Gafka," whispered Marie. She cleared her throat, spoke louder, self-consciously: "He's coming out of the forest quite a ways down."

"I can't tell one from the other," said Laoconia. "They all look alike and sound alike. Monsters."

"They do look alike," agreed Marie, "but the sound is quite individual."

"Let's not harp on my tone deafness!" snapped Laoconia. She joined Marie at the door. "If they'll only let us attend their Sing . . ."

A six-foot Easter egg ambled toward them on four of its five prehensile feet.

The crystal glistening of its vision cap, tipped slightly toward the field hut, was semi-lidded by inner cloud-pigment in the direction of the setting sun. Blue and white greeting colors edged a great bellows muscle around the torso. The bell extension of a mouth/ear—normally visible in a red-yellow body beneath the vision cap—had been retracted to a multicreased pucker.

"What ugly brutes," said Laoconia.

"Shhhh!" said Marie. "You don't know how far away he can hear you." She waved an arm. "Gaaafkaa!" Then: "Damn!"

"What's wrong?"

"I only made eight notes out of his name instead of nine."

Gafka came up to the door, picking a way through the

stubble spikes. The orange mouth/ear extended, sang a 22-note harmonica passage: "Maarriee Mmmmmmedillll." Then a 10-second concerto: "Laoconnnnia Wiiilkinnn-sonnnn!"

"How lovely!" said Marie.

"I wish you'd talk straight out the way we taught you," said Laoconia. "That singing is difficult to follow."

Gafka's vision cap tipped toward her. The voice shifted to a sing-song waver: "But polite sing greeting."

"Of course," said Laoconia. "Now." She took a deep breath. "Do we have permission to attend your Big Sing?"

Gafka's vision cap tipped toward Marie, back to Laoconia.

"Please, Gafka?" said Marie.

"Difficulty," wavered Gafka. "Not know how say. Not have knowledge your kind people. Is subject not want for talking."

"I see," said Laoconia, recognizing the metaphorical formula. "It has to do with your breeding habits."

Gafka's vision cap clouded over with milky pigment, a sign the two women had come to recognize as embarrassment.

"Now, Gafka," said Laoconia. "None of that. We've explained about science and professional ethics, the desire to be of real help to one another. You must understand that both Marie and I are here for the good of your people."

A crystal moon unclouded in the part of the vision cap facing Laoconia.

"If we could only get them to speak straight out," said Laoconia.

Marie said: "Please, Gafka. We only want to help."

"Understand I," said Gafka. "How else talk this I?" More of the vision cap unclouded. "But must ask question. Friends perhaps not like."

"We are scientists," said Laoconia. "You may ask any question you wish."

"You are to old for . . . breeding?" asked Gafka. Again the vision cap clouded over, sparing Gafka the sight of Laoconia shocked speechless.

Marie stepped into the breech. "Gafka! Your people and my people are . . . well, we're just too different. We couldn't. There's no way . . . that is . . ."

"Impossible!" barked Laoconia. "Are you implying that we might be sexually attacked if we attended your Big Sing?"

Gafka's vision cap unclouded, tipped toward Laoconia. Purple color bands ran up and down the bellows muscles, a sign of confusion.

"Not understand I about sex thing," said Gafka. "My people never hurt other creature." The purple bands slowed their upward-downward chasing, relaxed into an indecisive green. The vision cap tipped toward Marie. "Is true all like kinds start egg young same?" This time the clouding of the vision cap was only a momentary glimmerwhite.

"Essentially, that is so," agreed Laoconia. "We all *do* start with an egg. However, the fertilization process is different with different peoples." Aside to Marie, she said: "Make a note of that point about eggs. It bears out that they may be oviparian as I suspected." Then: "Now, I must know what you meant by your question."

Gafka's vision cap rocked left, right, settled on a point between the two women. The sing-song voice intoned: "Not understand I about different ways. But know I you see many thing my people not see. If breeding (glimmerwhite) different, or you too old for breeding (glimmerwhite) my people say you come Big Sing. Not want we make embarrass of you."

"We are scientists," said Laoconia. "It's quite all right. Now, may we bring our cameras and recording equipment?"

"Bring you much of things?" asked Gafka.

"We'll only be taking one large floater to carry our equipment," said Laoconia. "How long must we be prepared to stay?"

"One night," said Gafka. "I bring worker friends to help with floater. Go I now. Soon be dark. Come moonrise I return, take to Big Sing place you." The trumpet mouth fluted three minor notes of farewell, pulled back to an orange pucker. Gafka turned, glided into the forest. Soon he had vanished among reflections of glasswood boles.

"A break at last!" barked Laoconia. She strode into the hut, speaking over her shoulder. "Call the ship. Have them monitor our equipment. Tell them to get duplicate recordings. While we're starting to analyze the sound-sight record down here, they can be transmitting a copy to the master computers at Kampichi. We want as many minds on this as possible. We may never get another chance like this one!"

Marie said: "I don't—"

"Snap to it!" barked Laoconia.

"Shall I talk to Dr. Baxter?" asked Marie.

"Talk to Helen?" demanded Laoconia. "Why would you want to bother Helen with a routine question like this?"

"I just want to discuss—"

"That transceiver is for official use only," said Laoconia. "Transmit the message as I've directed. We're here to solve the Rukuchp breeding problem, not to chitchat."

"I feel suddenly so uneasy," said Marie. "There's something about this situation that worries me."

"Uneasy?"

"I think we've missed the point of Gafka's warning."

"Stop worrying," said Laoconia. "The natives won't give us any trouble. Gafka was looking for a last excuse to keep us from attending their Big Sing. You've seen how stupidly shy they are."

"But what if—"

"I've had a great deal of experience in handling native peoples," said Laoconia. "You never have trouble as long as you keep a firm, calm grip on the situation at all times."

"Maybe so. But—"

"Think of it!" said Laoconia. "The first humans ever to attend a Rukuchp Big Sing. Unique! You mustn't let the magnitude of our achievement dull your mind. Stay cool and detached as I do. Now get that call off to the ship!"

It was a circular clearing perhaps two kilometers in diameter, dark with moonshadows under the giant glaze trees. High up around the rim of the clearing, moonlight painted prismatic rainbows along every leaf edge. A glint of silver far above the center of the open area betrayed the presence of a tiny remote-control floater carrying night cameras and microphones.

Except for a space near the forest edge occupied by Laoconia and Marie, the clearing was packed with silent, shadowy humps of Rukuchp natives. Vision caps glinted like inverted bowls in the moonlight.

Seated on a portable chair beside the big pack-floater, Laoconia adjusted the position of the tiny remote unit high above them. In the monitor screen before her she could see what the floater lenses covered—the clearing with its sequin glitter of Rukuchp vision caps and the faintest gleam of red and green instrument lights between herself and Marie, seated on the other side of the floater. Marie was monitoring the night lenses that would make the scene appear as bright as day on the recording wire.

Marie straightened, rubbed the small of her back. "This clearing must be at least two kilometers across," she whispered, impressed.

Laoconia adjusted her earphones, tested a relay. Her feet ached. It had been at least a four-hour walk in here to this clearing. She began to feel latent qualms about what might be ahead in the nine hours left of the Rukuchp night. That stupid warning . . .

"I said it's a big clearing," whispered Marie.

Laoconia cast an apprehensive glance at the silent Rukuchp figures packed closely around. "I didn't realize there'd be so many," she whispered. "It doesn't look to me as though they're dying out. What does your monitor screen show?"

"They fill the clearing," whispered Marie. "And I think they extend back under the trees. I wish I knew which one was Gafka. I should've watched when he left us."

"Didn't he say where he was going?"

"He just asked if this spot was all right for us and if we were ready to help them."

"Well, I'm sure everything's going to be all right," said Laoconia. She didn't sound very convincing, even to herself.

"Isn't it time to contact the ship?" asked Marie.

"They'll be calling any—" A light flashed red on the panel in front of Laoconia. "Here they are now."

She flipped a switch, spoke into her cheek microphone. "Yes?"

The metallic chattering in Laoconia's earphones only made Marie feel more lonely. The ship was so far away above them.

"That's right," said Laoconia. "Transmit your record immediately and ask Kampichi to make an independent study. We'll compare notes later." Silence while she listened, then: "I'm sure there's no danger. You can keep an eye on us through the overhead lenses. But there's never been a report of a Rukuchp native offering violence to anyone. . . . Well, I don't see what we can do about it now. We're here and that's that. I'm signing off now." She flipped the switch.

"Was that Dr. Baxter?" asked Marie.

"Yes. Helen's monitoring us herself, though I don't see what she can do. Medical people are very peculiar sometimes. Has the situation changed with the natives?"

"They haven't moved that I can see."

"Why couldn't Gafka have given us a preliminary briefing?" asked Laoconia. "I detest this flying blind."

"I think it still embarrasses him to talk about breeding," said Marie.

"Everything's too quiet," hissed Laoconia. "I don't like it."

"They're sure to do something soon," whispered Marie.

As though her words were the signal, an almost inaudible vibration began to throb in the clearing. Glaze leaves started their sympathetic tinkle-chiming. The vibration grew, became an organ rumble with abrupt piping obligatto that danced along its edges. A cello insertion pulled a melody from the sound, swung it over the clearing while the glazeforest chimed louder and louder.

"How exquisite," breathed Marie. She forced her attention onto the instruments in front of her. Everything was functioning.

The melody broke to a single clear high note of harmonic brilliance—a flute sound that shifted to a second phase with expanded orchestration. The music picked up element after element while low-register tympani built a stately rhythm into it, and zither tinkles laid a counterpoint on the rhythm.

"Pay attention to your instruments," hissed Laoconia.

Marie nodded, swallowing. The music was like a song heard before, but never before played with this perfection. She wanted to close her eyes; she wanted to submit entirely to the ecstasy of sound.

Around them, the Rukuchp natives remained stationary, a rhythmic expansion and contraction of bellows muscles their only movement.

And the rapture of music intensified.

Marie moved her head from side to side, mouth open. The sound was an infinity of angel choirs—every sublimity of music ever conceived—now concentrated into one exquisite distillation. She felt that it could not possibly grow more beautiful.

But it did.

There came a lifting-expanding-floating . . . a long, gliding, suspenseful timelessness.

Silence.

Marie felt herself drifting back to awareness, found her hands limply fumbling with dials. Some element of habit assured her that she had carried out her part of the job, but that music . . . She shivered.

"They sang for 47 minutes," hissed Laoconia. She glanced around. "Now what happens?"

Marie rubbed her throat, forced her attention onto the luminous dials, the floater, the clearing. A suspicion was forming in the back of her mind.

"I wish I knew which one of these creatures was Gafka," whispered Laoconia. "Do we dare arouse one of them, ask after Gafka?"

"We'd better not," said Marie.

"These creatures did nothing but sing," said Laoconia. "I'm more certain than ever that the music is stimulative and nothing more."

"I hope you're right," whispered Marie. Her suspicion

was taking on more definite shape . . . *music, controlled sound, ecstasy of controlled sound* . . . Thoughts tumbled over each other in her mind.

Time dragged out in silence.

"What do you suppose they're doing?" hissed Laoconia. "They've been sitting like this for 25 minutes."

Marie glanced around at the ring of Rukuchp natives hemming in the little open space, black mounds topped by dim silver. The stillness was like a charged vacuum.

More time passed.

"Forty minutes!" whispered Laoconia. "Do they expect us to sit here all night?"

Marie chewed her lower lip. *Ecstasy of sound,* she thought. And she thought of sea urchins and the parthenogenetic rabbits of Calibeau.

A stirring movement passed through the Rukuchp ranks. Presently, shadowy forms began moving away into the glazeforest's blackness.

"Where are they going?" hissed Laoconia. "Do you see Gafka?"

"No."

The transmission-receive light flashed in front of Laoconia. She flipped the switch, pressed an earphone against her head. "They just seem to be leaving," she whispered into the cheek microphone. "You see the same thing we do. There's been no movement against us. Let me call you back later. I want to observe this."

A Rukuchp figure came up beside Marie.

"Gafka?" said Marie.

"Gafka," intoned the figure. The voice sounded sleepy.

Laoconia leaned across the instrument-packed floater. "What are they doing now, Gafka?" she demanded.

"All new song we make from music you give," said Gafka.

"Is the sing all ended?" asked Marie.

"Same," breathed Gafka.

"What's this about a new song?" demanded Laoconia.

"Not have your kind song before correct," said Gafka. "In it too much new. Not understand we how song make you. But now you teach, make right you."

"What is all this nonsense?" asked Laoconia. "Gafka, where are your people all going?"

"Going," sighed Gafka.

Laoconia looked around her. "But they're departing singly . . . or . . . well, there don't seem to be any mated pairs. What *are* they doing?"

"Go each to wait," said Gafka.

And Marie thought of caryocinesis and daughter nuclei.

"I don't understand," complained Laoconia.

"You teach how new song sing," sighed Gafka. "New song best all time. We keep this song. Better much than old song. Make better"—the women detected the faint glimmer-haze lidding of Gafka's vision cap—"make better young. Strong more."

"Gafka," said Marie, "is the song all you do? I mean, there isn't anything else?"

"All," breathed Gafka. "Best song ever."

Laoconia said: "I think we'd better follow some of these—"

"That's not necessary," said Marie. "Did you enjoy their music, Dr. Wilkinson?"

"Well . . ." There appeared to be embarrassment in the way the older woman turned her head away. "It was *very* beautiful."

"And you *enjoyed* it?" persisted Marie.

"I don't see what—"

"You're tone deaf," said Marie.

"It's obviously a stimulant of some sort!" snapped Laoconia. "I don't understand now why they won't let us—"

"They let us," said Marie.

Laoconia turned to Gafka.

"I must insist, Gafka, that we be permitted to study all phases of your breeding process. Otherwise we can be of no help to you."

"You best help ever," said Gafka. "Birthrate all good now. You teach way out from mixing of music." A shudder passed upward through Gafka's bellows muscles.

"Do you make sense out of this?" demanded Laoconia.

"I'm afraid I do," said Marie. "Aren't you tired, Gafka?"

"Same," sighed Gafka.

"Laoconia, Dr. Wilkinson, we'd better get back to the hut," said Marie. "We can improvise what we'll need for the Schafter test."

"But the Schafter's for determining *human* pregnancy!" protested Laoconia.

The red light glowed in front of Laoconia. She flipped the switch. "Yes?"

Scratching sounds from the earphones broke the silence. Marie felt that she did not want to hear the voice from the ship.

Laoconia said: "Of course I know you're monitoring the test of . . . Why should I tell Marie you've already given Schafter tests to yourself? . . ." Laoconia's voice climbed. "WHAT? You can't be ser—That's impossible! But, Helen, we . . . they . . . you . . . we . . . Of course I . . . Where could we have . . . Every woman on the ship . . ."

There was a long silence while Marie watched Laoconia listening to the earphones, nodding. Presently, Laoconia lifted the earphones off her head and put them down gently. Her voice came out listlessly. "Dr. Bax . . . Helen suspected that . . . she administered Schafter tests to herself and some of the others."

"She listened to that music?" asked Marie.

"The whole universe listened to that music," said Laoconia. "Some smuggler monitored the ship's official transmission of our recordings. Rebroadcast stations took it. Everyone's going crazy about our *beautiful* music."

"Oh, no," breathed Marie.

Laoconia said: "Everyone on the ship listened to our recordings. Helen said she suspected immediately after the broadcast, but she waited the full half hour before giving the Schafter test." Laoconia glanced at the silent hump of Gafka standing beside Marie. "Every woman on that ship who could become pregnant is pregnant."

"It's obvious, isn't it?" asked Marie. "Gafka's people have developed a form of group parthenogenesis. Their Big Sing sets off the blastomeric reaction."

"But we're humans!" protested Laoconia. "How can—"

"And parts of us are still very primitive," said Marie. "This shouldn't surprise us. Sound's been used before to induce the first mitotic cleavage in an egg. Gafka's people merely have this as their sole breeding method—with corresponding perfection of technique."

Laoconia blinked, said: "I wonder how this ever got started?"

"And when they first encountered our *foreign* music," said Marie, "it confused them, mixed up their musical relationships. They were fascinated by the new musical forms. They experimented for new sensations . . . and their birthrate fell off. Naturally."

"Then you came along," said Laoconia, "and taught them how to master the new music."

"Exactly."

"Marie!" hissed Laoconia.

"Yes?"

"We were right here during that entrie . . . You don't suppose that we . . . that I . . ."

"I don't know about you," said Marie, "but I've never felt more certain of anything in my life."

She chewed at her lower lip, fought back tears. "I'm going to have a baby. Female. It'll have only half the normal number of chromosomes. And it'll be sterile. And I . . ."

"Say I to you," chanted Gafka. There was an air of sadness in the singsong voice. "Say I to you: all life kinds start egg young same. Not want I to cause troubles. But you say different you."

"Parthenogenesis," said Laoconia with a show of her old energy. "That means, of course, that the human reproductive process need not . . . that is, uh . . . we'll not have to . . . I mean to say that men won't be . . ."

"The babies will be drones," said Marie. "You know that. Unfertile drones. This may have its vogue, but it surely can't last."

"Perhaps," said Laoconia. "But I keep thinking of all those rebroadcasts of our recordings. I wonder if these Rukuchp creatures ever had two sexes?" She turned toward Gafka. "Gafka, do you know if . . . "

"Sorry cause troubles," intoned Gafka. The singsong voice sounded weaker. "Must say farewell now. Time for birthing me."

"*You* are going to give birth?" asked Laoconia.

"Same," breathed Gafka. "Feel pain on eye-top." Gafka's prehensile legs went into a flurry of digging in the ground beside the floater.

"Well, you were right about one thing, Dr. Wilkinson," said Marie. "She-he is not a *him*."

Gafka's legs bent, lowered the ovoid body into the freshly dug concavity in the ground. Immediately, the legs began to shrink back into the body. A crack appeared across the vision cap, struck vertically down through the bellows muscles.

Presently, there were two Gafkas, each half the size of the original. As the women watched, the two half-sized Gafkas began extruding new legs to regain the normal symmetry.

"Oh, no," whispered Marie.

She had a headache.

NICE GIRL WITH FIVE HUSBANDS

Fritz Leiber

Here is one of those quiet, understated, poetic, nostalgic-for-the-future stories that once in a great while beautifies the science fiction scene. Characteristically, it has been bypassed by anthologists (including this one) for more than fourteen years; it just didn't make a loud enough noise to call attention to itself. It is a pleasure to give it an airing; better late than never.[1]

TO BE GIVEN PAID-UP LEISURE AND FIND YOURSELF unable to create is unpleasant for any artist. To be stranded in a cluster of desert cabins with a dozen lonely people in the same predicament only makes it worse. So Tom Dorset was understandably irked with himself and the Tosker-Brown Vacation Fellowships as he climbed with the sun into the valley of red stones. He accepted the chafing of his camera strap against his shoulder as the nagging of conscience. He agreed with the disparaging hisses of the grains of sand rutched by his sneakers, and he wished that the occasional breezes, which faintly echoed the same criticisms, could blow him into a friendlier, less jealous age.

He had no way of knowing that, just as there are winds that blow through space, so there are winds that blow through time. Such winds may be strong or weak. The strong ones are rare and seldom blow for short distances, or more of us would know about them. What they pick

[1] Ironically, just as we were going to press, another publisher issued a collection by Fritz Leiber. It included this story. I had a decision to make, and I have made it. I refuse to deprive you of the pleasure of reading our "Nice Girl." She stays!

up is almost always whirled far into the future or past.

This has happened to people. There was Ambrose Bierce, who walked out of America and existence, and there are thousands of others who have disappeared without a trace, though many of these may not have been caught up by time tornados and I do not know if a time gale blew across the deck of the *Marie Celeste*.

Sometimes a time wind is playful, snatching up an object, sporting with it for a season and then returning it unharmed to its original place. Sometimes we may be blown about by whimsical time winds without realizing it. Memory, for example, is a tiny time breeze, so weak that it can ripple only the mind.

A very few time winds are like the monsoon, blowing at fixed intervals, first in one direction, then the other. Such a time wind blows near a balancing rock in a valley of red stones in the American Southwest. Every morning at ten o'clock, it blows a hundred years into the future; every afternoon at two, it blows a hundred years into the past.

Quite a number of people have unwittingly seen time winds in operation. There are misty spots on the sea's horizon and wavery patches over desert sands. There are mirages and will o' the wisps and ice blinks. And there are dust devils, such as Tom Dorset walked into near the balancing rock.

It seemed to him no more than a spiteful upgust of sand, against which he closed his eyes until the warm granules stopped peppering the lids. He opened them to see the balancing rock had silently fallen and lay a quarter buried—no, that couldn't be, he told himself instantly. He had been preoccupied; he must have passed the balancing rock and held its image in his mind.

Despite this rationalization he was quite shaken. The strap of his camera slipped slowly down his arm without his feeling it. And just then there stepped around the gaint bobbin of the rock an extraordinarily pretty girl with hair the same pinkish copper color.

She was barefoot and wearing a pale blue playsuit rather like a Grecian tunic. But most important, as she stood there toeing his rough shadow in the sand, there was a complete naturalness about her, an absence of sharp edges, as if her personality had weathered without aging, just as the valley seemed to have taken another step toward eternity in the space of an instant.

She must have assumed something of the same gentleness in him, for her faint surprise faded and she asked him, as easily as if he were a friend of five years' standing, "Tell now, do you think a woman can love just one man? All her life? And a man just one woman?"

Tom Dorset made a dazed sound.

His mind searched wildly.

"I do," she said, looking at him as calmly as at a mountain. "I think a man and woman can be each other's world, like Tristan and Isolde or Frederic and Catherine. Those old authors were wise. I don't see why on earth a girl has to spread her love around, no matter how enriching the experiences may be."

"You know, I agree with you," Tom said, thinking he'd caught her idea—it was impossible not to catch her casualness. "I think there's something cheap about the way everybody's supposed to run after sex these days."

"I don't mean that exactly. Tenderness is beautiful, but—" She pouted. "A big family can be vastly crushing. I wanted to declare today a holiday, but they outvoted me. Jock said it didn't chime with our mood cycles. But I was angry with them, so I put on my clothes—"

"Put on—?"

"To make it a holiday," she explained bafflingly. "And I walked here for a tantrum." She stepped out of Tom's shadow and hopped back. "Ow, the sand's getting hot," she said, rubbing the grains from the pale and uncramped toes.

"You go barefoot a lot?" Tom guessed.

"No, mostly digitals," she replied and took something shimmering from a pocket at her hip and drew it on her foot. It was a high-ankled, transparent mocassin with five separate toes. She zipped it shut with the speed of a card trick, then similarly gloved the other foot. Again the metal-edged slit down the front seemed to close itself.

"I'm behind on the fashions," Tom said, curious. They

were walking side by side now, the way she'd come and he'd been going. "How does that zipper work?"

"Magnetic. They're on all my clothes. Very simple." She parted her tunic to the waist, then let it zip together.

"Clever," Tom remarked with a gulp. There seemed no limits to this girl's naturalness.

"I see you're a button man," she said. "You actually believe it's possible for a man and woman to love just each other?"

His chuckle was bitter. He was thinking of Elinore Murphy at Tosker-Brown and a bit about cold-faced Miss Tosker herself. "I sometimes wonder if it's possible for anyone to love anyone."

"You haven't met the right girls," she said.

"Girl," he corrected.

She grinned at him. "You'll make me think you really are a monogamist. What group do you come from?"

"Let's not talk about that," he requested. He was willing to forego knowing how she'd guessed he was from an art group, if he could be spared talking about the Vacation Fellowships and those nervous little cabins.

"My group's very nice on the whole," the girl said, "but at times they can be nefandously exasperating. Jock's the worst, quietly guiding the rest of us like an analyst. How I loathe that man! But Larry's almost as bad, with his shame-faced bumptiousness, as if we'd all sneaked off on a joyride to Venus. And there's Jokichi at the opposite extreme, forever scared he won't distribute his affection equally, dividing it up into mean little packets like candy for jealous children who would scream if they got one chewy less. And then there's Sasha and Ernest—"

"Who are you talking about?" Tom asked.

"My husbands." She shook her head dolefully. "To find five more difficult men would be positively Martian."

Tom's mind backtracked frantically, searching all conversations at Tosker-Brown for gossip about cultists in the neighborhood. It found nothing and embarked on a wider search. There were the Mormons (was that the word that had sounded like Martian?) but it wasn't the Mormon husbands who were plural. And then there was Oneida (weren't husbands and wives both plural there?) but that was nineteenth century New England.

"Five husbands?" he repeated. She nodded. He went on, "Do you mean to say five men have got you alone somewhere up here?"

"To be sure not," she replied. "They are my kwives."

"Kwives?"

"Co-wives," she said more slowly. "They can be fascinerously exasperating, too."

Tom's mind did some more searching. "And yet you believe in monogamy?"

She smiled. "Only when I'm having tantrums. It was civilized of you to agree with me."

"But I actually do believe in monogamy," he protested.

She gave his hand a little squeeze. "You are nice, but let's rush now. I've finished my tantrum and I want you to meet my group. You can fresh yourself with us."

As they hurried across the heated sands, Tom Dorset felt for the first time a twinge of uneasiness. There was something about this girl, more than her strange clothes and the odd words she used now and then, something almost—though ghosts don't wear digitals—spectral.

They scrambled up a little rise, digging their footgear into the sand, until they stood on a long flat. And there, serpentining around two great clumps of rock, was a many-windowed adobe ranch house with a roof like fresh soot.

"Oh, they've put on their clothes," his companion exclaimed with pleasure. "They've decided to make it a holiday after all."

Tom spotted a beard in the group swarming out to meet them. Its cultish look gave him a momentary feeling of superiority, followed by an equally momentary apprehension—the five husbands were certainly husky. Then both feelings were swallowed up in the swirl of introduction.

He told his own name, found that his companion's was Lois Wolver, then smiling faces began to bob toward his, his hands were shaken, his cheeks were kissed, he was even spun around like blind man's buff, so that he lost track of the husbands and failed to attach Mary, Rachel, Simone and Joyce to the right owners.

He did notice that Jokichi was an Oriental with a skin as tight as enameled china, and that Rachel was a tall, slim Negro girl. Also someone said, "Joyce isn't a Wolver, she's just visiting."

He got a much clearer impression of the clothes than the names. They were colorful, costly-looking, and mostly Egyptian and Cretan in inspiration. Some of them would have been quite immodest, even compared to Miss Tosker's famous playsuits, except that the wearers didn't seem to feel so.

"There goes the middle-morning rocket!" one of them eagerly cried.

Tom looked up with the rest, but his eyes caught the dazzling sun. However, he heard a faint roaring that quickly sank in volume and pitch, and it reminded him that the Army had a rocket-testing range in this area. He had little interest in science, but he hadn't known they were on a daily schedule.

"Do you suppose it's off the track?" he asked anxiously.

"Not a chance," someone told him—the beard, he thought. The assurance of the tones gave him a possible solution. Scientists came from all over the world these days and might have all sorts of advanced ideas. This could be a group working at a nearby atomic project and leading its peculiar private life on the side.

As they eddied toward the house, he heard Lois remind someone, "But you finally did declare it a holiday," and a husband who looked like a gay pharaoh respond, "I had another see at the mood charts and I found a subtle surge I'd missed."

Meanwhile the beard (a black one) had taken Tom in charge. Tom wasn't sure of his name, but he had a tan skin, a green sarong, and a fiercely jovial expression. "The swimming pool's around there, the landing spot's on the other side," he began, then noticed Tom gazing at the sooty roof. "Sun power cells," he explained proudly. "They store all the current we need."

Tom felt his idea confirmed. "Wonder you don't use atomic power," he observed lightly.

The beard nodded. "We've been asked that. Matter of esthetics. Why waste sunlight or use hard radiations needlessly? Of course, you might feel differently. What's your group, did you say?"

"Tosker-Brown," Tom told him, adding when the beard frowned, "the Fellowship people, you know."

"I don't," the beard confessed. "Where are you located?"

Tom briefly described the ranch house and cabins at the other end of the valley.

"Comic, I can't place it." The beard shrugged. "Here come the children."

A dozen naked youngsters raced around the ranch house, followed by a woman in a vaguely African dress open down the sides.

"Yours?" Tom asked.

"Ours," the beard answered.

"C'est un homme!"

"Regardez les vêtements!"

"No need to practice, kids; this is a holiday," the beard told them. "Tom, Helen," he said, introducing the woman with the air-conditioned garment. "Her turn today to companion *die Kinder.*"

One of the latter rapped on the beard's knee. "May we show the stranger our things?" Instantly the others joined in pleading. The beard shot an inquiring glance at Tom, who nodded. A moment later the small troupe was hurrying him toward a spacious lean-to at the end of the ranch house. It was chuckful of strange toys, rocks and plants, small animals in cages and out, and the oddest model airplanes, or submarines. But Tom was given no time to look at any one thing for long.

"See my crystals? I grew them."

"Smell my mutated gardenias. Tell now, isn't there a difference?" There didn't seem to be, but he nodded.

"Look at my squabbits." This referred to some long-eared white squirrels nibbling carrots and nuts.

"Here's my newest model spaceship, a DS-57-B. Notice the detail." The oldest boy shoved one of the submarine affairs in his face.

Tom felt like a figure that is being tugged about in a rococo painting by wide pink ribbons in the chubby hands of naked cherubs. Except that these cherubs were slim and tanned, fantastically energetic, and apparently of depressingly high IQ. (What these scientists did to children!) He missed Lois and was grateful for the single little girl solemnly skipping rope in a corner and paying no attention to him.

The odd lingo she repeated stuck in his mind: "Gik-lo, I-o, Rik-o, Gis-so. Gik-lo, I-o . . ."

Suddenly the air was filled with soft chimes. "Lunch," the children shouted and ran away.

Tom followed at a soberer pace along the wall of the ranch house. He glanced in the huge windows, curious about the living and sleeping arrangements of the Wolvers, but the panes were strangely darkened. Then he entered the wide doorway through which the children had scampered and his curiosity turned to wonder.

A resilient green floor that wasn't flat, but sloped up toward the white of the far wall like a breaking wave. Chairs like giants' hands tenderly cupped. Little tables growing like mushrooms and broadleafed plants out of the green floor. A vast picture window showing the red rocks.

Yet it was the wood-paneled walls that electrified his artistic interest. They blossomed with fruits and flowers, deep and poignantly carved in several styles. He had never seen such work.

He became aware of a silence and realized that his hosts and hostesses were smiling at him from around a long table. Moved by a sudden humility, he knelt and unlaced his sneakers and added them to the pile of sandals and digitals by the door. As he rose, a soft and comic piping started and he realized that beyond the table the children were lined up solemnly puffing at little wooden flutes and recorders. He saw the empty chair at the table and went toward it, conscious for the moment of nothing but his dusty feet.

He was disappointed that Lois wasn't sitting next to him, but the food reminded him that he was hungry. There was a charming little steak, striped black and brown with perfection, and all sorts of vegetables and fruits, one or two of which he didn't recognize.

"Flown from Africa," someone explained to him.

These sly scientists, he thought, living behind their security curtain in the most improbable world!

When they were sitting with coffee and wine, and the children had finished their concert and were busy at another table, he asked, "How do you manage all this?"

Jock, the gay pharaoh, shrugged. "It's not difficult."

Rachel, the slim Negro, chuckled in her throat. "We're just people, Tom."

He tried to phrase his question without mentioning money. "What do you all do?"

"Jock's a uranium miner," Larry (the beard) answered, briskly taking over. "Rachel's an algae farmer. I'm a rocket pilot. Lois—"

Although pleased at this final confirmation of his guess, Tom couldn't help feeling a surge of uneasiness. "Sure you should be telling me these things?"

Larry laughed. "Why not? Lois and Jokichi have been exchange-workers in China the last six months."

"Mostly digging ditches," Jokichi put in with a smile.

"—and Sasha's in an assembly plant. Helen's a psychiatrist. Oh, we just do ordinary things. Now we're on grand vacation."

"Grand vacation?"

"When all of us have a vacation together," Larry explained. "What do you do?"

"I'm an artist," Tom said, taking out a cigaret.

"But what else?" Larry asked.

Tom felt an angry embarrassment. "Just an artist," he mumbled, cigaret in mouth, digging in his pockets for a match.

"Hold on," said Joyce beside him and pointed a silver pencil at the tip of the cigaret. He felt a faint thrill in his lips and then started back, coughing. The cigaret was lighted.

"Please mutate my poppy seeds, Mommy." A little girl had darted to Joyce from the children's table.

"You're a very dirty little girl," Joyce told her without reproof. "Hold them out." She briefly directed the silver pencil at the clay pellets on the grimy little palm. The little girl shivered delightedly. "I love ultrasonics, they feel so funny." She scampered off.

Tom cleared his throat. "I must say I'm tremendously impressed with the wood carvings. I'd like to photograph them. Oh, Lord!"

"What's the matter?" Rachel asked.

"I lost my camera somewhere."

"Camera?" Jokichi showed interest. "You mean one for stills?"

"Yes."

"What kind?"

"A Leica," Tom told him.

Jokichi seemed impressed. "That is interesting. I've never seen one of those old ones."

"Tom's a button man," Lois remarked by way of explanation, apparently. "Was the camera in a brown case? You dropped it where we met. We can get it later."

"Good, I'd really like to take those pictures," Tom said. "Incidentally, who did the carvings?"

"We did," Jock said. "Together."

Tom was grateful that the scamper of the children out of the room saved him from having to reply. He couldn't think of anything but a grunt of astonishment.

The conversation split into a group of chats about something called a psych machine, trips to Russia, the planet Mars, and several artists Tom had never heard of. He wanted to talk to Lois, but she was one of the group gabbling about Mars like children. He felt suddenly uneasy and out of things, and neither Rachel's deprecating remarks about her section of the wood carvings nor Joyce's interesting smiles helped much. He was glad when they all began to get up. He wandered outside and made his way to the children's lean-to feeling very depressed.

Once again he was the center of a friendly naked cluster, except for the same solemn-faced little girl skipping rope.

A rather malicious but not very hopeful whim prompted him to ask the youngest, "What's one and one?"

"Ten," the shaver answered glibly. Tom felt pleased.

"It could also be two," the oldest boy remarked.

"I'll say," Tom agreed. "What's the population of the world?"

"About seven hundred million."

Tom nodded noncommittally and, grabbing at the first long word that he thought of, turned to the eldest girl. "What's poliomyelitis?"

"Never heard of it," she said.

The solemn little girl kept droning the same ridiculous chant: "Gik-lo, I-o, Rik-o, Gis-so."

His ego eased, Tom went outside and there was Lois.

"What's the matter?" she asked.

"Nothing," he said.

She took his hand. "Have we pushed ourselves at you too much? Has our jabbering bothered you? We're a loud-mouthed family and I didn't think to ask if you were loning."

"Loning?"

"Solituding."

"In a way," he said. They didn't speak for a moment. Then, "Are you happy, Lois, in your life here?" he asked.

Her smile was instant. "Of course. Don't you like my group?"

He hesitated. "They make me feel rather no good," he said, and then admitted. "but in a way I'm more attracted to them than any people I've ever met."

"You are?" Her grip on his hand tightened. "Then why don't you stay with us for a while? I like you. It's too early to propose anything, but I think you have a quality our group lacks. You could see how you fit in. And there's Joyce. She's just visiting, too. You wouldn't have to lone unless you wanted."

Before he could think, there was a rhythmic rush of feet and the Wolvers were around them.

"We're swimming," Simone announced.

Lois looked at Tom inquiringly. He smiled his willingness, started to mention he didn't have trunks, then realized that wouldn't be news here. He wondered whether he would blush.

Jock fell in beside him as they rounded the ranch house. "Larry's been telling me about your group at the other end of the valley. It's comic, but I've whirled down the valley a dozen times and never spotted any sort of place there. What's it like?"

"A ranch house and several cabins."

Jock frowned. "Comic I never saw it." His face cleared. "How about whirling over there? You could point it out to me."

"It's really there," Tom said uneasily. "I'm not making it up."

"Of course," Jock assured him. "It was just an idea."

"We could pick up your camera on the way," Lois put in.

The rest of the group had turned back from the huge oval pool and the dark blue and flashing thing beyond it, and stood gay-colored against the pool's pale blue shimmer.

"How about it?" Jock asked them "A whirl before we bathe?"

Two or three said yes besides Lois, and Jock led the way toward the helicopter that Tom now saw standing beyond the pool, its beetle body as blue as a scarab, its vanes flashing silver.

The others piled in. Tom followed as casually as he could, trying to suppress the pounding of his heart. "Wonder you don't go by rocket," he remarked lightly.

Jock laughed. "For such a short trip?"

The vanes began to thrum. Tom sat stiffly, gripping the sides of the seat, then realized that the others had sunk back lazily in the cushions. There was a moment of strain and they were falling ahead and up. Looking out the side, Tom saw for a moment the sooty roof of the ranch house and the blue of the pool and the pinkish umber of tanned bodies. Then the helicopter lurched gently around. Without warning a miserable uneasiness gripped him, a desire to cling mixed with an urge to escape. He tried to convince himself it was fear of the height.

He heard Lois tell Jock, "That's the place, down by that rock that looks like a wrecked spaceship."

The helicopter began to fall forward. Tom felt Lois' hand on his.

"You haven't answered my question," she said.

"What?" he asked dully.

"Whether you'll stay with us. At least for a while."

He looked at her. Her smile was a comfort. He said, "If I possibly can."

"What could possibly stop you?"

"I don't know," he answered abstractedly.

"You're strange," Lois told him. "There's a weight of sadness in you. As if you lived in a less happy age. As if it weren't 2050."

"Twenty?" he repeated, awakening from his thoughts with a jerk. "What's the time?" he asked anxiously.

"Two," Jock said. The word sounded like a knell.

"You need cheering," Lois announced firmly.

Amid a whoosh of air rebounding from earth, they jounced gently down. Lois vaulted out. "Come on," she said.

Tom followed her. "Where?" he asked stupidly, looking around at the red rocks through the settling sand cloud stirred by the vanes.

"Your camera," she told him, laughing. "Over there. Come on, I'll race you."

He started to run with her and then his uneasiness got beyond his control. He ran faster and faster. He saw Lois catch her foot on a rock and go down sprawling, but he couldn't stop. He ran desperately around the rock and into a gust of upwhirling sand that terrified him with its suddenness. He tried to escape from the stinging, blinding gust, but there was the nightmarish fright that his wild strides were carrying him nowhere.

Then the sand settled. He stopped running and looked around him. He was standing by the balancing rock. He was gasping. At his feet the rusty brown leather of the camera case peeped from the sand. Lois was nowhere in sight. Neither was the helicopter. The valley seemed different, rawer—one might almost have said younger.

Hours after dark he trailed into Tosker-Brown. Curtained lights still glowed from a few cabins. He was footsore, bewildered, frightened. All afternoon and through the twilight and into the moonlit evening that turned the red rocks black, he had searched the valley. Nowhere had he been able to find the soot-roofed ranch house of the Wolvers. He hadn't even been able to locate the rock like a giant bobbin where he'd met Lois.

During the next days he often returned to the valley. But he never found anything. And he never happened to be near the balancing rock when the time winds blew at ten and two, though once or twice he did see dust devils. Then he went away and eventually forgot.

In his casual reading he ran across popular science articles describing the binary system of numbers used in electronic calculating machines, where one and one make ten. He always skipped them. And more than once he saw the four equations expressing Einstein's generalized theory of gravitation:

$$\text{"}g_{\overset{i}{\underset{+-}{}}}K\text{;}\ell_{=0}\text{;}\Gamma_{i=0}\text{;}R_{ik=0}\text{;}\mathcal{G}\text{,}_{\overset{is}{\underset{s}{v}}}\text{=}o\text{"!}$$

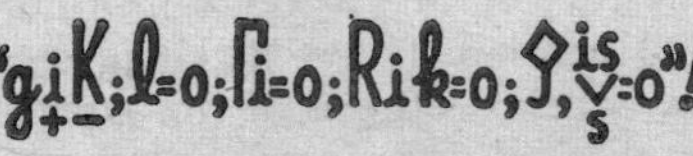

He never connected them with the little girl's chant: "Gik-lo, I-o, Rik-o, Gis-so."

PRONE

Mack Reynolds

Bet you that, if the Enemy involved in this story had been terrestrial, it would have appealed to the International Court of Justice at The Hague for protection against conduct not in accordance with the Ethics and Morals of Civilized Warfare. However, what the SupCom faced was an *extraterrestrial* Enemy who had no standing at The Hague, and his lack of ethics was as total as the kind of warfare he intended to wage. So (br-r-r-r!) read on.

SUPCOM BULL UNDERWOOD SAID IN A VOICE OMI-nously mild, "I continually get the impression that every other sentence is being left out of this conversation. Now, tell me, General, what do you mean *things happen around him*?"

"Well, for instance, the first day Mitchie got to the Academy a cannon burst at a demonstration."

"What's a cannon?"

"A pre-guided-missile weapon," the commander of the Terra Military Academy told him. "You know, shells propelled by gunpowder. We usually demonstrate them in our history classes. This time four students were injured. The next day sixteen were hurt in ground-war maneuvers."

There was an element of respect in the SupCom's tone. "Your course must be rugged."

General Bentley wiped his forehead with a snowy handkerchief even as he shook it negatively. "It was the first time any such thing happened. I tell you, sir, since Mitchie Farthingworth has been at the academy things have been chaotic. Fires in the dormitories, small arms exploding, cadets being hospitalized right and left. We've just got to expel that boy!"

"Don't be ridiculous," the SupCom growled. "He's the apple of his old man's eye. We've got to make a hero out of him if it means the loss of a battle fleet. But I still don't get this. You mean the Farthingworth kid is committing sabotage?"

"It's not that. We investigated. He doesn't do it on purpose, things just *happen* around him. Mitchie can't help it."

"Confound it, stop calling him Mitchie!" Bull Underwood snapped. "How do you know it's him if he doesn't do it? Maybe you're just having a run of bad luck."

"That's what I thought," Bentley said, "until I ran into Admiral Lawrence of the Space Marines Academy. He had the same story. The day Mitchie—excuse me, sir—Michael Farthingworth set foot in Nuevo San Diego, things started happening. When they finally got him transferred to our academy the trouble stopped."

It was at times like these that Bull Underwood regretted his shaven head. He could have used some hair to tear. "Then it *must* be sabotage if it stops when he leaves!"

"I don't think so, sir."

The SupCom took a deep breath, snapped to his secretarobot, "Brief me on Cadet Michael Farthingworth, including his early life." While he waited he growled under his breath, "A stalemated hundred-year war on my hands with those Martian *makrons* and I have to get things like this tossed at me."

In less than a minute the secretarobot began: "Son of Senator Warren Farthingworth, Chairman War Appropriations Committee. Twenty-two years of age. Five feet six, one hundred and thirty, blue eyes, brown hair, fair. Born and spent early youth in former United States area. Early education by mother. At age of eighteen entered Harvard but schooling was interrupted when roof of assembly hall collapsed killing most of faculty. Next year entered Yale, leaving two months later when 90 percent of the university's buildings were burnt down in the holocaust of '85. Next attended University of California but failed to graduate owing to the earthquake which completely . . ."

"That's enough," the SupCom rapped. He turned and stared at General Bentley. "What the hell is it? Even if the kid was a psychokinetic saboteur he couldn't accomplish all that."

The academy commander shook his head. "All I know is that, since his arrival at the Terra Military Academy, there's been an endless series of casualties. And the longer he's there the worse it gets. It's twice as bad now as when he first arrived." He got to his feet wearily. "I'm a broken man, sir, and I'm leaving this in your hands. You'll have my resignation this afternoon. Frankly, I'm afraid to return to the school. If I do, some day I'll probably crack my spine bending over to tie my shoelaces. It just isn't safe to be near that boy."

For a long time after General Bentley had left, SupCom Bull Underwood sat at his desk, his heavy underlip in a pout. "And just when the next five years' appropriation is up before the committee," he snarled at nobody.

He turned to the secretarobot. "Put the best psychotechnicians available on Michael Farthingworth. They are to discover . . . well, they are to discover why in hell things happen around him. Priority one."

Approximately a week later the secretarobot said, "May I interrupt you, sir? A priority-one report is coming in."

Bull Underwood grunted and turned away from the star chart he'd been studying with the two Space Marine generals. He dismissed them and sat down at his desk.

The visor lit up and he was confronted with the face of an elderly civilian. "Doctor Duclos," the civilian said. "Case of Cadet Michael Farthingworth."

"Good," the SupCom rumbled. "Doctor, what in the devil is wrong with young Farthingworth?"

"The boy is an accident prone."

Bull Underwood scowled at him. "A what?"

"An accident prone." The doctor elaborated with evident satisfaction. "There is indication that he is the most extreme case in medical history. Really a fascinating study. Never in my experience have I been—"

"Please, Doctor. I'm a layman. What is an accident prone?"

"Ah, yes. Briefly, an unexplained phenomenon first noted by the insurance companies of the nineteenth and twentieth centuries. An accident prone has an unnaturally large number of accidents happen either to him, or less often, to persons in his vicinity. In Farthingworth's case, they happen to persons about him. He himself is never affected."

The SupCom was unbelieving. "You mean to tell me there are some persons who just naturally have accidents happen to them without any reason?"

"That is correct," Duclos nodded. "Most prones are understandable. Subconsciously, the death wish is at work and the prone *seeks* self-destruction. However, science has yet to discover the forces behind the less common type such as Farthingworth exemplifies." The doctor's emphatic shrug betrayed his Gallic background. "It has been suggested that it is no more than the laws of chance at work. To counterbalance the accident prone, there should be persons at the other extreme who are blessed with abnormally good fortune. However . . ."

SupCom Bull Underwood's lower lip was out, almost truculently. "Listen," he interrupted. "What can be done about it?"

"Nothing," the doctor said, his shoulders raising and lowering again. "An accident prone seems to remain one as a rule. Not always, but as a rule. Fortunately, they are rare."

"Not rare enough," the SupCom growled. "These insurance companies, what did they do when they located an accident prone?"

"They kept track of him and refused to insure the prone, his business, home, employees, employers, or anyone or anything connected with him."

Bull Underwood stared unblinkingly at the doctor, as though wondering whether the other's whole explanation was an attempt to pull his leg. Finally he rapped, "Thank you, Doctor Duclos. That will be all." The civilian's face faded from the visor.

The SupCom said slowly to the secretarobot, "Have Cadet Farthingworth report to me." He added sotto voce. "And while he's here have all personnel keep their fingers crossed."

The photoelectric-controlled door leading to the sanctum sanctorum of SupCom Bull Underwood glided quietly open and a lieutenant entered and came to a snappy attention. The door swung gently shut behind him.

"Well?" Bull Underwood growled.

"Sir, a Cadet Michael Farthingworth to report to you."

"Send him in. Ah, just a minute, Lieutenant Brown. How do you feel after talking to him?"

"Me, sir? I feel fine, sir." The lieutenant looked blankly at him.

"Hmmm. Well, send him in, confound it."

The lieutenant turned and the door opened automatically before him. "Cadet Farthingworth," he announced.

The newcomer entered and stood stiffly before the desk of Earth's military head. Bill Underwood appraised him with care. In spite of the swank Academy uniform, Michael Farthingworth cut a wistfully ineffectual figure. His faded blue eyes blinked sadly behind heavy contact lenses.

"That'll be all, Lieutenant," the SupCom said to his aide.

"Yes, sir." The lieutenant about-faced snappily and marched to the door—which swung sharply forward and quickly back again before the lieutenant was halfway through.

SupCom Bull Underwood winced at the crush of bone and cartilage. He shuddered, then snapped to his secretarobot, "Have Lieutenant Brown hospitalized . . . and, ah . . . see he gets a Luna Medal for exposing himself to danger beyond the call of duty."

He swung to the newcomer and came directly to the point. "Cadet Farthingworth," he rapped, "do you know what an accident prone is?"

Mitchie's voice was low and plaintive. "Yes, sir."

"You do?" Bull Underwood was surprised.

"Yes, sir. At first such things as the school's burning

down didn't particularly impress me as being personally connected with me, but the older I get, the worse it gets, and after what happened to my first date, I started to investigate."

The SupCom said cautiously, "What happened to the date?"

Mitchie flushed. "I took her to a dance and she broke her leg."

The SupCom cleared his throat. "So finally you investigated?"

"Yes, sir," Mitchie Farthingworth said woefully. "And I found I was an accident prone and getting worse geometrically. Each year I'm twice as bad as the year before. I'm glad you've discovered it too, sir. I . . . didn't know what to do. Now it's in your hands."

The SupCom was somewhat relieved. Possibly this wasn't going to be as difficult as he had feared. He said, "Have you any ideas Mitchie, ah, that is . . . "

"Call me Mitchie if you want, sir. Everybody else does."

"Have you any ideas? After all, you've done as much damage to Terra as a Martian task force would accomplish."

"Yes, sir. I think I ought to be shot."

"Huh?"

"Yes, sir. I'm expendable." Mitchie said miserably. "In fact, I suppose I'm probably the most expendable soldier that's ever been. All my life I've wanted to be a spaceman and do my share toward licking the Martians." His eyes gleamed behind his lenses. "Why, I've . . ."

He stopped and looked at his commanding officer pathetically. "What's the use? I'm just a bust. An accident prone. The only thing to do is liquidate me." He tried to laugh in self-deprecation but his voice broke.

Behind him, Bull Underwood heard the glass in his office window shatter without seeming cause. He winced again, but didn't turn.

"Sorry, sir," Mitchie said. "See? The only thing is to shoot me."

"Look," Bull Underwood said urgently, "stand back a

few yards farther, will you? There on the other side of the room." He cleared his throat. "Your suggestion has already been considered, as a matter of fact. However, due to your father's political prominence, shooting you had to be ruled out."

From a clear sky the secretarobot began to say, "'Twas brillig, and the slithy toves did gyre and gimble in the wabe."

SupCom Bull Underwood closed his eyes in pain and shrunk back into his chair. "What?" he said cautiously.

"The borogoves were mimsy as all hell," the secretarobot said decisively and shut up.

Mitchie looked at it. "Slipped its cogs, sir," he said helpfully, "It's happened before around me."

"The best damned memory bank in the system," Underwood protested. "Oh, no."

"Yes, sir," Mitchie said apologetically. "And I wouldn't recommend trying to repair it, sir. Three technicians were electrocuted when I was . . ."

The secretarobot sang, "O frabjous day! Callooh! Callay!"

"Completely around the corner," Mitchie said.

"This," said Bull Underwood, "is too frabjous much! Senator or no senator, appropriations or no appropriations, with my own bare hands—"

As he strode impulsively forward, he felt the rug giving way beneath him. He grasped desperately for the edge of the desk, felt ink bottle and water carafe go crashing over.

Mitchie darted forward to his assistance.

"Stand back!" Bull Underwood roared, holding an ankle with one hand, shaking the other hand in the form of a fist. "Get out of here, confound it!" Ink began to drip from the desk over his shaven head. It cooled him not at all. "It's not even safe to destroy you! It'd wipe out a regiment to try to assemble a firing squad! It—" Suddenly he paused, and when he spoke again his voice was like the coo of a condor.

"Cadet Farthingworth," he announced, "after considerable deliberation on my part I have chosen you to perform the most hazardous operation that Terra's forces have undertaken in the past hundred years. If successful, this effort will undoubtedly end the war."

"Who, me?" Mitchie said.

"Exactly," SupCom Underwood snapped. "This war has been going on for a century without either side's being able to secure that slight edge, that minute advantage which would mean victory. Cadet Farthingworth, you have been chosen to make the supreme effort which will give Terra that superiority over the Martians." The SupCom looked sternly at Mitchie.

"Yes, sir," he clipped. "What are my orders?"

The SupCom beamed at him. "Spoken like a true hero of Terra's Space Forces. On the spaceport behind this building is a small spycraft. You are to repair immediately to it and blast off for Mars. Once there you are to land, hide the ship, and make your way to their capital city."

"Yes, sir! And what do I do then?"

"Nothing," Bull Underwood said with satisfaction. "You do absolutely nothing but live there. I estimate that your presence in the enemy capital will end the war in less than two years."

Michael Farthingworth snapped him a brilliant salute. "Yes, sir."

Spontaneous combustion broke out in the wastebasket.

Through the shards of his window, SupCom Bull Underwood could hear the blast-off of the spyship. Half a dozen miles away the flare of a fuel dump going up in flames lighted up the sky.

Seated there in the wreckage of his office he rubbed his ankle tenderly. "The only trouble is when the war is over we'll have to bring him home."

But then he brightened. "Perhaps we could leave him there as our occupation forces. It would keep them from ever recovering to the point where they could try again."

He tried to get to his feet, saying to the secretarobot, "Have them send me in a couple of medical corpsmen."

"Beware the Jabberwock," the secretarobot sneered.

THE EDUCATION OF TIGRESS MCCARDLE

C. M. Kornbluth

They evolved this method of controlling the population explosion around the year 2000; but they really should have had it 'way back in 1965, when there was still a chance that it might do some good—perhaps even save us from the future so grimly outlined for us in the chronicle that follows. In 1965 the Invention might have kept down the number of neurotics, psychotics, folk singers, juvenile delinquents, merchants of death, and cannon fodder quite successfully, thus saving us from a Fate Worse Than Death. . . . But never mind. Quite probably it is already too late. So just settle down and read. This is one of the few stories by the late and much-missed Cyril Kornbluth still unanthologized and uncollected. It is an honor to present it herewith.

WITH THE UNANIMITY THAT HAD ALWAYS CHARACTERIZED his fans, as soon as they were able to vote they swept him into office as President of the United States. Four years later the 28th Amendment was ratified, republican institutions yielded gracefully to the usages of monarchy, and King Purvis I reigned in the land.

Perhaps even then all would have gone well if it had not been for another major entertainment personage, the insidious Dr. Fu Manchu, that veritable personification of the Yellow Peril, squatting like some great evil spider in the center of his web of intrigue. The insidious doctor appeared to have so much fun on his television series, what with a lovely concubine to paw him and a dwarf to throw knives, that it quite turned the head of Gerald Wang, a hitherto-peaceable antique dealer of San Francisco. Gerald decided that he too would become a veritable personification of the Yellow Peril, and that he too would squat like some great evil spider in the center of a web of intrigue, and that he would *really* accomplish something. He found it remarkably easy since nobody believed in the Yellow Peril any more. He grew a mandarin mustache, took to uttering cryptic quotations from the sages, and was generally addressed as "doctor" by the members of his organization, though he made no attempt to practice medicine. His wife drew the line at the concubine, but Gerald had enough to keep him busy with his personifying and squatting.

His great coup occurred in 1986 when, after patient years of squatting and plotting, one of his most insidious ideas reached the attention of His Majesty via a recommendation ridered onto the annual population-resources report. The recommendation was implemented as the Parental Qualifications Program, or P.Q.P., by royal edict. "Ow rackon thet'll make um mahnd they P's and Q's," quipped His Majesty, and everybody laughed heartily—but none more heartily than the insidious Dr. Wang, who was present in disguise as Tuner of the Royal Git-tar.

A typical PQP operation (at least when judged typical by the professor of Chronoscope History Seminar 201 given by Columbia University in 2756 A.D., who ought to know) involved George McCardle . . .

George McCardle had a *good* deal with his girl friend, Tigress Moone. He dined her and bought her pretties and had the freedom of the bearskin rug in front of her wood-burning fireplace. He had beaten the game; he had achieved a delightful combination of bachelor irresponsibility and marital gratification.

"George," Tigress said thoughtfully one day . . . so they got married.

With prices what they were in 1998, she kept her job, of course—at least until she again said thoughtfully: "George . . ."

She then had too much time on her hands; it was absurd for a healthy young woman to pretend that taking care of a two-room city apartment kept her occupied . . . so she thoughtfully said, "George?" and they moved to the suburbs.

George happened to be a rising young editor in the Civil War Book-of-the-Week Club. He won his spurs when he got MIGHTIER THAN THE SWORD: A STUDY OF PENS AND PENCILS IN THE ARMY OF THE POTOMAC, 1863–1865 whipped into shape for the printer. They then assigned him to the infinitely more difficult and delicate job of handling writers. A temperamental troll named Blount was his special trial. Blount was writing a novelized account of Corporal Piggott's Raid, a deservedly obscure episode which got Corporal Piggott of the 104th New York (Provisional) Heavy Artillery Regiment deservedly court-martialled in the summer of '63. It was George's responsibility to see that Blount novelized the verdict of guilty into a triumphant acquittal followed by an award of the Medal of Honor, and Blount was being unreasonable about it.

It was after a hard day of screaming at Blount, and being screamed back at, that George dragged his carcass off the Long Island Rail Road and into the family car. "Hi, dear," he said to Mrs. McCardle, erstwhile tigress-Diana, and off they drove, and so far it seemed like the waning of another ordinary day. But in the car Mrs. McCardle said thoughtfully: "George . . ."

She told him what was on her mind, and he refrained from striking her in the face because they were in rather tricky traffic and she was driving.

She wanted a child.

It was necessary to have a child, she said. Inexorable logic dictated it. For one thing, it was absurd for just the two of them to live in a great barn of a six-room house.

For another thing, she needed a child to fulfill her womanhood. For a third, the brains and beauty of the Moone-McCardle strain should not die out; it was their duty to posterity.

(The students in Columbia's Chronoscope History Seminar 201 retched as one man at the words.)

For a fourth, everybody was having children.

George thought he had her there, but no. The statement was perfectly correct if for "everybody" you substituted "Mrs. Jacques Truro," their next-door neighbor.

By the time they reached their great six-room barn of a place she was consolidating her victory with a rapid drumfire of simple declarative sentences which ended with "Don't you?" and "Won't we?" and "Isn't it?" to which George, hanging onto the ropes, groggily replied: "We'll see . . . we'll see . . . we'll see . . ."

A wounded thing inside him was soundlessly screaming: *youth! joy! freedom! gone beyond recall, slain by wedlock, coffined by a mortgage, now to be entombed beneath a reeking Everest of diapers!*

"I believe I'd like a drink before dinner," he said. "Had quite a time with Blount today," he said as the Martini curled quietly in his stomach. He was pretending nothing very bad had happened. "Kept talking about his integrity. Writers! They'll never learn. . . . Tigress? Are you with me?"

His wife noticed a slight complaining note in his voice, so she threw herself on the floor, began to kick and scream, went on to hold her breath until her face turned blue, and finished by letting George know that she had abandoned her Career to assuage his bachelor misery, moved out to this dreary wasteland to satisfy his whim, and just once in her life requested some infinitesimal consideration in return for her ghastly drudgery and scrimping.

George, who was a kind and gentle person except with writers, dried her tears and apologized for his brutality. They would have a child, he said contritely. "Though," he added, "I hear there are some complications about it these days."

"For Motherhood," said Mrs. McCardle, getting off the floor, "no complications are too great." She stood profiled like a statue against their picture window, with its view of the picture window of the house across the street.

The next day George asked around at his office.

None of the younger men, married since the P.Q.P. went into effect, seemed to have had children.

A few of them cheerily admitted they had not had children and were not going to have children, for they had volunteered for D-Bal shots, thus doing away with a running minor expense and, more importantly, ensuring a certain peace of mind and unbroken continuity during tender moments.

"Ugh," thought George.

(The Columbia University professor explained to his students "It is clearly in George's interest to go to the clinic for a painless, effective D-Bal shot and thus resolve his problem, but he does not go; he shudders at the thought. We cannot know what fear of amputation stemming from some early traumatic experience thus prevents him from action, but deep-rooted psychological reasons explain his behavior, we can't be certain." The class bent over the chronoscope.)

And some of George's co-workers slunk away and would not submit to questioning. Young MacBirney, normally open and incisive, muttered vaguely and passed his hand across his brow when George asked him how one went about having a baby—red-tape-wise, that is.

It was Blount, come in for his afternoon screaming match, who spilled the vengeful beans. "You and your wife just phone P.Q.P. for an appointment," he told George with a straight face. "They'll issue you—everything you need." George in his innocence thanked him, and Blount turned away and grinned the twisted, sly grin of an author.

A glad female voice answered the phone on behalf of the P.Q.P. It assured George that he and Mrs. McCardle need only drop in any time at the Empire State Building and they'd be well on their way to parenthood.

The next day Mr. and Mrs. McCardle dropped in at the Empire State Building. A receptionist in the lobby was buffing her nails under a huge portrait of His Majesty. A beautifully lettered sign displayed the words with which His Majesty had decreed that P.Q.P. be enacted: "Ow Racken Theah's a Raht Smaht Ah-dee, Boys."

"Where do we sign up, please?" asked George.

The receptionist pawed uncertainly through her desk. "I *know* there's some kind of book," she said as she rummaged, but she did not find it. "Well, it doesn't matter. They'll give you everything you need in Room 100."

"Will I sign up there?" asked George nervously, conditioned by a lifetime of red tape and uncomfortable without it.

"No," said the receptionist.

"But for the tests—"

"There aren't any tests."

"Then the interviews, the deep probing of our physical and psychological fitness for parenthood, our heredity—"

"No interviews."

"But the evaluation of our financial and moral standing without which no permission can be—"

"No evaluation. Just Room 100." She resumed buffing her nails.

In Room 100 a cheerful woman took a Toddler out of a cabinet, punched the non-reversible activating button between its shoulderblades, and handed it to Mrs. McCardle with a cheery: "It's all yours, madame. Return with it in three months and, depending on its condition, you will, or will not, be issued a breeding permit. Simple, isn't it?"

"The little darling!" gurgled Mrs. McCardle, looking down into the Toddler's pretty face.

It spit in her eye, punched her in the nose and sprang a leak.

"Gracious!" said the cheerful woman. "Get it out of our nice clean office, *if* you please."

"How do you work it?" yelled Mrs. McCardle, juggling the Toddler like a hot potato. "How do you turn it off?"

"Oh, you *can't* turn it off," said the woman. "And you'd better not swing it like that. Rough handling goes down on the tapes inside it and we read them in three months and now if you *please,* you're getting our nice office *all wet*—"

She shepherded them out.

"Do something, George!" yelled Mrs. McCardle. George took the Toddler. It stopped leaking and began a ripsaw scream that made the lighting fixtures tremble.

"Give the poor thing to me!" Mrs. McCardle shouted. "You're hurting it holding it like that—"

She took the Toddler back. It stopped screaming and resumed leaking.

It quieted down in the car. The sudden thought seized them both—*too* quiet? Their heads crashed together as they bent simultaneously over the glassy-eyed little object. It laughed delightedly and waved its chubby fists.

"Clumsy oaf!" snapped Mrs. McCardle, rubbing her head.

"Sorry, dear," said George. "But at least we must have got a good mark out of it on the tapes. I suppose it scores us good when it laughs."

Her eyes narrowed. "Probably," she said. "George, do you think if you fell heavily on the sidewalk—?"

"No," said George convulsively. Mrs. McCardle looked at him for a moment and held her peace.

("Note, young gentlemen," said the history professor, "the turning point, the seed of rebellion." They noted.)

The McCardles and the Toddler drove off down Sunrise Highway, which was lined with filling stations; since their '98 Landcruiser made only two miles to the gallon, it was not long before they had to stop at one.

The Toddler began its ripsaw shriek when they stopped. A hollow-eyed attendant shambled over and peered into the car. "Just get it?" he asked apathetically.

"Yes," said Mrs. McCardle, frantically trying to joggle the Toddler, to change it, to burp it, to do anything that would end the soul-splitting noise.

"Half pint of white 90-octane gas is what it needs," mumbled the attendant. "Few drops of SAE 40 oil. Got one myself. Two weeks to go. I'll never make it. I'll crack. I'll—I'll . . ." He tottered off and returned with the gasoline in a nursing bottle, the oil in an eye-dropper.

The Toddler grabbed the bottle and began to gulp the gas down contentedly.

"Where do you put the oil?" asked Mrs. McCardle.

He showed her.

"Oh," she said.

"Fill her up," said George. "The car, I mean. I . . .

ah . . . I'm going to wash my hands, dear."

He cornered the attendant by the cash register. "Look," he said. "What, ah, would happen if you just let it run out of gas? The Toddler, I mean?"

The man looked at him and put a compassionate hand on his shoulder. "It would *scream*, buddy," he said. "The main motors run off an atomic battery. The gas engine's just for a sideshow and for having breakdowns."

"Breakdowns? Oh, my God! How do you fix a breakdown?"

"The best way you can," the man said. "And buddy, when you burp it, watch out for the fumes. I've seen some ugly explosions . . ."

They stopped at five more filling stations along the way when the Toddler wanted gas.

"It'll be better-behaved when it's used to the house," said Mrs. McCardle apprehensively as she carried it over the threshold.

"Put it down and let's see what happens," said George.

The Toddler toddled happily to the coffee table, picked up a large bronze ashtray, moved to the picture window and heaved the ashtray through it. It gurgled happily at the crash.

"You little—!" George roared, making for the Toddler with his hands clawed before him.

"George!" Mrs. McCardle screamed, snatching the Toddler away. "It's only a machine!"

The machine began to shriek.

They tried gasoline, oil, wiping with a clean lint-free rag, putting it down, picking it up and finally banging their heads together. It continued to scream until it was ready to stop screaming, and then it stopped and gave them an enchanting grin.

"Time to put it to—away for the night?" asked George.

It permitted itself to be put away for the night.

From his pillow George said later: "Think we did pretty well today. Three months? Pah!"

Mrs. McCardle said: "You were wonderful, George."

He knew that tone. "My Tigress," he said.

Ten minutes later, at the most inconvenient time in the

world, bar none, the Toddler began its ripsaw screaming.

Cursing, they went to find out what it wanted. They found out. What it wanted was to laugh in their faces.

(The professor explained: "Indubitably, sadism is at work here, but harnessed in the service of humanity. Better a brutal and concentrated attack such as we have been witnessing than long-drawn-out torments." The class nodded respectfully.)

Mr. and Mrs. McCardle managed to pull themselves together for another try, and there was an exact repeat. Apparently the Toddler sensed something in the air.

"Three months," said George, with haunted eyes.

"You'll live," his wife snapped.

"May I ask *just* what kind of a crack that was supposed to be?"

"If the shoe fits, my good *man*—"

So a fine sex quarrel ended the day.

Within a week the house looked as if it had been liberated by a Mississippi National Guard division. George had lost ten pounds because he couldn't digest anything, not even if he seasoned his food with powdered Equanil instead of salt. Mrs. McCardle had gained fifteen pounds by nervous gobbling during the moments when the Toddler left her unoccupied. The picture window was boarded up. On George's salary, and with glaziers' wages what they were, he couldn't have it replaced twice a day.

Not unnaturally, he met his next-door neighbor, Jacques Truro, in a bar.

Truro was rye and soda, he was dry martini; otherwise they were identical.

"It's the little whimper first that gets me, when you know the big screaming's going to come next. I could jump out of my skin when I hear that whimper."

"Yeah. The waiting. Sometimes one second, sometimes five. I count."

"I forced myself to stop. I was throwing up."

"Yeah. Me too. And nervous diarrhea?"

"All the time. Between me and that goddam thing the house is awash. Cheers." They drank and shared hollow laughter.

"My stamp collection. Down the toilet."

"My fishing pole. Three clean breaks and peanut butter in the reel."

"One thing I'll never understand, Truro. *What* decided you two to have a baby?"

"Wait a minute, McCardle," Truro said. "Marguerite told me that *you* were going to have one, so *she* had to have one—"

They looked at each other in shared horror.

"Suckered," said McCardle in an awed voice.

"Women," breathed Truro.

They drank a grim toast and went home.

"It's beginning to talk," Mrs. McCardle said listlessly, sprawled in a chair, her hand in a box of chocolates. "Called me 'old pig-face' this afternoon." She did look somewhat piggish with fifteen superfluous pounds.

George put down his briefcase. It was loaded with work from the office which these days he was unable to get through in time. He had finally got the revised court-martial scene from Blount, and would now have to transmute it into readable prose, emending the author's stupid lapses of logic, illiterate blunders of language and raspingly ugly style.

"I'll wash up," he said.

"Don't use the toilet. Stopped up again."

"Bad?"

"He said he'd come back in the morning with an eight-man crew. Something about jacking up a corner of the house."

The Toddler toddled in with a bottle of bleach, made for the briefcase, and emptied the bleach into it before the exhausted man or woman could comprehend what was going on, let alone do anything about it.

George incredulously spread the pages of the court-martial scene on the gouged and battered coffee table. His eyes bulged as he watched the thousands of typed words vanishing before his eyes, turning pale and then white as the paper.

Blount kept no carbons. Keeping carbons called for a minimal quantity of prudence and brains, but Blount was an author and so he kept no carbons. The court-martial scene, the product of six months' screaming, was *gone*.

The Toddler laughed gleefully.

George clenched his fists, closed his eyes and tried to ignore the roaring in his ears.

The Toddler began a whining chant:

"*Da*-dy's an *au*-thor!
Da-dy's an *au*-thor!"

"That did it!" George shrieked. He stalked to the door and flung it open.

"Where are you going?" Mrs. McCardle quavered.

"To the first doctor's office I find," said her husband in sudden icy calm. "There I will request a shot of D-Bal. When I have had a D-Bal shot, a breeding permit will be of no use whatever to us. Since a breeding permit will be useless, we need not qualify for one by being tortured for another eleven weeks by that obscene little monster, which we shall return to P.Q.P. in the morning. And unless it behaves, it will be returned in a basket, for them to reassemble at their leisure."

"I'm so glad," his wife sighed.

The Toddler said: "May I congratulate you on your decision. By voluntarily surrendering your right to breed, you are patriotically reducing the population pressure, a problem of great concern to His Majesty. We of the P.Q.P. wish to point out that your decision has been arrived at not through coercion but through education; i.e., by presenting you in the form of a Toddler with some of the arguments against parenthood."

"I didn't know you could talk that well," marveled Mrs. McCardle.

The Toddler said modestly: "I've been with the P.Q.P. from the very beginning, ma'am; I'm a veteran Toddler operator, I may say, working out of Room 4567 of the Empire State. And the improved model I'm working through has reduced the breakdown time an average thirty-five percent. I foresee a time, ma'am, when we experienced operators and ever-improved models will do the job in one day!"

The voice was fanatical.

Mrs. McCardle turned around in sudden vague apprehension. George had left for his D-Bal shot.

("And thus we see," said the professor to the seminar, "the genius of the insidious Dr. Wang in full flower." He snapped off the chronoscope. "The first boatloads of Chinese landed in California three generations—or should I say non-generations?—later, unopposed by the scanty, elderly population." He groomed his mandarin mustache and looked out for a moment over the great rice paddies of Central Park. It was spring; blue-clad women stooped patiently over the brown water, and the tender, bright-green shoots were just beginning to appear.

(The seminar students bowed and left for their next lecture, "The Hound Dog as Symbol of Juvenile Aggression in Ancient American Folk Song." It was all that remained of the reign of King Purvis I.)

NOW INHALE

Eric Frank Russell

For our second off-world excursion—see "Mating Call" for the first—we take you to the planet of Gombar, about which it can only be said that the planet itself was less unappetizing than the Gombarians. However, thanks to the fact that Our Hero, Wayne Taylor, knows a smattering of Eastern lore, has a handy way with games, and possesses the ability of a Stoic to resist boredom and panic, everything comes out all right in the end. They generally do, when Eric Russell pits one or more of his space-scout types against the myriad nasties of deep space with which he has dealt during his almost thirty years of writing science fiction. Indeed, Russell is one of England's most honored pre-war gifts to the American s.f. field, having published his first story here back in 1937.

HIS LEG IRONS CLANKED AND HIS WRIST CHAINS jingled as they led him into the room. The bonds on his ankles compelled him to move at an awkward shuffle and the guards delighted in urging him onward faster than he could go. Somebody pointed to a chair facing the long table. Somebody else shoved him into it with such force that he lost balance and sat down hard.

The black brush of his hair jerked as his scalp twitched and that was his only visible reaction. Then he gazed across the desk with light gray eyes so pale that the pupils seemed set in ice. The look in them was neither friendly nor hostile, submissive nor angry; it was just impassively and impartially cold, cold.

On the other side of the desk seven Gombarians surveyed him with various expressions: triumph, disdain, satisfaction, boredom, curiosity, glee and arrogance. They were a humanoid bunch in the same sense that gorillas are humanoid. At that point the resemblance ended.

"Now," began the one in the middle, making every third syllable a grunt, "your name is Wayne Taylor?"

No answer.

"You have come from a planet called Terra?"

No response.

"Let us not waste any more time, Palamin," suggested the one on the left. "If he will not talk by invitation, let him talk by compulsion."

"You are right, Eckster." Putting a hand under the desk Palamin came up with a hammer. It had a pear-shaped head with flattened base. "How would you like every bone in your hands cracked finger by finger, joint by joint?"

"I wouldn't," admitted Wayne Taylor.

"A very sensible reply," approved Palamin. He placed the hammer in the middle of the desk, positioning it significantly. "Already many days have been spent teaching you our language. By this time a child could have learned it sufficiently well to understand and answer questions." He favored the prisoner with a hard stare. "You have pretended to be abnormally slow to learn. But you can deceive us no longer. You will now provide all the information for which we ask."

"Willingly or unwillingly," put in Eckster, licking thin lips, "but you'll provide it anyway."

"Correct," agreed Palamin. "Let us start all over again and see if we can avoid painful scenes. Your name is Wayne Taylor and you come from a planet called Terra?"

"I admitted that much when I was captured."

"I know. But you were not fluent at that time and we want no misunderstandings. Why did you land on Gombar?"

"I've told my tutor at least twenty times that I did it involuntarily. It was an emergency landing. My ship was disabled."

"Then why did you blow it up? Why did you not make

open contact with us and invite us to repair it for you?"

"No Terran vessel must be allowed to fall intact into hostile hands," said Taylor flatly.

"Hostile?" Palamin tried to assume a look of pained surprise but his face wasn't made for it. "Since you Terrans know nothing whatever about us what right have you to consider us hostile?"

"I wasn't kissed on arrival," Taylor retorted. "I was shot at coming down. I was shot at getting away. I was hunted across twenty miles of land, grabbed and beaten up."

"Our soldiers do their duty," observed Palamin virtuously.

"I'd be dead by now if they were not the lousiest marksmen this side of Cygni."

"And what is Cygni?"

"A star."

"Who are you to criticize our soldiers?" interjected Eckster, glowering.

"A Terran," informed Taylor as if that were more than enough.

"That means nothing to me," Eckster gave back with open contempt.

"It will."

Palamin took over again. "If friendly contact were wanted the Terran authorities would send a large ship with an official deputation on board, wouldn't they?"

"I don't think so."

"Why not?"

"We don't risk big boats and important people without knowing what sort of a reception they're likely to get."

"And who digs up that information?"

"Space scouts."

"Ah!" Palamin gazed around with the pride of a pygmy who has trapped an elephant. "So at last you admit that you are a spy?"

"I am a spy only in the estimation of the hostile."

"On the contrary," broke in a heavily jowled specimen seated on the right, "you are whatever we say you are—because we say it."

"Have it your own way," conceded Taylor.

"We intend to."

"You can be sure of that, my dear Borkor," soothed Palamin. He returned attention to the prisoner. "How many Terrans are there in existence?"

"About twelve thousand millions."

"He is lying," exclaimed Borkor, hungrily eying the hammer.

"One planet could not support such a number," Eckster contributed.

"They are scattered over a hundred planets," said Taylor.

"He is still lying," Borkor maintained.

Waving them down, Palamin asked, "And how many ships have they got?"

"I regret that mere space scouts are not entrusted with fleet statistics," replied Taylor coolly. "I can tell you only that I haven't the slightest idea."

"You must have *some* idea."

"If you want guesses, you can have them for what they are worth,"

"Then make a guess."

"One million."

"Nonsense!" declared Palamin. "Utterly absurd!"

"All right. One thousand. Or any other number you consider reasonable."

"This is getting us nowhere," Borkor complained.

Palamin said to the others, "What do you expect? If we were to send a spy to Terra, would we fill him up with top-secret information to give the enemy when caught? Or would we tell him just enough and only enough to enable him to carry out his task? The ideal spy is a shrewd ignoramus, able to take all, unable to give anything."

"The ideal spy wouldn't be trapped in the first place," commented Eckster maliciously.

"Thank you for those kind words," Taylor chipped in. "If I had come here as a spy, you'd have seen nothing of my ship much less me."

"Well, exactly where were you heading for when forced

to land on Gombar?" invited Palamin.

"For the next system beyond."

"Ignoring this one?"

"Yes."

"Why?"

"I go where I'm told."

"Your story is weak and implausible." Palamin lay back and eyed him judicially. "It is not credible that a space explorer should bypass one system in favor of another that is farther away."

"I was aiming for a binary said to have at least forty planets," said Taylor. "This system had only three. Doubtless it was considered relatively unimportant."

"What, with us inhabiting all three worlds?"

"How were we to know that? Nobody has been this way before."

"They know it now," put in Eckster, managing to make it sound sinister.

"This one knows it," Palamin corrected. "The others do not. And the longer they don't, the better for us. When another life form starts poking its snout into our system, we need time to muster our strength."

This brought a murmur of general agreement.

"It's your state of mind," offered Taylor.

"What d'you mean?"

"You're taking it for granted that a meeting must lead to a clash and in turn to a war."

"We'd be prize fools to assume anything else and let ourselves be caught unprepared," Palamin pointed out.

Taylor sighed. "To date we have established ourselves on a hundred planets without a single fight. The reason: we don't go where we're not wanted."

"I can imagine that," Palamin gave back sarcastically. "Someone tells you to beat it and you obligingly beat it. It's contrary to instinct."

"Your instinct," said Taylor. "We see no sense in wasting time and money fighting when we can spend both exploring and exploiting."

"Meaning that your space fleets include no warships?"

"Of course we have warships."

"Many?"

"Enough to cope."

"Pacifists armed to the teeth," said Palamin to the others. He registered a knowing smile.

"Liars are always inconsistent," pronounced Eckster with an air of authority. He fixed a stony gaze upon the prisoner. "If you are so careful to avoid trouble, why do you *need* warships?"

"Because we have no guarantee that the entire cosmos shares our policy of live and let live."

"Be more explicit."

"We chevvy nobody. But someday somebody may take it into their heads to chevvy us."

"Then you will start a fight?"

"No. The other party will have started it. We shall finish it."

"Sheer evasion," scoffed Eckster to Palamin and the rest. "The technique is obvious to anyone but an idiot. They settle themselves upon a hundred planets—if we can believe that number, which I don't! On most there is no opposition because nobody is there to oppose. On the others the natives are weak and backward, know that a struggle is doomed to failure and therefore offer none. But on any planet sufficiently strong and determined to resist—such as Gombar for instance—the Terrans will promptly treat that resistance as unwarranted interference with themselves. They will say they are being chevvied. It will be their moral justification for a war."

Palamin looked at Taylor. "What do you say to that?"

Giving a deep shrug, Taylor said, "That kind of political cynicism has been long out of date where I come from. I can't help it if mentally you're about ten millennia behind us."

"Are we going to sit here and allow ourselves to be insulted by a prisoner in chains?" Eckster angrily demanded of Palamin. "Let us recommend that he be executed. Then we can all go home. I for one have had enough of this futile rigmarole."

Another said, "Me, too." He looked an habitual me-tooer.

"Patience," advised Palamin. He spoke to Taylor. "You claim that you were under orders to examine the twin system of Halor and Ridi?"

"If by that you mean the adjacent binary, the answer is yes. That was my prescribed destination."

"Let us suppose that instead you had been told to take a look over our Gombarian system. Would you have done so?"

"I obey orders."

"You would have come upon us quietly and surreptitiously for a good snoop around?"

"Not necessarily. If my first impression had been one of friendliness, I'd have presented myself openly."

"He is dodging the question," insisted Eckster, still full of ire.

"What would you have done if you had been uncertain of our reaction?" continued Palamin.

"What anyone else would do," Taylor retorted. "I'd hang around until I'd got the measure of it one way or the other."

"Meanwhile taking care to evade capture?"

"Of course."

"And if you had not been satisfied with our attitude, you'd have reported us as hostile?"

"Potentially so."

"That is all we require," decided Palamin. "Your admissions are tantamount to a confession that you are a spy. It does not matter in the least whether you were under orders to poke your inquisitive nose into this system or some other system, you are still a spy." He turned to the others. "Are we all agreed?"

They chorused, "Yes."

"There is only one proper fate for such as you," Palamin finished. "You will be returned to your cell pending official execution." He made a gesture of dismissal. "Take him away."

The guards took him by simple process of jerking the chair from under him and kicking him erect. They tried to rush him out faster than he could go, he stumbled in his leg irons and almost fell. But he found time to throw one swift glance back from the doorway and his strangely pale eyes looked frozen.

When the elderly warder brought in his evening meal, Taylor asked, "How do they execute people here?"

"How do they do it where you come from?"

"We don't."

"You don't?" The warder blinked in amazement. Putting the tray on the floor, he took a seat on the bench beside Taylor and left the heavily barred grille wide open. The butt of his gun protruded from its holster within easy reach of the prisoner's grasp. "Then how do you handle dangerous criminals?"

"We cure the curable by whatever means are effective no matter how drastic, including brain surgery. The incurable we export to a lonely planet reserved exclusively for them. There they can fight it out between themselves."

"What a waste of a world," opined the warder. In casual manner he drew his gun, pointed it at the wall and pressed the button. Nothing happened. "Empty," he said.

Taylor made no remark.

"No use you snatching it. No use you running for it. The armored doors, multiple locks and loaded guns are all outside."

"I'd have to get rid of these manacles before I could start something with any hope of success," Taylor pointed out. "Are you open to bribery?"

"With what? You have nothing save the clothes you're wearing. And even those will be burned after you're dead."

"All right, forget it." Taylor rattled his irons loudly and looked disgusted. "You haven't yet told me how I'm to die."

"Oh, you'll be strangled in public," informed the warder. He smacked his lips for no apparent reason. "All executions take place in the presence of the populace. It is not enough that justice be done, it must also be seen to be done. So everybody sees it. And it has an excellent disciplinary effect." Again the lip smacking. "It is quite a spectacle."

"I'm sure it must be."

"You will be made to kneel with your back to a post, your arms and ankles tied behind it," explained the warder in tutorial manner. "There is a hole drilled through the post at the level of your neck. A loop of cord goes round your neck, through the hole and around a stick on the other side. The executioner twists the stick, thereby tightening the loop quickly or slowly according to his mood."

"I suppose that when he feels really artistic he prolongs the agony quite a piece by slackening and retightening the loop a few times?" Taylor ventured.

"No, no, he is not permitted to do that," assured the warden, blind to the sarcasm. "Not in a final execution. That method is used only to extract confessions from the stubborn. We are a fair-minded and tenderhearted people, see?"

"You're a great comfort to me," said Taylor.

"So you will be handled swiftly and efficiently. I have witnessed many executions and have yet to see a sloppy, badly performed one. The body heaves and strains against its bonds, the eyes stick out, the tongue protrudes and turns black and complete collapse follows. The effect is invariably the same and is a tribute to the executioner's skill. Really, you have nothing to worry about, nothing at all."

"Looks like I haven't, the way you put it," observed Taylor dryly. "I'm right on top of the world without anything to lose except my breath." He brooded a bit, then asked, "*When* am I due for the noose?"

"Immediately after you've finished your game," the warder informed.

Taylor eyed him blankly. "Game? What game? What do you mean?"

"It is conventional to allow a condemned man a last game against a skilled player chosen by us. When the game ends he is taken away and strangled."

"Win or lose?"

"The result makes no difference. He is executed regardless of whether he is the winner or the loser."

"Sounds crazy to me," said Taylor frowning.

"It would, being an alien," replied the warder. "But

surely you'll agree that a person facing death is entitled to a little bit of consideration if only the privilege of putting up a last minute fight for his life."

"A pretty useless fight."

"That may be. But every minute of delay is precious to the one concerned." The warder rubbed hands together appreciatively. "I can tell you that nothing is more exciting, more thrilling than a person's death-match against a clever player."

"Is that so?"

"Yes. You see, he cannot possibly play in normal manner. For one thing, his mind is obsessed by his impending fate while his opponent is bothered by no such burden. For another, he dare not let the other win—and he dare not let him lose, either. He has to concentrate all his faculties on preventing a decisive result and prolonging the game as much as possible. And, of course, all the time he is mentally and morally handicapped by the knowledge that the end is bound to come."

"Bet it gives you a heck of a kick," said Taylor.

The warder sucked his lips before smacking them. "Many a felon have I watched playing in a cold sweat with the ingenuity of desperation. Then at last the final move. He has fainted and rolled off his chair. We've carried him out as a limp as an empty sack. He has come to his senses on his knees facing a crowd waiting for the first twist."

"It isn't worth the bother," decided Taylor. "No player can last long."

"Usually they don't but I've known exceptions, tough and expert gamesters who've managed to postpone death for four or five days. There was one fellow, a professional *alizik* player, who naturally chose his own game and contrived to avoid a decision for sixteen days. He was so good it was a pity he had to die. A lot of video-watchers were sorry when the end came."

"Oh, so you put these death-matches on the video?"

"It's the most popular show. Pins them in their chairs, I can tell you."

"Hm-m-m!" Taylor thought a bit, asked, "Suppose this

video-star had been able to keep the game on the boil for a year or more, would he have been allowed to do so?"

"Of course. Nobody can be put to death until he has completed his last game. You could call it a superstition, I suppose. What's more, the rule is that he gets well fed while playing. If he wishes he can eat like a king. All the same, they rarely eat much."

"Don't they?"

"No—they're so nervous that their stomachs refuse to hold a square meal. Occasionally one of them is actually sick in the middle of a game. When I see one do that I know he won't last another day."

"You've had plenty of fun in your time," Taylor offered.

"Quite often," the warder admitted. "But not always. Bad players bore me beyond description. They give the video-watchers the gripes. They start a game, fumble it right away, go to the strangling-post and that's the end of them. The greatest pleasure for all it when some character makes a battle of it."

"Fat chance I've got. I know no Gombarian games and you people know no Terran ones."

"Any game can be learned in short time and the choice is yours. Naturally you won't be permitted to pick one that involves letting you loose in a field without your irons. It has to be something that can be played in this cell. Want some good advice?"

"Give."

"This evening an official will arrive to arrange the contest, after which he will find you a suitable partner. Don't ask to be taught one of our games. No matter how clever you may try to be, your opponent will be better because he'll be handling the familiar while you're coping with the strange. Select one of your own planet's games and thus give yourself an advantage."

"Thanks for the suggestion. It might do me some good if defeat meant death—but victory meant life."

"I've told you already that the result makes no difference."

"There you are then. Some choice, huh?"

"You can choose between death in the morning and death the morning after or even the one after that." Getting up from the bench, the warder walked out, closed the grille, said through the bars, "Anyway, I'll bring you a book giving full details of our indoor games. You'll have plenty of time to read it before the official arrives."

"Nice of you," said Taylor. "But I think you're wasting your time."

Left alone, Wayne Taylor let his thoughts mill around. They weren't pleasant ones. Space scouts belonged to a high-risk profession and none knew it better than themselves. Each and every one cheerfully accepted the dangers on the ages-old principle that it always happens to the other fellow, never to oneself. But now it had happened and to him. He ran a forefinger around the inside of his collar, which felt a little tight.

When he'd dived through the clouds with two air-machines blasting fire to port and starboard, he had pressed alarm button D. This caused his transmitter to start flashing a brief but complicated number giving his co-ordinates and defining the planet as enemy territory.

Earlier and many thousands of miles out in space he had reported his intention of making an emergency landing and identified the chosen world with the same co-ordinates. Button D, therefore, would confirm his first message and add serious doubts about his fate. He estimated that between the time he'd pressed the button and the time he had landed the alarm-signal should have been transmitted at least forty times.

Immediately after the landing he'd switched the delayed-action charge and taken to his heels. The planes were still buzzing around. One of them swooped low over the grounded ship just as it blew up. It disintegrated in the blast. The other one gained altitude and circled overhead, directing the search. To judge by the speed with which troops arrived he must have had the misfortune to have dumped himself in a military area full of uniformed goons eager for blood. All the same, he'd kept them on the run for six hours and covered twenty miles before they got him. They'd expressed their disapproval with fists and feet.

Right now, there was no way of telling whether Terran listening-posts had picked up his repeated D-alarm. Odds were vastly in favor of it since it was a top-priority channel on which was kept a round-the-clock watch. He didn't doubt for a moment that, having received the message, they'd do something about it.

The trouble was that whatever they did would come too late. In this very sector patrolled the *Macklin*, Terra's latest, biggest, most powerful battleship. If the *Macklin* happened to be on the prowl, and at her nearest routine point, it would take her ten months to reach Gombar at maximum velocity. If she had returned to port, temporarily replaced by an older and slower vessel, the delay might last two years.

Two years was two years too long. Ten months was too long. He could not wait ten weeks. In fact it was highly probable that he hadn't got ten days. Oh, time, time, how impossible it is to stretch it for a man or compress it for a ship.

The warder reappeared, shoved a book between the bars. "Here you are. You have learned enough to understand it."

"Thanks."

Lying full length on the bench, he read right through it swiftly but comprehensively. Some pages he skipped after brief perusal because they described games too short, simple and childish to be worth considering. He was not surprised to find several games that were alien variations of ones well-known upon Terra. The Gombarians had playing cards, for instance, eighty to a pack with ten suits.

Alizik proved to be a bigger and more complicated version of chess, with four hundred squares and forty pieces per side. This was the one that somebody had dragged out for sixteen days and it was the only one in the book that seemed capable of such extension. For a while he pondered *alizik*, wondering whether the authorities—and the video audience—would tolerate play at the rate of one move in ten hours. He doubted it. Anyway, he could not prevent his skilled opponent from making each answering move in five seconds.

Yes, that was what he really wanted: a game that slowed down the other fellow despite his efforts to speed up. A game that was obviously a game and not a gag because any fool could see with half an eye that it was possible to finish it once and for all. Yet a game that the other fellow could not finish, win or lose, no matter how hard he tried.

There wasn't any such game on the three worlds of Gombar or the hundred worlds of Terra or the multimillion worlds yet unfound. There couldn't be because, if there were, nobody would play it. People like results. Nobody is sufficiently cracked to waste time, thought and patience riding a hobbyhorse that got nowhere, indulging a rigmarole that cannot be terminated to the satisfaction of all concerned, including kibitzers.

But nobody!

No?

"When the last move is made God's Plan will be fulfilled; on that day and at that hour and at that moment the universe will vanish in a mighty thunderclap."

He got off the bench, his cold eyes expressionless, and began to pace his cell like a restless tiger.

The official had an enormous potbelly, small, piggy eyes and an unctuous smile that remained permanently fixed. His manner was that of a circus ringmaster about to introduce his best act.

"Ah," he said, noting the book, "so you have been studying our games, eh?"

"Yes."

"I hope you've found none of them suitable."

"Do you?" Taylor surveyed him quizzically. "Why?"

"It would be a welcome change to witness a contest based on something right out of this world. A genuinely new game would give a lot of satisfaction to everybody. Providing, of course," he added hurriedly, "that it was easy to understand and that you didn't win it too quickly."

"Well," said Taylor, "I must admit I'd rather handle something I know than something I don't."

"Good, good!" enthused the other. "You prefer to play a Terran game?"

"That's right."

"There are limitations on your choice."

"What are they?" asked Taylor.

"Once we had a condemned murderer who wanted to oppose his games-partner in seeing who could be the first to catch a sunbeam and put it in a bottle. It was nonsensical. You must choose something that obviously and beyond argument can be accomplished."

"I see."

"Secondly, you may not select something involving the use of intricate and expensive apparatus that will take us a long time to manufacture. If apparatus is needed, it must be cheap and easy to construct."

"Is that all?"

"Yes—except that the complete rules of the game must be inscribed by you unambiguously and in clear writing. Once play begins, those rules will be strictly followed and no variation of them will be permitted."

"And who approves my choice after I've described it?"

"I do."

"All right. Here's what I'd like to play." Taylor explained it in detail, borrowed pen and paper and made a rough sketch. When he had finished the other folded the drawing and put it in a pocket.

"A strange game," admitted the official, "but it seems to me disappointingly uncomplicated. Do you really think you can make the contest last a full day?"

"I hope so."

"Even two days perhaps?"

"With luck."

"You'll need it!" He was silent with thought a while, then shook his head doubtfully. "It's a pity you didn't think up something like a better and trickier version of *alizik*. The audience would have enjoyed it and you might have gained yourself a longer lease of life. Everyone would get a great kick out of it if you beat the record for delay before your execution."

"Would they really?"

"They sort of expect something extra-special from an alien life form."

"They're getting it, aren't they?"

"Yes, I suppose so." He still seemed vaguely dissatisfied. "Oh, well, it's your life and your struggle to keep it a bit longer."

"I'll have only myself to blame when the end comes."

"True. Play will commence promptly at midday tomorrow. After that, it's up to you."

He lumbered away, his heavy footsteps dying along the corridor. A few minutes later the warder appeared.

"What did you pick?"

"Arky-malarkey."

"Huh? What's that?"

"A Terran game."

"That's fine, real fine." He rubbed appreciative hands together. "He approved it, I suppose?"

"Yes, he did."

"So you're all set to justify your continued existence. You'll have to take care to avoid the trap."

"What trap?" Taylor asked.

"Your partner will play to win as quickly and conclusively as possible. That is expected of him. But once he gets it into his head that he can't win, he'll start playing to lose. You've no way of telling exactly when he'll change his tactics. Many a one has been caught out by the sudden switch and found the game finished before he had time to realize it."

"But he must keep to the rules, mustn't he?"

"Certainly. Neither you nor he will be allowed to ignore them. Otherwise the game would become a farce."

"That suits me."

Somewhere outside sounded a high screech like that of a bobcat backing into a cactus. It was followed by a scuffle of feet, a dull thud and dragging noises. A distant door creaked open and banged shut.

"What goes?" said Taylor.

"Lagartine's game must have ended."

"Who's Lagartine?"

"A political assassin." The warder glanced at his watch. "He chose *ramsid,* a card game. It has lasted a mere four hours. Serves him right. Good riddance to bad rubbish."

"And now they're giving him the big squeeze?"

"Of course." Eying him, the warder said, "Nervous?"

"Ha-ha," said Taylor without mirth.

The performance did not commence in his cell as he had expected. A contest involving an alien life form playing an alien game was too big an event for that. They took him through the prison corridors to a large room in which stood a table with three chairs. Six more chairs formed a line against the wall, each occupied by a uniformed plug-ugly complete with hand gun. This was the knock-down-and-drag-out squad ready for action the moment the game terminated.

At one end stood a big, black cabinet with two rectangular portholes through which gleamed a pair of lenses. From it came faint ticking sounds and muffled voices. This presumably contained the video camera.

Taking a chair at the table, Taylor sat down and gave the armed audience a frozen stare. A thin-faced individual with the beady eyes of a rat took the chair opposite. The potbellied official dumped himself in the remaining seat. Taylor and Rat-eyes weighed each other up, the former with cold assurance, the latter with sadistic speculation.

Upon the table stood a board from which arose three long wooden pegs. The left-hand peg held a column of sixty-four disks evenly graduated in diameter, the largest at the bottom, smallest at the top. The effect was that of a tapering tower built from a nursery do-it-yourself kit.

Wasting no time, Potbelly said, "This is the Terran game of Arky-malarkey. The column of disks must be transferred from the peg on which it sits to either of the other two pegs. They must remain graduated in the same order, smallest at the top, biggest at the bottom. The player whose move completes the stack is the winner. Do you both understand?"

"Yes," said Taylor.

Rat-eyes assented with a grunt.

"There are three rules," continued Potbelly, "which will be strictly observed. You will make your moves alternately, turn and turn about. You may move only one disk at a time. You may not place a disk upon any other smaller than itself. Do you both understand?"

"Yes," said Taylor.

Rat-eyes gave another grunt.

From his pocket Potbelly took a tiny white ball and carelessly tossed it onto the table. It bounced a couple of times, rolled across and fell off on Rat-eyes' side.

"You start," he said.

Without hesitation Rat-eyes took the smallest disk from the top of the first peg and placed it on the third.

"Bad move," thought Taylor, blank of face. He shifted the second smallest desk from the first peg to the second.

Smirking for no obvious reason, Rat-eyes now removed the smallest disk from the third peg, placed it on top of Taylor's disk on the second. Taylor promptly switched another disk from the pile on the first peg to the empty third peg.

After an hour of this it had become plain to Rat-eyes that the first peg was not there merely to hold the stock. It had to be used. The smirk faded from his face, was replaced by mounting annoyance as hours crawled by and the situation became progressively more complicated.

By bedtime they were still at it, swapping disks around like crazy, and neither had got very far. Rat-eyes now hated the sight of the first peg, especially when he was forced to put a disk back on it instead of taking one off it. Potbelly, still wearing his fixed, meaningless smile, announced that play would cease until sunrise tomorrow.

The next day provided a long, arduous session lasting from dawn to dark and broken only by two meals. Both players worked fast and hard, setting the pace for each other and seeming to vie with one another in effort to reach a swift conclusion. No onlooker could find cause to complain about the slowness of the game. Four times Rat-eyes mistakenly tried to place a disk on top of a smaller one and was promptly called to order by the referee in the obese shape of Potbelly.

A third, fourth, fifth and sixth day went by. Rat-eyes now played with a mixture of dark suspicion and desperation while the column on the first peg appeared to go up as often as it went down. Though afflicted by his emotions he was no fool. He knew quite well that they were making progress in the task of transferring the column. But it was progress at an appalling rate. What's more, it became worse as time went on. Finally he could see no way of losing the game, much less winning it.

By the fourteenth day Rat-eyes had reduced himself to an automation wearily moving disks to and fro in the soulless, disinterested manner of one compelled to perform a horrid chore. Taylor remained as impassive as a bronze Buddha and that fact didn't please Rat-eyes either.

Danger neared on the sixteenth day though Taylor did not know it. The moment he entered the room he sensed an atmosphere of heightened interest and excitement. Rat-eyes looked extra glum. Potbelly had taken on added importance. Even the stolid, dull-witted guards displayed faint signs of mental animation. Four off-duty warders joined the audience. There was more activity than usual within the video cabinet.

Ignoring all this, Taylor took his seat and play continued. This endless moving of disks from peg to peg was a lousy way to waste one's life but the strangling-post was lousier. He had every inducement to carry on. Naturally he did so, shifting a disk when his turn came and watching his opponent with his pale gray eyes.

In the midafternoon Rat-eyes suddenly left the table, went to the wall, kicked it good and hard and shouted a remark about the amazing similarity between Terrans and farmyard manure. Then he returned and made his next move. There was some stirring within the video cabinet. Potbelly mildly reproved him for taking time off to advertise his patriotism. Rat-eyes went on playing with the surly air of a delinquent whose mother has forgotten to kiss him.

Late in the evening, Potbelly stopped the game, faced the video lenses and said in portentious manner, "Play will resume tomorrow—the seventeenth day!"

He voiced it as though it meant something or other.

When the warder shoved his breakfast through the grille in the morning, Taylor said, "Late, aren't you? I should be at play by now."

"They say you won't be wanted before this afternoon."

"That so? What's all the fuss about?"

"You broke the record yesterday," informed the other with reluctant admiration. "Nobody has ever lasted to the seventeenth day."

"So they're giving me a morning off to celebrate, eh? Charitable of them."

"I've no idea why there's a delay," said the warder. "I've never known them to interrupt a game before."

"You think they'll stop it altogether?" Taylor asked, feeling a constriction around his neck. "You think they'll officially declare it finished?"

"Oh, no, they couldn't do that." He looked horrified at the thought of it. "We mustn't bring the curse of the dead upon us. It's absolutely essential that condemned people should be made to choose their own time of execution."

"Why is it?"

"Because it always has been since that start of time."

He wandered off to deliver other breakfasts, leaving Taylor to stew the explanation. "Because it always has been." It wasn't a bad reason. Indeed, some would consider it a good one. He could think of several pointless, illogical things done on Terra solely because they always had been done. In this matter of unchallenged habit the Gombarians were no better or worse than his own kind.

Though a little soothed by the warder's remarks he couldn't help feeling more and more uneasy as the morning wore on without anything happening. After sixteen days of moving disks from peg to peg, it had got so that he was doing it in his sleep. Didn't seem right that he should be enjoying a spell of aimless loafing around his cell. There was somehing ominous about it.

Again and again he found himself nursing the strong suspicion that officialdom was seeking an effective way of ending the play without appearing to flout convention. When they found it—if they found it—they'd pull a fast one on him, declare the game finished, take him away and fix him up with a very tight necktie.

He was still wallowing in pessimism when the call came in the afternoon. They hustled him along to the same room as before. Play was resumed as if it had never been interrupted. It lasted a mere thirty minutes. Somebody tapped twice on the inside of the video cabinet and Potbelly responded by calling a halt. Taylor went back to his cell and sat there baffled.

Late in the evening he was summoned again. He went with bad grace because these short and sudden performances were more wearing on the nerves than continual day-long ones. Previously he had known for certain that he was being taken to play Arky-malarkey with Rat-eyes. Now he could never be sure that he was not about to become the lead character in a literally breathless scene.

On entering the room he realized at once that things were going to be different this time. The board with its pegs and disks still stood in the center of the table. But Rat-eyes was absent and so was the armed squad. Three people awaited him: Potbelly, Palamin, and a squat, heavily built character who had the peculiar air of being of this world but not with it.

Potbelly was wearing the offended frown of someone burdened with a load of stock in a nonexistent oil well. Palamin looked singularly unpleased and expressed it by snorting like an impatient horse. The third appeared to be contemplating a phenomenon on the other side of the galaxy.

"Sit," ordered Palamin, spitting it out.

Taylor sat.

"Now, Marnikot, you tell him."

The squat one showed belated awareness of being on Gombar, said pedantically to Taylor, "I rarely look at the video. It is suitable only for the masses with nothing better to do."

"Get to the point," urged Palamin.

"But having heard that you were about to break an ages-old record," continued Marnikot, undisturbed, "I watched the video last night." He made a brief gesture to show that he could identify a foul smell at first sniff. "It was immediately obvious to me that to finish your game would require a minimum number of moves of the order of two to the sixty-fourth power minus one." He took flight into momentary dreamland, came back and added mildly, "That is a large number."

"Large!" said Palamin. He let go a snort that rocked the pegs.

"Let us suppose," Marnikot went on, "that you were to transfer these disks one at a time as fast as you could go, morning, noon and night without pause for meals or sleep, do you know how long it would take to complete the game?"

"Nearly six billion Terran centuries," said Taylor as if talking about next Thursday week.

"I have no knowledge of Terran time-terms. But I can tell you that neither you nor a thousand generations of your successors could live long enough to see the end of it. Correct?"

"Correct," Taylor admitted.

"Yet you say that this is a Terran game?"

"I do."

Marnikot spread hands helplessly to show that as far as he was concerned there was nothing more to be said.

Wearing a forbidding scowl, Palamin now took over. "A game cannot be defined as a genuine one unless it is actually played. Do you claim that this so-called game really is played on Terra?"

"Yes."

"By whom?"

"By priests in the Temple of Benares."

"And how long have they been playing it?" he asked.

"About two thousand years."

"Generation after generation?"

"That's right."

"Each player contributing to the end of his days without hope of seeing the result?"

"Yes."

Palamin fumed a bit. "Then *why* do they play it?"

"It's part of their religious faith. They believe that the moment the last disk is placed the entire universe will go bang."

"Are they crazy?"

"No more so than people who have played *alizik* for equally as long and to just as little purpose."

"We have played *alizik* as a series of separate games and not as one never-ending game. A rigmarole without possible end cannot be called a game by any stretch of the imagination."

"Arky-malarkey is not endless. It has a conclusive finish." Taylor appealed to Marnikot as the indisputed authority. "Hasn't it?"

"It is definitely finite," pronounced Marnikot, unable to deny the fact.

"So!" exclaimed Palamin, going a note higher. "You think you are very clever, don't you?"

"I get by," said Taylor, seriously doubting it.

"But we are cleverer," insisted Palamin, using his nastiest manner. "You have tricked us and now we shall trick you. The game is finite. It can be concluded. Therefore it will continue until it reaches its natural end.

You will go on playing it days, weeks, months, years until eventually you expire of old age and chronic frustration. There will be times when the very sight of these disks will drive you crazy and you will beg for merciful death. But we shall not grant that favor—and you will continue to play. He waved a hand in triumphant dismissal. "Take him away."

Taylor returned to his cell.

When supper came the warder offered, "I am told that play will go on regularly as from tomorrow morning. I don't understand why they messed it up today."

"They've decided that I'm to suffer fate worse than death," Taylor informed.

The warder stared at him.

"I have been very naughty," said Taylor.

Rat-eyes evidently had been advised of the new setup because he donned the armor of philosophical acceptance and played steadily but without interest. All the same, long sessions of repetitive motions ate corrosively into the armor and gradually found its way through.

In the early afternoon of the fifty-second day, Rat-eyes found himself faced with the prospect of returning most of the disks to the first peg, one by one. He took off the clompers he used for boots. Then he ran barefooted four times around the room, bleating like a sheep. Potbelly got a crick in the neck watching him. Two guards led Rat-eyes away still bleating. They forgot to take his clompers with them.

By the table Taylor sat gazing at the disks while he strove to suppress his inward alarm. What would happen now? If Rat-eyes had given up for keeps it could be argued that he had lost, the game had concluded and the time had come to play okey-chokey with a piece of cord. It could be said with equal truth that an unfinished game remains an unfinished game even though one of the players is in a mental home giving his hair a molasses shampoo.

If the authorities took the former view, his only defense was to assert the latter one. He'd have to maintain with all the energy at his command that, since he had not won or lost, his time could not possibly have come. It wouldn't be easy if he had to make his protest while being dragged by the heels to his doom. His chief hope lay in Gombarian unwillingness to outrage an ancient convention. Millions of video viewers would take a poor look at officialdom mauling a pet superstition. Yes, man, there were times when the Idiot's Lantern had its uses.

He need not have worried. Having decided that to keep the game going would be a highly refined form of hell, the Gombarians had already prepared a roster of relief players drawn from the ranks of minor offenders whose ambitions never rose high enough to earn a strangling. So after a short time another opponent appeared.

The newcomer was a shifty character with a long face and hanging dewlaps. He resembled an especially dopey bloodhound and looked barely capable of articulating three words, to wit, "Ain't talking, copper." It must have taken at least a month to teach him that he must move only one disk at a time and never, never, never place it upon a smaller one. But somehow he had learned. The game went on.

Dopey lasted a week. He played slowly and doggedly as if in fear of punishment for making a mistake. Often he was irritated by the video cabinet, which emitted ticking noises at brief but regular intervals. These sounds indicated the short times they were on the air.

For reasons best known to himself, Dopey detested having his face broadcast all over the planet and, near the end of the seventh day, he'd had enough. Without warning he left his seat, faced the cabinet and made a number of swift and peculiar gestures at the lenses. The signs meant nothing to the onlooking Taylor. But Potbelly almost fell off his chair. The guards sprang forward, grabbed Dopey and frogmarched him through the door.

He was replaced by a huge-jowled, truculent character who dumped himself into the chair, glared at Taylor and wiggled his hairy ears. Taylor, who regarded this feat as one of his own accomplishments, promptly wiggled his own ears back. The other then looked fit to burst a blood vessel.

"This Terran sneak," he roared at Potbelly, "is throwing dirt at me. Do I *have* to put up with that?"

"You will cease to throw dirt," ordered Potbelly.

"I only wiggled my ears," said Taylor.

"That is the same thing as throwing dirt," Potbelly said mysteriously. "You will refrain from doing it and you will concentrate upon the game."

And so it went on, with disks being moved from peg to peg hour after hour, day after day, while a steady parade of opponents arrived and departed. Around the two hundredth day, Potbelly himself started to pull his chair apart with the apparent intention of building a campfire in the middle of the floor. The guards led him out. A new referee appeared. He had an even bigger paunch, and Taylor promptly named him Potbelly Two.

How Taylor himself stood the soul-deadening pace he never knew. But he kept going while the others cracked. He was playing for a big stake while they were not. All the same, there were times when he awoke from horrid dreams in which he was sinking through the black depths of an alien sea with a monster disk like a millstone around his neck. He lost count of the days, and once in a while his hands developed the shakes. The strain was not made any easier by several nighttime uproars that took place during this time. He asked the warder about one of them.

"Yasko refused to go. They had to beat him into submission."

"His game had ended?"

"Yes. The stupid fool matched a five of anchors with a five of stars. Immediately he realized what he'd done, he tried to kill his opponent." He wagged his head in sorrowful reproof. "Such behavior never does them any good. They go to the post cut and bruised. And if the guards are angry with them, they ask the exectioner to twist slowly."

"Ugh!" Taylor didn't like to think of it. "Surprises me that none have chosen my game. Everybody must know of it by now."

"They are not permitted to," said the warder. "There is now a law that only a recognized Gombarian game may be selected."

He ambled away. Taylor lay full length on his bench and hoped for a silent, undisturbed night. What was the Earth-date? How long had he been here? How much longer would he remain? How soon would he lose control of himself and go nuts? What would they do with him if and when he became too crazy to play?

Often in the thought-period preceding sleep, he concocted wild plans of escape. None of them were of any use whatever. Conceivably he could break out of this prison despite its grilles, armored doors, locks, bolts, bars and armed guards. It was a matter of waiting for a rare opportunity and seizing it with both hands. But suppose he got out, what then? Any place on the planet he would be as conspicuous as a kangaroo on the sidewalks of New York. If it were possible to look remotely like a Gombarian, he'd have a slight chance. It was not possible. He could do nothing save play for time.

This he continued to do. On and on and on without cease, except for meals and sleep. By the three hundredth day he had to admit to himself that he was feeling somewhat moth-eaten. By the four hundredth he was under the delusion that he had been playing for at least five years and was doomed to play forever, come what may. The four-twentieth day was no different from the rest except in one respect of which he was completely unaware—it was the last.

At dawn of day four twenty-one, no call came for him to play. Perforce he waited a couple of hours and still no summons. Maybe they'd decided to break him with a cat-and-mouse technique, calling him when he didn't expect it and not calling him when he did. A sort of psychological water torture. When the warder passed along the corridor, Taylor went to the bars and questioned him. The fellow knew nothing and was as puzzled as himself.

The midday meal arrived. Taylor had just finished it when the squad of guards arrived accompanied by an officer. They entered the cell and removed his irons. Ye gods, this was something! He stretched his limbs luxuriously, fired questions at the officer and his plug-uglies. They took no notice, behaved as if he had stolen the green eye of the little yellow god. Then they marched him out of the cell, along the corridors and past the games room.

Finally they passed through a large doorway and into an open yard. In the middle of this area stood six short steel posts each with a hole near its top and a coarse kneeling-mat at its base. Stolidly the squad tramped straight toward the posts. Taylor's stomach turned over. The squad pounded on past the posts and toward a pair of gates. Taylor's stomach turned thankfully back and settled itself.

Outside the gates they climbed aboard a troop-carrier which at once drove off. It took him around the outskirts of the city to a spaceport. They all piled out, marched past the control tower and onto the concrete. There they halted.

Across the spaceport, about half a mile away, Taylor could see a Terran vessel sitting on its fins. It was far too small for a warship, too short and fat for a scout-ship. After staring at it with incredulous delight he decided that it was a battleship's lifeboat. He wanted to do a wild dance and yell silly things. He wanted to run like mad toward it, but the guards stood close around and would not let him move.

They waited there for four long tedious hours, at the end of which another lifeboat screamed down from the sky and landed alongside its fellow. A bunch of figures came out of it, mostly Gombarians. The guards urged him forward.

He was dimly conscious of some sort of exchange ceremony at the halfway mark. A line of surly Gombarians passed him, going the opposite way. Many of them were ornamented with plenty of brass and had the angry faces of colonels come fresh from a general demotion. He recognized one civilian, Borkor, and wiggled his ears at him as he went by.

Then willing hands helped him through an airlock and he found himself sitting in the cabin of a ship going up. A young and eager lieutenant was talking to him but he heard only half of it.

". . . Landed, snatched twenty and beat it into space. We cross-examined them by signs . . . bit surprised to learn you were still alive . . . released one with an offer to exchange prisoners. Nineteen Gombarian bums for one Terran is a fair swap, isn't it?"

"Yes," said Taylor, looking around and absorbing every mark upon the walls.

"We'll have you aboard the *Thunderer* pretty soon . . . *Macklin* couldn't make it with that trouble near Cygni . . . got here as soon as we could." The lieutenant eyed him sympathetically. "You'll be heading for home within a few hours. Hungry?"

"No, not a all. The one thing they didn't do was starve me."

"Like a drink?"

"Thanks, I don't drink."

Fidgeting around embarrassedly, the lieutenant asked, "Well, how about a nice, quiet game of draughts?"

Taylor ran a finger around the inside of his collar and said, "Sorry, I don't know how to play and don't want to learn. I am allergic to games."

"You'll change."

"I'll be hanged if I do," said Taylor.

THE BACK OF OUR HEADS

Stephen Barr

I find it impossible to do anything about introducing this extraordinary story other than to tell you to read it with a strong hold on your sense of reality. It is a thoroughly unsettling tale, and one that might unhinge any overly susceptible mind.

IN READING THIS REPORT, IT MUST BE BORNE IN mind that, when the word "they" is used, it does not refer necessarily to separate entities as individuals.

It is possible that a closer analogy would be the cells of an organism—which, in a sense, we ourselves become when we are in a pack or forming a mob.

On the other hand, that particular cell or entity which this report deals with exhibited at all times marked individuality—even eccentricity—and will hereinafter be referred to as "she." This is because "she" invariably assumed a female form when visiting us, and because she furthermore gave every indication of that type of mind and point of view which is generally met with in the more noticeable, effective or contentious members of that sex.

As she put it herself during the hearing, she was always in hot water.

The four teen-agers—one girl, three boys—weren't allowed in the bar, so they went down the street to a joint where there were a soda fountain, booths and a jukebox. They sat in a booth and a waitress came to take the orders: three hot dogs and three cokes.

"What about you, dear?"

"Just a glass of water." The waitress started to leave. "No, wait—gimme a white on rye, too."

The waitress left, then came back again. "What was that you wanted, dear? Some kind of rye-bread sandwich?"

"Changed my mind. Make it a buttered pecan, but tell'em to go easy on the butter. And I don't want no French dressing. Make it on whole wheat."

The waitress look uncertain. "You mean a *nut* sandwich?"

"Yeah, only malted. With lettuce and chocolate sprinkles."

"Who you kiddin?" the waitress said, and turned to go.

"No, hold it. Tell Joe to please scramble them on both sides."

"What you *talkin'* about?" the waitress said. "We ain't got no one here called Joe."

"So okay, Joseph, then. Tell him just a boiled egg sunny side up."

The waitress left, frowning.

"Our Miss Framis," one of the boys said, meaning the girl, and the others smiled. They looked as though they were sneering at the same time and hoped they would be taken for juvenile delinquents.

There were two very odd-looking men in the booth opposite and they were listening to the conversation. Their oddness lay in an atmosphere rather than in any physical abnormality. The girl noticed them and nudged one of the boys.

The three boys looked at the men resentfully and one of them said something under his breath, but the girl said, "Button it." Then she asked the men opposite, "Lookin' for someone, mister?"

The two men looked away, and this made the boys feel brave. One of them said, "Let's give 'em the works."

"No, leave it to me." The girl got up and went across to the two men. "Me and my friends was wondering. Maybe you gentlemen would like to come to a trake in the gort later?"

The three boys snickered and the men looked up at the girl and waited with blank faces.

"Or maybe you'd rather we put on a hanse for you?" she said.

"No, sit down," one of the men—the bigger one—said, and moved back to make room for her. She glanced at him with surprise for a moment and sat down next to him.

One of the boys started to get up when he saw this, but the others pulled him down again.

"What did you say to us just now?" the big man asked. "It was too small in here."

She shook her head and frowned.

"Why, that was just . . . I said did you want for us to put on a hanse, is all." She had a rather feeble grin.

"Yes," the big man said. "We do."

She glanced back at her friends nervously, and then at the man again. "I don't get you," she said.

"Neither do we," the smaller man said.

The boys across the room were listening quietly and then one of them said, "Go on, tell'em, Miss Framis."

"We just want you to quint," the big man said, "and don't thursday on it."

She stared at him without expression and got up slowly. She went over to her friends. "Let's get out of here," she said.

She was shivering.

Q. You say you object to this line of questioning?

A. *(She)* No, I just don't like being spied on. And it made the kids . . . mad. They wrecked the car and that meant starting all over again.

Q. The car?

A. Yes, their hot-rod. When we got outside, they acted the way teen-agers do and went too fast. They were sore at those spies—they took it out on the car, so it went off the road. It turned over three times and we were all killed.

Q. They were not spies. They were acting on their own.

A. *I* didn't know that. I just knew something was funny. Anyway, how can you say that? They're a waste. And I would have been part of you, just as I am. It would have been more of a waste if I hadn't been split. The other part was only about eleven years old and I had to wait another six years to—

Q. It is your own fault if you were split. You cannot

blame us. This has happened before—you have aimed badly and arrived wrong. Don't forget about the kelp.

A. Well, in this case it's a lucky thing I did; otherwise the whole thing would have been wasted. And the kelp—that was dreadfully dull. I wanted to try a really primitive form, but not *that* primitive. Then I got washed up and it led to the cat. After they got the iodine out of the kelp, I was suddenly a cat.

Q. This has not been reported.

A. I'm reporting it now. It wasn't dull in the least, but they were very superstitious about cats in those days, and they decided I was possessed.

Q. They saw through you?

A. Oh, yes. People usually do.

Q. You couldn't have been very successful if they saw through you.

A. It doesn't make any difference if they see through you. The important thing is to see through them.

Q. But you were a cat.

A. Cats are in a very good position to see through people. I think they sensed that. Anyway, I was . . . done away with.

Q. Burned again?

A. Yes.

Q. Seems to be a habit of yours. What happens? How does it feel?

A. I cannot explain it to you, but I know what to do. It's not *my* habit—it's one of theirs, but it's dying out in most places now. And there was a time when it would never have occurred to them. They were too frightened of it.

Q. Frightened of what?

A. Of fire. It was very new then. . . .

The hunters came back to the cave at dusk, and one of them went to the fire that was kept going constantly in front of the opening. He took a dry branch and held it in the fire until the end caught. Then he held it up. "If we take this, we can hunt in the dark," he said. "And when it is nearly eaten by the fire, we can take another branch and start it again. That way we do not need the moon."

"That way we can hunt until we are tired," said the other.

"That way we can kill twice as much game," said the first.

"There is so much game in the cave now," a young woman said, "that it is beginning to smell."

The older hunter glanced at her apprehensively; she made him feel foolish, always finding fault with his plans. "Perhaps so," he said. "But at other times we starve."

"Besides," she said, "if you take the fire with you to see where you are going and to see the game, the game will see you."

The hunters looked at one another and shrugged. The woman went into the cave and returned with an earthenware pot. There were pieces of raw meat and some water in it, and she put it on the fire, propping it in position with three stones. The second hunter looked at the pot curiously. He was a younger brother from the other side of the valley, where he lived with his mates. He pointed at the pot and looked inquiringly at the older brother.

"She made it out of mud," the older brother said.

"Why doesn't it fall apart with the water in it?"

"I put it into the fire first, for a long time," the young woman said. "A very big fire. The mud gets red—and then it gets hard so it won't melt when the water is in it."

The younger man looked surprised. "Magic?"

"Yes," said the other man.

"Nonsense," said the woman. She went back into the cave and the young man put the end of his spear into the fire and tried to scrape the side of the pot with the flint head, but the flint was cold and it cracked. He pulled it back and was looking angrily at it when she came out again and sat on the ground. She had an armful of roots which she began to scrape with a sharp stone. "The spearhead is made of the wrong sort of stone," she said, without looking up. "That is why it broke in the fire."

"It's made of the *right* kind!" the young man shouted. "All spearheads are made of that kind! They always have been and they always will be! How did *you* know it broke in the fire? You weren't looking."

"I heard it make the sound it makes when the fire breaks it."

The young man glowered and pushed his under lip out. "This kind of stone was put in the cave for us to make knives and spears. And it makes a very sharp edge when you know how to form it."

"No sharper than this knife," she said, holding up the stone in her hand. "This doesn't break so easily."

The young man took it and examined it carefully. "How do you strike it to make it this shape?" he said, and then, grudgingly, "It is very smooth—a very good shape."

"You don't strike it," she said, taking it back and going on scraping the roots. "You rub it on another stone—first on the kind that has the bright sparkles in it, and then under water on the flat gray kind. It's much better that your knives and the fire doesn't break it so easily."

She finished with the roots and put them in the pot with the meat.

"Where do you find such big roots?" the young man asked his brother.

"Over there," the brother said, pointing to a patch of earth nearby. *She* finds them there."

"I don't find them," she said. "I put them there in the first place."

"You mean you store them in the earth?" the young man said.

"No. I put the tops in the ground—the blue and yellow flowers—and next warm season I dig and there are the new roots. You have to put water on the earth when it gets dry. Also you have to put up all the small plants that grow there among them. It's very hard work."

"More magic," said the young man.

"It's not magic!" she said. "You are stupid. Haven't you noticed that when you leave an acorn on the ground, it breaks open and a finger goes down into the earth? And then, after the next rains, it makes little leaves—and if you leave it alone, it grows and in time becomes a young tree?"

"Everyone knows that," the young man said disdainfully.

"Well, this is the same."

"Yes, but what makes the roots so big? I never saw any like these."

"That's because I only take the flowers from the plants that have the biggest roots. And if any of the new roots are little, I throw away the flowers from them. Far away."

"What do you do with the little roots?"

"Eat them."

"I don't understand. If you eat the little roots, why don't you get little roots?"

"You are being foolish again!" the young woman said. "A tall man has tall sons."

"*If* he eats the meat of a tall animal," said the young man.

"That has nothing to do with it."

"My friend's father, who lives near the river, always eats the fat of the game they kill, and *he* is fat. So you see!"

"That has nothing to do with it," she said, and went into the cave.

The young man walked up and down angrily. "Why does she talk that way? Is she one of our sisters? I don't remember her."

"No," said the other. "She was with the people we fought with three seasons ago. She is my new mate and she is very good at magic, only I advise you not to pay any attention to what she says."

The other picked up the scrapping-stone she had left and looked at it with grudging envy. "The very tall man who killed the aurochs by himself has a son," he said, "and the son is short."

The other shrugged. "Don't pay any attention to her."

The woman came out again and looked at the sky, then went to the fire and stirred the pot with a stick. "I wish you would try to get the young animals," she said. "You always bring home the biggest ones and they are hard to chew unless I cook the meat all day."

"My father said if you wish to be brave, powerful and swift, you must eat only the animals that are brave, powerful and swift," said the young man obstinately.

"Didn't he eat roots, too?"

"Yes."

"Well, then."

The young man threw the scraping-stone hard against the side of the cave opening and split it in two. "Roots are not animals!"

The young woman picked up the pieces and said, "I think I can make a small scraper out of the big piece and a throwing tip out of the little one, but this is a foolish way to get little stones. There are more little ones than big ones."

"Show him your bent stick with the animal sinew," said her mate. "She has a way of throwing very small spears with a bent stick," he said to his brother. He had a dim feeling that there should be peace between the other two, since they were near his cave, but he was scarcely aware of the feeling.

The young woman looked pleased and went into the cave and brought back a stick of springy wood with a thong attached to one end, and a few dried reeds.

"See," she said, and took a dried reed which had a small sharp stone stuck in the end of it. Then she bent the stick and strung the sinew from end to end. The younger man had his first view of a bow and arrow. "This was the way my mother showed me to throw little spears."

She fitted the arrow into the bow and, pulling it back, shot it at a pine tree on the other side of the fire. The bowstring twanged and the arrow wobbled, having no fletching, but it stuck into the tree trunk. The young man jumped back in alarm and blinked his eyes. Then he went to the tree and pulled at the arrow. It came loose, leaving the tip stuck in the bark.

"What good is it?" he said derisively, to conceal his astonishment. "It is a child's plaything!" He tried to pry out the arrowhead with his thumb, and broke his nail.

"If any child of mine played with this," said the young woman, "I should beat him." She put a larger arrow into the bow—one that had a heavier tip—and shot it into the same tree. Owing to its superior balance, this arrow did not wobble; it swished through the air and sank its tip deep into the soft wood.

"You have no child," said her mate, "so how can you beat it?"

The young woman said nothing, but she looked angry.

"My other women have children," he went on tauntingly. "They laugh at you."

"You have no child younger than ten seasons!" she said, and stamped her foot. "*That* is why I have no child! You are an old man!"

He started toward her with a look of furious intention. He had no spear in his hand, but he held a club with flint splinters stuck in the heavy head. She ran back to the cave mouth and put another arrow in her bow and aimed it at him. They both stood silently staring at one another. Then he threw down his club and turned away.

"Peace," he said.

"Peace," she replied, and dropped her bow. She went to the pot over the fire and sniffed it, poking at the meat with a sharp stick. "The food is ready," she said. "Will you take the pot off the fire? You have braver hands than I."

Q. How are we to find out anything about them, when you are so slow?
A. What are we supposed to find out?
Q. That is what you are supposed to find out.
A. I am to find out what I am to find out? You sound like them—like men.
Q. Like Man?
A. No, men. The women aren't quite the same. That's why I always choose to be one, but I wish you would send somebody else—another part of our Organism. I'm tired.
Q. Absurd. Besides, you are the best; you cannot be tired.
A. The best! How am I the best? You do nothing but criticize. You send me because I understand the intentions—the leanings—of live things. You say I

understand understanding. I suppose that makes me some kind of epistemologist: the father confessor of the inscrutable.

Q. Wouldn't it be mother confessor?

A. Not with them; they don't like women to be priests. They can be holy, but they don't like women to tell them what to do. It's called nagging. They get especially angry if the woman is right.

Q. Hmm. Now you say that we criticize you. You surely are not going to claim to be above criticism *here*, are you?

A. Oh, no. I'm beneath it.

Q. Then why do you resent it?

A. Because it doesn't apply. If a mother is not a fool, she will correct her child, but she won't blame it. You can't go looking for good and evil motives in everything that happens. Does a stone have a motive when it falls to the ground?

Q. If this is the way you always talked, I'm not surprised you angered them.

A. I am sorry.

Q. You turn everything around that's said to you.

A. I will try not to. It's like the bishop—he complained about the same thing, and I was only trying to—

Q. What bishop?

A. I forgot his name. He was the thin one; he was much cleverer than the others. He gave me an impossible choice, so I chose to make another start.

Q. You mean you got yourself burned again?

A. Yes! They did it to all their best people. Both sides did. I would have looked a precious fool if I'd backed down.

Q. Can't you bear to admit you are wrong?

A. But I wasn't wrong. Anyway, they'd have made me out in the wrong either way.

Q. Did they only burn the women, when they thought the women were wrong?

A. No, of course not. And it was usually when they suspected the women were right. Then there were the women who were thought to be possessed by what they thought were evil spirits.

Q. They didn't suspect *they* were right, surely?

A. No, but they were afraid they might be. They were very unsure of themselves and their beliefs. That's when they burned people.

Q. It sounds very wasteful. They must be very careless of their possessions.

A. No, not in the least. I'll explain—

Q. I wish you wouldn't.

A. There, you see? They were just like you—they kept asking me questions and getting more and more enraged when I answered them. So, to shut me up, they tied me to a stake.

Q. You are too interested in your own reactions to things. Tell us about something more constructive—about what you found in other guises. I understand you led an insurrection?

A. If you call throwing an armed robber out of your house an insurrection. The trouble was that on that occasion a lot of my friends thought I was right. That's called conspiracy. . . .

The captain led a small group of foot soldiers into the village at what, to the Romans, was the Twelfth Hour, which is sunset. The soldiers had light armor and carried only the small shields—not the enormous *testudines*—but they had been warned to keep their eyes open as the British were tricky, even treacherous. The captain greatly disliked to take such raw troops so far north, where the treaties were uncertain and the Pax Romana was held lightly, if at all. An ancestor of his, also a captain, had been killed near here in one of Hadrian's marches, and no one was quite sure what had happened.

The earth wall that Hadrian's men subsequently built across the British island was intended to keep out the more unruly natives of the North, and later the emperor Severus built another one of stone, but it was by now in a state of disrepair and only a few of the guard towers were manned. Even the Great North Road made an attenuated and unreliable line of supply, and the captain could expect neither reinforcements nor food from the camps farther south, like Eboracum or Lancastrium.

Live off the land, he was told, and that meant quartering his troops—a risky thing because it separated them—or sending foraging parties to the surly farmers for "contributions." Since he was here to collect back-taxes, the inhabitants would not take kindly to feeding the collectors.

The village had a stockade of undressed logs and wide gates at either end. These were surmounted by arched wooden structures that were supposed to serve as watchtowers, but beyond spears and knives for hunting and the necessary farming implements, the villagers were not allowed to carry weapons of any kind. The stockade was not big enough to enclose all the houses, and the majority of these were on the outside and huddled against the walls.

The small body of Roman troops—barely a *manipulus*—were not surprised to notice that all the windows and booths had been shuttered, and in the exact center of the village, the local chieftain and heads of families were gathered in a respectful and anxious group. It annoyed the captain that it was impossible to make an unexpected arrival anywhere in Britain; news traveled faster than Roman foot soldiers.

"Hail, Caesar!" said the captain, putting his arm up, the palm of his hand facing forward.

"Hail, Caesar!" said the villagers.

"We come for the taxes which were not paid last year."

The villagers shook their heads and made regretful sounds.

"Nor the year before, nor the year before that. Which is your headman? I shall require food for my men at once—they are tired after a day's march."

A gray-bearded, very tall man stood forward. "The food will be ready at once, noble decemvir, and I hope you will honor me with your presence for dinner."

"Thank you very much." said the captain, "but I prefer to stay with my men until I see them taken care of. And I am not a decemvir. My rank is captain—Caesar's captain."

The bearded man bowed and said, "Then, after the arrangements have been made, Captain will you not take a cup of wine?"

"Don't press him, Grandfather," a voice said from above them, and, looking up, the captain saw a girl's face at a second-story window. She had very dark skin, red hair and blue eyes. "If he's been walking all day, I expect he wants to go to bed early. You'll only keep him up all night talking about boar hunts."

"Silence!" the headman shouted. "Get back, girl! You insult our . . . our guest!"

"No, let her stay," the captain said with an amused smile. "Better still, have her come down. I think I shall accept your offer about the wine later."

In the evening, the captain came to the headman's house with his two lieutenants as guard. They were received with deference and given wolf-hides to sit on. The wine was brought by the granddaughter and served in horn cups.

"What is your name, young lady?" asked the captain politely. "This is excellent wine, by the way."

"Thank you, Captain," she said. "We have had a cask taken to your men. I made it myself, three years ago. My name is Boadicea."

"Boadicea?" said the captain in astonishment.

"No, no, Captain!" the headman said hurriedly. "She's joking—her name is Flavia; the other is the name she takes for herself. I apologize for her."

"It is not a joke," she said. "Boadicea is my heroine and I have taken her name. I don't like the name Flavia—it's Roman. Do I look like a Roman to you, Captain?"

"You look very beautiful," the captain said, laughing, "and there is no need for apology. I admire Boadicea myself; she very nearly drove Caesar's men into the sea. It was a long time ago." He drained his wine cup. "A long, long time ago."

"But we have not forgotten her, Captain," the girl said, filling his cup again.

"You insult our honored guest, girl!" her grandfather said. "Go to bed!"

"No, I beg you—please don't send her to bed," said the captain. "I'm not in the least insulted. After all, it's ancient history now. I don't think people think of us as conquerors any more. We are protectors. While we are here, the Picts stay where they belong, and the Scots, too."

"The Picts say they used to live hereabouts," said the girl.

"The Picts say, the Picts say! What do you know of what they say?"asked her grandfather.

"The cook's mother is a Pict," she replied.

"Well, she'd better not come *here!*" said the headman. "We want no Celts!"

"But, Grandfather, we *are* Celts!"

"No, girl, we are Romans," he answered, looking sideways at the captain.

The captain nodded. "That is true. All members of the Empire are Romans. Not citizens, perhaps, but Romans just the same, and all live by Caesar's law."

"But suppose people don't want to live by his law?" said the girl.

The two lieutenants looked shocked, but the captain smiled. "That would be most foolish and uncivilized of them. Don't you think it's better for the whole world to live as members of one community and cease all this useless warfare?"

"It seems to me," the girl said, "that warefare is the result of somebody trying to take somebody else's land and subject him to a law that is alien to him."

The captain raised his eyebrows and put his head to one side quizzically. The headman coughed and attempted to change the subject. "The taxes, Captain," he said, "are very much on my mind. . . ."

"And on mine," the captain said. The two lieutenants tried to look businesslike, but they looked more as if they were falling asleep.

"And I hope I may say that this time we will have them ready for you," said the headman.

"I hope so, too," said the captain.

"But there are other levies that have not been made, which we had rather expected to be made . . ."

"Other levies?" The captain held out his cup and the girl poured more wine into it.

"I refer to troops, Captain," the headman said. "You levy no troops from us up here."

"You put me in rather an embarrassing position," the captain said. "You must realize that while I make no comparison to yourself, there are some people living at the outer boundaries of the Empire, people not yet wholly reconciled to Caesar's dominion, people who—to give another example—think of themselves as, say, Helvetiae first and Romans second. It is the Imperial policy in such cases not to levy troops because—"

"In other words," the girl interrupted, "you think we are not to be trusted. It quite passes my understanding why anyone should expect loyalty unless it is freely offered."

"But, my dear young lady, you are not slaves! You are given the civilizing benefits of Roman rule, and you are taxed very much less than people living in Rome itself, I can assure you of that." He felt terribly sleepy—the wine was stronger than he had thought and he found it difficult to think of the right words. He was beginning to sound to himself like a senator, a race of men he secretly despised. "Let me put it this way," he went on. "A child does not *offer* loyalty to his parents—it comes by nature."

"Perhaps grown people do not like to be treated as children," she said. "*I* don't."

"You behave like one, Granddaughter!" the headman said. "Go to your room!"

Rather unexpectedly, she got up and walked to the door. "Good night, Captain," she said, but he did not answer. He was asleep and so were his lieutenants, and, since there were poppyheads in the wine, they did not wake up even when, an hour later, the shouting began outside.

Almost the entire detachment of the Roman troops was killed, and the captain and his lieutenants were being held hostage by the Pictish Decaledonae who had swarmed over the broken Wall—the break having been enlarged by the headman's granddaughter and her friends during the previous night.

The headman and his companions were horrified; they pleaded with the Pictish leaders to spare the Roman officers. "Caesar will send a legion," the headman said, "many legions to avenge this! Leave them unharmed and go back to the North, and the Roman captain will soften the blow that will fall on us all. . . . "

The Picts told him to shut up and called for wine. The headman and his companions took advantage of the carousing to slip out the back way and, taking some of the villagers, including Flavia, they hid themselves in a cottage in the forest. Except for the girl, they were shaking with terror. She was triumphant.

"Now Caesar will withdraw again," she said. "He no longer moves north—but slowly southward. The next Imperial rampart will be below us, and we shall be free!"

"You are mad," her grandfather said. "Under Roman rule, we are safe. What can we expect from these Pictish barbarians?" He looked at her as though she were some new kind of snake.

"I should rather be occasionally robbed by my cousins than taxed to death by strangers," she said, her dark face flushed.

"But the Romans are civilized!" said her grandfather.

"Their civilization stands on slavery," she replied. "I'd rather be a free barbarian. The Romans are doomed."

"This is revolt!" the headman said. "In the name of freedom, you deliver us into the hands of the Picts—you are a traitor to your own people!"

"The Picts won't stay," she said. "They never do; they hate farming. What does it matter if they burn the village and steal some of the farm animals? It will come to less than what you would have to pay in taxes to Caesar."

"Caesar's men will return," said her grandfather, "and we shall have to pay ten times over. And if the Picts kill the captain, the Romans will have my life for it! You are a traitor! Who was with you in this infernal plot?"

Q. Why didn't you tell them? Why are you always so stubborn? You might have stayed on and found out many useful things.
A. There would have been nothing useful to find out. Men who submit to autocracy cease to be a living, growing organism. Look at Egypt—it stayed that way almost uninterruptedly for four thousand years. However, I did find out one very surprising thing.
Q. I'm glad to hear it. What was that?
A. My grandfather was a Druid! I thought all that was dead and gone with the Roman occupation—but there was a secret sect and he was their high priest! So all the time he was in a conspiracy, too! I couldn't help laughing.
Q. How did you learn this?
A. They took me to an oak tree, put a wreath of mistletoe on my head, and he executed me with a stone sickle. Also all my friends who didn't have the sense to escape north over the Wall of Severus. But it made no difference in the end. The next emperor withdrew the army to the southeast part of the island and the next—or the one after; I forget which—took them all back to Rome. This was after we invited the Saxons in—they made it hot for Caesar's men, I can tell you! They also made things rather hot for us, but everything calmed down in time.
Q. It doesn't sound like much of an improvement.
A. Well, the Saxons may have been pretty bloodthirsty, but they hated slavery. They had sort of half-slaves—housekarls—but their heart wasn't in it. Also, although they were extremely rough, they didn't go in for official torture.
Q. But surely the civilized Romans didn't either?
A. I think you are being quite funny.
Q. I don't know what you mean.

A. I know you don't. That's the one really appealing thing about men: they sometimes have a sense of humor—when the joke is not on them. I think I must have caught it from them.

Q. Keep in mind that you are not an irreplaceable part of this organism!

A. How can I forget it?

Q. One gets the impression that Man felt that you were not irreplaceable either. When they want war, you are against it, and when they want peace—like your North Britons—you are all for war. How did you hear about Caesar withdrawing from Britain?

A. I was supposed to go back a little later, but I missed again, and that time I was in real trouble—with both sides at once. It was just about a thousand years later, when the French and English were fighting each other.

Q. You seem to have made a rather dismaying number of mistakes.

A. I would never have learned anything if I had been afraid of making mistakes. Anyway, the bishops were the ones I had to fear the most, and when they started questioning me, I—

Q. Was it they who told you about the Saxons being invited to come in?

A. No, indeed. By that time, scarcely anyone knew anything any more, except prayers, recipes and how to cure warts. Later on, there was a revival and everyone became very clever, but I was in Italy at the time and I never got to hear about the Saxons until long afterward—my last trip but two, in fact. I was at a school in England. . . .

The headmistress of St. Agatha's prided herself on being fair. Her way of being fair was to avoid favoritism by being equally unfair to all the girls and to those of the assistant teachers who would stand for it. Some of them didn't, and they usually left after their first term, as the headmistress didn't believe in contracts. Besides, at the beginning of the twentieth century, contracts for teachers were a novelty.

The result of this policy was a rapid turnover in the young and intelligent teachers, and a small permanent staff of compliant sheep. That St. Agatha's had any scholastic standing was due to the fact that Miss Wakefield had taken honors at Girton, and the school's social standing was due to her being the cousin of a Peer of the Realm. The girls were fed almost enough, the school uniform was expensive, and nobody had much free time. French was well taught—by Miss Wakefield herself—and so was Latin, but games were also stressed. The school was run on what Miss Wakefield called the Honor System, which had the effect of dividing the pupils into tale-bearers and secret rebels.

On a raw November afternoon, Miss Wakefield sent a prefect for Sarah Stone, who was one of the new girls. "Tell her to come straight to my office. She can have her shower later," she said, and Sarah arrived in the jersey and serge skirt she had been wearing on the hockey field. Her bare knees were blue and her nose was running. She stood waiting while the headmistress looked with prominent eyes at some papers on her desk. Sarah could see that they were examination papers and one of them was in her own handwriting.

Without looking up, Miss Wakefield said, "I hear that your mother is in trouble with the police."

"But she—"

"Do not interrupt. I asked you no question and no answer is called for. It is a fact, which I have just read in the *Morning Post,* that your mother is in trouble with the police. Again—is that not true?"

"No."

The headmistress looked up in amazement. "Do you mean to stand there and tell me the newspaper is *lying?* Do you tell me to my face that your mother is not involved with the . . . the authorities?" Miss Wakefield also taught English Composition and woe betide the girl who used the same word twice in the same context. "We are blessed with the richest of all languages," she would say, "so let us explore it—let us make use of it—for to do otherwise would be tautology." She never made clear what tautology meant, but the girls got her drift.

"I don't know whether the newspapers are lying or merely mistaken, Miss Wakefield," Sarah said, "although my mother says that it's hard to tell the difference with most journalists. At any rate, she is not in trouble with the police. They are the ones that are in trouble."

The headmistress stared hard at Sarah; she was rather good at this with small girls of thirteen. (You and I might find it difficult to stare down a child, and impossible in the case of a kitten, but Miss Wakefield was, after all is said, the cousin of a Peer of the Realm.)

"I believe I can understand that," she said. "In fact, I pity the arresting officer. Here is a woman who breaks shop windows for the sake of attracting attention to her political *clique,* and he is no doubt subjected to scratching and biting. Votes for women, indeed! Does breaking shop windows prove that people like her should have the . . . the franchise?"

"She didn't break the window," Sarah said. "She was pushed against it by the policeman. And she never scratches unless a mosquito happens to—"

"You were not there, Stone," said the headmistress, "so how can you say that?"

"I know my mother. And she doesn't bite, either," Sarah said, looking at Miss Wakefield's neck. "Unless it's a tough old hen!"

Miss Wakefield had enough sense to refuse the bait, but she flushed. "I do not feel that it is at all suitable for the mother of one of our girls to be a Militant Suffragette! The reputation of the School . . ." The sentence was left unfinished.

She picked up the sheets of paper. "I have here two of the midterm examination papers in arithmetic, yours and Angela Harvey's. There is a curious, a *very* curious similarity between them. All the answers are correct except for problems five, seven and twelve, and they have precisely the same mistakes in both papers!" She paused and stared hard at Sarah, who blinked but refused to lower her eyes. "You and Harvey sit next to one another," Miss Wakefield said meaningly.

Sarah said nothing. She sniffed because her nose was running and there was no pocket in her games uniform for a handkerchief.

"Well?" said Miss Wakefield. "Have you nothing to say?"

"No, Miss Wakefield," Sarah said, "except I didn't copy from Angela, if that's what you mean."

"Then it would appear that she copied from you."

"That's a beastly thing to say! It was a coincidence! She's not a cheat!"

The headmistress felt on secure ground: the child was losing her temper. It was Miss Wakefield's favorite strategem to make people lose their tempers—that is, if they were children or underlings.

"Blow your nose, Stone," she said, and then, seeing that Sarah had no handkerchief, she gave her her own, with a look of distaste. "I think perhaps you might do better at some other school."

"So do I, Miss Wakefield," Sarah said. "Mother wanted to get me into Mr. Russell's school, but it was full up."

"*Bertrand* Russell?"

Sarah nodded, blowing her nose again. She was shivering.

"*Well!*" said Miss Wakefield. "I never heard the like! He's an Atheist! Why, he believes in *Free Love!*"

"I don't know what he believes," Sarah said. "I know he was awfully nice when he came to tea. He said I had some kind of a guiding somebody standing over me. He said he would like awfully to have me at his school, but it was full up. I know one of the boys there and he says it's simply ripping."

"*Well!* Of course, if your mother thinks of us as Second Best . . . Perhaps Mr. Russell believes it is all right to cheat in examinations, but we have a Tradition at St. Agatha's." She rang a bell on her desk and a scrawny little housemaid came in. "Send one of the girls for Angela Harvey," Miss Wakefield said. "Tell her to come here directly." The little housemaid bobbed respectfully and went out. "Now we shall see what *she* has to say," the headmistress said.

"She'll only be frightened and cry." Sarah said, "and she'll say anything you want her to. She wouldn't *dare* cheat in an examination."

"Then you admit that you copied from her?"

"I do not!" Sarah said, her teeth chattering. "I tell you it was a fluke! Miss Somerville jolly well knows I wouldn't do it!" Miss Somerville was the new and still enthusiastic math teacher, but her enthusiasm would be gone by the end of the term, and so would Miss Somerville.

"That will do!" said the headmistress. "Impertinence will not improve matters."

There was a timid knock on the door and a girl of Sarah's age, but smaller, came in. She had changed into the school uniform and wore steel-rimmed spectacles.

"Stand beside Stone, Harvey," the headmistress said. "Now I want you to think very carefully before you answer what I'm going to ask you."

Angela Harvey looked terrified and began to cry.

"There, you see?" Sarah said. "You're only doing this because you don't like my mother! You want me to leave school, and it's the only excuse you can find!"

"Be quiet," Miss Wakefield said with an unpleasant smile. She never lost her temper. "Did you, or did you not," she went on to the damp Angela, "copy the answers in your arithmetic from Stone?"

"Oh, no! Oh, I *wouldn't,* Miss Wakefield!"

"Then how is it you have seventeen right answers? You never do as well as that, and you got the same three wrong that Stone did."

"I don't know, Miss Wakefield! I don't *know!*" Angela sobbed loudly and became smaller than ever.

"I'm afraid," said Miss Wakefield, who looked quite otherwise, "that unless your *friend* here can explain this curious—this odd coincidence by admitting she copied *your* answers, I shall have to ask your parents to remove you from St. Agatha's at once."

Sarah's face was bright red, but it had the look of

fever. "How simply rotten of you! You're just trying to get me to confess to something I didn't do, to save Angela!"

The headmistress felt her heart beat with excitement and pleasure. Why, the child was positively crimson with temper! "You are not helping her by behaving like a common guttersnipe. At this school, we try to behave like ladies. Perhaps at Mr. Russell's—"

"At Mr. Russell's school," Sarah interrupted, "I'm sure nobody would think it was worthwhile to cheat."

"Then you admit you cheated?"

Sarah looked at Angela, and back at the headmistress. "Yes!"

Miss Wakefield smiled. "Well, then, I think there is nothing more to be said. You may go, Harvey."

"You," Sarah said, looking at Miss Wakefield with blazing fury, "are a coward and a—a *blackmailer!*"

Tiny cracks seemed to appear in the headmistress's porcelain composure. Angela had not yet left the room and heard Sarah's outburst. She stopped at the door and turned around with wide eyes.

"Go at once!" cried the headmistress to her, and waited until the door closed. "You are to be expelled publicly from the school!" she said to Sarah in a low, unsteady voice. "And first you will be publicly thrashed!"

Sarah's face was patchy now, red on white, and her skin looked dry as paper. "If you touch me, I will kill you. I'm not afraid of anyone like you. I didn't cheat in the exam. I said it to keep you from expelling Angela, and you knew it all the time. Everything you say is a lie. You just want to get rid of me because of my mother. You are against votes for women because you are a liar. You told us in history class about government by consent, but how can it be when half the population have nothing to say in the matter? I'm going to pack and leave, and if you try and stop me, I'll . . ."

She went fiery red, and then white, and fainted.

The headmistress was breathing hard, and later, when Sarah was taken to the san, she was frightened. Sarah's temperature was 107 and she had the most virulent kind of pneumonia the school doctor had yet come across. He was almost more curious in watching the course of the disease than he was concerned with the patient, but he did not have very long to watch it, for Sarah died shortly before sunrise.

Q. As far as one can follow your line of reasoning, you claim that the head woman of your school was untruthful, but was against untruth.
A. Yes. Quite a lot of them are.
Q. They sound mad.
A. Well, they are and they aren't. They lie to themselves, mainly; that's what causes most of the trouble. They have a saying: Know Thyself, but nobody ever—
Q. They have? Who said it?
A. All sorts of people are said to be the ones who said it first, but actually I think I was. I was living on an island in the Aegean Sea, and the mainland Greeks thought women shouldn't be writing poetry, so there was a row about it. They said I invented hexameters—which was nonsense—and that made them angry for some reason. So, later on, they decided I was a myth.
Q. Is this the Sappho you mentioned earlier in this hearing?
A. No, no. She was later and she didn't become a myth. My name was Phemonoë. I meant to tell you about that trip. My father was—
Q. Never mind. We've heard enough of the early trips. What we should like to hear about is your last. A decision must be made about these people—we've waited long enough. While it must be admitted that you are the best we have for the task, you not only take a long time and make error after error, but in the very process of examining them, you alter the subject of examination.
A. Yes, I know. They have a new phrase for that. They call it the Uncertainty Principle. For example, you can't determine the mass and velocity of a particle

and at the same time its position. If you measure the one, you alter the other.

Q. We are quite aware of that.

A. I just thought I'd remind you.

Q. Unnecessary.

A. That's what men usually say; they dislike being reminded. Am I to stop making trips?

Q. That will be decided in the light of the rest of your report. I may tell you now that there will probably be no further trips. You will be reabsorbed into the Unity.

A. I see. I remember you said the same thing after I reported on the time they hanged Haman. You seemed to side with him. Anyway, if I get reabsorbed, it won't be a Unity any more—not the way things are going.

Q. You overrate yourself. Contact with Mankind has changed you.

A. Oh, it has! I've changed them a bit, but it's the principle of uncertainty again: it changes me, too.

Q. The Unity is greater than its parts.

A. Not if it's infinite, the way you say it is. You know, it's a funny thing, but I've never been quite clear just what's behind all this decision you talk about. What is our purpose?

Q. Does a stone have a purpose when it falls?

A. I'm not talking about values. What are the alternatives you imply in the decision?

Q. There are three. We destroy them; we absorb them; we ignore them.

A. I'm afraid they can't be ignored.

Q. Why not?

A. It's too late. The Unity should have started ignoring them right at the beginning—we are already changed. And if they are absorbed, we shall be still more changed.

Q. *They* will be changed. The Unity is eternal and—

A. You ought to talk to a man called Heisenberg. He called it the inexactitude principle, but it's the same thing. For example, men are always going around asking each other questions; they call it taking a poll, only when you try to find out that way what people are thinking, you change them. Or anthropology—when you study a tribe, you alter its way of life. Furthermore, it alters yours.

Q. It would appear that you have lost your sense of objectivity.

A. That's the way my last husband talks. There is no such thing. It's a strange fact, but it seems that the mathematicians are the only ones who have a glimmering of the truth—they and the physicists. I was beginning to think that mankind as a whole was progressing quite nicely.

Q. I thought you said they were. It seems you're never satisfied.

A. Well, some things improve, but their point of view keeps changing with regard to what should and what should not improve. It's hard to say whether the Greeks really believed in progress: they thought there had been a golden age and that the world had degenerated from it. Some of them may have wanted to return to it, but I always suspected their motives—by their own showing, they were decadent. During the Middle Ages, it was felt that art was on the way up—part of an evolutionary process—whereas science was not. Aristole and the Thomists had science all cut and dried. Nowadays it's fashionable to say the art was as "good" in primitive times as it is now, while science on the other hand is evolving to a higher state of truth. The latter happens to be true, but they still have war.

Q. Perhaps it's inevitable.

A. If it is, we are wasting our time.

Q. That is for the Unity to decide. You set yourself up as Mankind's conscience.

A. Not conscience. I plead for self-examination—for a reappraisal of ideas.

Q. Yet you only succeed in irritating them.

A. That may be the best way. And you confuse conscience with consciousness. If there's one thing I've found out, it's that Man differs from the animal in having more consciousness, just as animals have more than plants. I don't suppose that hydrogen has any at all.

Q. But you have turned what was intended to be a field trip for examination and analysis into a crusade. With all your nagging and irritating them, there have been no results—no real advances.

A. I thought you were complaining that I *was* altering what I was sent to examine. You talk about unification—or absorption—as if it were a catchword. That's the trouble with generalities: they're not necessarily true in all cases.

Q. You mean they are too general?

A. I mean that they are not general enough. I agree that men progress too slowly toward unification, but we mustn't confuse it with domination. We cannot *impose* it on them. That would lead to a world divided into the ruled and the rulers—not a unity.

Q. Then you are for absorption?

A. You know, you twist things around much worse than I do.

Q. The Unity is incapable of—

A. Furthermore, I think you have been altered more than I have.

Q. You are part of the Unity.

A. And the least altered part. You won't be able to absorb them the way you can reabsorb me without destroying them as entities.

Q. You set yourself up as the only one to know this. Why?

A. Because I have been the one to make the trips. I have been your eye.

Q. But the others—the ones you called the spies?

A. They weren't there to look at Man, only to watch *me*. They weren't even sightseeing—they were slumming. However, I think I am ceasing to be the only one. I think you are coming to know these things, too.

Q. Very gratifying. Now, as to the latest trip?

A. There seems to have been a slip-up. . . .

Q. *Another* one?

A. Different. The ones *I* made were errors in time; this one is not mine, and it's in hypertime. I was trying to explain it to a friend, but he already knew all about it and that led to the slip-up. It caused it, yet it came afterward.

Q. How annoying for you. How did you explain hypertime?

A. I said that when an object moves or changes, time is needed as one of the coordinates to describe that change. I said that consciousness moves *through* time—from Monday to Tuesday—otherwise we would be merely aware of differences without experiencing them as change. I said that to describe this motion of consciousness along the dimension of time, *another* coordinate is needed: hypertime.

Q. And the slip-up—which you claim is not yours?

A. Is in hypertime. It is the result of the Unity and Mankind affecting one another. You have, through my efforts, examined them—and thus changed them. Now they begin to examine you—with the result that *you* change.

Q. They begin to examine *us?* You must mean they have examined *you*.

A. There is a man—a young physicist—and he has found out something. I think that without quite knowing it, he has detected you. At all events, he has found out where you are, and I think that perhaps you are aware.

Q. What makes you say that?

A. Obviously these things work both ways. Heisenberg's principle says—

Q. We want to hear no more of Heisenberg's principle! There's enough confusion as it is, without that!

A. I admit it. That's why I decided to—to close my eyes to everything but essentials on this trip.

Q. It is gratifying to hear you admit something for a change. What are you "closing your eyes to" in this case?

A. Appearances.
Q. Why?
A. Appearances are deceitful. That is, they are now; they weren't before, when the Unity was the Unity and Mankind was Mankind, not something of each. You ask me to keep my objectivity and you don't tell me how. You can't, of course—your own is too lost for you even to know it's gone. So I have to work out my way alone and the best method seems to be to work with as few senses as possible. That won't give me real objectivity, but it will mean somewhat less involvement.
Q. The less you see, the more you can observe? Does that make sense?
A. Nothing does any more. Oh, if you had only stopped in time—no, that wasn't possible.
Q. Why not?
A. Because, being in hypertime, the slip-up is both in the past and the future in simple time. The last trip is going on now. . . .

Katherine was lying on the lab sofa with her hands behind her head. The sofa was shabby and was alleged to have belonged at one time to a psychoanalyst. Its present function was to offer temporary rest to anyone working late in the lab. Today was Sunday and no undergraduates were there.

"What are you fiddling around with, Phil?" Katherine asked.

"The electron microscope," he said. Phil Kaufman was an assistant physics professor, short, bony and intense looking, and at the moment he was engaged in extracurricular research.

"You know, I bet this old chaise longue could many a tale unfold," she said.

"Well, according to rumor, many have been unfolded on it."

"Professor, your mind wanders. I'm thinking of its previous condition of servitude. Think of the dreams it used to hear."

Phil Kaufman didn't answer. There was a pause and she said, "This afternoon you're working with the microscope, and last night it was the telescope. You were in the observatory until dawn."

"How did you find that out?"

"I have my methods, Watson. I don't see how you expect to keep going on no sleep at all. Russ is worried about you."

"Pro or con?"

"Pro, of course. He likes you very much. In fact, he thinks you are the best brain on the faculty."

"Coming from the president, that's praise indeed." Phil got up and went to a desk, where he looked at some notes. "Speaking as my boss's wife, would you say he was pro or con about this work I'm doing?"

"I would say he can't make it out. Alternating between the Microcosm and the Macrocosm. Incidentally, why don't they call that thing in the observatory a macroscope? I don't think Russ is very good at understanding the unfamiliar. I was telling him about the concept of hypertime the other day, and his reaction was one of solicitude—he got me a drink." Katherine stretched her arms. "What are you doing now?"

"Checking some figures. You know, that was odd, your bringing up the business of hypertime. This thing I'm working on seems to involve it."

"Oh?" Katherine put her arms behind her head again. "Tell me something, Phil—what does he look like?"

"Doctor Russell Farley?"

"Yes. I suppose it's a funny sort of question to ask about one's husband. How does he look to you?"

"Like the youngest college president in America, I guess. Brawny but brainy. You make what they call a handsome couple."

"Yes, I was going to ask you what I looked like, only it's a waste of time. People never tell you."

"I can," Phil said, "but I won't, for fear of giving you a swelled head."

"As a matter of fact, it's silly of me to ask," she went on. "I wouldn't understand. I don't even know what 'pretty' means, although I have a dim idea what 'ugly' does. Color is another enigma to me. Somebody once told me it's like a smell, but when I get a bad cold, I can't remember what smells are like. It's like not being able to think of the word 'bubble' when your mouth is wide open—you think of '*Ah*-uh.' "

"I'll tell you one thing about yourself," Phil said. "You don't look as though . . ."

"As though I was blind?"

"Correct. And it's incredible the way you get around. You never bump into anything, and you look people right in the eye when they talk to you."

"They say it's hearing faint echoes from an obstacle—like a bat. Personally, I *feel* the wall in front of me. I admit when my ears are stopped up I can't hear the wall, but I'm not so sure that's a convincing proof. It's the same with pit vipers—some smart investigator discovered that when you plug up their little heat-detecting organs—I guess those are the pits—they can't locate warm prey in the dark. Conversely, in the dark and not plugged up, they will strike at a hot-water bottle."

"Sounds pretty convincing to me," Phil said, and went back to the electron microscope.

"Tush," Katherine said. "How about people not wanting to smoke in the dark? Does that prove that the sense of taste depends on sight? *I* smoke. In fact, you might bring me a cigarette and an ashtray. The only reason most blind people don't smoke is they're afraid of fire." She took the cigarette Phil brought her. "Thanks."

"Aren't you afraid of fire?" he asked.

"Of course not. I can detect a match flame at fifteen feet."

"You ought to go to Duke University sometime and have Rhine take a look at you."

"I did. All he said was 'Hmm,' and I joined the other statistics."

There was silence for a while, interrupted at one point by a muffled "Damn!" from Phil peering into the electron microscope, and the warm sun lay across Katherine's lap. Finally he straightened up and switched off the current. "Well, it's there, all right," he said, and got up and went to the couch and sat at her feet.

"What is?"

"The red shift."

"Aren't you confusing things?" she said. "You're not in the observatory now, Buster; this is the lab. I thought the red shift was the recession of the distant galaxies . . . whatever 'red' is."

"Quite right, Holmes. However, in this case, it's the recession of the not-so-distant atoms. They are small-sized solar systems, too, in a way, and when I say 'red' I mean something I can only infer mathematically, because I'm not dealing with light in the ordinary sense."

"You mean they're *receding?"*

"Only in this context," he said. "Motion is length over time; in this case, it's length over hypertime, so they're still here in the lab."

"I'm relieved to hear it," she said. "However, I should think they'd be receding into tomorrow."

"They are, but into yesterday, and new ones from tomorrow are continually coming in to take their place. It's like Fred Hoyle's theory of the continuous birth of hydrogen."

"You're making me feel like my poor husband," Katherine said. "I understand the necessity of hypertime to describe the motion of consciousness along time, but what's this got to do with the atoms?"

There was a knock at the door and Phil stood up, just as Doctor Russell Chalmers Farley came in without waiting for an answer. Phil and Katherine felt faintly embarrassed—there was scarcely any need to knock on the door to the physics lab; it somehow suggested that the door should be kept open when entertaining callers.

Doctor Farley was a handsome man of thirty-eight with a blond mustache that gave him the look of a Kipling colonial officer.

"Ah, there you are, Katherine," he said cheerfully. "Hello, Kaufman. How's the Research Magnificent?"

"It's beginning to show signs of life," Phil said. "I think I can detect a sort of fetal pulse."

Doctor Farley blinked his pale eyelashes and smiled. He sat down at the end of the couch where Phil had been sitting and looked up at him. Part of his charm was that, when he talked to a man shorter than himself, he got below him and looked up. At his evening "sherries" at home, he had a way of deferring to the newest and least important visitor, who was thus raised to the temporary rank of philosopher, while Russell Chalmers Farley was reduced to the position of listener.

The role of humble servitor of the Truth was his most useful one—it had worked rather well with Katherine, and he had an adroit and imaginative way of expressing his ideas, which usually disguised the fact that they were generally borrowed.

They had met at a street corner in New York City where she was waiting for the sound of traffic to abate so that she could cross. He was on the opposite side, and with his extraordinary eyesight and intuition instantly recognized that the beautiful, odd-looking girl facing him on the other side of the street was blind. He was at her side before the light—and the sound of traffic—had changed, and said, "I hope you don't think I'm being forward, but let me offer you my arm. Taxis have a way of making illegal turns sometimes. . . ."

"You are very kind," she replied, pulling him back from the path of a taxi making an illegal turn. "You have a very nice voice," she said as they got to the other side. "I guess being blind makes one . . . forward!" She laughed and started to walk on.

"No, please wait!" he said, and caught up with her. "I wish you hadn't said that. It can be taken in another way: that I am forward because you are blind. I should like to say that *you* have a very nice voice."

She stopped and laughed again. "That's one of the nicest things I've ever had said to me!"

"Do let's . . . I mean would you let me . . ." He floundered, and laughed, too. "Can't we have a drink together? Now?"

"I think it would be lovely," she said.

Later on, he said to her, "You may think this impertinent of me, but you make me envy you. If I were braver, I should wish that I were blind. You actually see more than I do."

Katherine was intrigued. She had been told this before, but always with mystical and pseudo-religious implications. This man, with the attractive voice and smell, had no trace of the mystic.

"Let me tell you a fable to illustrate what I mean," he went on. "There was a man who was born blind, and he went to work as a coal miner because the darkness was no hindrance to him. One day while he was working alone in an unlighted gallery, his sight was miraculously given to him . . . He shouted out in amazement and awe, and the other miners came stumbling to him in the total darkness.

" 'What is it?' they cried. 'What's the matter?'

" 'I can see!' he told them. But they were puzzled, for they had brought no lights.

" 'What can you see?' they asked. 'There is nothing to be seen here in the dark.'

" 'I see *black!*' he said. 'In front of my face is blackness—however, at the back of my head, I'm still blind and I see nothing.' "

Katherine was delighted. "I'm not quite sure I understand."

"Why, to the blind there are no shadows," Farley said. "Another drink?"

"I think it would be lovely," she had said, and since she could see no shadows, she had begun to fall in love.

Doctor Russell Chalmers Farley looked up at Phil and smiled. It was a charming smile and it was as genuine as a guaranteed, ten-carat, real, honest-to-goodness zircon. "As Katherine has probably told you," he said, "what you are doing is completely over my bowed head. I am enormously impressed and at the same time unable to comprehend."

"I find it hard to comprehend, too," Phil Kaufman said. "And I suppose that's what leads me on."

"Well, the thing is," Farley continued, "Washington

seems to have gotten wind of it, and you know how they are. They don't like things to be over their heads."

Phil Kaufman looked at him in astonishment and sat on a lab stool. "I don't understand. How can they possibly be interested in what I'm doing? It's purely theoretical research."

"Surely you don't deny that Lise Meitner's researches began by being theoretical? And look what *they* led to. The point is, Kaufman, that I have been informed that we are about to receive a visit from a man from the A.E.C. He's arriving here sometime this afternoon."

"But that's absurd! I'm not *doing* anything to atoms. I'm merely examining them!"

Katherine frowned when he said this. Phil knew better. Worse yet, so did she.

"When the A.E.C. hears of somebody working in atomic research," Farley said, "they want to know what's cooking. I hate you to be subjected to this, but it won't do any harm to be polite to the fellow and let him, as it were, look over your shoulder."

"I'm damned if I see why I should!" Phil said. "What does he expect to do? Classify me?"

Farley laughed placatingly. "I know it seems high-handed, but I think we all ought to remember there is such a thing as Security."

"Security, my foot!" Phil said. "It was that kind of demented thinking that caused Germany to lose Lise Meitner! *And* Einstein."

"What strikes *me* as rather odd," Katherine said, "is their sending someone here on a Sunday. When did you hear about it, Russ?"

"A little while ago. On the phone."

"Curiouser and curiouser."

"He was very polite and apologetic."

"Quite typical," Phil said. "It's the velvet-glove touch."

Farley looked at his wristwatch. "He won't be here for a while, so I wish you could brief me about the inwardness of what you are doing, Phil." He'd never used his first name before, and Phil became a little wary. "I know you can't give me a ten-year course in advanced physics this afternoon, but—well, I'd like to know what kind of stand to take. I'll be representing the university, after all."

Phil Kaufman looked down from his perch on the stool at the earnest, kindly face and wondered what really lay behind it. So far as he could see, Doctor Farley had no reason to take any stand on the question at all, except to tell the A.E.C. man to go sit on a tack. If he wanted to represent the university, let him do it in the name of Academic Freedom. Phil glanced at Katherine. She was sitting very still and he had the impression that she was thinking about something else.

"All right, I'll give it a try," he said. "There's an idea that's been around for quite a while that there is an analogy between the stars and the atoms."

Doctor Farley's face lighted. "I believe I've heard of it. Back in the twenties, by a man called Dunn, wasn't it?"

Phil shook his head. "Twenty years earlier by a man called Fournier-d'Albe. He wrote a book called *Two New Worlds*, in which he suggested that the solar systems are actually atoms in some vast cloud of super-gas. Of course, this notion ignores the celestial absence of molecular structure—unless you count double stars as molecules—but it might be accounted for by assuming a high temperature. Then he said that the newly hypothesized Rutherford model of the atom was a submicroscopic solar system, but he didn't stop there.

"The atoms and their electrons, he said, were in turn made up of sub-atoms and were perhaps populated by sentient beings who looked through their telescopes and counted the atoms in their vicinity, no doubt arranging them into constellations. You can carry this imaginary process in both directions and as far as you like, but are we to decide arbitrarily that it goes on infinitely? Or is it like Einsteinian space, finite but unbounded?

"I have asked myself this question and I believe the latter statement to be in a sense correct, but what does it mean? Well, it means that if you move further and further into larger universes, you eventually get to where you started. Not that Big is the same thing as Small, but that from wherever you happen to be, the ones in the direction—outward—look successively bigger, while the ones in the other direction—inward—look successively smaller. Now if there were some kind of super-telescope that could look beyond our universe of super-atoms, and beyond the next and so on indefinitely, you would find yourself staring up through a super-microscope at your own eye."

"Get along with you!" Katherine said. "This is the pipe dream to end all pipe dreams. Tell us more."

"Well, I'll revise it to this extent," said Phil. "It wouldn't be your eye that you'd see, any more than you'd see your own face if you looked far enough across ordinary intergalactic space. You'd see the back of your head—or, rather, the other side of the Earth—provided there was nothing in the way."

"And in this case it would be what?" she asked.

"I don't know," Phil said, looking worried. "What *is* the equivalent of the back of your head—looked at along the direction of hypertime? Could it be that what you saw would not be from behind, but from . . . inside?"

Katherine's beautiful sightless eyes seemed to be turned inward, and she sat very still. Then she said, "You evoke something in my mind like the echo of a picture I once knew, and will know again."

Farley looked at her sharply.

"You mean something in your subconscious?" Phil asked.

"Perhaps that's what it is, and yet they say that you try to escape knowledge of your subconscious—that it frightens you. I am not frightened, Phil. I feel . . . expectant."

"I'd feel more expectant," he said, "if I were quite sure of what I was doing. The trouble is that while ordinary light could in theory show you the super-astronomy of the stars and planets that are made up of atoms consisting of *our* stars and planets, it won't work the other way."

"Why not?" Farley wanted to know.

"Wavelength. As it is, we have to use an electron

microscope to see the larger molecules; the wavelength of visible light is too coarse-grained to show anything that small. So just try to imagine how impossible it would be to see the sub-atoms—infra-atoms—that I'm talking about if one had to rely on ordinary light! The electron microscope wouldn't help, either. It would be exactly as though some gigantic, super-researcher were trying to look at one of *our* molecules by bombarding it with a shower of planets."

"Then how can you see this 'red shift'?" Katherine asked.

"I can't," he said. "I detect it by a kind of mathematical diagnosis. It's an inferential process—as most forms of observation are, in modern physics."

Farley was looking as intelligent as he possibly could, but it was plain that he was out of his depth. He had heard of the red shift, but he decided he had better not have it explained.

"There's another thing," Phil said. "The time it would take light to make the round trip of our Einsteinian finite universe would be so great—in the order of $4\pi \times 10^8$ years—that not only would you not see your not-yet born self, but the Earth wouldn't have been formed either. The light you saw would be that many years out of date. However, in this case the elapsed time would be hypertime, and you'd be there in ordinary time."

Doctor Farley got up and walked to one of the windows and stood looking out at the observatory across the campus. "Am I to understand then," he said, "that you are trying to formulate a new atomic theory?"

"Not in the sense of in any way modifying the accepted one," Phil said. "If I'm right, it will merely be a new way of looking at the Universe as a whole, and it won't have the slightest effect on anything."

"I should have thought," Katherine said, "that being able to see inside one's own head would have all sorts of interesting effects." She got up. "I've got to get back to the house. We've got people coming to dinner, Russ, and I'd better get things organized. Are you coming?"

"I'll be along in a little while, Katherine," he said. "I

want to hear more of what Kaufman has to say." He refrained from guiding his wife to the door because of long habit, and again sat down on the couch. After the door closed, he and Phil listened to her sure footsteps going down the corridor. They looked at one another a little guardedly.

"You know I'm on your side," Farley said when they could no longer hear Katherine's footsteps. "Surely you know I don't like this any more than you do, Phil."

"I suppose you don't."

"You won't mind very much if I ask you a favor, will you?" Farley said. Having asked a rhetorical question, he seemed to be illogically waiting for an answer. Phil was unaware of the chess game, but wondered uneasily what was coming.

"Will you please leave her alone?" Farley said.

"I—" Phil started to say, but Farley held his hand up, palm forward.

"My dear chap, you are one of the most sensitive and kind people I know. But you are a little thoughtless. You imagine that, because Katherine is blind, you are doing her a favor by—by giving her companionship. You feel that her interest in the world can be furthered by your interest in her. This is not the case. I ask you please to leave us alone."

"Us?"

"Yes. You put me in the embarrassing position of having to say that we are very well as we are. I know that Katherine is impressed by your—your mind, and I know that your sympathy is well-intended, but it is misplaced. She needs no sympathy."

"Why not?"

Doctor Farley spread his hands, a gesture usually meant to substitute for words. "Do the strong need sympathy?"

"I think so," Phil said.

Doctor Farley smiled. "Well, then, think of *me* as the strong one—the one who needs sympathy as the guardian of something precious. Will you give me your sympathy?" He smiled still.

Phil realized that when the A.E.C. man came—when any

pretext presented itself—Doctor Farley would throw him to the wolves.

"Katherine is not in love with me," Phil said.

"But are you with her?"

"No. At least . . . I don't know."

"Then you are."

Phil said nothing.

Farley had abandoned his usual pose of sitting and looking up. He looked down at Phil—in fact, he looked down his nose and past his blond mustache.

Phil said, "I think Katherine ought to be the one to decide whether she wants to go on seeing me."

"And I disagree."

"And I," Phil said, "shall stop seeing her when—and only when—*she* wants me to! I refuse to be ordered around like this. We're not doing anything wrong!"

"I think you're forgetting—"

"I'm forgetting nothing!" Phil interrupted. "You're acting as though I were having an affair with your wife, and you're trying to pull rank on me! I don't intend to be browbeaten and threatened!"

"I'm not threatening you, my dear man," Farley said, his eyebrows raised. "I ask you as a favor, that's all. I think I know my wife's—mind better than perhaps she does herself. And certainly better than an outsider can."

"And you regard me as an outsider?" Phil's voice was loud.

"You know perfectly well what I mean!" Farley replied angrily. "You are not her husband and consequently do not know—"

"I know her a damn sight better than you do, you stuffed shirt!"

Like most blond men, Farley became red very easily. At the moment, he resembled a tomato with yellow hair. "Why, you little—"

"*Really!*" At the sound of Katherine's voice, they both swung around. They had been making too much noise to hear her return, and she stood at the open door. "Isn't this a bit undignified?" she said. "I could hear you outside."

Farley was breathing heavily. "What brought you back, Katherine?" he asked, finally.

She walked past them to the psychiatrical sofa and sat on it without answering the question. She looked as though her mind was on something else—and then, suddenly, startled and intent.

Yes! I am here . . .

Neither Phil Kaufman nor Russell Farley heard her—they were intent on avoiding one another's eyes, but they would not have heard her anyway.

Q. You were right. He knows where the Unity is—if not what it is, yet.
A. Oh, he will.
Q. Are you so sure? And will you at last admit that we are right? *Unification*—it's the only way . . . now,
A. (*She has her face toward the electron microscope; her blind eyes seem to probe it*) One cannot impose it on them. What kind of unity can come from imposition?
Q. And are things to go on as they are?
A. No, it's too late. Things have already changed. . . .
Q. The history of Man has been the history of his integration—from families to tribes, to communities, to city states, to nations, to hemispheres, to—what next? Is it to stop here, and the hemispheres to beat each other down to the tribal or family level?
A. You will be destroyed in the process.
Q. *We?* In the process of unification?
A. Of course.
Q. And you?
A. I'm always being destroyed.
Q. Ridiculous. Unification can scarcely destroy the Unity.
A. If you unite with Disunity?
Q. The decision has been made: Absorption.
A. By whom? Of whom?
Q. The joining of the collective subconscious to the mutually antagonistic egos of all men. Freud of Vienna had this as a goal—you told us that yourself and I quote it back to you.

A. Or the reverse—men's mutually antagonistic egos in combat with the Unity?

Q. We will take that chance. Now watch—look at the world around you and you will see a dominion of universal brotherhood, the moment Unification is imposed!

A. I will look, but is that what I'll see?

Q. Now! Look!

She looked at Phil and then at her husband, who looked back at her questioningly.

"You were going to say something?" he asked.

She shook her head, and he shrugged his shoulders.

"This business I'm working on—" Phil began, and hesitated.

"Oh, yes. That reminds me," Farley said. "How's the Research Magnificent?"

"It's beginning to show signs of life," Phil said. "I think I can detect a sort of fetal pulse."

Dr. Farley blinked his pale eyelashes and nodded. He sat down at the end of the couch where Phil had been sitting and looked up at him. "Well," he said, "I just thought I'd drop by and see how you were doing. I'll never be able to understand it, though."

"I was going to say, do you think the A.E.C. might conceivably be interested?" Phil said. "After all, it is sort of vaguely connected with atomic stuff."

"I can't imagine why they would be," Farley said, and glanced at Katherine. She had gotten up and was standing at the window.

"The sun's going in," she said, "and it looks as though it may rain. I've got to get back to the house." She turned around with a smile. "How about having dinner with us tonight, Phil? We've got some people coming who'd like to meet you. Don't you think that would be nice, Russ?"

Dr. Farley didn't look as though he thought it would be nice at all, but he said nothing, and neither did Phil Kaufman.

"If you're coming, you'd better straighten your tie," Katherine said. "It's under your ear, as usual."

Phil reached up absently and pulled at it with one hand.

"Sorry." "You put me in an embarrassing position," Farley said. "I think I had better say what I have to say now. Better to have it out, before things go any further."

"Before *what* things go any further?" Phil asked, with a trace of belligerence. "Of course, if you don't want me for dinner—"

"Wait!" Katherine said in distress. "This isn't . . . But it should be . . ." She looked from one to the other and smiled a tentative, hopeful little smile. "We don't have to go on with this, do we . . . *now?*"

"What do you mean, 'now'?" Farley said, his face becoming red. "I think it's high time I got this off my chest. Katherine, I don't believe in letting things drift. I want this out in the open!"

(Oh, but this wasn't the way things were to be! This is all wrong—what can have happened?—There was no answer.)

Phil's face was pale and he started for the door. "I guess I'd better leave you two alone."

"No!" Farley said abruptly. "I want you here! I want you to hear this. Well, Katherine?" He turned to her again.

"I . . . I can't answer you," she said miserably.

"You mean you are in love with him, don't you?" Farley said, with a kind of angry triumph. "All the time, behind my back, you—"

"Dry up, Farley!" Phil said, coming back from the door. "And stop acting like a bully!"

"Why, you—"

The telephone rang, and Katherine picked it up. "It's for you, Russ," she said, and handed it to him.

"Yes?" Farley snapped into it. "Put him on." He listened for a few moments and his eyes traveled to Phil. "All right," he said. "When do you want to come?—I see. Well, I'll arrange to have him here. Three o'clock tomorrow, then. Right. Good-by." He hung up. "You were right in one respect," he said to Phil. "That was a man from the Atomic Energy Commission and he wants to have a look at what you're doing. He'll be here tomorrow and

I shall expect your full cooperation. Sorry, but it can't be helped."

Phil looked at him steadily for a moment. "So that's your way of getting back at me," he said. "Academic freedom means a lot to you! Of all the cowardly, spineless, rotten—"

Farley's face was now dark red and he held up his hand. "That's enough from you!"

"What the hell does he want to come nosing around here for?" Phil said. "My research is purely theoretical—"

"You yourself suggested they might," Farley reminded him. "And don't forget Lise Meitner's work was theoretical, and look where it led!"

"Very cute!" Phil said. "In fact, Jesuitical! What I'm objecting to is having you dump me in their laps! I know your real motive—it stands out a mile!"

Farley's neck veins became noticeable, but he kept himself in control. "You tend to overrate your position here."

"Ha!" Phil said. "You can't bear me in my position of the man your wife loves!"

Farley's control went and he rushed at Phil and grabbed him by the collar.

"*Stop* it!" Katherine cried. "Stop it at once! Are you going to act like a pair of apemen? I'm not in love with Phil—I like him very, very much, but it's you I love, you ox!" She pushed and pulled, and they came apart like a bread sandwich, and she got between them. "For heaven's *sake!*"

"I'm sorry," Farley muttered, and looked ashamed of himself. "I wasn't *dumping* you into their laps, Kaufman—I had no choice. If I'd objected, they'd have got just that much tougher."

"It's okay," Phil said dispiritedly. "I guess."

"Oh, forget the whole thing, you two," Katherine said. "Come on, we'll be late for dinner." Taking their arms, she led them out onto the campus.

BUTTON, BUTTON

Isaac Asimov

When the Good Doctor[1] (a favorite label, among his friends, for one of the most prolific[2] and readable science and science fiction writers of our time) decides to take a day off and be funny, he can be very funny indeed, as the following tricky jape proves. It seems remarkable to me that this Asimov story has managed to escape inclusion in a book for over twelve years. But that omission is our gain: here you have a vintage, never-before-booked story by a master craftsman of the art of science fiction.

IT WAS THE TUXEDO THAT FOOLED ME, AND FOR TWO seconds I didn't recognize him. To me, he was just a possible client, the first that had whiffed my way in a week and he looked beautiful.

Even wearing a tuxedo at 9:45 A.M., he looked beautiful. Six inches of bony wrist and ten inches of knobbly hand continued on where his sleeve left off; the top of his socks and the bottom of his trousers did not quite join forces; still he looked beautiful.

Then I looked at his face and it wasn't a client at all. It was my uncle Otto. Beauty ended. As usual, my uncle Otto's face looked like a bloodhound that had just been kicked in the rump by his best friend.

[1] Doctor? Yes. What they call in the profession a "phony doctor"—Ph.D. In biochemistry. Associate Professor of Biochemistry at Boston University School of Medicine, along with all his other activities.

[2] Sixty-plus titles as this book went to press in mid-1965. Pretty good for a fellow born as recently as 1920!

I wasn't very original in my reaction. I said, "Uncle Otto!"

You'd know him, too, if you saw that face. When he was featured on the cover of *Time* about five years ago (it was either '80 or '81), 204 readers by count wrote in to say that they would never forget that face. Most added comments concerning nightmares. If you want my uncle Otto's full name, it's Otto Schemmelmayer. But don't jump to conclusions. He's my mother's brother. My own name is Smith.

He said, "Harry, my boy," and groaned.

Interesting, but not enlightening. I said, "Why the tuxedo?"

He said, "It's rented."

"All right. But why do you wear it in the morning?"

"Is it morning already?" He stared about him, then went to the window and looked out.

That's my uncle Otto Schemmelmayer.

I assured him it was morning and with an effort he deduced that he must have been walking the city streets all night.

He took a handful of fingers away from his forehead to say, "But I was so upset, Harry. At the banquet—"

The fingers waved about for a minute and then folded into a quart of fist that came down and pounded holes in my desk top. "But it's the end. From now on I do things my own way."

He'd been saying that since the business of the "Schemmelmayer Effect" first started up. Maybe that surprises you. Maybe you think it was the Schemmelmayer Effect that made my uncle Otto famous. Well, it's all how you look at it.

He discovered the Effect back in 1966 and the chances are you know as much about it as I do. In a nutshell, he devised a germanium relay of such a nature as to respond to thoughtwaves, or anyway, to the electromagnetic fields of the brain cells. He worked for years to build such a relay into a flute, so that it would play music under the pressure of nothing but thought. It was his love, his life, it was to revolutionize music. Everyone would be able to play. No skill was necessary. Only thought.

Then, five years ago, this young fellow at Consolidated Arms, Stephen Wheland, modified the Schemmelmayer Effect and reversed it. He devised a field of supersonic waves that could activate the brain via a germanium relay, fry it, and kill a rat at twenty feet. Also, they found out later, men.

After that, Wheland got a bonus of ten thousand dollars and a promotion, while the major stockholders of Consolidated Arms proceeded to make millions when the government bought the patents and placed its orders.

My uncle Otto? He made the cover of *Time*.

After that, everyone who was close to him, say within a few miles, knew he had a grievance. Some thought it was the fact he had received no money. Others that his great discovery had been made an instrument of war and killing.

Nuts! It was his flute! That was the real tack on the chair of his life. Poor Uncle Otto. He loved his flute. He carried it with him always, ready to demonstrate. It reposed in its special case on the back of his chair when he ate and at the head of his bed when he slept. Sunday mornings in the University physics laboratories were made hideous by the sounds of my uncle Otto's flute, under imperfect mental control, flatting its way through some tearful German folksong.

The trouble was that no manufacturer would touch it. As soon as its existence was unveiled, the musicians' union threatened to silence every demiquaver in the land; the various entertainment industries called its lobbyists to attention and marked them off in brigades for instant action; and even old Pietro Faranini stuck his baton behind his ear and made fervent statements to the newspapers about the death of art.

Uncle Otto never recovered.

He was saying, "Yesterday were my final hopes. Consolidate informs me they will in my honor a banquet give. Who knows, I say to myself. Maybe they will my flute buy." Under stress, my uncle Otto's word order tends to shift from English to German.

The picture intrigued me.

"What an idea," I said. "A thousand giant flutes secreted in key spots in enemy territories blaring out singing commercials just flat enough to—"

"Quiet! Quiet!" My uncle Otto brought down the flat of his hand on my desk like a pistol shot, and the plastic calendar jumped in fright and fell down dead. "From you also mockery? Where is your respect?"

"I'm sorry, Uncle Otto."

"Then listen. I attended the banquet and they made speeches about the Schemmelmayer Effect and how it harnessed the power of mind. Then when I thought they would announce they would my flute buy, they give me this!"

He took out what looked like a two-thousand-dollar gold piece and threw it at me. I ducked.

If it had hit the window, it would have gone through and brained a pedestrian, but it hit the wall. I picked it up. You could tell by the weight that it was only gold-plated. On one side it said: "The Elias Bancroft Sudford Award" in big letters and "to Dr. Otto Schemmelmayer for his contributions to science" in small letters. On the other side was a profile, obviously not of my uncle Otto. In fact, it didn't look like any breed of dog; more like a pig.

"That," said my uncle Otto, "is Elias Bancroft Sudford, chairman of Consolidated Arms."

He went on, "So when I saw that was all, I got up and very politely, said: 'Gentlemen, dead drop!' and walked out."

"Then you walked the streets all night," I filled in for him, "and came here without even changing your clothes. You're still in your tuxedo."

My uncle Otto stretched out an arm and looked at its covering. "A tuxedo?" he said.

"A tuxedo!" I said.

His long, jowled cheeks turned blotchy red and he roared. "I come here on something of first-rate importance and you insist on about nothing but tuxedos talking. My own nephew!"

I let the fire burn out. My uncle Otto is the brilliant one in the family so, except for trying to keep him from falling into sewers and walking out of windows, we morons try not to bother him.

I said, "And what can I do for you, Uncle?"

I tried to make it sound businesslike; I tried to introduce the lawyer-client relationship.

He waited impressively, and said, "I need money."

He had come to the wrong place. I said, "Uncle, right now I don't have—"

"Not from you," he said.

I felt better.

He said, "There is a new Schemmelmayer Effect, a better one. This one I do *not* in scientific journals publish. My big mouth shut I keep. It entirely my own is." He was leading a phantom orchestra with his bony fist as he spoke.

"From this new Effect," he went on, "I will make money and my own flute factory open."

"Good," I said, thinking of the factory and lying.

"But I don't know how."

"Bad," I said, thinking of the factory and lying.

"The trouble is my mind is brilliant. I can conceive concepts beyond ordinary people. Only, Harry, I can't conceive ways of making money. It's a talent I do not have."

"Bad," I said, not lying at all.

"So I come to you as a lawyer."

I sniggered a little deprecating snigger.

"I come to you," he went on, "to make you help me with your crooked, lying, sneaking, dishonest lawyer's brain."

I filed the remark, mentally, under Unexpected Compliments and said, "I love you, too, Uncle Otto."

He must have sensed the sarcasm because he turned purple with rage and yelled. "Don't be touchy. Be like me, patient, understanding, and easygoing, lumphead. Who says anything about you as a man? As a man, you are an honest dunderkopf, but as a lawyer, you have to be a crook. Everyone knows that."

I sighed. The Bar Association warned me there would be days like this.

"What's your new Effect, Uncle Otto?" I asked.

He said, "I can reach back into Time and bring things out of the past."

I acted quickly. With my left hand I snatched my watch out of the lower-left vest pocket and consulted it with all the anxiety I could work up. With my right hand I reached for the telephone.

"Well, Uncle," I said heartily, "I just remembered an extremely important appointment I'm already late for. Always glad to see you. And now, I'm afraid I must say good-by. Yes, sir, seeing you has been a pleasure. Well, good-by. Yes, sir—"

I failed to lift the telephone out of its cradle. I was pulling up all right, but my uncle Otto's hand was on mine and pushing down. It was no contest. Have I said my uncle Otto was once on the Heidelberg wrestling team in '32?

He took hold of my elbow gently (for him) and I was standing. It was a great saving of muscular effort (for me).

"Let's," he said, "to my laboratory go."

He to his laboratory went. And since I did not have a knife handy with which to cut my left arm off at the shoulder, I to his laboratory also went.

My uncle Otto's laboratory is down a corridor and around a corner in one of the University buildings. Ever since the Schemmelmayer Effect had turned out to be a big thing, he had been relieved of all course work and left entirely to himself. His laboratory looked it.

I said, "Don't you keep the door locked any more?"

He looked at me slyly, his huge nose wrinkling into a sniff. "It *is* locked. With a Schemmelmayer relay, it's locked. I think a word and the door opens. Without it, nobody can get in. Not even the president of the University. Not even the *janitor*."

I got a little excited, "Great guns, Uncle Otto. A thought-lock could bring you—"

"Hah! I should sell the patent for someone else rich to

get? After last night? Never. In a while, I will myself rich become."

One thing about my uncle Otto. He's not one of these fellows you have to argue and argue with before you can get him to see the light. You know in advance he'll never see the light.

So I changed the subject. I said, "And the time machine?"

My uncle Otto is a foot taller than I am, thirty pounds heavier, and strong as an ox. When he puts his hands around my throat and shakes, I have to confine my own part in the conflict to turning purple.

I turned purple accordingly.

He said, "Ssh!"

I got the idea.

He let go and said, "Nobody knows about Project X." He repeated, heavily. "Project X. You understand?"

I nodded. I couldn't speak anyway with a larynx that was only slowly healing.

He said, "I do not ask you to take my word for it. I will for you a demonstration make."

I tried to stay near the door.

He said, "Do you have a piece of paper with your own handwriting on it?"

I fumbled in my inner jacket pocket. I had notes for a possible brief for a possible client on some possible future day.

My uncle Otto said, "Don't show it to me. Just tear it up. In little pieces tear it up and in this beaker the remnants put."

I tore it into one hundred and twenty-eight pieces.

He considered them thoughtfully and began adjusting knobs on a—well, on a machine. It had a thick opal-glass slab attached to it that looked like a dentist's tray.

There was a wait. He kept adjusting.

Then he said, "Aha!" and I made a sort of queer sound that doesn't translate into letters.

About two inches above the glass tray there was what seemed to be a fuzzy piece of paper. It came into focus while I watched and—oh, well, why make a big thing out of it? It was my notes. My handwriting. Perfectly legitimate.

"Is it all right to touch it?" I was a little hoarse, partly out of astonishment and partly because of my uncle Otto's gentle ways of enforcing secrecy.

"You can't," he said, and passed his hand through it. The paper remained behind untouched. He said, "It's only an image at one focus of a four-dimensional paraboloid. The other focus is at a point in time before you tore it up."

I put my hand through it, too. I didn't feel a thing.

"Now watch," he said. He turned a knob on the machine and the image of the paper vanished. Then he took out a pinch of papers from the pile of scrap, dropped them in an ashtray and set a match to them. He flushed the ash down the sink. He turned a knob again and the paper appeared, but with a difference. Ragged patches in it were missing.

"The burned pieces?" I asked.

"Exactly. The machine must trace in time along the hyper-vectors of the molecules on which it is focused. If certain molecules are in air dispersed—pff-f-ft."

I had an idea. "Suppose you just had the ash of a document."

"Only those molecules would be traced back."

"But they'd be so well distributed," I pointed out, "that you could get a hazy picture of the entire document."

"Hmm. Maybe."

My idea became more exciting. "Well, then, look, Uncle Otto. Do you know how much police departments would pay for a machine like this. It would be a boon to the legal—"

I stopped. I didn't like the way he was stiffening. I said, politely "You were saying, Uncle?"

He was remarkably calm about it. He spoke in scarcely more than a shout. "Once and for all, Nephew. All my inventions I will myself from now on develop. First I must some initial capital obtain. Capital from some source other than my ideas selling. After that, I will for my flutes a factory to manufacture open. That comes first. Afterward, afterward, with my profits I can time-vector machinery manufacture. But first my flutes. Before anything, my flutes. Last night, I so swore.

"Through selfishness of a few the world of great music is being deprived. Shall my name in history as a murderer go down? Shall the Schemmelmayer Effect a way to fry men's brains be? Or shall it beautiful music to mind bring? Great, wonderful, enduring music?"

He had a hand raised oracularly and the other behind his back. The windows gave out a shrill hum as they vibrated to his words.

I said, quickly, "Uncle Otto, they'll hear you."

"Then stop shouting," he retorted.

"But look," I protested, "how do you plan to get your initial capital if you won't exploit this machinery?"

"I haven't told you. I can make an image real. What if the image is valuable?"

That did sound good. "You mean, like some lost document, manuscript, first edition. Things like that."

"Well, no. There's a catch. Two catches. Three catches."

I waited for him to stop counting, but three seemed the limit.

"What are they?" I asked.

He said, "First, I must have the object in the present to focus on or I can't locate it in the past."

"You mean you can't get anything that doesn't exist right now where you can see it."

"Yes."

"In that case, catches two and three are purely academic. But what are they, anyway?"

"I can only remove about a gram of material from the past."

A gram! A thirtieth of an ounce!

"What's the matter? Not enough power?"

My uncle Otto said impatiently, "It's an inverse exponential relationship. All the power in the universe more than maybe two grams couldn't bring."

This left things cloudy. I said, "The third catch?"

"Well." He hesitated. "The further the two foci separated are, the more flexible the bond. It must a certain length be before into the present it can be drawn. In other words, I must at least one hundred fifty years into the past go."

"I see," I said (not that I really did). "Let's summarize."

I tried to sound like a lawyer. "You want to bring something from the past out of which you can coin a little capital. It's got to be something that exists and which you can see so it can't be a lost object of historical or archaeological value. It's got to weigh less than a thirtieth of an ounce so it can't be the Kullinan diamond or anything like that. Its got to be at least one hundred and fifty years old, so it can't be a rare stamp."

"Exactly," said my uncle Otto. "You've got it."

Got what? I thought two seconds. "Can't think of a thing," I said. "Well, good-by, Uncle Otto."

I didn't think it would work, but I turned to go.

It didn't work. My uncle Otto's hands came down on my shoulders and I was standing tiptoe on an inch of air.

"You'll wrinkle my jacket, Uncle Otto."

"Harold," he said. "As a lawyer to a client, you owe me more than a quick good-by."

"I didn't take a retainer," I managed to gargle. My shirt collar was beginning to fit very tightly about my neck. I tried to swallow and the top button pinged off.

He reasoned, "Between relatives a retainer is a formality. As a client and as an uncle, you owe me absolute loyalty. And besides, if you do not help me out, I will tie your legs behind your neck and dribble you like a basketball."

Well, as a lawyer, I am always amenable to reason. I said, "I give up. I surrender. You win."

He let me drop.

And then—this is the part that seems most unbelievable to me when I look back at it all—I got an idea.

It was a whale of an idea. A piperoo. The one in a lifetime that everyone gets once in a lifetime.

I didn't tell my uncle Otto the whole thing at the time. I wanted a few days to think about it. But I told him what to do. I told him he would have to go to Washington. It wasn't easy to argue him into it, but, on the other hand, if you know my uncle Otto, there are ways.

I found two ten-dollar bills lurking pitifully in my wallet and gave them to him.

I said, "I'll make out a check for the train fare and you can keep the two tens if it turns out I'm being dishonest with you."

He considered. "A fool to risk twenty dollars for nothing you aren't," he admitted.

He was right, too.

He was back in two days and pronounced the object focused. After all it was on public view. It's in a nitrogen-filled, airtight case, but my uncle Otto said that didn't matter. And back in the laboratory, four hundred miles away, the focusing remained accurate. My uncle Otto assured me of that, too.

I said, "Two things, Uncle Otto, before we do anything."

"What? What? What?" He went on at greater length, "What? What? What? What?"

I gathered he was growing anxious. I said, "Are you sure that if we bring into the present a piece of something out of the past, that piece won't disappear out of the object as it now exists."

My uncle Otto cracked his large knuckles and said, "We are creating new matter, not stealing old. Why else should we enormous energy need?"

I passed on to the second point. "What about my fee?"

You may not believe this, but I hadn't mentioned money till then. My uncle Otto hadn't either, but then, that follows.

His mouth stretched in a bad imitation of an affectionate smile. "A fee?"

"Ten percent of the take," I explained, "is what I'll need."

His jowls drooped, "But how much is the take?"

"Maybe a hundred thousand dollars. That would leave you ninety."

"Ninety thousand—*Himmel!* Then why do we wait?"

He leaped at his machine and in half a minute the space above the dentist's tray was agleam with an image of parchment.

It was covered with neat script, closely spaced, looking like an entry for an old-fashioned penmanship prize. At the bottom of the sheet there were names: one large one and fifty-five small ones.

Funny thing! I choked up. I had seen many reproductions, but this was the real thing. The real Declaration of Independence!

I said, "I'll be damned. You did it."

"And the hundred thousand?" asked my uncle Otto, getting to the point.

Now was the time to explain. "You see, uncle, at the bottom of the document there are signatures. These are the names of great Americans, fathers of their country, whom we all reverence. Anything about them is of interest to all true Americans."

"All right," grumbled my uncle Otto, "I will accompany you by playing the 'Stars and Stripes Forever' on my flute."

I laughed quickly to show that I took that remark as a joke. The alternative to a joke would not bear thinking of. Have you ever heard my uncle Otto playing the "Stars and Stripes Forever" on his flute?

I said, "But one of these signers, from the state of Georgia, died in 1777, the year after he signed the Declaration. He didn't leave much behind him and so authentic examples of his signature are about the most valuable in the world. His name was Button Gwinnett."

"And how does this help us cash in?" asked my uncle Otto, his mind still fixed grimly on the eternal verities of the universe.

"Here," I said, simply, "is an authentic real-life signature of Button Gwinnett, right on the Declaration of Independence."

My uncle Otto was stunned into absolute silence, and to bring absolute silence out of my uncle Otto, he's really got to be stunned!

"I said, "Now you see him right here on the extreme left of the signature space along with the two other signers for Georgia, Lyman Hall and George Walton. You'll notice they crowded their names although there's plenty of room above and below. In fact, the capital 'G' of 'Gwinnett' runs down into practical contact with Hall's name. So we won't try to separate them. We'll get them all. Can you handle that?"

Have you ever seen a bloodhound that looked happy? Well, my uncle Otto managed it.

A spot of brighter light centered about the names of the three Georgian signers.

My uncle Otto said, a little breathlessly, "I have this never tried before."

"What!" I screamed. *Now* he told me.

"It would have too much energy required. I did not wish the University to inquire what was in here going on. But don't worry! My mathematics cannot wrong be."

I prayed silently that his mathematics not wrong were.

The light grew brighter and there was a humming that filled the laboratory with raucous noise. My uncle Otto turned a knob, then another, then a third.

Do you remember the time when all of upper Manhattan and the Bronx were without electricity for twelve hours because of the damndest overload cutoff in the main powerhouse? I won't say we did that, because I am in no mood to be sued for damages. But I will say this. The electricity went off when my uncle Otto turned the third knob.

Inside the lab, all the lights went out and I found myself on the floor with a terrific ringing in my ears. My uncle Otto was sprawled across me.

We worked each other to our feet and my uncle Otto found a flashlight.

He howled his anguish. "Fused. Fused. My machine in ruins is. It has to destruction devoted been."

"But the signatures?" I yelled at him. "Did you get them?"

He stopped in mid-cry. "I haven't looked."

He looked, and I closed my eyes. The disappearance

of a hundred thousand dollars is not an easy thing to watch.

He cried, "Ah, ha!" and I opened my eyes quickly. He had a square of parchment in his hand some two inches on a side. It had three signatures on it and the top one was that of Button Gwinnett.

Now, mind you, the signature was absolutely genuine. It was no fake. There wasn't an atom of fraud about the whole transaction. I want that understood. Lying on my uncle Otto's broad hand was a signature indited with the Georgian hand of Button Gwinnett himself on the authentic parchment of the honest-to-God, real-life Declaration of Independence.

It was decided that my uncle Otto would travel down to Washington with the parchment scrap. I was unsatisfactory for the purpose. I was a lawyer. I would be expected to know too much. He was merely a scientific genius, and wasn't expected to know anything. Besides, who could suspect Dr. Otto Schemmelmayer of anything but the most transparent honesty.

We spent a week arranging our story. I bought a book for the occasion, an old history of colonial Georgia, in a secondhand shop. My uncle Otto was to take it with him and claim he had found a document among its leaves; a letter to the Continental Congress in the name of the State of Georgia. He had shrugged his shoulders at it and held it out over a Bunsen flame. Why should a physicist be interested in letters? Then he became aware of the peculiar odor it gave off as it burned and the slowness with which it was consumed. He beat out the flames but saved only the piece with the signatures. He looked at it and the name "Button Gwinnett" had stirred a slight fiber of memory.

He had the story cold. I burnt the edges of the parchment so that the lowest name, that of George Walton, was slightly singed.

"It will make it more realistic," I explained. "Of course, a signature, without a letter above it, loses value, but here we have three signatures, all signers."

My uncle Otto was thoughtful. "And if they compare the signatures with those on the Declaration and notice it is all even microscopically the same, won't they fraud suspect?"

"Certainly. But what can they do? The parchment is authentic. The ink is authentic. The signatures are authentic. They'll have to concede that. No matter how they suspect something queer they can't prove anything. Can they conceive reaching through time for it. In fact, I hope they do try to make a fuss about it. The publicity will boost the price."

The last phrase made my uncle Otto laugh.

The next day he took the train to Washington with visions of flutes in his head, long flutes, short flutes, bass flutes, flute tremolos, massive flutes, micro-flutes, flutes for the individual and flutes for the orchestra. A world of flutes for mind-drawn music.

"Remember," his last words were, "the machine I have no money to rebuild. This must work."

And I said, "Uncle Otto, it can't miss."

Ha!

He was back in a week. I had made long-distance calls each day and each day he told me they were investigating.

Investigating.

Well, wouldn't you investigate? But what good would it do them?

I was at the station waiting for him. He was expressionless. I didn't dare ask anything in public. I wanted to say, "Well, yes or no?" but I thought, let *him* speak.

I took him to my office. I offered him a cigar and a drink. I hid my hands under the desk but that only made the desk shake, too, so I put them in my pocket and shook all over.

He said, "They investigated."

"Sure! I told you they would. Ha, ha, ha! Ha, ha?"

My uncle Otto took a slow drag at the cigar. He said, "The man at the Bureau of Documents came to me and said, 'Professor Schemmelmayer,' he said, 'you are the victim of a clever fraud.' I said, 'So? And how can it a fraud be? The signature a forgery is?' So he answered, 'It certainly doesn't look like a forgery, but it must be!' 'And why must it be?' I asked."

My uncle Otto put down his cigar, put down his drink and leaned across the desk toward me. He had me so in suspense, I actually leaned forward toward him, so in a way I deserved everything I got.

"Exactly," I babbled, "why must it be? They can't prove a thing wrong with it, because it's genuine. Why must it be a fraud, eh? Why?"

My uncle Otto's voice was terrifyingly sweet. He said, "We got the parchment from the past?"

"Yes. Yes. You know we did."

"Well in the past."

"Over a hundred fifty years in the past. You said—"

"And a hundred fifty years ago the parchment on which the Declaration of Independence was written pretty new was. No?"

I was beginning to get it, but not fast enough.

My uncle Otto's voice switched gears and became a dull, throbbing roar, "and if Button Gwinnett in 1777 died, you Godforsaken, dungheaded lump, how can an authentic signature of his be on a new piece of parchment found?"

After that it was just a case of the whole world rushing backward and forward about me.

I expect to be on my feet soon. I still ache, but the doctors tell me no bones were broken.

Still, he didn't have to make me swallow the parchment.

THE DEEP DOWN DRAGON

Judith Merril

Psychotherapy today undoubtedly is a valuable tool for ego reinforcement, confidence-building, and all that. But what of its uses from here on out? Judith Merril has done some thinking about it, and when you consider the sort of problems that must be faced and coped with on the far frontiers of our tomorrows, you will see why her curious sort of transistorized psychodrama might make excellent sense in some not too distant era of planet colonizing.

THE GIRL'S ONE DUTY WAS TO LOOK—AND UNDERstand:

White flatness of the wide wall dissolved into mist as the room dimmed. Then whiteness itself broke apart, from all-color to each component.

Pinpoints of brightness swirled and coalesced into new patterns of color and shape. Pinks and yellows here. Silver, blue, black there. Brown, gray, green. Rainbow stripes.

First flat, like a painted scene, then deepening to its own kind of reality, the scene glowed in the center of nothingness where the wall had been before.

The scene had been exactly the same before, she remembered. There was the strangely clear-air atmosphere, thin and sharp. The sketched-in effect of the background —hills, oddly shaped? A domed structure closer?— was simply a matter of her focused attention, not distance haze. Through this transparent air detailed vision would be possible at a far distance. And the background hills were far; for the moment, however, they were only background.

What counted was front-center, bright-colored . . . as real as when she had seen it the first time for herself.

The three footprints. The shoe. The square of cloth. The three bushes. In color, focus and meaning they were identical. Her own shoe, with the silly spike heel and lacy strap unfastened, was lying where it dropped on the pink-hued sand, alongside the alien prints. The first time she had not known why, exactly, the prints were "alien." Now she saw it was the shoe that accomplished the effect. Plenty of three-toed things left prints in sand, but nothing exactly the length of her own foot was tripartite.

Nothing on Earth.

It was the same thing with the brown-gray-green thorn bushes . . . planted, she suddenly realized, by some insane gardener, to landscape that circular blockhouse thing in the background! Or maybe not so insane. Nowhere else in sight was there a growing or green thing at all. Poor green was better than none. Spikes, spines and thorns did grow. They were alive, if still—alien? Why? Of course, the same thing. The patterned robe. A square of cloth, from the same bolt from which she had made the robe, only last week, hung impaled on the farthest bush.

Farthest? Nearest! Nearest to the door of the house, from which the strange footprints curved down and off-scene.

Half the wall was filled now. Inch by slow fraction of inch the scene widened. She sat forward, breathing almost not at all, tensed with knowing the next print, or the one beyond it, would contain the print-maker, the—alien.

Alien? What an odd thought! That was the second —the third?—time she'd thought it. She did not remember the thought from the first seeing of the same scene. "Strange," maybe. "Unknown." Not "alien."

Odd. . . . Odder still, as her eyes went unwillingly from the forming print at the far edge of the scene, she saw her own sandal alongside the trail, silly spike heel and lacy strap, still fastened as it had been on her foot. . . .

That wasn't just odd. It was wrong! And the torn strip of fabric ripped from her robe by the thornbush—

"That's not how it was! That's not the way it went," she thought, and the scene faded out.

The light brightened in the room as the wall came back to normality, and she realized that she had not just thought it, but spoken aloud.

"This is *his,* remember?" Gordon was smiling. "Only the very first frame is identical. It starts branching off right away. The colors, for instance?"

Ruth thought back and of course he was right. *Hers* had been much yellower. Pink sand was absurd.

She laughed out loud, at the absurdity of thinking anything in the projection absurd. Then she explained. "Pink sand. I was thinking how silly that was, and then I remembered that *mine* had little pink clouds floating over my pure yellow desert! Why on Earth do you think he'd have pink sand, though?"

Gordon smiled again as she realized how her own question had answered itself. ". . . on Earth . . ." she had said. Of course. Why should it be Earth at all?

With the questioning thought came concern. Why had *hers* been on Earth? Did that mean . . . ? Were they showing her Charles's sequence just to explain, in the kindest way, why she failed?

She wouldn't finish the thoughts, even in her own head. But Gordon was chuckling quietly as he watched her. Of course he knew what had been crossing her—face, she decided, as well as her mind! Other people had been through this whole thing before. Half of them must have gone through the same thoughts.

Half of them would have been worried . . . and how many of them had good cause to be?

"Relax, Ruth," he said warmly. "You haven't failed or passed yet. There's a lot more to it than the sequence. But I can tell you that it makes no difference where you make the setting, or when. At least—" he frowned faintly, and she knew it was impatience with his own imprecision in a vital communication. "At least, it makes no more difference—and no less—than your choice of colors or textures. A good bit less difference than clothing, for instance."

She looked at him gratefully.

"All right," she said. "I'll try to forget my own sequence."

"The best way is just to let yourself go, as completely as you can. There's no harm in being aware of the difference, just so you aren't contrasting. It won't rationalize. But you don't have to stop being you to be *him* for a while, you know." He smiled again.

She nodded and grinned. Some things did not have to be verbalized.

She shivered and settled back, ready to watch—to feel, to know, be, exist—in *his* mind and body.

Gordon didn't say any more. The room dimmed again, and once more the misting wall focused the scene.

When it had covered the wall, Ruth had forgotten that there was a wall there at all. Or that she was herself.

More completely than ever before, or again (unless and until they fused to a new person, their child) she was one with the man who had made her his own.

The trail of prints led tantalizingly out of sight, curving away behind a low ridge of dunes. Unless the creature, whatever it was, moved much more swiftly than the prints promised, it had been more than a few minutes since it happened.

He looked again at her slipper dropped on its side in the sand. The first glimpse had been more incongruous than anything else. The alienness of the prints contrasted ridiculously with the spiced femininity of Ruth's shoe on the orange-pink sand. Now it seemed to him that the slipper was not dropped but thrown. Or kicked.

Kicked off her foot? For the first time, fear grabbed him, a clawed fist or ice in his belly that turned him to look again at the bright rainbow of stuff draped and torn on the edge of the bush near the door. It was part of the skirt of the new robe, the one she made herself last week, after he noticed the new fabric in the shop window. He had liked it; so she had bought it and fashioned into a garment to please him. Now it hung cruelly torn by spiked thorns. And she—

He tore himself loose from the immobility of anxiety, and ran for the house. Somewhere in back of his mind the question was registered: What shop? Where? The nearest shop was forty million miles away. The question was registered, filed, and ticketed for later thought.

Right now he could not even stop to wonder why he had not noticed the door before. He had to have seen it, when he saw the bush. How do you not notice that the thick door of a pressure hut has been torn loose from its hinges? What kind of wild man speculates about his wife's robe when his home, in which he left her safe and protected, no more then five hours ago, has been violated?

That was a dangerous word. He unthought it, and the red haze cleared away. He could see again.

"Ruth!" he shouted. *"Ruth!"*

No answer. He had known there could not be one. "Ruth!" he kept shouting to thin-aired emptiness inside the dome that had been—five short hours ago—rich with Earth air and scents, sounds and solidity: Ruth.

His gun hung by the door. It had been a joke, he remembered. Pioneers ought to keep a gun by the front door. Damn right they should! He grabbed it as he ran, stride unbroken. He tore off down the trail of the monstrous prints, past the bushes and the sandal, fifty feet more. His lungs were on fire inside him. He would have cursed in his futility, but there was no strength or breath for self-anger; not even, just now, for anger better placed. It was not even possible now to run back to the copter. He had wasted too much strength. He had to drag himself full length along the sand, catching and holding the thin concentration of lichen's oxygen at the sand surface.

Inside the copter, lungs full again, he was coasting along fifteen feet above the prints of horned three-toed feet. He had time enough, and more than he wanted, to think and to question his idiocies. As if he had forgotten where he was. At the first hint of danger they faced he went into shock. As if he were back on Earth, wrapped in her warm air, strong-armed gravity.

Ancestral memories reacting for him in moment of panic? He sneered back at himself for that kind of excuse. The only part that applied was the single word "panic."

He'd panicked. Okay. Don't forget it, boy. But don't let it slow you down, either. File for future reference. Take it out and examine it—later. Meantime, what counts is down there. Right now, you're just a pair of eyes. Later you may get to be arms and legs, a back, if you're lucky a gun. Right now—just eyes. And a computer.

He studied the prints. Two-footed or four? He couldn't decide—and then he saw the pattern, and it was not two or four, but three. Three? Distribute *N* pounds of weight—divided at any time on two of three feet, in prints that each dug in deeper than his own foot would, with his full weight on it. The damn thing was big. *N* pounds was too many.

That didn't make sense. What kind of Thing made prints like that on Mars? On a planet whose largest life-form was adapted to breathing air no more than two feet above ground? And even those didn't cross desert dryness. They lived in the still thinly moist and green valley of old sea bottoms.

The error was obvious. What kind of creature could make a print like a man's, on Mars? Largest *native* life-form, he had meant. So this Thing, with three-toed, three-legged stride, hard-bottomed foot digging too deep in dry sand, had a stride barely more than a man's, one meter maybe from print to print along the trail. It was not long enough to be that heavy. Not man, not Martian. Something else.

Alien.

He tried to think more, but either there were no more clues or the block was too great. Alien, from where? No way to know. What for? Where to? Why? When?

For the moment, the "when" was what counted the most. Whatever and whyever, It had Ruth with It. Was she still alive? Did she have an oxytank?

He tried to remember, aside from the door, what signs of violence, struggle or damage he'd seen in the house. He remembered none. The door, the robe and the slipper. That was all.

Ten minutes after the copter lifted, he came to the first rock outcroppings. For a while after that he could still follow the trail without too much trouble. The creature tended to stay on the sand-drifted crevices between hills. There were still plenty of prints clear enough to be seen from the height he had to maintain to stay clear of the jagged-edged, sand-scoured shapes of bare hilltops. But as the ground level rose, there was less and less sand between rocks to catch imprints, and it was more difficult to peer down and navigate at the same time.

Hard to say if he would be better off on the ground. He could spend hours trying wrong passages, backing and trying again, to search out the scattered prints that made the only trail now. Circling above, he could save time—maybe. Certainly, if he could stay in the air, he kept an advantage he'd never have face to face. (Face to chest? belly? thigh? No way at all to judge relative height.) Not to mention armament, general equipment. Inside the copter, he had the distilled and neatly packaged essence of Earth technology to fight for him. On foot in the hills, with whatever he could carry on his own back—?

It was obvious he had no choice. He had just noticed the time. Twilight would fall fast and dark across him in a half hour or less. Moonless, or as good as moonless, dark would follow short minutes after. The kind of cross-eyed trail-following and peak-hopping he could barely manage in sunlight would then be impossible. Find a place where he could land, then. Now, quickly, while he still could.

The copter dropped, and he found a ledge just firm and wide enough. Charles went methodically through lockers, picking and choosing, till at last he had a pile he thought he could manage, with all the essentials, in one form or other.

Searchlight, rope, hand pickaxe, knife. Pistol-grip torch, which he thought of as a flame thrower. Plain old pistol. Extra airtank. Extra mask. Light warm blanket. Bullets, and gas for the torch. Food concentrates. Two water flasks. He climbed into his heat suit, discarded the blanket, and took her suit instead. He had thought to make a knapsack of the blanket, carrying the rest of the stuff on his back, but that was silly. He had to be able to get at whatever he needed but fast. He got out a package of clip-back hooks and studded his suit with them, hanging himself like a grim Christmas tree inside-out: bright flame-red suit underneath; dull gray, brown and black tanks, handles, tools and weapons dangling all around.

He practiced bending over, sitting, squatting, reaching. He could climb. Okay. The weight was going to be hard to handle, but not impossible.

He added one more airtank, and one more flask. If it all got too heavy, he could leave a trail of his own behind him. At least the stuff would be nearer than here in the copter. He was half out of the hatch when he remembered it: the first aid kit.

He started into the hills with his searchlight flooding the pass at his feet just as darkness collapsed from the sky. He wondered as he stumbled forward and up —following an edge of toe here, of heel there—what else he had not thought to take.

Then the glare of light glinted of redness on rockside. A smear, that's all. Red blood. Not alien. Ruth's!

His gloved hand reached out, and the red smudged.

Still wet? Impossible. In this atmosphere, the seconds they'd need to get out of sight would have dried blood. He looked closely at his gauntlet and moved forward more swiftly, with an exultation of knowledge and purpose he had not dared let himself hold until then. It was not blood. It was spilled red powder. Rouge! She was alive, able to think, to act! She knew he would have to come after, and she was helping by leaving a trail.

He no longer followed footprints. He followed the crimson trail blazes. And wondered how far back they'd started, how much time he might have gained had he abandoned the copter sooner.

No use wondering. No use thinking back. Now it was only the next moment and the next. Was he gaining or losing? This he had to know. He was traveling at his best speed. He went faster. If he lost ground now, he had no chance. The creature was making a path as straight as the hard rockside hills would permit; It knew where It was headed. The Thing could not climb, that was clear, so It would not have gone through the hills without cause. But wherever It was headed, presumably that spot offered It some protection. He had to find It and head It off first.

He found he could go faster still. And then, suddenly, he knew he'd better slow down. It was nothing he'd seen—surely nothing he'd heard. Inside the suit hood, even such sounds as carried through the thin air were stilled. Well, then.

He opened the mask, and he did hear. Maybe it was some vibration of the Thing's tread through the rock that had warned him first. Well, he would not give himself away by the same carelessness. He knew he was very close to It now.

He moved so carefully after that, it seemed agonizingly as if he were once more crawling belly-flat. But he knew he was gaining on them. The Thing was really slow!

He was close. Fool! he thought angrily, as he switched his light off. Creep up on the Thing with a searchlight to flood the scene in advance! The suit had an infra-scope in the visor. He'd have had to close it soon any-how. Five minutes was about maximum breathing with-out a tank; unless you cared to drag yourself flat as he'd done earlier.

The black-light scope came on. Charles paused with a new certainty under an overhang of rock at the next bend. And saw the Thing. And his wife.

He noticed, in a detached and extremely calm way, that what happened next all happened in seconds. Maybe a minute at most. No more, because with the sharp self-awareness exploding inside him, he could count his breaths while he did all the rest.

He inhaled exactly three times—deeply, evenly—while it occurred.

Before the first breath, there was again the ice-fingered grip of fear twisting his gut, squeezing the strength and air out of him.

He inhaled then. And let the retinal image go to his brain, instead of his belly.

It was twice the height of a man, weirdly elongated, the tripod base all ropy tendon, thin and hard. The trunk—thorax?—chest?—well, whatever, shelled or spacesuited or something, but shiny-hard—bulked enor-mous, four feet around surely at the center. At least four. And the Thing's head was turned just far enough to the side so that Charles could see clearly that his wife's face was in the gaping, reptilian maw of the Thing.

It held her under one arm. Her feet kicked at its side. It seemed not to notice. Her arm, with the bright metal cosmetic case clutched in her hand, swung wide, reaching to hit the canyon wall whenever it could. Her head was half into the creature's mouth, firmly held, chin and forehead, by its enormous stretched lips.

While he drew in the first breath, he saw all this clearly and knew he dared not act in such a way as to make It bite down—from fear or anger, made no difference. Charles could not see inside the great maw. What kind of teeth, what harm had been done, what could be done, he did not know . . . and knew he could not risk. He thought through and rejected five separate plans, while his hands found the items he'd need. He drew a new breath, and his legs moved beneath him.

He could not shoot first. And he could not simply follow and learn more about the Thing. Because another image came through from somewhere—the same eyes that watched every move of the Thing? Unlikely, but it had to be—of the gleaming column of metal too close ahead. A Thing-ship. So: no time.

He leaped, knife in hand. Pricked the creature, and jumped back.

It worked, as he'd prayed; no; as he had known, not just hoped or prayed, that it must. The Thing jumped, turned to look—and released his wife's head.

He did not waste effort in looking, but saw anyhow that her face was unharmed. He jumped again, drawing the third breath, and pricked at the arm that held her. She squirmed and pushed, exactly on time, like a part of himself—which she was—and her body was clear of his as he emptied the pistol at Its head.

He reached for the torch.

By that time he could not stop himself. He would have avoided the torch if he could. As it was he thundered at Ruth, above the explosion: "*Down!* Keep down, babe!" And the blue flame of released oxygen missed her head by a foot . . .

He carried her back to the copter with strength he had not believed he could find. Nobody pursued.

She sat up, dazed, as the lights brightened slowly, and the white wall turned serenely opaque. She looked across at Gordon, and her face glowed with pleasure.

"No sillier than mine was," she said, laughing. "Was it?"

"Not at all," Gordon said.

She sat politely, waiting.

Gordon stood up, grinned down at her, and offered

his hand. "I think they must be done in there," he told her, nodding in the direction of the screenwall. "I imagine you'd like . . ." He let it trail off.

"You're a smart old thing, aren't you?" She took the hand and came to her feet. Then, on impulse, astonished at herself, she stood on tiptoe and placed a quick kiss on his cheek. "What's more, you're a doll." She turned and ran, glad but embarrassed.

The door closed behind her. A mirrored door on the opposite wall opened, and a young man entered. Gordon greeted him warmly. "Well—what did you think?" His own enthusiasm was unmistakable.

"Outside of its being a great racket? Do they all react that way?"

"Well, not all. Matter of fact, this pair is practically classical. You don't often get a mesh like this one—you saw hers, didn't you?"

"I don't think so," the other said. "Unless it was one of the bunch you ran for us last night?"

"Could be. She worked out a sort of a junior-size Tyrannosaur. Out of Professor Challenger maybe? Future-past uncertainty, here on Earth. Had it threaten the children, and just when she was about to sacrifice herself to save them, old Charlie showed up in the nick of time to do the slaying."

The other nodded. "It's a fascinating technique," he said. "Damn glad to have this chance to see it work. One thing I don't follow—why do you show them each other's? That's pretty much against basic theory on joint therapy, isn't it?"

Gordon was smiling again. "Well," he said slowly. "This pair didn't really take the runs for therapy." He had a surprise to spring, and he was enjoying it. "You've heard about the new screening technique for colonists? You know the last expedition had only one broken couple and two psychotic collapses, out of fifty-six?"

The younger man whistled. Then he understood. "This is how you're doing it? Let them fantasy their own reactions? Well, hell. Sure! What's surprising is, nobody thought of using it before!"

"Of course not. It was right under our noses," Gordon said.

They both laughed.

"In this case," he added, "we've got everything. His sequence stressed readiness, thoughtful preparation, careful action. You saw that. Hers was strongest on instinct, physical wisdom, that whole set. He was moved to do things he couldn't possibly do—and knows he can't, by the way—in real life, because *she* was in danger. Her stimulus was a threat to home and children. And even then, she made sure he did the actual dragon-slaying job." He flicked a switch. Through the wall, now, they saw Ruth and Charles, standing, holding hands, smiling and squeezing a little. That was all.

The two doctors smiled as the pale-skinned, ninety-five-pound, five-foot product of slum-crowded Earth threw a proud arm around his wife's narrow shoulder, and led her out.

"Doesn't look like much of a dragon-slayer," the younger one said.

"No. But as long as he *is* . . ." He paused, looked the visitor over with care, and said. "You asked about showing them to each other? Ever think how much more therapy there might be for him in knowing she *knows* he can handle a dragon? Or for her, knowing that he really *can?*"

THE KAPPA NU NEXUS

Avram Davidson and Morton Klass

Only one word is needed to introduce this rococo piece of baroque titillation: WOW.

THERE ARE CERTAIN PRINCIPLES WHICH FLOURISH (to use Addison's felicitous phrase) midst the Crash of Matter and the Wrack of Worlds. Facts, we believe we may safely say, are facts. When the supple and suntanned young woman clad in two (or at most three) wisps of an astonishingly non-opaque material walked out of the closet and into the guest bedroom of the Kappa Nu Fraternity House, the goggling and gaping occupant of the bed—and here we take our stand—was young Hank Gordon.

But how *come?* you ask, and with justice and commendable tenseness. Why would he, now the Biggest of the Big Men on Campus, and an experienced (not to say, polished) womanizer, goggle and gape in such a situation? No matter. We affirm that it was to Hank Gordon's imbecile stare of disbelief—and to no one else's—that the young female person responded with a smile of infinite lubricity as she removed from over her left *mamma* a large name-pin reading *Thaïs,* and tossed it in the direction of the closet shelf.

The pin, that is.

It may also come as a shock to learn of the anti-fraternity statements for which Henry Gordon had been noted in school prior to his successful assault upon the College Entrance Boards. The world is scarcely aware at all that it was he who remarked to the other components of the stag line (Hank? In a stag line? Even so.) on the occasion of the Senior Hop, "Frats? Strictly from Oldsville. Besides, y'think I got rocks? I mean, my old man would flip his wig if I asked for more money. Anyway—I mean, like frats? Who needs 'em?"

Thus Henry, pre-college. At other times he had been known to insist that he was going to college to "work hard" (though he did not specify at what, or with what purpose, save it might be to deceive his draft board) and not to "horse around." There are even witnesses to the fact that he accused the entire American fraternity system of being *undemocratic*! We mean, how callow can one get?

Was Voltaire right in saying that the adjective is the enemy of the noun? Properly to understand Hank's inability to make deed jibe with word, we must leave him for the moment struggling to extricate himself from the Kappa Nu guest bedclothes, gazing with wild surmise at the declared sweetheart of wicked Alexandria. Let us go back in time only a few hours, and in space to the bus traversing its customary route between the metropolis (train going no farther) and College Hill.

Here, then, slumped on the seat directly over the rear wheel is Hank Gordon, cynic, iconoclast, freshman-designate. He is no great spectacle—young, callow (see above), as tall as he will ever be, though by no means yet fully formed; dishwater-blond hair, a wide mouth quick to smile, eager, fearful, hopeful, lustful. His clothes? Altogether the wrong sort of clothes. Enough about his clothes.

In short, a young man with all his parts, though as yet some of them, etcetera, etcetera; and full of what are often called "juices."

Note that we are calling him *Hank*. He had left "Henry" at home, along with six suits of ankle-length underwear. In the unlikely circumstance of a fellow bus rider's asking of him if he still held forth against the frats, he would have stammered a stout affirmative. Most of his mind, however, was engaged in rueing the previous evening: a date with a hometown cocktail waitress whose pelvic structure had long enchanted him. But all the waitress had wanted was to sample the charcoal broil at a different bar.

But, now, frats. . . . Hank's position would have not

surprised Professor Eamon De V. Mulcahy of the Psych Department (he of the full-grown taste for full-blown women, who was in the near future to trade a more than passing grade for an introduction to Catherine, she of All the Russias.) Unhesitatingly, E. D. V. Mulcahy would have pronounced Hank's attitude to be a simple defense mechanism: the young man feared he might not be asked to join a fraternity, and in this not very brave manner he thought to defend himself. It may be. Let us not be quick to criticize him. He was very young. We have never been as young as he was.

Then, too, we might with profit turn to the opinions of Professor C. B. Yelg of the Anthro Department on the subject of secret societies (ancient, modern, and primitive) and initiation rites. His rollicking accounts of circumand sub-incision techniques would alone repay us. But time and space, alas, do not permit. To Hank, again.

Into the town bus station, already half-sunk in the torpors of the night, the dirty floors flecked with cigarette butts and scraps of newspapers, the peeling walls engraved with coarse graffiti, steps our man, laden with suitcases. In his mind at this moment are two hopes: secondly, that he find a beautiful female freshman (preferably a sex-fiend) who will give him a lift in her automobile; and firstly, that the men's room in the station will be plainly marked, thus saving him the agony of inquiry.

While these two thoughts, each a messy mixture of spiritual and physical, danced in his head like visions of, shall we say, sugar plums, he became cognizant of a figure standing in front of him and saying something or other with every appearance of affability.

This was the almost life-sized Thorwald ("Swede") Thorwaldson, deputed by the brethren of Kappa Nu to go down to the depot and not return without a cargo of human flesh. Recruiting had been bad, had been bad for years and *years*, and although, the Kappa Nu interpretation of what constituted fraternity material was pathetically liberal, this had nothing helped. (The cleverness of the gambit was something less than needle-sharp. It is hardly necessary to point out that neither Rho Gamma nor Beta

Tau, nor yet Lambda Mu, ever posted scouts at the bus station—and for the late bus, no less—to greet likely freshmen. No man who didn't drive up in his own car was a likely freshman in the eyes of the Big Three.)

But now something like a fresh wind was beginning to blow through the becobwebbed halls of Kappa Nu. One suspects the fine Italian hand of Pietro Di Guglielmo, this year's president.

"I beg your pardon?" asked Hank, introducing dialogue into these pages as he peered at the figure out of travel-gummed eyes, and let his suitcases find their own way to the floor.

"Said, I was wondering if you'd seen Bill Northrup on the bus?"—Thorwald knowing damned well he hadn't, there being no such person.

"Well, I don't—"

"Tall, good-looking fellow, probably with a letter-sweater," said canny Thorwald.

"Gee, I don't *think*—but—"

"You must know him: Big Man On Campus," Thorwald proceeded, cunningly.

"Well, um, I've never even seen the campus. I'm *uh* freshman," admitted Hank, producing before the last word in his embarrassment, a glottal stop of a richness which would have delighted Courtney T. Armbruster, sometime Professer of Chaditic, Cushitic, and Hamito-Semitic Languages. (Here let us interrupt the silken-swift flow of our narrative for a respectful pause in memory of Professor Armbruster. A man may depart this mortal vale in many ways, few of them pleasant. For Courtney T. Armbruster, Kismet decreed that he was to be discovered by a highly volatile wife whilst in flagrant delight with Salomé daughter to Herodias; and how can man die better?) But we are peeping into Volume II again. Our concern should be in Volume I with Thorwald's magnificently simulated astonishment.)

"Really?" the sly Swede exclaimed. "You—a freshman? Why, I certainly would have thought you were an upperclassman!" And to the blushing Gordon he offered his hand and declaimed the Runic syllables of his own name.

This young man, Thor thought, promised well: he had only one head, no visible jerks or twitches, one could gaze at his face without shuddering, and his voice gave no indication of palatal cleavage. In all, superior grist for the decrepit Kappa Nu mill.

"He's not on this bus, he won't be in tonight," said the wily soul-snatcher of the mythical Northrup. "Fixed up a room for him at the Kappa Nu House . . . all for nothing . . ." he mused aloud "Shame. . . . Say!" A thought struck him, he struck his forehead, and almost staggered. "If you're not expected anywhere else, and this late at night it'd be kind of hard for you to find a place—"

"Meant to take an earlier bus," mumbled Gordon.

"—I mean, kind of irregular, but I can fix it up with the guys, I guess." And so he rattled on, securing one of Hank's suitcases and moving toward the door.

"Well, uh, *yuh,*" said Hank, pleased no end at this totally unexpected offer. "Thanks, I mean." Kappa Nu, he was beginning to suspect, gave indication of being so delightfully democratic that he might needs release himself of all rash vows never to join a fraternity.

His victim safely in the car—a stripped-down, souped up Tortoni-Thung belonging to Tom Schmertz, frat brother and idiot scion of Schmertz's Cheese, who could be bullied with only moderate difficulty into make the rod available for lodge business—his victim safely in the car, to repeat and the car on its way, Thor confided a bit of news. "Had a little fire at the frat house last week. Staying now in temporary quarters. Just until."

Such deceit, in the face of the dark-rushing, sweet-scented night, was regrettable, and may now be exposed. The chances of Kappa Nu's then rebuilding any structure larger than a three-hole privy were slightly less than those of the Canarsie Indians getting back Manhattan Island.

"Naming no names," Thor observed, in tones hard and putative, "but it wouldn't surprise *me* . . . certain elements . . . jealous of Kappa Nu. Of course," hastily, "no danger *now*. But when we move back *in*—You know how to use a gun?" he shot at Hank.

"Gosh!" breathed Hank, delightedly. "I mean, well, I used to have this Daisy—"

"Good man!" Thorwald gripped his knee. Then he chuckled. "Of course—I know we can trust *you*—fact is, the liquor fed the flames! Damn, but those bottles were well hid! And not just bottles, haw, the Dean raided us twice, but couldn't find a drop—or a dame!"

Note well our dispassionate fairness. In making this last comment Kappa Nu's enterprising representative was not entirely untruthful. He neglected only to mention that the Dean in question had died still deploring the loss to the nation occasioned by the departure from the political scene of the Whig Party, for which he had regularly voted with youthful enthusiasm. Ah, yes! Though currently devoid of so much as a single lizard, not to speak of lions, Kappa Nu, too, had known a time when Jamshyd gloried and drank deep. The cow in the belfry, the skeleton in the chapel, cane rush, pear-shaped tennis rackets, fringe-topped surreys; and the frat as a body rushing to join the Cadet Corps, hastily formed in '98 to repel the Royal Spanish Fleet from sailing up the Wabash and glutting their vile Iberic lusts upon the local virgins—*Ichabod, Ichabod (or—for we wish to keep nothing from our readers—The glory hath departed).*

Exactly *why* the glory had departed, it would be difficult now to say. Thirty years ago Kappa Nu was still, if not top banana on the Grecian tree, at least respectable. Fifteen years ago, however, saw the damage already done, and its so-called house parties were a scorn and a laughter in every sorority (the College itself being non-co-ed) between Marietta, Ohio, and Muscadine, Iowa. . . . But of all of this, Hank knew but nothing.

Au contraire. Guns . . . liquor . . . dean-led raids . . . woman . . . *women!* Hank was all of a delighted tremble.

"Here we are," said Bring-'Em-Back-Alive Thorwaldson as the Tortoni-Thung snarled to a halt in the weed-choked front yard of the *pro tem.* frat-house. He intercepted young Gordon's gaze of dismayed shock and almost fumbled. "You understand this is not permanent. It's just until. Only just until."

Thus, the background. And now we return to Hank, enmeshed in the patched sheets of the bed in what he still thought of, innocently, as "Bill Northrup's room." (Unbeknownst to our man, B. Northrup, mythical busrider, was presently the subject of impassioned debate in the Kappa Nu conference room on the floor below. President Di Guglielmo proposed that the inconvenient Northrup be disposed of through a sudden onset of Hodgkin's Disease—which he vaguely thought of as being amorous in origin—whereas Thor Thorwaldson, having developed an affection for this creature of his invention, insisted that Northrup be permitted to run off and join the Foreign Legion.) We are now at the very moment when Thaïs makes her entrance, so let us rummage a bit in Hank Gordon's mind.

It had been quite an evening, Hank was telling himself. All the leading figures of Kappa Nu had shaken him by the hand and assured him that they Had A Great Little Fraternity Here, *videlicet* Sam Swack the Baseball Player (not delineated in his precise position as utility outfielder on the third scrub), Prexy Di Guglielmo as chairman and ranking player of the Checkers Club ("Really creamed the Sarah Stillwell Junior College Team!"), the Tom Schmertz of Schmertz's Cheese aforementioned, and other, lesser, luminaries. They had discussed Sports, Liquor, and Women—though not in that order.

Innocent Hank was not, of course, aware that the less presentable members of Kappa Nu (i.e., most of the members) were being carefully screened from his view. As for the fire which burned out the old frat hutch having been of incendiary origin, ha! a likely story. The antique pile, unpainted since the days when Cactus Jack Garner presided over the U. S. Senate, had gone up like a matchhead as a result of defective wiring. The new (or Just Until) longhouse was some distance from the campus, and had been obtained through shenanigans with a local realestatenik which would not bear close scrutiny. Though it had supposedly not been dwelt in for years, the manselike mass was in a rather good shape. Its exterior flaunted the scars inflicted long years ago by a carpenter who had run amuck with a scroll-saw, and its interior was clean enough (though not so clean as it had been before the blood brothers moved in.)

Necessary paint, plaster, and wallpaper were far beyond the slender resources of the local's treasury; national, appealed to for aid, indicated that only the high cost of postage prevented revocation of the local's charter. But a sufficiency of the heads of antlered ungulates, splintered oars, triangular banners bearing strange devices, tarnished loving-cups, genuine imitation Heidelberg beer steins, and notices of athletic victories some ten college generations old, plus group photos of turtle-necked young men, and brightly colored pictures of well endowed young women who—if they existed at all and were not mere lensmen's tricks—ought to have been working for Borden's; a sufficiency of such equipment, we say, had been disposed about the place to give it an air which satisfied Hank's imaginings of what a well-furnished frat house ought to be.

And now the action begins. Thaïs (dark, she was, and looked delicious), you may remember, was smiling lewdly at Hank, Hank was garroting himself with his blanket by way of response. Both we and Hank appear to have too long delayed: the door closes softly behind Thaïs's utterly enchanting haunches.

For yet another moment Hank remained horizontal, reflecting (as it might be academically) that the vision had patently stood in need of neither falsies nor uplifts, nor indeed any such foolish fictions. Then, after first thrashing about and then flinging away blanket and sheet like a finally triumphant Laocoön, he jumped out of bed and in two great leaps bounded to the door. He threw it open and gazed wildly about him.

The hall was empty, unless one be picayune enough to count two frat brothers engaged in conversation on the rickety stair landing down the hall. Sam Swack had just finished doing one of Tom Schmertz's papers, overdue from the previous term, for him; and Tom was laboriously expressing his gratitude and the hope that no suspicion as to authorship would be aroused by the paper's earning more than a C. Sam assured him, heartily, that there was no chance of this.

Both young men looked up as the pajama'd Gordon emerged from the guest room (soon to be his and his alone —well, almost alone—that is, by no means alone, but . . .).

"Did you guys see—?" Hank paused in mid-question. Even in his present fevered state he was capable of a certain minimal amount of ratiocination. An Einstein he was not, but against the Tom Schmertz's of the world Hank Gordon at least flickered if he did not shine. It now occurred to him that if they had seen Thaïs they would scarcely be sitting there discussing grades, and if they had *not* seen her, no matter how carefully he construed his question it stood a good chance of getting a bad response.

"Uh, *yuk,*" he concluded, with an involuntary and rather nicely Hottentotish click, and withdrew into his bedroom. He closed the door, though not swiftly enough to avoid hearing Sam Swacks exasperated: "One guy, only, to rush—and he turns out to be a sleepwalker! Whatta creepjoint!"

Blushing quietly, Hank walked back to his bed, slowly and automatically wiped off the sole of each foot against the opposite pajama leg, and pensively clambered in.

In a second he was out again. Had he been Lars Porsena, by the nine gods he would have sworn that he *had* seen an attractive and underdressed young woman saunter out of his closet and through his bedroom door. Being Hank, however, and not Clusium's leading warlord, he could only burble inarticulately, but the point was still the same. In the air of his room there seemed to linger a scent which he thought might be musk. The word *patchouli* glided into Hank's mind, banked, and was gone as he was in the very act of asking himself whether it weren't a game one played with dice.

Walking, oh, ever so cautiously to the closet, he paused, then threw wide the door. Darkness there, and nothing more. He pulled the light cord and was rewarded by the sight of a cross-bar holding four wire-hangers, on one of which was draped his favorite and only drip-dry shirt. Crumpled and forgotten in the corner lay an athletic supporter from which the bloom had long since departed.

Hank reached up and moved a hand around the surface of the closet shelf. He harvested two dead cockroaches and a splinter, but not the slightest trace of a large name-pin carrying the word *Thaïs.*

He tapped the walls, pulled the cross-bar, examined the floor for signs of a trapdoor. He backed out, closing the door, and sat heavily on the bed.

"She must be one of those 'dames' Thorwald was talking about: hidden so the Dean couldn't find her," himself told himself, but not with what you could call real confidence.

Bing! the closet door, and out came *another* member of the female persuasion to meet without flinching Hank's instant exhibition of exophthalmia, or popeyes. She was perhaps a trifle more mature than the first visitor, but undeniably unstaled and distinctly unwithered. Her eyelids were painted blue and her palms were tinted with henna. Upon the bit of flimsy fabric which emphasized, rather than concealed, her bosom, was a large name-pin reading *Cleopatra.* This she removed, the action revealing to astonished Hank two small but distinct areas on which he had never till this moment realized that rouge might be applied, and —an imitation of her predecessor—tossed the button back on the closet shelf.

"Heyyy!" cried our eager, impetuous Hank Gordon, leaping still again to his feet and so blundering forward like a dim-sighted giraffe that he bumped boorishly into the lady as she paced her stately way across the floor on tiny, perfectly formed feet.

"Podden *me!*" said she, with a regal hauteur that became her well, and pattered away and out the door with all the imperiousness of a true daughter of a hundred belted Ptolemies.

This time Hank knew better than to follow. He ran to attack the closet instead, but once again it yielded nothing. "It could be part of the fraternity initiation," he whispered, awed at the thought, as even Professor Yelg might be.

Hank sat on the by now well-warmed side of the bed. And as he stared into the open closet he saw, to his infinite consternation, the figure of another woman materialize therein, her charms, alas! to an extent covered by a dress of antique cut; our man was already becoming a connoisseur of appartitions (which was only fair, since he had already done more business in this field than the average member of the Psychic Research Society). Haply and happily, however, the newcomer found it necessary to bend over to adjust her garter, thus revealing the advantages inherent in a neckline so low as to be only a moderately high waistline. What red-blooded American boy would have had the ingratitude to avert his eyes? Just so. Not Hank, either.

Holding up her voluminous skirts and swaying slightly from side to side so that her elaborate headdress trembled a bit, she headed for the door as if she had done this a hundred times before. Hank held out a hand and said, "Uhnk." She ignored this barbaric monosyllable—reminiscent though it is to students of classical Algonkian (who shudder, to a man, at the common mistransliteration: "Ugh")—and evaded his touch, with a comment he (owing to a curious ringing in his ears) did not clearly comprehend. He was able to note only that it had contained the barest hint of a Gallic accent; and *pouf!* she was gone.

The button on *her* bosom had read, *Mme. Pompadour.*

Thrilled almost beyond his power of containment, baffled and vexed, excited and unfulfilled, Hank stood in the middle of the room, wondering *What the hell?* to beat the band. When he reflected on the beauty of the ladies he had just seen, his heart beat fast. But as he considered the mystery of it all, plus his youth and inexperience, he fell a prey to every variety of despair.

Reader, if you have smiles, prepare to exhibit them now. Hank is at the very nadir; we have nowhere to go but up. At this very moment the door opened—*not* the closet door: no. The *bedroom* door—and in galloped a well-developed cutie dressed in still another variety of ancient mode. On one arm she held a basket of oranges, and so sudden was her entrance that she had made it to the closet door, plucked up from the shelf a button labeled *Nell Gwynn,* and pinned it to her half-laced upper torso before Hank was able to switch on the ignition.

Then, accumulated repressions bursting like overfilled balloons, H. Gordon leaped between Nell and the cross-bar and spread his arms wide. "You aren't going in—not until you tell me what this is all about!"

Nell gave an enchanting little giggle. "Ow, come awn, Ducks," she protested, pushing with her free hand against his chest—or, conceivably, just a bit below it. As Hank—whose ticklishness had been a byword on the local basketball circuit—guffawed and involuntarily relaxed his stance, she lowered her head and charged beneath his left armpit. Instinctively, he seized her by the panniers and swung her about.

The session of free-style wrestling which ensued was not disagreeable to Hank, and Nell's own small squeals of laughter hinted at least a modicum of amusement on her part.

"Coo, my horanges!" she exclaimed at last. "You 'aven't arf spilled them!"

Reluctantly, Hank returned to the matter at issue. "Say, listen here," he said, with that keen mastery of repartee which characterizes the youth of this great republic. There was an annoyed and unappreciative cough, such as could have proceeded only from a throat masculine (lady Soviet athletes perhaps excepted), and, by its sound, at the closet door. Not letting go for a second of the little orange-girl's hand, Hank swiveled.

The man who stepped into his field of vision was undeniably looking harassed. But it was not that which caused Hank's lower jaw to dangle, his brows to rise. Not to keep the facts stored up in our bosoms, the new visitor was wearing a plaid breechclout, heavy side-whiskers, and a thick fur boa. Hank, into whose mind had darted, at the first cough, thoughts of janitors and house detectives and deans, was forced to reconsider. Dark though the ways of deans may be, and equally obscure the *mores* of janitors and house-dicks, young Gordon was reasonably certain that none of these classes were represented in his room. Which did not, of course, bring him any closer to the category which *was* represented. Reader, let us steal a march on our man, Gordon. The man in the quasi-Caledonian Bikini was a temporal expediter.

He was also pointing a beringed finger. "What by Hell goes on here?" he demanded, voice thundering from massy chest.

" 'Ello, hAngstrom," Nell greeted. "Harsk *'im—*" indicating Hank.

Vainly trying to reassure himself that the visitor was doubtless musclebound, Hank gathered himself for battle behind a thrust-out chin and lower lip. After all there had been Gordons at Drummossie Moor (known to the Sassenachs as Culloden—and may the sod rest heavy on the heavy Duke of Cumberland.) "It's *my* room," said this heir of the lawless and turbulent gillies of Gight, with no little truculence—an effect slightly impaired by his next words: "Well, *isn't* it?" ending in a squeak.

Breechclout tugged at a side-whisker. "True," he conceded; adding, with the air of one quoting, "Occupancing is nine *snurgs*—as indefinite-you said. Have saying? Unperfect tense?" He waved an impatient and glittering hand at synthetic niceties and pushed on. "Still, *we* have were first here. Previous tenantry, and all thus."

The shredded English had Hank gaping again, then a dim light seemed to flicker and he headed for it like a glowworm in sore need of refueling.

"You a Kappa Nu?" he asked, eagerly. It was all so clear to him so suddenly. His frat-brothers-to-be. What a bunch of cards!

Breechclout scowled, and with a large hand pulled his fur-piece tight. Hank noted that the head on it had three eyes. Somewhere in the far reaches of his mind a feverish censor promptly disposed of the notation. "I!" said Fur Boa, loudly. "Me, that are, is Angstrom IV—latelish upleveled from III—and none of your barbaric epithets!" He thrust his ring-encrusted fist under Hank's nose. "See?

Saw? Pleasure to count? Me, that are, is Expediter for M*ark*-TIME, Incorporealated."

Hank took a step back, colliding with Nell, who at once pinched him and guffawed at his leap. All he could find to say was, "How, how about that?"

Angstrom IV—for so, it would seem, he of breechclout and fur boa was officially known—clutched Hank by the arm and led him gently to the bed; Nell, to whom a bed was as the magnetic pole to a lodestone, followed. "I have-will to explain how. But first. Utter promisory. Hele, conceal, and never more reveal. Honor word?"

Gulping somewhat, Hank held up three fingers. "Honor word," he said.

Happily, we are not bound by H. Gordon's oath. Unhappily, we are as birdlimed as you are by Angstrom's garbled grammar. If we have it right, what emerged from his brief lecture was the stuff of dreams itself. He was, he instructed Hank, from the year 831 S.M.—roughly 1,200 years from our time, a closer approximation being difficult owing to the Great Timequake—and he expedited diligently for MARK-TIME, Incorporealated, an inter-eon freight and messenger service chartered under the *nids* of the Freemanship of Delaware. The Ninth Century, S.M., it would appear, is going to be an exciting and richly rewarding time to be alive in, if the fact that MARK-TIME was (will be) under contract to PLANETARY PANDERERS, Limitless, is any criterion.

"The motto of PP, me young cock-sparrer," interjected Little Nell, deftly peeling an orange and offering it to Hank, "is, 'Femyles, hany plyce, hany time.' *hAnd* the motto of hold hAngstrom's company is, 'We got the right time.' One 'and washes the hother, see-wot-I-means?" she demanded, and, with a pretty trill of laughter, dug her pretty elbow into Hank's ribs. The skinless citrus fell from his fingers and landed on the floor with a soggy plunk.

"Uh, *yuh!*" said Hank. "I mean—*no!* You mean, these —uh—*pan*derers supply famous beauties to the future from the past? And you really *are* Nell Gwynn, and you're a . . . a . . . that is—" He tried to swallow, it turned into a gulp which almost choked him.

"Ow, yus," said the orange girl, complacently. "Read abaht me in the books, 'ave you? 'Ow the mob thought hI was the King's French doxie, and hI said 'Prithee, good people, hI'm 'is Protestant 'ore,' hand all that clobber." She pushed a stray wisp of hair at the back of her neck, and in a tone of infinite boredom added, "No popery.'"

Hank ran a distracted hand over his face. That this was no mere jape or masquerade, he was by now well-convinced: Had he not *seen* them appear from—and vanish into—apparently nothing? Still . . . "But—you, and all the others—the women and Angstrom IV—were you born in the past, or in the future?"

Nell clapped her hands and kicked her feet in the air. "Stone the crows, Duckie—hyn't you the flipping limit? We was born in *bofe,* hof course! Forgot your *Gundslag's Laws of Time Paradox,* didn't you, love?" She waggled a playful finger under his eagerly twitching nose. "The Union mykes it required reading—" She sat up, suddenly, putting her finger in her rosebud mouth. "Ow! hI *was* forgetting, wasn't hI? You're not *hin* the Union, cockie—"

"No!" burst out Angstrom IV, jumping to his feet, allowing his boa to flap free in this excitement, "But *you* (vocative positively) are in Union, so getting to work? You wish to be wharfed. Piered?" He seemed suddenly uncertain. "Jettied?"

Nell curled her lips at him in splendid Restoration disdain. "Stow it, myte!" she tapped the big insigne on her bosom with triumph. "Long's the Union button's on, hofficially, hI *ham* working. Read the contract. hAnd pippin, 'ere," thumb over her half-bare shoulder (milky white, it was, and void of spots) into Hank's face; *"e's* the gallant wot 'eld me hup. So you can just dock'*im,* see?"

Angstrom danced wildly on one leg, for so urgent was his desire to express himself that he required the aid of both hands and one foot.

"But you admits he is not *in* Union! Time wastes, midwhile—Charlie Two is making clamor for you, and if we don't clear this nexus, Mary Antonetta will got her head cat—cat? cut—for true-blue this time around. The

San Kulaks—" he gabbled, neatly confusing two (or perhaps even three) Revolutions in his haste.

Miss Sunkist of 1665 smoothed her skirts complacently, and twitched her panniered hips. "Now you just leave Charlie to me, hAngstrom," she smiled.

"And if he refuses to give us his head, ah, what?"

Hank, who had picked up some motes of European History on the run between basketball and bathing, said, with a touch of proud severity, "Now, just hold on. It was Charles the *First* whose head was cut off, not—"

But Angstrom waved away this erudition impatiently. "Customer is Arcturus Territory with collective of King Charles's heads. Don't make troubles! Supposed you think the librarian of Alexandria was will burned up, eh. Business, little shot, business: I of the four rings expediting into your past, so—pleasure to get out of way."

Nellie winked. Lust and rage struggled, in Hank, for mastery. The choleric Celtic chromosomes, for the instant, won. He doubled his fists. "Whaddaya mean, 'Get out of way'?" he shrieked. *"It's my room!"*

The man in the plaid breechclout calmed at once, and looked sly. "Cannot, you knew," he whispered, conspiratorially, with a finger alongside his nose. "Cannot, that be, go elsewhere. This room, from closet to door, is best nexus between past-future and future-past to be found. Quick, direct, economicful. Also, safe. Copper-bobbies cannot dast disturb this nexus—see case of Ginsbury vs Oligarcny. We go elsewhere and get clapped in vile durance; also, expensic. Further—" He looked at Hank in mild reproach. "—it *were* our room both before and after it were *your* room."

Hank considered this surprise bit of intelligence. "You mean, this room—the house?—used to belong to one of your agents before the frat got it? Well, where *is* he?"

Angstrom sighed, with evident embarrassment. "This one, myself," he said, "has the greatest respectful to all religionry—Brotherness Bond, Thou Art, Gourmandizing, All One, and even have best friend member Sons of Pincus—but moderating in all things, not? We pat—putted:—

Fletchworth IV here, and he has offed to become a placed minister of the Auld Licht Kirk in Echlefauchen, Scotia, of your 1823! Damn chap has gone native!"

Nellie, on the bed, had begun to pout. Though not a beauty, Hank (her expression seemed to say) certainly promised well after all those gouty old kings and flatulent magnates; but if all he was going to do was *talk*, well . . . Then the pout gave away to smile which was almost a grin, and she leaped to her feet, letting fall her fruit. "hI've gottit!" she shrilled. "Wot abaht myking 'im—" she gestured at Hank—the nexus hagent?"

The temporal expediter pulled at a side whisker thoughtfully. "Mmmm—forhaps," he said, half-conceding, half-dubious. "But with what we paid? No good to he, Arcurian script, Galactic gumpkins, Delaware nidsdollars . . ."

Nell cast a modest glance downward at the basket of tumbled navels. "Well, naow . . . there's *me* . . . there's the hother gels . . ." She looked up, winked at Hank, whose eyes were getting rounder and rounder and rounder. "We *do* 'ave to pass through 'is room to 'n' from work, carn't avoid that: the nexus. Well, I meantersay—honly polite to stop and natter a bit wif the tenant, wot?"

"Well, and so?" Angie was earnestly considering. "PP Company warrantees the merchandise—"

A loud and irritated pounding at the door interrupted the three of them. It had escaped all their minds that they were not alone in the house, and an annoyed and puzzled committee was now demanding admittance.

"Either he goes or I go!" Sam Swack was heard threatening. "It'd better to have no pledge at all than a sleepwalker who talks to himself a whole damn night—and in three different voices, too!"

"Come on, Gordon!" Thorwald shouted. "Open wide this pearly gate!"

And then it was that inspiration of a rare and radiant sort came to Hank Gordon. "Just a minute, guys!" he yelled, doorwards. He clutched at Angstrom IV's boa.

"What about the rest of the fraternity?" he demanded, in urgent whisper. "I means, can I let *them* in on The Deal? I mean, it's *my* room, but it's *their* house—

The noise at the door subsided to a low, spasmodic thumping. Angstrom IV smoothed his fur boa. He consulted his earring watch and listened to it announce the hour and minute in four spatial and four temporal terms. Finally, he capitulated. After all, the business of an expediter is to expedite; Coolidge could have agreed to that.

"All rights," he mumbled. "Girls to visit boys as they are passes through nexus. And we shall make it part of portage and portal pay, so no charge. *But!*" He shook a ringed finger at Hank. "Nobodies else learns where and how and which and whether. Honor word?"

"Honor word," whispered Hank, exchanging a long look with Our Nell. And it is here that we shall leave him.

True enough, because of this brief transaction, the entire football team was to become pledged to Kappa Nu in the course of a single spectacular day and night—and would go on to achieve such fabulous upset victories over Pershing Military Academy, Lake Hopatcong Teacher's Normal, Mizpah Baptist, and Lubavitcher Rabbinical, as very shortly resulted in their being invited to play in a far superior conference. After that the Big 3 was nothing, and Kappa Nu everything. Soon there would be no happier, healthier, or more popular Big Man On Campus (and expert on Restoration Drama)—beloved of student, faculty member, and even trustee—than Hank Gordon; and as a result of endeavors to be made on his behalf by various Kappa Nu Old Grads anxious to participate in certain undergraduate extracurricular activities, he will be tendered lucrative offers of postgraduation employment by our largest corporations.

But all this lies, narrationwise, in the not-as-yet, and will not detain us now. Better far to take leave of Hank as he strides towards the reverberating door, a light of pure joy in his heart and eyes, and news—such news—all of a tremble on his lips. He opens the door . . .

IDIOT SOLVANT

Gordon R. Dickson

What could be worse than an adolescent Superman? A grown-up one, perhaps; but we will never know from this story. All we can do is imagine. And to tell you the truth, I think that the grown-up guy that Art may become will be quite wonderful. Maybe he will even be good enough to Save the World, which, at the time of writing this note, seemed to be in need of saving. Of course, supermen develop more slowly than men, so that Art, even though well on in his peculiar college career, is still really just an emotional teen-ager as this story opens.

THE AFTERNOON SUN, SHOOTING THE GAP OF THE missing slat in the Venetian blind on the window of Art Willoughby's small rented room, splashed fair in Art's eyes, blinding him.

"Blast!" muttered Art. "Got to do something about that sun."

He flipped one long, lean hand up as an eyeshield and leaned forward once more over the University newssheet, unaware that he had reacted with his usual gesture and litany to the sun in his eyes. His mouth watered. He spread out his sharp elbows on the experiment-scarred surface of his desk and reread the ad.

Volunteers for medical research testing. $1.60 hr., rm., board. Dr. Henry Rapp, Room 432, A Bldg., University Hospitals.

"Board—" echoed Art aloud, once more unaware he had spoken. He licked his lips hungrily. *Food,* he thought. Plus wages. And hospital food was suposed to be good. If they would just let him have all he wanted . . .

Of course, it would be worth it for the $1.60 an hour alone.

"I'll be sensible," thought Art. "I'll put it in the bank and just draw out what I need. Let's see—one week's work, say—seven times twenty-four times sixteen. Two-six-eight-eight—to the tenth. Two hundred sixty-eight dollars and eighty cents. . . ."

That much would support him for—mentally, he totted up his daily expenses. Ordinary expenses, that was. Room, a dollar-fifty. One-and-a-half-pound loaf of day old bread at half price—thirteen cents. Half a pound of peanut butter, at ninety-eight cents for the three-pound economy-size jar—seventeen cents roughly. One all-purpose vitamin capsule—ten cents. Half a head of cabbage, or whatever was in season and cheap—approximately twelve cents. Total, for shelter with all utilities paid and a change of sheets on the bed once a week, plus thirty-two hundred calories a day—two dollars and two cents.

Two dollars and two cents. Art sighed. Sixty dollars and sixty cents a month for mere existence. It was heartbreaking. When sixty dollars would buy a fine double magnum of imported champagne at a half a dozen of the better restaurants in town, or a 1954 used set of the *Encyclopedia Britannica,* or the parts from a mail-order house so that he could build himself a little ocean-hopper shortwave receiver so that he could tune in on foreign-language broadcasts and practice understanding German, French, and Italian.

Art sighed. He had long ago come to the conclusion that, since the two billion other people in the world could not very well all be out of step at the same time, it was probably he who was the odd one. Nowadays he no longer tried to fight the situation, but let himself reel uncertainly through life, sustained by the vague, persistent conviction that somewhere, somehow, in some strange fashion destiny would eventually be bound to call on him to have a profound effect on his fellowmen.

It was a good twenty-minute walk to the university. Art scrambled lankily to his feet, snatched an ancient leather jacket off the hook holding his bagpipes, put his slide rule up on top of the poetry anthologies in the bookcase so he would know where to find it again—that being the most unlikely place, Q.E.D.—turned off his miniature electric furnace in which he had been casting up a gold pawn for his chess set, left some bread and peanut butter for his pet racoon, now asleep in the wastebasket, and hurried off, closing the door.

". . . There's one more," said Margie Hansen, Dr. Hank Rapp's lab assistant. She hesitated. "I think you better see him." Hank looked up from his desk, surprised. He was a short, cheerful, tough-faced man in his late thirties.

"Why?" he said. "Some difficulties? Don't sign him up if you don't want to."

"No. No. . . . I just think maybe you better talk to him. He passed the physical all right. It's just . . . well, you have a look at him."

"I don't get it," said Hank. "But send him in."

She opened the door behind her and leaned out through it.

"Mr. Willoughby, will you come in now?" She stood aside and Art entered. "This is Dr. Rapp, Mr. Willoughby. Doctor, this is Art Willoughby." She went out rather hastily, closing the door behind her.

"Sit down," said Hank, automatically. Art sat down; and Hank blinked a little at his visitor. The young man sitting opposite him resembled nothing so much as an unbearded Abe Lincoln. A *thin* unbearded Abe Lincoln, if it was possible to imagine our sixteenth president as being some thirty pounds lighter than he actually had been.

"*Are* you a student at the University here?" asked

Hank, staring at the decrepit leather jacket.

"Well, yes," said Art, hoping the other would not ask him what college he was in. He had been in six of them, from Theater Arts to Engineering. His record in each was quite honorable. There was nothing to be ashamed of—it was just always a little bit difficult to explain.

"Well—" said Hank. He saw now why Margie had hesitated. But if the man was in good enough physical shape, there was no reason to refuse him. Hank made up his mind. "Has the purpose of this test been explained to you?"

"You're testing a new sort of stay-awake pill, aren't you?" said Art. "Your nurse told me all about it."

"Lab assistant," corrected Hank automatically. "There's no reason you can think of yourself, is there, why you shouldn't be one of the volunteers?"

"Well, no. I . . . I don't usually sleep much," said Art, painfully.

"That's no barrier." Hank smiled. "We'll just keep you awake until you get tired. How much do you sleep?" he asked, to put the younger man at his ease at least a little.

"Oh . . . six or seven hours."

"That's a little less than average. Nothing to get in our way . . . why, what's wrong?" said Hank, sitting up suddenly; for Art was literally struggling with his conscience, and his Abe Lincoln face was twisted unhappily.

"A . . . a week," blurted Art.

"A week! Are you—" Hank broke off, took a good look at his visitor and decided he was not kidding. Or at least, believed himself he was not kidding. "You mean, less than an hour a night?"

"Well, I usually wait to the end of the week—Sunday morning's a good time. Everybody else is sleeping then, anyway. I get it over all at once—" Art leaned forward and put both his long hands on Hank's desk, pleadingly. "But can't you test me anyway, doctor? I need this job. Really, I'm desperate. If you could use me as a control, or something—"

"Don't worry," said Hank, grimly. "You've got the job. In fact if what you say is true, you've got more of a job than the rest of the volunteers. This is something we're all going to want to see!"

"Well," said Hank, ten days later. "Willoughby surely wasn't kidding."

Hank was talking to Dr. Arlie Bohn, of the department of psychology. Arlie matched Hank's short height, but outdid him otherwise to the tune of some fifty pounds and fifteen years. They were sitting in Hank's office, smoking cigarettes over the remains of their bag lunches.

"You don't think so?" said Arlie, lifting blond eyebrows toward his half-bare, round skull.

"Arlie! Ten days!"

"And no hallucinations?"

"None."

"Thinks his nurses are out to poison him? Doesn't trust the floor janitor?"

"No. No. No!"

Arlie blew out a fat wad of smoke.

"I don't believe it," he announced.

"I beg your pardon!"

"Oh—not you, Hank. No insults intended. But this boy of yours is running some kind of a con. Sneaking some sort of stimulant when you aren't looking."

"Why would he do that? We'd be glad to give him all the stimulants he wants. He won't take them. And even if he was sneaking something—ten days, Arlie! Ten days and he looks as if he just got up after a good eight hours in his own bed." Hank smashed his half smoked cigarette out in the ashtray. "He's not cheating. He's a freak."

"You can't be that much of a freak."

"Oh, can't you?" said Hank. "Let me tell you some more about him. Usual body temperature—about one degree above normal average."

"Not unheard of. You know that."

"Blood pressure a hundred and five systolic, sixty-five diastolic. Pulse, fifty-five a minute. Height, six feet four, weight when he came in here a hundred and forty-two. We've been feeding him upwards of six thousand calories a day since he came in and I swear he still looks hungry. No history of childhood diseases. All his wisdom teeth. No cavities in any teeth. Shall I go on?"

"How is he mentally?"

"I checked up with the University testing bureau. They rate him in the genius range. He's started in six separate colleges and dropped out of each one. No trouble with grades. He gets top marks for a while, then suddenly stops going to class, accumulates a flock of incompletes, and transfers into something else. Arlie," said Hank, breaking off suddenly, lowering his voice and staring hard at the other, "I think we've got a new sort of man here. A mutation."

"Hank," said Arlie, crossing his legs comfortably, "when you get to be my age, you won't be so quick to think that Gabriel's going to sound the last trump in your own particular back yard. This boy's got a few physical peculiarities, he's admittedly bright, and he's conning you. You know our recent theory about sleep and sanity—"

"Of course I—"

"Suppose," said Arlie, "I lay it out for you once again. The human being deprived of sleep for any length of time beyond what he's accustomed to, begins to show signs of mental abnormality. He hallucinates. He exhibits paranoid behavior. He becomes confused, flies into reasonless rages, and overreacts emotionally to trifles."

"Arthur Willoughby doesn't."

"That's my point." Arlie held up a small, square slab of a hand. "Let me go on. How do we explain these reactions? We theorize that possibly sleep has a function beyond that of resting and repairing the body. In sleep we humans, at least, dream pretty constantly. In our dreams we act out our unhappiness, our frustrations, our terrors. Therefore sleep, we guess, may be the emotional safety valve by which we maintain our sanity against the intellectual pressures of our lives."

"Granted," said Hank, impatiently. "But Art—"

"Now, let's take something else. The problem-solving mechanism—"

"Oh, Arlie!"

"If you didn't want my opinion, why did you ring me in on this . . . what was that you just said, Hank?"

"Nothing. Nothing."

"I will pretend I didn't hear it. As I was saying—the problem-solving mechanism. It has been assumed for centuries that man attacked his intellectual problems consciously, and consciously solved them. Recent attention to this assumption has caused us to consider an alternate viewpoint of which I may say I"—Arlie folded his hands comfortably over his bulging shirtfront—"was perhaps the earliest and strongest proponent. It may well be—I and some others now think—that Man is inherently incapable of consciously solving any new intellectual problem."

"The point is, Art Willoughby—what?" Hank broke off suddenly and stared across the crumpled paper bags and wax paper on his desk, at Arlie's chubby countenance. "What?"

"Incapable. Consciously." Arlie rolled the words around in his mouth. "By which I mean," he went on, with a slight grin, "Man has no *conscious* mechanism for the solution of new intellectual problems." He cocked his head at Hank, and paused.

"All right. All right!" fumed Hank. "Tell me."

"There seems to be a definite possibility," said Arlie, capturing a crumb from the piece of wax paper that had enwrapped his ham sandwich, and chewing on it thoughtfully, "that there may be more truth than poetry to the words *inspiration, illuminating flash,* and *stroke of genius.* It may well turn out that that new-problem-solving mechanism is not under conscious control at all. Hm-m-m, yes. Did I tell you Marta wants me to try out one of these new all-liquid reducing diets? When a wife starts that—"

"Never mind Marta!" shouted Hank. "What about nobody being consciously capable of solving a problem?"

Arlie frowned.

"What I'm trying to say," he said, "is that when we try to solve a problem consciously, we are actually only utilizing an attention-focusing mechanism. Look, let me define a so-called new problem for you—"

"One that you haven't bumped into before."

"No," said Arlie. "No. Now you're falling into a trap." He waggled a thick finger at Hank; a procedure intensely irritating to Hank, who suffered a sort of adrenalin explosion the moment he suspected anybody of lecturing down to him. "Does every hitherto undiscovered intersection you approach in your car constitute a new problem in automobile navigation? Of course not. A truly new problem is not merely some variation or combination of factors from problems you have encountered before. It's a problem that for you, at least, previously, did not even exist. It is, in fact, *a problem created by the solution of a problem of equal value in the past.*"

"All right. Say it is," scowled Hank. "Then what?"

"Then," said Arlie, "a true problem must always pose the special condition that no conscious tools of education or experience yet exist for its solution. Ergo, it cannot be handled on the conscious level. The logic of conscious thought is like the limb structure of the elephant, which, though ideally adapted to allow seven tons of animal a six-and-a-half-foot stride, absolutely forbids it the necessary spring to jump across a seven-foot trench that bars its escape from the zoo. For the true problem, you've got to get from hyar to thar without any stepping stone to help you across the gap that separates you from the solution. So, you're up against it, Hank. You're in a position where you can't fly but you got to. What do you do?"

"You tell me," glowered Hank.

"The answer's simple," said Arlie, blandly. "You fly."

"But you just said I couldn't!" Hank snapped.

"What I said," said Arlie, "was two things. (1) You can't fly. (2) You got to fly. What you're doing is clinging to (1), which forces you to toss out (2). What I'm pointing out is that you should cling to (2), which tosses out (1). Now, your conscious, experienced, logical mind *knows* you can't fly. The whole idea's silly. It won't even consider the problem. But your unconscious—aha!"

"What about my unconscious?"

"Why, your unconscious isn't tied down by any ropes of logical process like that. When it wants a solution, it just goes looking for it."

"Just like that."

"Well," Arlie frowned, "not just like that. First it has to fire up a sort of little donkey-engine of its own which we might call the 'intuitive mechanism.' And that's where the trickiness comes in. Because the intuitive mechanism seems to be all power and no discipline. It's great usefulness comes from the fact that it operates under absolutely no restrictions—and of course this includes the restriction of control by the conscious mind. It's a sort of idiot savant . . . no, idiot solvant would be a better term." He sighed.

"So?" said Hank, after eying the fat man for a moment. "What's the use of it all? If we can't control it, what good is it?"

"What good is it?" Arlie straightened up. "Look at art. Look at science! Look at civilization. You aren't going to deny the existence of inspirations, are you? They exist —and one day we're going to find some better method of sparking them than the purely inductive process of operating the conscious, attention-focusing mechanism in hopes that something will catch."

"You think that's possible?"

"I know it's possible."

"I see," said Hank. There was a moment or so of silence in the office. "Well," said Hank, "about this little problem of my own, which I hate to bring you back to, but you did say the other day you had some ideas about this Art Willoughby. Of course, you were probably only speaking inspirationally, or perhaps I should say, without restriction by the conscious mind—"

"I was just getting to that," interrupted Arlie. "This Art Willoughby obviously suffers from what educators like to call 'poor work-habits.' Hm-m-m, yes. Underdevelopment of the conscious, problem-focusing mechanism. He tries to get by on a purely intuitive basis. When this fails him, he is helpless. He gives up—witness his transfers from college to college. On the other hand, when it works good, it works very, very good. He has probably come up with some way of keeping himself abnormally stimulated, either externally or internally. The only trouble will be that he probably isn't even conscious of it, and he certainly has no control over it. He'll fall asleep any moment now. And when he wakes up you'll want him to duplicate his feat of wakefulness but he won't be able to do it."

Hank snorted disbelievingly.

"All right," said Arlie. "All right. Wait and see."

"I will," said Hank. He stood up. "Want to come along and see him? He said he was starting to get foggy this morning. I'm going to try him with the monster."

"What," wondered Arlie, ingenuously, rising, "if it puts him to sleep?"

Hank threw him a glance of pure fury.

"Monster!" commanded Hank. He, Arlie, and Margie Hansen were gathered in Art's hospital room, which was a pleasant, bedless place already overflowing with books and maps. Art, by hospital rules deprived of such things as tools and pets, had discovered an interest in the wars of Hannibal of Carthage. At the present moment he was trying to pick the truth out of the rather confused reports following Hannibal's escape from the Romans, after Antiochus had been defeated at Magnesia and surrendered his great general to Rome.

Right now, however, he was forced to lay his books aside and take the small white capsule which Margie, at Hank's order, extended to him. Art took it; then hesitated.

"Do you think it'll make me very jittery?" he asked.

"It should just wake you up," said Hank.

"I told you how I am with things like coffee. That's why I never drink coffee, or take any stimulants. Half a cup and my eyes feel like they're going to pop out of my head."

"There wouldn't," said Hank a trifle sourly, "be much point in our paying you to test out the monster if you refused to take it, now would there?"

"Oh . . . oh, no," said Art, suddenly embarrassed. "Water?"

Margie gave him a full glass and threw an unkind glance at her superior.

"If it starts to bother you, Art, you tell us right away," she said.

Art gulped the capsule down. He stood there waiting as if he expected an explosion from the region of his stomach. Nothing happened; and after a moment of two, he relaxed.

"How long does it take?" he asked.

"About fifteen minutes," said Hank.

They waited. At the end of ten minutes, Art began to brighten up and said he was feeling much more alert. At fifteen minutes, he was sparkling-eyed and cheerful; almost, in fact, bouncy.

"Awfully sorry, doctor," he said to Hank. "Awfully sorry I hesitated over taking the monster that way. It was just that coffee and things—"

"That's all right," said Hank, preparing to leave. Margie'll take you down for tests, now."

"Marvelous pill. I recommend it highly," said Art, going out the door with Margie. They could hear him headed off down the corridor outside toward the laboratory on the floor below, still talking.

"Well?" said Hank.

"Time will tell," said Arlie.

"Speaking of time," continued Hank. "I've got the plug-in coffeepot back at the office. Have you got time for a quick cup?"

". . . Don't deny it," Hank was saying over half-empty cups in the office a short while later. "I heard you; I read you loud and clear. If a man makes his mind up to it, he can fly, you said."

"Not at all. And besides, I was only speaking academically," retorted Arlie, heatedly. "Just because I'm prepared to entertain fantastic notions academically doesn't mean I'm going to let you try to shove them down my throat on a practical basis. Of course nobody can fly."

"According to your ideas, someone like Willoughby could if he punched the right buttons in him."

"Nonsense. Certainly he can't fly."

There was the wild patter of feminine feet down the hallway outside the office, the door was flung open, and Margie tottered in. She clung to the desk and gasped, too out of wind to talk.

"What's wrong?" cried Hank.

"Art—" Margie managed, "flew out—lab window."

Hank jumped to his feet, and pulled his chair out for her. She fell into it gratefully.

"Nonsense!" said Arlie. "Illusion. Or—" he scowled at Margie, "collusion of some sort."

"Got your breath back yet? What happened?" Hank was demanding. Margie nodded and drew a deep breath.

"I was testing him," she said, still breathless, "he was talking a blue streak and I could hardly get him to stand still. Something about Titus Quintus Flaminінius, the three-body problem, Sauce Countess Waleska, the family Syrphidae of the order Diptera—all mixed up. Oh, he was babbling! And all of a sudden he dived out an open window."

"Dived?" barked Arlie. "I thought you said he *flew?*"

"Well, the laboratory's on the third floor!" wailed Margie, almost on the verge of tears.

Further questioning elicited the information that when Margie ran to the window, expecting to see a shattered ruin on the grass three stories below, she perceived Art swinging by one arm from the limb of an oak outside the window. In response to sharp queries from Arlie, she asserted vehemently that the closest grabable limb of the oak was, however, at least eight feet from the window which Art had jumped, fallen or dived.

"And then what?" said Hank.

Then, according to Margie, Art had uttered a couple of

tarzanlike yodels, and swung himself to the ground. When last seen he had been running off across the campus through the cool spring sunlight, under the budding trees, in his slacks and shirt unbuttoned at the throat. He had been heading in a roughly northeasterly direction—i.e., toward town—and occasionally bounding into the air as if from a sheer access of energy.

"Come on!" barked Hank, when he had heard this. He led the way at a run toward the hospital parking lot three stories below and his waiting car.

On the other side of the campus, at a taxi stand, the three of them picked up Art's trail. A cab driver waiting there remembered someone like Art taking another cab belonging to the same company. When Hank identified the passenger as a patient under his, Hank's, care; and further identified himself as a physician from the University hospitals, the cab driver they were talking to agreed to call in for the destination of Art's cab.

The destination was a downtown bank. Hank, Arlie and Margie piled back into Hank's car and went there.

When they arrived, the learned that Art had already come and gone, leaving some confusion behind him. A vice-president of the bank, it appeared, had made a loan to Art of two hundred and sixty-eight dollars and eighty cents; and was now, it seemed, not quite sure as to why he had done so.

"He just talked me into it, I guess," the vice-president was saying unhappily as Hank and the others came dashing up. It further developed that Art had had no collateral. The vice-president had been given the impression that the money was to be used to develop some confusing but highly useful discovery or discoveries concerning Hannibal, encyclopedias, the sweat fly and physics—with something about champagne and a way of preparing trout for the gourmet appetite.

A further check with the cab company produced the information that Art's taxi had taken him on to a liquor store. They followed. At the liquor store they discovered that Art had purchased the single jeroboam of champagne (Moet et Chandon) that the liquor store had on hand; and had mentioned that he was going on to a restaurant. What restaurant, the cab company was no longer able to tell them. Art's driver had just announced that he would not be answering his radio for the next half hour.

They began checking the better and closer restaurants. At the fourth one, which was called the Calice d'Or, they finally ran Art to ground. They found him seated alone at a large, round table, surrounded by gold-tooled leather volumes of a brand-new encyclopedia, eating and drinking what turned out to be Truite Sauce Countess Waleska and champagne from the jeroboam, now properly iced.

"Yahoo!" yelped Art, as he saw them approaching. He waved his glass on high, sloshing champagne liberally about. "Champagne for everybody! Celebrate Dr. Rapp's pill!"

"You," said Hank, "are coming back to the hospitals."

"Nonsense! Glasses! Champagne for m'friends!"

"Oh, Art!" cried Margie.

"He's fried to the gills," said Arlie.

"Not at all," protested Art. "Illuminated. Blinding flash. Understand everything. D'you know all knowledge has a common point of impingement?"

"Call a taxi, Margie," commanded Hank.

"Encyclopedia. Champagne bubble. Same thing."

"Could I help you, sir?" inquired a waiter, approaching Hank.

"We want to get our friend here home—"

"All roads lead knowledge. Unnerstand ignorance, unnerstand everything—"

"I understand, sir. Yes sir, he paid the check in advance—"

"Would *you* like to speak three thousand, four hundred and seventy-one languages?" Art was asking Arlie.

"Of course," Arlie was saying, soothingly.

"My assistant has gone to get a taxi, now. I'm Dr. Rapp of the University hospitals, and—"

"When I was child," announced Art, "thought as child, played child; now man—put away childish things."

"Here's the young lady, sir."

"But who will take care of pet racoon?"

"I flagged a taxi down. It's waiting out front."

"Hoist him up," commanded Hank.

He and Arlie both got a firm hold on a Willoughby arm and maneuvered Art to his feet.

"This way," said Hank, steering Art toward the door.

"The universe," said Art. He leaned confidentially toward Hank, almost toppling the three of them over. "Only two inches across."

"That so?" grunted Hank.

"Hang on to Arlie, Art, and you won't fall over. There—" said Margie. Art blinked and focused upon her with some difficulty.

"Oh . . . there you are—" he said. "Love you. Naturally. Only real woman in universe. Other four point seven to the nine hundred seventeenth women in universe pale imitations. Marry me week Tuesday, three P.M. courthouse, wear blue." Margie gasped.

"Open the door for us, will you?"

"Certainly sir," said the waiter, opening the front door to the Calice d'Or. A pink and gray taxi was drawn up at the curb.

"Sell stock in Wehauck Cannery immediately," Art was saying to the waiter. "Mismanagement. Collapse." The waiter blinked and stared. "News out in ten days."

"But how did you know I had—" the waiter was beginning as they shoved Art into the back seat of the cab. Margie got in after him.

"Ah, there you are," came Art's voice from the cab. "First son Charles Jonas—blond hair, blue eyes. Second son, William . . ."

"I'll send somebody to pick up that encyclopedia and anything else he left," said Hank to the waiter and got into the taxi himself. The taxi pulled away from the curb.

"Well," said the waiter, after a long pause in which he stared after the receding cab, to the doorman who had just joined him on the sidewalk, "how do you like that? Ever see anything like that before?"

"No, and I never saw anyone with over a gallon of champagne in him still walking around, either," said the doorman.

". . . And the worst of it is," said Hank to Arlie, as they sat in Hank's office, two days later, "Margie *is* going to marry him."

"What's wrong with that?" asked Arlie.

"What's wrong with it? Look at that!" Hank waved his hand at an object in the center of his desk.

"I've seen it," said Arlie.

They both examined the object: It appeared to be an ordinary movable telephone with a cord and wall plug. The plug, however, was plugged into a small cardboard box the size of a cheese carton, filled with a tangled mess of wire and parts cannibalized from a cheap portable radio. The box was plugged into nothing.

"What was that number again . . . oh, yes," said Arlie. He picked up the phone and dialed a long series of numbers. He held the phone up so that they could both hear. There was a faint buzzing ring from the earphone and then a small, tinny voice filled the office.

" . . . The time is eight forty-seven. The temperature is eighteen degrees above zero, the wind westerly at eight miles an hour. The forecast for the Anchorage area is continued cloudy and some snow with a high of twenty-two degrees, a low tonight of nine above. Elsewhere in Alaska—"

Arlie sighed, and replaced the phone in its cradle.

"We bring him back here," said Hank, "stewed to the gills. In forty minutes before he passes out, he builds this trick wastebasket of his that holds five times as much as it ought to. He sleeps seven hours and wakes up as good as ever. What should I do? Shoot him, or something? I must have some responsibility to the human race—if not to Margie."

"He seems sensible now?"

"Yes, but what do I do?"

"Hypnosis."

"You keep saying that. I don't see—"

"We must," said Arlie, "inhibit the connection of his conscious mind with the intuitive mechanism. The wall between the two—the normal wall seems to have been freakishly thin in his case. Prolonged sleeplessness, combined with the abnormal stimulation of your monster, has caused him to break through—to say to the idiot solvant, *'Solve!'* And the idiot solvant in the back of his head has provided him with a solution."

"I still think it would be better for me to shoot him."

"You are a physician—"

"You would remind me of that. All right, so I can't shoot him. I don't even want to shoot him. But, Arlie, what's going to happen to everybody? Here I've raised up a sort of miracle worker who can probably move the North American continent down to the South Pacific if he wants to—only it just happens he's also a feather-headed butterfly who never lit on one notion for more than five minutes at a time in his life. Sure, I've got a physician's responsibility toward him. But what about my responsibility to the rest of the people in the world?"

"There is no responsibility being violated here," said Arlie patiently. "Simply put him back the way you found him."

"No miracles?"

"None. At least, except accidental ones."

"It might be kinder to shoot him."

"Nonsense," said Arlie sharply. "It's for the good of everybody." Hank sighed, and rose.

"All right," he said. "Let's go."

They went down the hall to Art's room. They found him seated thoughtfully in his armchair, staring at nothing, his books and maps ignored around him.

"Good morning, Art," said Arlie.

"Oh? Hello," said Art, waking up. "Is it time for tests?"

"In a way," said Arlie. He produced a small box surmounted by a cardboard disk on which were inked alternate spirals of white and black. He plugged the box in to a handy electric socket by means of the cord attached to it, and set it on a small table in front of Art. The disk began to revolve. "I want you to watch that," said Arlie.

Art stared at it.

"What do you see?" asked Arlie.

"It looks like going down a tunnel," said Art.

"Indeed it does," said Arlie. "Just imagine yourself going down that tunnel. Down the tunnel. Faster and faster . . ." He continued to talk quietly and persuasively for about a minute and a half, at the end of which Art was limply demonstrating a state of deep trance. Arlie brought him up a bit for questioning.

" . . . And how do these realizations, these answers come to you?" Arlie was asking, a few minutes later,

"In a sort of a flash," replied Art. "A blinding flash."

"That is the way they have always come to you?"

"More lately," said Art.

"Yes," said Arlie, "that's the way it always is just before people outgrow these flashes. They do outgrow these flashes—you know that."

There was a slight pause.

"Yes," said Art.

"You have now outgrown these flashes. You have had your last flash. Flashes belong to childhood. You have had a delayed growing-up; but from now on you will think like an adult. Logically. You will think like an adult. Repeat after me."

"I will think like an adult," intoned Art.

Arlie continued to hammer away at his point for a few more minutes; then he brought Art out of his trance, with a final command that, if Art felt any tendency to a recurrence of his flashes, he should return to Arlie for further help in suppressing them.

"Oh, hello, doctor," said Art to Hank, as soon as he woke up. "Say, how much longer are you going to need me as a test subject?"

Hank made a rather unhappy grimace.

"In a hurry to leave?" he said.

"I don't know," said Art, enthusiastically, rubbing his long hands together as he sat up in the chair, "but I was just thinking maybe it's time I got to work. Settled down. As long as I'm going to be a married man shortly."

"We can turn you loose today, if you want," said Hank.

When Art stepped once more into his room, closing the door behind him and taking off his leather jacket to hang it up on the hook holding his bagpipes, the place seemed so little changed that it was hard to believe ten full days had passed. Even the raccoon was back asleep in the wastebasket. It was evident the landlady had been doing her duty about keeping the small animal fed—Art had worried a little about that. The only difference Art thought, was that the room seemed to feel smaller.

He sighed cheerfully and sat down at the desk, drawing pencil and paper to him. The afternoon sun, shooting the gap of the missing slat on the Venetian blind at the window, splashed fair in Art's eyes, blinding him.

"Blast!" he said aloud. "Got to do something about that—"

He checked himself suddenly with one hand halfway up to shield his eyes; and smiled. Opening a drawer of the desk, he took out a pair of heavy kitchen scissors. He made a single cut into the rope slot at each end of the plastic slat at the bottom of the blind, snapped the slat out of position, and snapped it back in where the upper slat was missing.

Still smiling, he picked up the pencil and doodled the name *Margie* with a heart around it in the upper left-hand corner as he thought, with gaze abstracted. The pencil moved to the center of the piece of paper and hovered there.

After a moment, it began to sketch.

What it sketched was a sort of device to keep the sun out of Art's eyes. At the same time, however, it just happened to be a dome-shaped all-weather shield capable of protecting a city ten miles in diameter the year around.

The "skin" of the dome consisted of a thin layer of carbon dioxide such as one finds in the bubbles of champagne, generated and maintained by magnetic lines of force emanating from three heavily charged bodies, in rotation about each other at the apex of the dome and superficially housed in a framework the design of which was reminiscent of the wing structure found in the family Syriphidae of the order Diptera.

Art continued to smile as the design took form. But it was a thoughtful smile, a mature smile. Hank and Arlie had been quite right about him. He had always been a butterfly, flitting from notion to notion, playing.

But then, too, he had always been a bad hypnotic subject, full of resistances.

And he was about to have a wife to care for. Consequently it is hard to say whether Arlie and Hank would have been reassured if they could have seen Art at that moment. His new thinking was indeed adult, much more so than the other two could have realized. Where miracles were concerned, he had given up *playing*.

Now, he was *working*.

COUNTER SECURITY

James White

Britishers do this sort of thing so well! Here is mastery of the English style of detailed, workmanlike, understated realism that can make even the most unlikely of fantastic situations seem inevitably real. We are given a picture of a business (department store), a profession (security officer, otherwise known as night watchman), and an Event (capital E, indeed!), with a vividness which seems astonishing when you examine the tale for signs of excitement. No real dialogue, almost no action in the melodramatic sense, great long paragraphs, and very little verbal effort to arouse your emotions (that is left to the nature of the Event itself!)—and yet the reader is continuously enthralled from start to ironic last word. At least, *I* was!

THE OBJECT LYING ON MR. STEELE'S DESK WAS the remains of a large, black plastic doll, Tully saw as he took the chair which the Store Manager indicated to him. The doll had lost a leg and both arms, one eye socket was empty and the nose had been pulled out of shape. There were also patches of hair missing from the scalp, and a narrow band of spotted material—the collar of the doll's dress, no doubt—still encircled its neck. Altogether it was an intriguing and rather pitiable object, Tully thought, but hardly the sort of thing to cause the Store Manager to send for the night security man as soon as he came on duty.

Tully was about to voice his curiosity when Steele's

receptionist announced Tyson of Hardware and Dodds, the Toy buyer. The SM waited until they had stopped moving in their chairs, then cleared his throat and began to speak.

"In the ordinary way, Mr. Tully," he said in his soft, unhurried voice, "all cases of malicious damage to stock by members of the staff are dealt with by the departmental buyer or floor supervisor and are not usually the concern of the night security people. Neither, I might add, are they the direct concern of the Store Manager, since I have slightly more important matters to occupy me."

His tone became gently sarcastic and he looked pointedly at the Toy buyer, who looked at the carpet.

". . . However," he went on, "this seems to be an unusual case, in that neither Mr. Dodds nor the supervisor on that floor have been able to do anything beyond establishing the fact that these occurrences do not take place during shop hours. Meanwhile the Toy department is being terrorized by an epidemic of armless dolls—"

"That sounds like an exaggeration," Dodds broke in quickly, strong emotion doubling the volume of his naturally loud voice, "but believe me it isn't! My staff are all girls, some of them colored, and this sort of thing . . ."

The SM silenced Dodds with a coldly disapproving look. Mr. Steele detested all unnecessary noises. He liked to think of his Store as an efficient, smoothly running machine and he was fond of reminding people that any part of it which operated loudly rendered its efficiency suspect.

"The retail value of the dolls is of no importance," Steele resumed. "What concerns us is the way in which the culprit can do such damage without being caught. That and the bad effect it is having on the Toy department staff. On the surface it looks like a practical joke, but—"

"A *joke!*" Dodds burst out. "I tell you my girls are terrified! At first they treated it as a joke, but then they kept finding them nearly every morning and the rumor started that there was a psychopath loose in the Store . . .!"

"Very *well,* Mr. Dodds," said the Store Manager irritably. "You tell it."

". . . Just look at the *facts!*" the Toy buyer rushed on, plainly too excited to notice the danger signals flying on the other side of the desk. "During the past two weeks nine dolls in all have been mutilated like this. Nine *black* dolls. All had a leg and both arms pulled off, the hair twisted or pulled out, the faces disfigured and their dresses torn off. One or two such incidents might be attributed to simple malicious damage, but nine of them in two weeks points to something much more sinister. . . ."

Tully found himself looking at the doll, which no longer seemed such an innocent object, and thinking about the implications of the word *mutilate* as opposed to *damage.*

". . . I'm not saying the rumor is true," Dodds went on, "but the facts support it. They point towards a perverted mind, a mind with some dreadful obsession about Negro dolls. I mean Negro girls. . . ."

Dodds stopped for breath and the Store Manager rejoined the conversation. He said, "Despite what you have just heard, Mr. Tully, we are not faced with a general walkout. But the rumor is causing trouble and I want it killed. The quickest way to do that will be to find out who is pulling these dolls apart, and that is where you come in. . . ."

It had already been established that whatever it was that happened was occurring outside of normal shop hours, Steele told him. The dolls were always found by staff arriving in the mornings, usually by the cleaners, who were always first in. Either the culprit was someone, not necessarily a member of the staff, who was hiding in the store at night, or the store was being broken into from the street. It was suggested that Mr. Tully keep a closer watch on the entrances to the Toy department. . . .

At that point Tully felt like reminding him that the store was reputed to be burglar-proof from the ground up, that the Toy department occupied the basement and that to gain access to it from the street would call for a fair-sized mining operation. He did not say anything, however, because the Store Manager knew these things as well as he did. And he noticed that the other had made no reference to his failure to notice anything peculiar going on during the past two weeks, when dolls must have been having their arms pulled off nearly every night. But now that the matter had been brought officially to his attention he knew that Steele would have plenty to say if he did not put a stop to it.

". . . This is an odd business whose solution may require a certain amount of imagination," the SM said, his eyes flicking briefly towards the inch or so of magazine showing in Tully's jacket pocket, "but then I see that that is something with which you are well supplied. Have you any questions?"

Before Tully could reply, Dodds broke in again. "Sir, you didn't mention the—"

That was as far as he got. Furiously, but still quietly, Steele said, "Mr. Dodds, there are some misdemeanors committed in this store which I, or Mr. Tully here are *not* obliged to investigate personally, and complaints of people spitting on the back staircase is one of them . . .!"

More to take the heat off the loud-voiced but kindly Dodds than from any strong curiosity over the matter, Tully nodded toward the Hardware buyer and said, "What is Mr. Tyson's connection with this?"

"Eh? Oh, very slight," said Steele, regaining his composure with a visible effort. "He is having trouble with shortages. Some power tools, and a motorized lawnmower, missing from packing cases which have the manufacturer's seals unbroken. There is some kind of hanky panky going on, but pilfering at this end is not suspected so it is not a matter for you. He may also have come to lend moral support to Mr. Dodds, who is going to need it. . . ."

He stood up suddenly, smiled and said, "Thank you, Mr. Tully." Then he began quietly to draw Dodds' attention to the Toy department's trading figures for the preceding week in comparison to the same week last year. This was a matter which Mr. Steele *was* obliged to investigate in person, and as Tully closed the office door softly behind him, the inquisition was just beginning to warm up.

Tully walked slowly out onto the sales floor, trying to make his mind think in a positive and constructive manner and not succeeding at all. Around him stretched the polished, square ocean of the Hardware department with its bright display islands of Do-It-Yourself, electrical goods, refrigerators, *et al.* There were only a few customers about, it being only half an hour to closing time, and he decided to have a chat with the people in the Hardware stockroom. Steele had told him that the shortages did not concern him, but Tully disliked having his mind made up for him even when he knew that the other party was right.

A few minutes later he was getting all the details from Carswell, Tyson's assistant. Carswell was an extremely conscientious type who expected everybody else to be the same, and the fact that everybody else wasn't had had a bad effect on his disposition over the years.

"Either the packers were drunk or the maker is trying to pull a fast one," Carswell said hotly. Then tolerantly, for him, he went on, "There might be an excuse for three power-drills being missing from a case which was supposed to contain twenty—an error in packing, no doubt, because the maker's seals on the cases were unbroken. But when we told them about it they insisted that there was no error, that they had packed twenty power-drills and if their seals were intact then we had received and in due course would be billed for twenty power-drills. And the trouble is, we've been holding them in storage unopened for a couple of weeks, which weakens our case considerably. . . ."

Except where they had been severed by Carswell's wire-cutters, the thin metal bands sealing the cases were in one piece, smooth and shining apart from a few tiny discolored sections which looked as if they were beginning to rust. The packing inside had fallen to the bottom of the case, but there was a suggestion of shaping to it as if the case had contained something which had been taken out rather than that the packing had merely been pushed into an empty case. For several minutes Tully poked around in it without quite knowing why, and lifted a handful up to his nose. It smelled of dust and dry straw and, vaguely, of peppermint, he thought, before he nearly blew over the case with the grandaddy of all sneezes.

Tully left Hardware and took the elevator to the ground floor, intending to ask some questions in the Toy department while its Buyer was still engaged with the Store Manager—he felt that he would get a more valuable reaction if he talked to the staff without Dodds shouting everybody down. But at the top of the basement stairs he changed his mind. There was another possibility which he should try to eliminate first.

When he reached the Nurse's Office a few minutes later he coughed gently in the manner of one intent on signalling one's presence rather than displaying symptoms of a respiratory malfunction. Through the frosted glass door which separated the tiny waiting room from the dispensary proper, he saw a white shadow approach and resolve itself into the Nurse as the door was opened.

She looked down at him, the soft brown eyes in her rather severe face scanning him automatically for signs of physical injury or distress, then she said quietly, "Good afternoon, Mr. Tully. Is something troubling you?"

"Well . . . yes," said Tully, standing up. He outlined what was troubling him, the Store Manager and a lot of other people, then ended awkwardly, ". . . Maybe I shouldn't ask this sort of question, I mean, what you find out or even guess at might be privileged information —I'm not sure what your position is in cases like this. But I was wondering if—"

"If," the Nurse broke in firmly, "there was anyone who came to see me who was as mentally disturbed as you and this rumor you mention suggests, I might or might not divulge his name. That would depend on the circumstances. I would, however, declare him unfit for work and immediately send him to his doctor, who would take over from there. I would not allow him to run around loose. Does that answer your question, Mr. Tully?"

"Thank you, Nurse," said Tully, and left.

The possibility of a Negro-hating psychopath among the staff was not completely eliminated, he thought as he resumed his journey to the Toy department; all the talk with Nurse had proved was that the psychopath, if there was one, had not revealed himself to her.

On his way down the basement stairs Tully was caught by a stampeding mass of chattering femininity on their way up. It was quitting time, which meant that he wouldn't be able to ask the Toy girls any questions today. His only possible source of information seemed to be Miss Barr, Dodd's assistant, who was still standing by the model railway display putting on her outdoor face.

But he learned very little from his talk with her. According to Miss Barr every doll had been found in the same condition—missing both arms, one leg, one eye, the nose pulled out of shape, hair disarranged and clothing, if the doll had been wearing any, ripped off. The only minor variation was that sometimes it was the right and sometimes the left eye that had been poked out, just as it could be the right or left leg that was missing. When she began to grow agitated and started repeating herself, a condition highly unusual in the competent and level-headed Miss Barr, Tully made gentle reassuring noises, helped her on with her coat and said goodnight.

When Tully was alone in the department he closed, bolted and locked the door at the top of the stairs, then he went on the prowl. His eyes missed nothing and he kept his lips pressed together so that he breathed in a long series of sniffs. This was routine, because his job required keen eyes and a very sensitive nose.

Few people realized that the Store, equipped as it was with the latest security devices and well covered by police patrols, was in no danger of being robbed, that the greatest and only danger was from fire. There was a sprinkler system installed, of course, which could be made so sensitive that a whole department could be instantly flooded—and its stock ruined, incidently—if someone switched on an electric fire. Or it could be made less sensitive so that a fire could gain an unbreakable hold which the spray from the ceiling would be unable to check. For despite its imposing facade the store was one of the oldest buildings in the city, and much of its stock was even more inflammable than its structure.

So the primary job of the night security man was to guard against fire and the causes of fire. Every stockroom, locker room and cubbyhole—the only exceptions were the washrooms—had its No Smoking notices. But despite the eagle eyes of the buyers and floor supervisors, the staff continued to sneak off for a smoke in all those places at every opportunity. Tully did not mind them smoking; the trouble arose when they were interrupted at it and were forced to hide the evidence quickly. They hid it in some very odd places, and the evidence smoldered sometimes for hours before Tully's nose led him to it and he rendered it safe.

On this occasion he was not simply looking for smoldering cigarette ends. He intended sealing the basement from outside and before he did so, he had to be sure that there was nobody hiding in it. He looked behind and under every counter and display stand and with his Master opened every locker in the Toy staff room, and finally he was satisfied that the department was empty. He spent ten minutes then at the model railway display, taking the 4-6-2 tank loco around the layout and performing a few simple shunting operations, then he killed all the lights and headed for the Dugout.

The total floor area of the basement was only a fraction of that of the ground floor, it being merely two cellars joined by a narrow corridor. A floor plan of the basement resembled a dumb-bell with square weights, the square representing the Toy department being twice the size of the one enclosing the Dugout. In the middle of the corridor was a heavy swing door which was kept permanently dogged open. There were two lights in the corridor which he switched off as he passed them.

The Dugout was a large untidy room which served as the supply base and—unofficially—rest room for the cleaning staff. Drawn up in the center of the room like some alien armored division were the rubberwheeled bogies which carried the electric polishers and vacuum cleaners, and ranged around the walls were storage cupboards filled with floor polish, liquid soap and an incredible quantity of rags, most of which were oily. Of all the places in the store, this was the one in which a fire would be most likely to start. Tully searched and sniffed meticulously, as he did every night in this potential danger spot, but without finding either a hiding place or a trace of tobacco smoke. He gave a last look around, then mounted the ramp which replaced a stairway at this end to facilitate movement of the wheeled cleaners. He switched off the lights, then closed, locked and bolted the door from the outside.

An odd thing happened while he was locking the door. One of the keys in his bunch, the thin, lightweight Master for the Wages Office lockers, flipped up suddenly and stuck to the bar. A few minutes testing showed him that the bolt and surrounding casing of the Dugout door was strongly magnetized.

If Tully had been asked to write down his thoughts just then, he would have put down a row of question marks. He thought of checking to see if there was an electrician working late and asking him how and why the lock should have become magnetic, then decided that before doing anything else he should complete the sealing off of the basement.

Still keeping his eye on the two entrances to the basement he paid a quick visit to the Haberdashery counter and a cigarette and confectionery kiosk which were on the same floor. At Haberdashery he took a spool of black thread, leaving a chit with his signature on it stating that the goods were being used in the store's business, and at the confectionary counter be opened a large packet of chewing gum. He thought of paying for this at first, but then reminded himself that he didn't *like* gum and he was chewing it solely in the line of duty. He left a chit for that, too, knowing full well that the people in accounting would have some very sarcastic things to say about it tomorrow. Tully grinned to himself and, chewing furiously, headed for the nearest basement door.

Fifteen minutes later the entrance to the Toy end of the basement was bolted both inside and out and had a length of black thread stretched across it approximately six inches from the floor level. The Dugout door had been similarly treated except that it was bolted and locked only from outside. He had also rigged threads at one-floor intervals on the staff stairway. The thread in each case was held by gum so that it would pull away rather than break, because there was a chance that his man might hear or feel a thread break and so have warning of the trap. Tully was assuming that any surreptitious movements which took place would be via the staff stairs, because the store's main stairway, which wound around the central well and elevators, was kept brightly illuminated all through the night. It was also in sight of Tully's night station at the Book counter as well as being in full view of anyone passing the main entrance in the street.

As well, the staff stairway would be in total darkness

while the main one would be lighted, so there was no reason for the men working late to break his threads. No innocent reason, that was.

With the feeling that he had taken all the precautions it was possible to take at that time, Tully began the first and most important of his six nightly rounds. Except for the well and the center of light and activity where *some* display staff and carpenters were working on the Fashion Theatre, the Store was in darkness. The floor supervisor on Lock-up whose job was also to keep tabs on the people working late, had already checked all doors and windows and killed the lights. Tully's first nightly duty was to make sure he had done these things properly, which he always had—floor supervisors were just as security minded as Tully himself, and none of them wanted to be caught out by the night man. It was a point of honor with them. Tully laughed wryly to himself as he paced the darkened sales floor, thinking that the competition which was fostered between departments—so fierce at times that it put an unfair strain on the word friendly—touched even the night watchman.

Gravely, Tully begged his own pardon; he meant the Night Security Officer. . . .

All around him the store began settling down for the night. The light and heating fixtures made soft pinging noises as they cooled, or creaked eerily just above the threshold of audibility. The woodwork ticked and sighed and the floor, relieved of the day-long pressure of thousands of pairs of feet, stretched minutely and moved itself into a more comfortable position. The sounds it made varied from those of a herd of running mice to the noise of distant gunfire. Later the store would come to rest, but during his first few patrols the sound effects could be quite startling.

Some people would have been bothered by these sounds. They would have let their imaginations loose among the eerie creakings and tinklings and scufflings and peopled the darkness with formless horrors. Not that Tully didn't have a good imagination. To the contrary, but he prided himself in that his imagination was properly under control. He had no time for gothic horrors or brooding menaces or fantasy of any kind. Tully liked his science fiction straight.

So he patrolled up and down behind the shadowy counters, ignoring the noises off and with most of his attention concentrated in his nose, thinking the sort of thoughts he always thought around this time of night. He thought about his job, which was easy and, because few people would work the hours he worked, very well paid. Then he would think about the day job at the counter which was not so well paid and which he had held for so many years without getting any farther up the ladder. He had been good at his job, but then so had about two thousand others in the store, and he must have lacked that extra bit of push which would have led to promotion. Finally he would think about himself.

He was an intelligent, well-read—he by no means restricted himself to science fiction although he preferred it—and essentially lazy person. His few close friends credited him with high intelligence by inference and did not, because they were his friends, mention laziness at all. But others came straight out and asked him if he was so intelligent why didn't he have a better job? Tully had asked himself the same question often without finding a satisfactory answer. Apparently there *were* no jobs which demanded a calm, easygoing disposition allied with detailed, but not specialist, knowledge on such widely varied subjects as Stellar Evolution, the history of the Roman Empire, the latest work being done on the psychology of worms and similar unrelated items. At the moment his job gave him plenty of time to read and think, and gave him security while he was doing these things, so he had no real cause for complaint. Tully now knew that he had not been happy in his job at the counter. The pay had been lower even though the chance of promotion had been much higher. But basically all he had had was a chance, and Tully's reading had included data on the Laws of Chance, so after due consideration he had gone after the job which was a fairly well paid dead end—he had chosen Security.

Pun unintentional, he thought wryly.

His watch said eight-thirty and he was just finishing the Third floor, walking from the brightly lit well towards the staff stairway. Around the well everything stood out bright and sharp and clear, but as he moved away from it objects began to throw long shadows, which eventually grew so hazy that the objects themselves became shadows. The vast, unlighted portion of the shop seemed to have become unreal, as if God had switched it off because nobody was using it. This was a very fanciful line of thought for Tully, but he sometimes indulged in such thinking when he wanted to mentally change the subject.

He did not like to think that he was a highly intelligent, well-read failure. . . .

On the way to the Fourth floor he checked his thread and found it unbroken. The sight of the thin black thread turned dusty white by the narrow beam of his torch sent the odd business of the dolls rushing back into his mind, and immediately his dark mood lifted. He had been given a problem which he did not think any ordinary night watchman could solve. Mr. Steele had suggested as much, although there was the possibility that the Store Manager had simply been making a crack about his taste in literature. This doll business was a challenge and Tully felt that, if he met it successfully, he might be able to stop thinking of himself as a complete failure.

Tully spent longer than usual on the Fourth, particularly in Mr. Steele's office. His reason for that was that he wanted to have a closer look at the mutilated doll. He found it in Mr. Steele's wastebasket, rescued it and placed it on Mr. Steele's blotter. Then he switched on Mr. Steele's desklamp and, with a slight qualm of something he couldn't put a name to, he sat down in Mr. Steele's chair.

His second examination of the doll told him nothing new, at first. It was still just a one-eyed, one-legged, armless black doll with a lot of its hair missing. But then he noticed that the hair might have been pulled out accidentally, that it had not simply been yanked out but rather that somebody had been trying to twist it into all-over pig-tails. Tully grunted; it seemed a useless bit of information. Almost automatically he lifted the doll and smelt its hair.

And got a faint, almost indetectable odor of something which could have been peppermint.

Suddenly impatient with himself Tully threw the doll back into the wastebasket. He was imagining things, either that or his nose was suffering from persistence of smell. It was stupid to suppose that his dolls and Tyson's missing lawnmower had any connection. . . .

On the Fifth floor, which housed the store's administrative offices, and on the roof above it there were no smoldering cigarette ends or signs of anyone skulking in the elevator housings. By the time he had finished the roof check it was nine-twenty, so he hurried down to the Time Office to make coffee for his first supper and watch the overtime men clocking out.

Ten minutes later he was standing at the only unlocked exit from the store, with the floor supervisor in charge of Lock-up and Overtime, watching the late workers troop out. Tully did not know what exactly he was looking for, but he did know that nobody left the place chewing peppermints or with a lawnmower under their coat. He chatted for a few minutes with the supervisor, offered him a cup of coffee which was accepted, then let him out.

By nine-forty-five Tully was alone inside a tightly sealed department store.

After his coffee and sandwiches, he did his second round, then set up a folding chair in the Book department. He sat down, drew the magazine which had arrived that morning out of his pocket and prepared to face the night. He was supposed to make his rounds at random intervals, the theory being that nobody would know where he was going to be at any given time. It being next to impossible to devise completely random intervals, Tully mixed business with pleasure by reading his magazine for the night and patrolling between stories. Sometimes he read the short stories first, sometimes last, just to make it more difficult for any hypothetical observer who might be trying to beat his system. . . .

He began his third round at eleven-fifty-eight, thinking that there were some people who could handle psi—Bester, Sturgeon and a few others—and some who most definitely could not. When they tried, their stories read like fantasy; instead of natural laws and controlled experiments, there was chaos and a sort of aseptic witchcraft. Still seething quietly, Tully finished his round and read another story. He had his second supper, it being close to one-thirty, then made his fourth patrol.

All the threads were intact, he saw nothing unusual, not a thing was stirring, not even a . . . But then, he reminded himself, the store did not have mice.

It was during his third story that Tully heard something—something unusual, that was. The floors and lighting fixtures still ticked and creaked at intervals, but this sounded exactly like a bolt being drawn. As he strained his ears to listen it was followed by the sounds of a door being opened and closed quietly and a muffled, slapping sound. It seemed to be coming from the Dugout entrance.

Tully put down his magazine, sheer habit making him mark his place with a used bus ticket, and moved from behind the counter. He glanced quickly at the department telephone, which at night was connected to an outside line in case he suddenly needed to call the Police or the Fire Department, then shook his head —he didn't need help, at least, not yet. With his torch in one hand and his shoes in the other he sprinted silently toward the Dugout entrance, pausing only long enough to check that the Toy door was still bolted and its thread unbroken.

The other door had been opened and the thread pulled from its anchoring gum. For a moment Tully dithered between entering the Dugout and checking where the person who had entered it had come from, then he made up his mind and ran up the stairs.

The threads were dislodged from the First to the Fourth floors, but not the Fifth. Whoever it was must have been hiding on the fourth floor, although Tully didn't see how anyone could have remained hidden after the going over he had given the place. On the way downstairs again his light picked out a small, damp patch on one of the stairs, as if someone had spat and scuffed over it with their shoe. He paused, sniffing. There was a distinct smell of peppermint.

So Steele had been wrong, Tully thought wildly; the dolls and Tyson's missing lawnmower and now even the spitting on the staff stairway were all part of the same problem. He hurried down the stairs with the pieces of what he thought had been three separate puzzles whirling around in his mind, trying to form a picture of the person who was responsible for the disappearance of various tools and one large, motorized lawnmower, who mutilated black dolls, who was fond of eating peppermints and who spat.

It was as well that in a few minutes he would be meeting this person face to face, Tully thought grimly; otherwise he thought that he would have died out of sheer curiosity. . . .

Still in his stockinged feet, Tully opened the Dugout door. Fanning the beam of his torch he painted the room with fast zigzags of light. It was empty. But there was a narrow, vertical band of light coming from the corridor leading to the Toys. It took him a couple of seconds to realize that someone had partly closed the door halfway along the connecting corridor, the door which had been dogged open for so long that Tully had almost forgotten it had hinges. He moved forward carefully, keeping the door between the source of light and himself, until he was just behind it. Then he looked into the Toy department.

There were enough lights switched on to show him the scene in detail. The mouth of the corridor framed the corner of a counter, a large square of floor, and something on the floor that was five feet long and black and sluglike. The sluglike something was curled around a large black doll, pulling one of its arms off. . . .

Tully staggered back against the wall, instinctively seeking a prop for his shaking body while he tried to steady his whirling mind.

The wall wasn't there.

Tully opened his mouth, to scream, and grunted instead as his shoulder hit a hard, sloping surface and he began to roll. The roll lasted only for a few yards before he crashed into an irregular metal object which knocked the breath out of him. His shoes and torch thudded gently against his body, and when he could breathe again he groped for the flash and switched it on.

He was lying close to the bottom of a hollow sphere twenty-five feet in diameter which had been cut out of the store's foundation material. He could see where the concrete, masonry and even the steel reinforcing had been sheered off along a perfect, spherical plane, and where the loose earth and clay was kept from falling into it by a thin film of hard, transparent material. The only break in the sphere was the opening which Tully had fallen through.

A smaller spherical object rested at the bottom of the hollow, surrounded thickly by metal objects some of which he recognized as having once been powered hand tools. There was also a six-foot circle of brickwork which was obviously the plug for the entrance, and the motorized lawnmower which he had collided with on the way in. All the tools had been . . . changed . . . in days that would have given their designers nightmares, and what had been done to the lawnmower verged on the obscene. The smell of peppermint was overpowering. Tully climbed to his feet and, carefully, began to explore.

The beam of his flash bobbed and vibrated along

the hull of the small, spherical ship with its not quite transparent shell and alien internal plumbing. It jerked because his hands were shaking, because his whole body was shaking. He had the shakes because part of him was afraid, the part which was thinking like a store night-watchman, but mostly he was shaking with sheer excitement as his mind stretched and his imagination soared to accept the reality of what was before him.

An alien ship, probably forcelanded and needing repairs, skillfully concealed while the repairs were being carried out. The evidence lay all around him—tools, human tools, modified and used to make other tools which made other tools which might be capable of making the repairs. It was a unique situation, probably the first time such a thing had happened on Earth, but at the same time it was one that was very familiar to Tully.

Many times he had discussed just this situation with those few friends who shared his taste in literature. What would you do, the question usually went, if an alien spaceship landed in your back yard? Would you try to talk, would you run, or would you call out the militia? The answer which Tully and his friends preferred had invariably been the first one—you would try to talk, try to work out a method of communication. Then if the visitor needed help, or was trying to help you, you would be able to discover which. Of course, there might be a third alternative—it might be hostile, completely inimical. . . .

Neither Tully nor his friends liked that third alternative. For one thing they had come up against that situation far too often in stories and they thought it corny. Another reason, a much more subtle and complex one, was their feeling that the Universe was such a big place that it was ridiculous to think of anyone coveting one tiny mote in it to such an extent that they would contemplate war to get it, together with a strong, philosophically based belief that anyone who was advanced enough to cross interstellar space must be highly civilized as well. If there was any hostility, any *apparent* hostility, it would come about through misunderstanding.

Tully would have to see to it that he managed his First Contact without misunderstandings. . . .

He shivered again with sheer excitement and swept his torch around the hideout which the alien had built in the middle of the store's foundations. It had been using and modifying Earth-type tools for its repairs, that seemed obvious. But there were other questions to which Tully itched to have the answers. How had the alien been able to materialize inside the solid foundations and create this place? And how was it able to pick out a place where tools were readily available? Had it detected them, or did it already know they were there? Had the ship been traveling, not through interstellar space but through Time . . . ? The answers, he knew, could come only from the alien.

Abruptly Tully came to a decision. He tied his shoes together by their laces, hung them around his neck and with the torch sticking out of his mouth like a metal trunk, scrambled up to the opening. At the lip of the hole he paused, sniffed, then hurried quietly along the corridor and out into the store. He replaced the thread across the door so that he would know if the alien left the basement while he was making his preparations.

Much of the equipment he needed was already in the basement in the shape of children's blackboards and chalks. And a measure of contact had already been made in that he knew what the alien looked like and, by virtue of its detection gear, the alien was used to the sight of Tully's species. At the same time he would have to render his general aspect less frightening to the alien. One, the most important, method would be not to carry a weapon or anything which might be mistaken for such. Then there was another, more positive method. . . .

Grinning suddenly, Tully headed for the confectionery counter. There he uncapped the big glass jar that was labelled "Extra Strong Peppermints" and began stuffing his mouth and pockets with the hard, white sweets. The way Tully saw it, the alien's body odor smelled of peppermint, or of something very like peppermint. The smell was not unpleasant to Tully, but the human body smell might be quite distressing to the alien, and if he tried to conceal it with the nearest equivalent he could manage to the alien's own smell, that should further reassure it of his friendly intentions.

Completely disregarding the bad effects to his teeth, Tully began to crunch and chew. Within minutes his tongue, mouth and throat were practically paralyzed by the hot-cold burn of the peppermints and his breath was stinking up the whole department. Tully popped in a few replacements and hurried back to the Dugout.

He paused on he way to look again at the phone in the Book department, wondering if he should call somebody. Not the Police or the Fire Department. Definitely not Mr. Steele, at least, not yet. One of his friends maybe, except that even then what he had to say might not sound believable at three o'clock in the morning. He wasn't frightened, Tully told himself; just excited and a little worried. He couldn't help thinking of all those armless dolls and wondering how they fitted into the alien's purpose.

The theory of a sex-maniac wandering the Toy department had been demolished. Tully now knew what exactly it was that wandered the Toy department at night, but what bothered him was its behavior towards the dolls. Had it, in some obscure fashion, been trying to communicate with *him* . . . ?

Tully went into the Dugout quietly, closing and locking the door behind him, and along the corridor. At the partly open dividing door he put his torch on the floor and continued towards the Toy department whistling and putting his feet down firmly so as to give the alien warning of his coming. But just before he entered the basement he stopped whistling when it occurred to him that high-pitched sounds might not be pleasant to alien ears—the noise he was making was not even pleasant to his own ears, Tully had to admit. Then suddenly he was in the Toy department and the alien was on the floor less than five yards away.

It was long and black and sluglike, with a soft bulginess about its body which suggested that internally it must be nearly all liquid. It moved by altering its center of gravity rapidly back and forwards, in a series of tumbling lurches accompanied by a wet slapping sound. The head section—Tully guessed it was the head by its direction of motion—had a grey, shining bulge which might have been a single eye over a long, conelike proboscis, and five long, thin tentacles sweeping forward. Its direction of motion was away from Tully and it was moving fast. Obviously it was afraid of him.

Tully stuffed more peppermints into his mouth and followed it, but slowly so as not to frighten it further. So far as he could see it wasn't wearing or carrying anything so that he was in no danger from extraterrestrial weapons. He showed his empty hands continually and made reassuring noises, and tried to attract its attention by drawing non-scale diagrams of the Solar System and Pythagorus' Thereom on one of the children's blackboards. But it was no good, it kept running away from him and trying to get back into the corridor where its ship was.

Tully could not allow that, at least, not yet. While the e-t was still excited and afraid of him, he didn't want it getting its hands on a weapon.

He was standing in the mouth of the corridor trying to think of some other approach when he heard a noise which caused the cold sweat to pop on his forehead.

He had been blind, stupid—Tully could see that now. He had made a gross tactical blunder. The broken threads between the dugout and Hardware department indicated the passage of someone between the fourth floor and the basement, but they could just as well have shown movement in the opposite direction. There were *two* aliens and the other one was coming back. Tully could hear it working at the locked Dugout door. . . .

His first thought was that he had to keep the two aliens apart, until he could make the one he was chasing understand that he meant no harm. If the second alien came on the scene it might misunderstand and Tully would not be able to stop it going to its ship for a weapon—always supposing it wasn't already carrying one. He must close the door in the corridor. He had already taken a step in that direction when he remembered that it was a simple bolt fastening, and locks and bolts did not a prison make for these aliens—he remembered the way his key's had stuck to the Dugout lock. The aliens could open locks magnetically. He would have to wedge it shut.

A set of kiddies building blocks gave him what he wanted and he ran back to the dividing door. By that time the second alien was on the way down the ramp and Tully used his torch briefly to have a look at it.

It was bigger, thicker and somehow meaner-looking than the one behind him. *The male of the species,* he thought. When it saw him it began to hurry, humping and lurching down the corridor and making high-pitched gobbling sounds. Behind him the other one began gobbling, too. Tully slammed the door and began kicking in the wedges just as a large, soft, heavy weight made its hinges creak.

A few seconds later one of the wedges was pushed from under the door . . .

Tully had just decided that he had made another blunder. That the second alien, with the devices in its ship available, could probably blast through the door in nothing flat, and probably blast through Tully as well. But now it seemed that it was not going to be as quick and dramatic as that. The second alien did not want to destroy the door because that would leave unmistakable evidence of its presence in the store, but no doubt Tully could be made to disappear tracelessly. He kicked the wedge in again, just as the one beside it popped out.

The smaller alien behind him had amused itself by pulling the arms off dolls. The second one . . . Tully wondered sickly what it would feel like to have his arms and leg pulled off, his nose mutilated and his eye . . . He tried desperately not to think about it, tried to think about good, civilized aliens, but his mind kept turning back to the other sort. The sort that Lovecraft used to write about.

According to Lovecraft, the whole of Time and Space was peopled with cruel, debased, unspeakably foul entities, beings as cold and malignant and uncaring as the interstellar wastes in which they dwelt. Humanity with its concern over Right and Wrong inhabited a single dust-mote, unknown and unknowing, in a continuum that was one vast, blasphemous obscenity. Tully had not liked Lovecraft's ideas, but they had been written up so well that they had stuck in his mind despite this. And Lovecraft's aliens were the type who *would* pull another living, intelligent creature apart with less feeling than an unthinking boy would pull the legs off a fly. . . .

Two more wedges jerked from under the door, and Tully couldn't move to replace them. All he could do was shake. His mind seemed to be a tight, hard ball of panic. He was beginning to realize that it was an *alien* at the other side of the door, a being whose civilization and philosophy and thought processes were such that there might be no common ground between them. And even if understanding was possible, he had spoiled any chance he had ever had of gaining it by closing the door.

Judging by its reactions his attempt to contact the first alien had simply driven it into a panic, and then, when the second one had come rushing to its aid, he had barred the way. So far as the e-t outside was concerned he might be doing anything to its mate, and the longer he kept them apart the less likely the larger alien would be to stop and think. And he couldn't run himself because the Toy door was bolted on the outside.

It occurred to him suddenly that he had met this situation before also—the bug-eyed monster, the girl and the hero dashing to the rescue. Only this time *he* was the bug-eyed monster . . .!

Somehow that thought brought him out of his panic state. Basically his problem was to show that he was a kindly disposed bug-eyed monster and not the other sort, and to show it unmistakably and fast. Tully was getting the glimmering of an idea, based on an assumption that might be all wrong, but he needed time to try it out. At least ten minutes. Abruptly he started kicking in the wedges again, kicking them in so hard and far that he ruined the toe-caps of his shoes and nearly broke a couple of toes. Then he sprinted back to the Toy basement and started tearing open a box of modeling clay.

Pulling and kneading at the stuff, Tully tried to work it into a shape that was shapeless. The clay was an improbable green color, but this did not worry him because the modelling set included a sprayer which, as well as giving the finished model a thin, hard skin within seconds, allowed it to be painted any desired color. While he worked Tully tried not to think of the gamble he was taking, or the scraping as wedge after wedge was pushed away, or of the gobbling which came from the other side of the door.

His theory, he told himself desperately, was supported by all the facts. It explained why one alien was careful to hide all traces of itself and its work, by plugging its bolt-hole and probably doing some sort of self-welding job on the metal strapping around the packing cases it had pilfered, while the other one left mutilated dolls lying around. . . .

He finished it just as the last wedge shot out and the door banged against the wall. Tully tried to ignore the heavy, slapping sounds of the second alien coming along the corridor and moved instead towards the other alien—slowly, so as to frighten it as little as possible. It was in a corner, still making agitated gobbling noises. It occurred to Tully that his height might frighten it so he got onto his knees, then flat on his stomach, and crawled towards it holding out the thing he had made in one hand. Behind him the slapping grew louder and the smell of something that wasn't peppermint grew stronger.

He was gambling everything on his theory's being right; lying flat on his stomach, defenseless, not even looking at his potential attacker. And his main reason for taking such a suicidal risk, Tully thought wildly, was that he did not want to think of the Galaxy's being peopled with Lovecraft aliens. . . .

He was only a few feet away from the smaller alien when the big one lurched to a halt beside Tully. It didn't look at him, but shot its five, whiplike tentacles out at the other e-t. Five smaller tentacles came out to meet them, touched, and almost tied themselves in five separate knots. Tully held his breath, afraid even to hope. It was not until the smaller e-t had left for the ship carrying the doll which Tully had made for it, and its parent began drawing a solar system with seventeen planets in it on the blackboard, that Tully knew he had guessed right.

Later that morning, as he tidied up the corridor and Toy department after aliens had gone underground for the day, Tully thought that it had been obvious from the very start that a child had been responsible for the doll business. While its parent had been up in Hardware searching for the proper tools, Junior had grown bored. It had wanted to play with a dolly, but all the dollies in the Toy Department were the wrong shape. So it had chosen one that was the nearest in color and pulled off the arms, and a leg to give it a more "human" shape. Twisting out its nose and hair to resemble the five tentacles and conelike proboscis and removing the surplus eye had been further attempts toward that end. Looked at objectively, the mutilated dolls did look a little like the aliens. But not much, because the small alien had never thought enough of them to bring them back into the ship.

It had kept, and had seemed delighted with, the doll which Tully had made for it. Which meant that the Toy department reign of terror was over. As for the spitting on the staircase, well, the aliens were not built for climbing stairs and they sometimes lost small amounts of body fluid when forced to do so. That, too, would stop in a few days' time when the repairs to the ship were complete. And the tools borrowed from Hardware would be returned to their former shape and replaced. No doubt this would cause widespread consternation, Tully thought wryly, but Tyson could not very well *complain*. All in all everybody should be happy.

Tully yawned and looked at his watch. It was six-thirty. He had just time to remove all his thread and chewing gum from the doors and stairway, make some coffee and finish the last story in his magazine before he unlocked the staff entrance for the cleaners arriving at seven-thirty. It had looked like being a very good story, he thought as he walked slowly up the Dugout ramp, which had been his reason for saving it until last.

He hoped it wouldn't be an anticlimax.

THE DREISTEIN CASE

J. Lincoln Paine

This little chiller only goes to prove that FDR was very smart indeed in not trusting the military alone to handle a Certain Famous Inquiry presented to him in the summer of 1939, but made the war agencies share with civilians the evaluation of that Inquiry's potentialities.[1]

Advanced Research Institute
Cambridge, Massachusetts
2 August 1971

The President of the United States
The White House
Washington, D.C.

Esteemed Sir:

Some recent work by my colleague, Prof. Hauck of Pretoria, has been communicated to me in manuscript. His findings lead me to believe that scientists may be able to counteract the forces of gravity in the near future. Undoubtedly, if Hauck's new discoveries are further developed and applied, a vast new area of space exploration and missile development will open.

The situation which has arisen seems to call for watchfulness and, if necessary, quick action on the part of the Administration. My colleagues here have urged me to

[1] It is also interesting to note that about four months before the Certain Famous Inquiry of 1939, a direct attempt to interest the Navy in the subject took place. The only result of that effort was that the Navy "expressed interest." See Paragraph 3.4 of the Smyth Report.

bring this obviously significant development to the attention of the appropriate government authorities. I believe, therefore, that it is my duty to bring to your attention some of the scientific facts which are attached in a separate memorandum.

Of course, my colleagues and I offer our full services toward the further development of this discovery.

Very truly yours,
Egbert Dreistein

THE WHITE HOUSE
Office of the Special Assistant
to the President

16 August 1971

To: The Secretary of Defense

Attached is copy of letter from Prof. Egbert Dreistein. Draft reply for my signature. Be polite. Incidentally, is there anything to this?

Grant Quincey

INTEROFFICE
MEMORANDUM

Date: 2 September 1971
Ref.: CPT-201/1

To: Col. T. Lee, OPS
From: The Secretary

Prepare reply to attachment. Is the Institute under contract to the DOD? Quote me their budget figures for the last three fiscal years.

Official Use Only
INTEROFFICE
MEMORANDUM

Date: 29 June 1972
Ref.: CPT-201/179

To: The Secretary
From: Col. T. Lee, OPS

The matter referred to in your memorandum CPT-201/1 of 2 September 1971 has been referred to an Inter-

Service Ad Hoc Committee of staff-rank representatives. The committee concurred that there was no consensus on the problem.

Individual views were as follows:

I. The Army feels that ordinary gravity is not fully understood yet and sees little purpose in extending studies into the field of antigravity.

II. The Air Force has been conducting small-scale research on antigravity at the TOP SECRET level. However, since it is impossible to extend the concept to fit existing weapons systems, a low priority has been assigned.

III. The Navy has recommended a high priority to anti-antigravity investigations under the code name of PLOP.

There is no record in DOD files of a facility clearance for the Advanced Research Institute. Prof. Dreistein has never applied for a "Q" clearance. Given the sensitive nature of the antigravity question and the extenuating circumstances, the attached draft reply to Prof. Dreistein has been made as clear as classification permits.

The committee reached agreement on a single point: Prof. Dreistein should not be encouraged. A permanent subcommittee has been set up to provide similar assistance in expediting the handling of any future suggestions from members of the scientific community.

DEPARTMENT OF DEFENSE
Office of the Secretary

2 July 1972

To: Special Assistant to the President

In reference to your request of 16 August 1971, attached is draft reply to Prof. Egbert Dreistein.

The receipt of Prof. Dreistein's letter has stimulated reexamination of the status of antigravity research in the Department of Defense. Estimated future budgetary allocations for that type of research do not warrant continuation of the projects which have been under way. Accordingly, I have issued an order that they be curtailed.

Frank Watt

THE WHITE HOUSE
Office of the Special Assistant
to the President

5 July 1972

Prof. Egbert Dreistein
The Advanced Research Institute
Cambridge, Massachusetts
Dear Prof. Dreistein:

The President has directed me to reply to your letter of 2 August 1971. We thank you for your interest and assure you that the matter has been investigated by appropriate government agencies.

Your patriotic interest is very much appreciated and the President is always interested in receiving stimulating ideas of that nature.

Yours very truly,
Grant Quincey

MOSCOW, Aug. 5 [1974].—A Soviet spokesman announced today that a manned space station has been established as a satellite around Mars and is now observing landing conditions on that planet.

The achievement was credited to the revolutionary discoveries of Prof. Otto Hauck, formerly of South Africa and now in the Soviet Union. He has been awarded three Lenin prizes for his work. . . .

THE WHITE HOUSE

6 August 1974

Prof. Egbert Dreistein
The Advanced Research Institute
Cambridge, Massachusetts
Dear Prof. Dreistein:

My advisers report to me that you have been interested in the subject of antigravity research. Because of the grave circumstances in which our Government finds itself as a result of the announcement from Moscow yesterday, I am asking you to lead a new high-priority project in that direction.

If you will come to Washington the early part of next week, a briefing will be arranged by representatives of the military services and the Central Intelligence Agency who will be able to give you a little of the historical development of Prof. Hauck's work.

I, as President, personally hope that you and your colleagues will rise to the challenge of this new emergency.

Yours very truly,
Horatio Calvin